Born at the End of the World

[illegible]
[illegible] መንግሥት
በከፍተኛ 14 ቀበሌ [illegible]
ሥራ ማኅበር ጽ/ቤት
አዲስ አበባ

ቁጥር ከ14 ቀ13/1835/72
ቀን 17/12/72 ዓ.ም

ወ/ሮ [illegible] 631
[illegible] 18 [illegible] 1972 ዓ.ም [illegible]
[illegible] 10 ቀን 1972 ዓ.ም [illegible]
[illegible]
[illegible]

[illegible]

Born at the End of the World

A Novel

Donica Merhazion

CATALYST PRESS
El Paso, Texas

Published by Catalyst Press.
www.catalystpress.org

Author representation by the Pontas Literary & Film Agency

In North America, this book is distributed by Consortium Book Sales & Distribution, a division of Ingram. Phone: 612/746-2600
cbsdinfo@ingramcontent.com
www.cbsd.com

In South Africa, Namibia, and Botswana, this book is distributed by Protea Distribution. For information, email orders@proteadistribution.co.za.

First edition, first printing
1 3 5 7 9 8 6 4 2

ISBN 978-1-960803-33-7
Library of Congress Control Number: 2025936341

Cover design by Karen Vermeulen

The bus pass opposite the title page reads: "Woizero Wubet Haile, who resides in house number 631 in Higher Kebele district 14, will be traveling through Sidamo from August 18 through September 10, 1972. We confirm that she is a resident of our Kebele and we request that all necessary assistance be given to her."

ማማ ፍቓርኺ ብርሃን እዩ።

ብሰንኪ ሓይልኺ ጽቡቕ ህይወት ይነብር ኣለኹ። መዓልታዊ እየ ዝመስግን።

ባባ ኩሉ ግዜ ንቕድሚት ዝኸይድ መንገዲ ከምዘሎ ስለ ዝመሃርካኒ ኣዝየ እየ ዘመስግን።

ኣካል ታሪኽካ ምዃን ክብሪ እዩ።

Noah, Gabriel, and Maria, this is for you.
You come from greatness.
The best thing I've ever been and ever will be
is your mother.
May the spirit of uplifting others
be woven into your lives
just as it is in your grandparents.

Moges, thank you for all the ways you make me whole.
You are the quiet in my storm.
You are the home where my sense of belonging lives.
Thank you for everything.

Part 1

To Be a Girl

Adi Nefas, Ethiopia, 1962

Perception equals truth.
Evade the impurity of a boy's gaze.
Reputation is a measure of your worth.

Your purity is the weight of the dowry
that feeds our fields from harvest to harvest.
You are—
currency

Remain pure
until
your monthly blood unlocks the door
to womanhood

Then you shall wear the betrothal necklace,
the sign of a promise
of your delivery
to the hands of the man
of your father's choosing.

Your obedience is our family's honor.
Stray from this path
and you will fall alone
into a place from which you can never return
to us.

1

Adi Nefas, Ethiopia, 1962

"You are a woman now," her mother Selas said after Elen showed her the stain on her underwear. Selas fumbled behind her sleeping space on the cowhide floor, extracted a wad of folded rectangular rags, and placed them into her thirteen-year-old daughter's shaking palm. "You'll need these for the next few days and every month for the rest of your life." Her mother sighed, heading toward the door.

"All my life?" Elen gasped. The edges of the rags shivered to the rhythm of her pulse.

Selas stopped mid-stride but didn't turn back. "It will stop whenever you carry a child," she added quietly. "I'll let your father know."

Why does Baba need to know? Elen sank to her sleeping space on the floor, trying to understand.

Four cycles later, the answer came when a beaded sisal necklace branded her a bride-to-be. "This gobagub is a mark of pride for you and our family," her father Ghebrekidan said, beaming as he fastened the engagement necklace around her neck. He stood tall before her, and she sensed the crease of his smile far above, where she dared not look. Elen's heartbeat quickened under the weight of the necklace. She stifled the urge to pull it apart, imagining the beads scattering so far that one would never find the other.

I could just leave, she thought.

Baba's gabi, worn for negotiating her bride price, blurred as her gaze focused on the clump of distant eucalyptus trees marking the end of the family's plot. Dry dust swirled aimlessly between them as if it, too, faced a dismal future. She had never been past those trees. Beyond them lay Adwa town. Her neighbor and friend Birikti called it "a place with options. A place where girls don't have to get married unless they want to, where they can go to school like their brothers, and where they can be—"

Elen lowered her face, blinking away the moisture filling her eyes, wishing she could talk to her friend.

Baba placed a giant palm on her shoulder and gave her an encouraging shake. "You will wear this until your wedding day," he said.

Elen felt a visceral hatred for the necklace burning through the back of her neck and searing into her gut.

"Lucky for us, your new home with your future husband is not far away. We shall visit you often."

Her mother hovered behind Elen's father at the entrance to the family hut, stoic and silent. Her brother Solomon and sisters Alem and Semaynesh stood beside her, their faces heavy with emotion. Elen had seen what happened to Tsehainesh. Her beautiful, tall, and lithe sister became a shadow of her former self with each visit home. She'd just turned sixteen and already had two children, with another on the way. She no longer sang.

"Sometimes I can't hold in my pee," Tsehainesh told Elen once. "The last baby must have been too big." She laughed it off. Elen had been too young to understand what she meant, but it all became clear as Baba fastened the necklace on her and pivoted her life toward marriage and motherhood.

Is this what you want for me, Mama? Elen closed her eyes against the orange glow of the afternoon, feeling the hope just out of reach beyond the trees. *Who am I kidding? Mama has nothing to do with this. She's just like me—powerless.*

"Like your sister before you," Baba continued, breaking the silence. "I know you will make us proud." He leaned down, lifted her chin, and frowned. "Selas! Have you been putting the holy water on her face like we discussed? She needs more."

Her mother disappeared into the hut as if expecting that very request. Moments later, she returned with the precious clay jar.

The wound on Elen's cheek had started as no more than a pimple months before. It festered under the village dust, sweat, and Elen's constant prodding, morphing into an oozing crevice on her otherwise smooth face. As stubborn as the resilient weeds on their family farm, it now pushed up against her lower eyelid, obstructing every downward glance.

"This will heal you, my daughter," Selas said as she uncovered the clay jar, dipped her fingers into the holy water, and flicked it onto Elen's face. Now that they had agreed upon the nuptials, Ghebrekidan watched his young daughter's wound with concern.

"This needs to heal before the wedding," he said as Selas flicked more water onto the wound.

"God willing, it will," her mother murmured between her prayers.

Birikti's father, Gebre, had delivered the water the week before at Ghebrekidan's special request. It came from Mai Chelot, the natural springs in Asmara, a three-hour bus ride away. Selas murmured prayers to heal the stubborn wound as she dipped and sprinkled the water. Elen kept her eyes closed, picturing the trees behind her eyelids.

In some ways, Elen was grateful for the sores.

Maybe Baba won't go ahead with the wedding if I'm ugly.

"Elen, now go and fetch the water for the evening," Ghebrekidan instructed once Selas finished and covered the pot. "Your aunt Tsehay may visit soon, and we will need extra water. Solomon and Alem, clean the yard and make sure to feed the bull. He worked hard for me in the field today."

"Please watch that Semaynesh doesn't wander out again," Selas called to the younger siblings as she withdrew into the hut.

Elen, her shoulders stiff from the foreign weight on her neck and chest, picked up two buckets from their usual place beside the hut's entrance and followed the path to the well. The sisal of the gobagub grated against her with each step. She pumped water into each bucket as slowly as possible, her eyes fixed on the trees.

After lingering as long as she could, Elen dragged herself home, ignoring the water sloshing over the bucket rims. She set them down beside her mud-caked feet, dabbed her wet face with the hem of her dress, and yanked at the necklace, wincing as the sisal pinched the raw skin on her neck.

How am I supposed to wear this all day?

Taking a deep breath, she yanked at the necklace, picked up the buckets, and shuffled through the wooden gate into the mud compound. Solomon's voice floated from behind the hut, beyond the two cows munching the hay Alem had laid out for them. Their youngest sister, Semaynesh, giggled at something Solomon said.

Life goes on, just as it will when I'm gone.

The hut that served as the family kitchen, where her eldest sister Tsehainesh used to bake injera, stood empty. Elen helped Selas make the injera now, but it was never the same after her sister left. Her absence took away Mama's singing voice too.

Village life slowed down for no one. Survival demanded that everyone work every waking moment. Day and night, the villagers of Adi Nefas and their neighbors sent fervent prayers skyward. They begged for rain as they worked the fields, putting their faith in the Almighty to deliver them from the starvation that loomed with a poor harvest. They fed the cows, tilled the land, gathered and stacked hay in the makeshift storage corner, and cooked the meals.

With firewood scarce, they used a mixture of wood and dehydrated cow dung as a fire starter. After harvesting the teff, Selas and Tsehainesh had carefully cleaned, sieved, and stored it, saving every precious grain. This food would sustain them for the rest of the year. Any slip-up or slowdown could force them into a future of rationing meals.

Give us this day our daily bread.

During lean times, they ate once a day. Selas constantly brewed coffee in the traditional pot, serving it to anyone who needed to suppress their appetite. When the harvest was abundant, Ghebrekidan passed some of it to Gebre, who sold it in the Adwa marketplace, an hour away. Then they had the luxury of eating different vegetables and, on rare occasions, meat.

Otherwise, they strung each day together, staving off the hunger pangs until the next shared plate of injera and watery shiro. The orange chickpea sauce provided just enough nutrients to sustain them. If they were lucky, the hens occasionally blessed them with eggs.

With Elen gone, it would be one less mouth to feed. The one comforting thought was that Elen's siblings wouldn't go hungry with the dowry money Ghebrekidan was getting in exchange for her.

Ghebrekidan did his best to care for his family. Elen knew that. He carefully tended the small patch of earth on the family farm from dawn till dusk. A cup of coffee—or three—during the afternoon break would ease his hunger before he returned to coaxing his beloved field to produce teff.

"You can't do this to your daughter. She needs medical help!"

Elen froze mid-stride a few feet from the hut entrance at the sound of a raised female voice from inside. She instantly recognized Tsehay's voice—her vivacious aunt from Asmara who refused to conform to the old traditions ingrained in every village girl since birth. Her vibrant make-up accentuated her sharp features, with red lipstick unapologetically drawing attention to her mouth. Her hair, freed from the traditional braids typical of village women, flowed in shiny waves down her back over clothes that showed no signs of the brown dust that burrowed into every fiber of villagers' clothing.

More water spilled onto Elen's feet as she lowered the buckets. She flattened herself against the wall, moved closer to the open doorway, and craned her neck. Her view extended only to the empty part of the communal room.

Elen had never seen a woman command such respect wherever she went, so she took every opportunity to be near Tsehay whenever she visited. She soaked in her commanding presence, absorbing tales from the big city and trying to construct images of the cars, buildings, and people her aunt spoke about.

Elen had seen Tsehay wearing a brand-new zuria at a wedding over the weekend. The traditional dress she had tailored for the festivities shone a brilliant white, even whiter than the bride's.

The bride, a girl several huts down the road, had been matched up to an older man from southern Tigray.

Selas had been busy talking to her friends, and Elen stood alone on the fringes of the celebrations, where her aunt spotted her. Tsehay's red fingernails sparkled in the sunlight as she grasped Elen's chin.

Elen shrank into her dusty dress, motionless under her aunt's attention. Tsehay's mascara-lined eyes narrowed at Elen's sores, her forehead folding into an elegant frown as she examined Elen's cheek.

"What is happening here?" Tsehay's gaze made all the wedding festivities recede. Elen focused on her aunt's full, red lips as she searched her mind for a coherent response. Her hand instinctively went up to feel her engorged cheek.

"No! Don't touch it. You'll get infected. In fact, it looks like you already are." Her perfume engulfed Elen as she leaned in, squinting at her cheek. She moved Elen's chin to get a better look.

"You need to keep it clean. It looks terrible." Elen silently basked in her aunt's attention as the festivities continued around them. She wanted to stay in that moment forever, imagining her patchy dress replaced by a brilliant one like Tsehay's. Elen longed for that life, that freedom—the yearning burned in her chest.

Why do I have to get married?

"Has a doctor looked at this yet?" Tsehay's voice had cut through the music, her grip still firm on Elen's chin. Behind Tsehay's bent shoulders, muscular arms lifted the new bride's reluctant body onto the back of a donkey, ready to head off to her new home.

"Mama sprinkles it with holy water," Elen managed. "She says that will make it go away."

Tsehay let go and straightened up, her lips pressed into a tight line. "I will be around for a few days." She turned to watch the dejected bride jostling back and forth as her new husband led the donkey away, ululations urging the newlyweds into their future. "I will come visit."

And here she is! She must have walked in while I was out getting water.

Elen remained glued to the wall and craned her head toward the open entrance of the hut. Her siblings' noisy chatter at the far end of the yard drifted toward her, their laughter interfering with the voices inside. She inched closer to the entrance and caught a whiff of Tsehay's familiar rosy perfume intertwined with the smell of coffee beans roasting over the open fire.

"She is too young to get married," Tsehay said. "Putting aside her age, do you see what is happening to her face? Is the dowry worth that much?" The urgency in Tsehay's voice was sharp and insistent, quickening Elen's heartbeat. "We have doctors in Asmara who can help her heal. The Italians have set up services at the Catholic hospital with free medical help. Let me take her there. She can stay with me while she gets treatment—then you can marry her off when she is well."

"There is no time for that." Elen recognized the steely, unmovable tone in her father's voice. "We have already completed the arrangements. I have found a good suitor for her."

When her father decided something would happen, that's how it would be.

"The dowry is an offer our family cannot refuse," Ghebrekidan continued. "Changing the agreement terms at this point will mean a fine. We can't afford that right now. Our family needs the dowry. Besides, he is a respectable man from a good family."

"That is complete nonsense." Tsehay's sharp tone sliced through the popping of the roasting coffee beans. "Why would you do that to her? She is still just a child. Please, let her return with me to Asmara so she can heal. Her face won't get any better without medical treatment."

Elen's sweating palms left wet imprints on the mud wall of the hut when she peeled them off. She rubbed them together, smearing the moist dirt on her skin. Her hope rose with the pitch of Tsehay's voice. She instantly imagined her face smooth as she walked free, wearing a white zuria, her unknown husband evaporating from her life. Time and space compressed as her mind flew to a city she could not imagine, to a life where she lived with Tsehay—unanchored to a faceless husband or archaic rules.

Surely, Tsehay will persuade Baba. He has to listen. Her thoughts raced. *Maybe I can go back with her when she leaves. Maybe—*

"We already talked to his family and agreed," Selas said, cutting Tsehay off. "We will not back out. As Ghebrekidan said, we cannot afford to pay the fine for breaking the agreement now."

Elen heard the three-legged wooden stool creak in protest as Tsehay shifted in her seat. "Selas, listen! It doesn't have to be this way—"

"Stop!" Selas's voice cut into Tsehay's pleas. For a moment, the only sound was the popping of roasting coffee beans lying heavy between the three figures inside.

"I don't want you giving Elen any ideas. She should hear none of this nonsense. You came to visit, so do that in peace. I don't want to talk about this anymore."

The crushing anvil of her mother's tone shattered Elen's momentary euphoria.

She reached for the hem of her dress, dabbing furiously at her tears, not bothering to avoid the pus-filled blisters on her cheek.

2

Asmara, Eritrea, 1957

"Stop!"

A shot of adrenalin jolted through Girmai's bony legs at the sound of the municipal officer's voice. As he ran faster, the basket's sisal handles dug deeper into his shoulders, clinging to him as tightly as he clung to it. The bananas inside were his lifeline.

I can't lose this.

Each banana he sold increased his chances of a decent meal. Losing the basket would plunge him back into an indefinite cycle of hunger. Like many other scrawny street boys in rags and with dirty fingernails, Girmai sold paper cones of peanuts, or bananas whenever he could, using the money to buy a hot meal. Street boys were known for their relentless sales tactics, and Girmai learned quickly. He imitated them, hawking whatever he could to people in cars stopped at traffic lights. He watched how they chatted up window shoppers and appealed to old mamas returning from the market with groceries.

Anything for a meal. When there was nothing to sell, the boys begged.

I am not a beggar.

Girmai's feet pounded hard and fast on the sidewalk. The battered sole of his left shoe flapped, threatening to peel away. He pinned the basket tighter to his side, pumping his left arm to propel himself forward. He winced mid-leap, knowing the force of his run was crushing the last of his bananas.

Not again.

"I said STOP!"

Girmai heard another officer joining the first. A swift backward glance filled his vision with a baton waving perilously close to his back. He pushed forward harder than he thought possible, almost feeling the officer's breath on his neck.

Usually, they gave up by now.

With its clean streets and art deco buildings, Asmara was a replica of an Italian city, with no place for street boys and beggars. The Italians were long gone, but Eritrean urbanites clung to the illusion of the European life that colonization had denied them.

Desperate for a few birr for his next meal, Girmai ventured into a part of the city he'd never visited. Officers didn't allow street boys in this part of town. They patrolled the manicured streets to keep downtown Asmara pristine for the gentrified folk. It had to be immaculate in case Emperor Haile Selassie visited from Addis Ababa.

Asmara's mid-morning crowd spilled from offices, flowing toward the open-air cafés for their essential cappuccino break. Conservative mamas, white netselas draped over their heads, wove through the crowd toward Edaga Hamus market. Young university students filled the pasticcerie lining every block, killing time before their classes.

Girmai slipped through the crowd, his father's gabi trailing behind him, its edges whipping at faces as he wove through. Sweat soaked the traditional cotton blanket, his only keepsake from his father. The delicious smell of freshly baked croissants wafted from the popular Dolce Vita Café, wedging itself into the pit of his stomach as he pivoted around the corner into Viale Buonarroti.

Distracted, he rammed into a girl in a tight skirt. He leaped over her as she tumbled and was meters away by the time she hit the ground. The commotion behind him stalled his pursuers for a few precious moments.

His thigh muscles burned as he raced into another intersection. A car skidded to a stop, its hood inches from his leg. Girmai plunged into a narrow gap between the slow-moving yellow cabs. Sending brief, silent apologies to the waving fists inside, he charged toward the broad steps of La Fontana, eyes fixed on the quiet Geza Banda neighborhood beyond the giant fountain.

I can't lose everything again, not this time.

As the pavement rose to the hill's swell, the crowd thinned. Girmai bounded up the stairs, barely noticing the cool spray of the fountain's tiny droplets.

No matter how hard he ran, the officers stayed on him. He blinked rapidly to clear his vision from the sweat streaming into his eyes.

I am not a beggar. I worked hard to earn this.

If he lost his stash, he couldn't repay the two birr he borrowed to start his banana and snack-selling business. He used everything he had, including a small scale for weighing peanuts and the few bananas in the basket. Now they were getting deformed.

No one will buy them now.

Losing this bunch meant more nights sleeping on the hard floor of the mosque, where he has been staying since arriving in the city empty-handed almost a year ago. Or worse—Girmai would have to go back home.

I can't go back.

His father's funeral three years ago marked a turning point in Girmai's life. The sounds of shovels slicing into freshly dug dirt, dropping pile after pile onto his father's malaria-ravaged body, echoed relentlessly in Girmai's mind. A part of Girmai would always lie within the folds of the white burial shroud that wrapped Isaac's body. Isaac was the only person who had loved him. The only other person who might have loved him was his mother, but life had seeped out of her on the floor of their family's mud hut, with his younger sibling still kicking inside her. Girmai was only three then, with barely enough cognizance to hold on to memories of her.

Isaac's extended family had dealt with his widowhood swiftly. Girmai was fifteen now, and the only mother he knew was Zaid, his stepmother, who had come into their lives barely a year after his mother died. Young and energetic, she entered the arranged marriage expecting to possess all of Isaac's affections. It didn't take long for Zaid to turn bitter, realizing she was married to Isaac's grief and unwavering love for his son. Her resentment at playing second fiddle overflowed onto Girmai.

She grew tired of the comparisons and the constant nostalgia that hung over her, even after she bore Isaac's two sons. The tendrils of her jealousy permeated every crevice of their lives, hardening into a wooden spoon that often came down on Girmai's backside whenever he was unfortunate enough to be alone with her. After his father died, Zaid's relentless beatings became the end to each of his back-breaking, laborious days in the field. She found other ways to make him suffer when he grew too big for the wooden spoon.

With his father gone, she decided how and when to serve food. While Girmai was out in the field, she fed herself and her sons. "There is no more food. We don't have enough for you," she'd greet his growling stomach.

He scavenged pieces of injera and cups of tea, willing them to sustain his dwindling body until he could no longer endure it. One morning, he walked past the field, kept going until he boarded an Asmara-bound bus, and never looked back.

"You need to get an education," his father had said when Girmai was old enough to walk the three kilometers to the nearest school alone. "It's the only way out of this hard life. You are such a clever boy. You deserve more than what this village offers."

His father had enrolled him in a school set up by Swedish missionaries. It was a small, one-room stone schoolhouse in a nearby village, teaching literacy and math to over fifty boys from surrounding areas. Girmai learned quickly and reached the sixth grade before his father died.

"We don't have time for that," Zaid spat at him soon after the obligatory forty-day mourning period ended. "You will take over your father's duties here. My children and I need to eat."

I will make you proud, Baba. I promise. I will make something of myself.

Past the fountain, the high walls surrounding each house in Geza Banda loomed. Desperation gripped his throat as he entered a narrow street grid, searching for an open gate to slip through. Skidding around another corner into a quiet, tree-lined street, he tested each gate with a little push as he sprinted past. A gate gave way, offering a narrow opening. He skidded to a stop, backtracked, slipped through, and gingerly closed it behind him.

The bougainvillea-lined garden in the front compound glowed with serene protection. Girmai opened his mouth wide to quiet his rapid breathing and shifted the basket to his other shoulder. A dark-blue car parked at the end of a narrow pathway winding around the house would give him the cover he needed.

Optimistic about this hiding place, he bent lower as he followed the walkway until the startled eyes of a washerwoman immobilized him mid-stride. Her eyes widened at the sight of the tattered boy. She took a deep breath and readied her mouth to scream.

He knew that look very well; he saw it daily as he hawked his wares on the Asmara streets. The same look was etched on Zaid's face just before she hurled insults at him.

"Please help me!" he spluttered. Bending low, he put his hands together as if in prayer. The woman's hesitation gave him a chance to continue. "I am only trying to sell bananas so I can eat. I don't know why they are after me. I'm so hungry. Please let me stay until they leave, and I will go. I need nothing else from you."

The woman's face softened as she took in the sight of him. Her indecision grew as her eyes moved from his ragged clothes to his basket and back to his desperate face. She opened her mouth to speak but was stilled by the sound of the municipal officer's voice on the other side of the wall.

"I saw him go in here." The officer stood just outside the gate, his voice projecting as if he were beside them.

Wild-eyed, Girmai silently pleaded with the woman.

A bang on the gate made them both jump. The woman motioned with her eyes toward a small laundry room behind her, separated from the main house by a narrow walkway. She dried her hands on her dress to intercept the officers as Girmai leaped toward the open door.

He scuttled in, closed the door gingerly, and blinked to adjust to the muted light. Crouching just under the window in the furthest corner from the door, he released his hold on the basket and frantically began peeling the bananas. He had only a few minutes before they reached the door.

Each bite of the crushed bananas pushed Zaid's voice further away. One after another, he shoved them into his mouth, forcing chunks down his throat. He managed to eat four before heavy footsteps approached and paused outside the door.

"We know he came in here." An officer was talking to the woman, who mumbled a reply unintelligible to Girmai, folded into the corner.

He had six ripe bananas left. Girmai stood, twisted his body, and quickly threw them out the open window above his head.

I'll come back for them later, God willing.

The door burst open as he crouched back down, casting him into the spotlight. A tall man filled the doorway.

"I told you I never wanted to see you again," he hissed, his teeth clenched.

The man grabbed Girmai's gabi with one hand and heaved him up, snatching the basket with the other. He threw Girmai out of the room, sending him sprawling at the silent woman's feet.

"You're ruining our streets with your shouting and pestering!"

Another officer standing beside the woman bent to lift Girmai. They both dragged him through the garden and into the street. Once out of the gate, the basket slammed into his shoulder, sending him skittering onto the pavement. He barely stood before the officer delivered a heavy kick to his backside.

The basket seemed to shrink in the officer's enormous fist. The only sounds Girmai registered were broken pieces of his scale rattling inside. The grating metallic squeaks told him it was beyond repair. Girmai glanced back toward the bananas beyond the house walls. His hesitation earned him another kick, throwing him off his feet and sprawling onto the pavement.

"This is going into the trash," the officer shook the tattered basket. "You'll get jail time if we see you again."

Girmai didn't move fast enough to avoid the boot, which landed another vicious kick on his hip, throwing him several feet further onto the sidewalk.

"I said go!" The officer's rabid face resembled the dogs Girmai had seen fighting for scraps. "You'll never see this again!"

He risked one glance back at his basket as he started running. It was everything he had.

Back to zero.

3

Adi Nefas, 1962

"Elen!" A hand shook her shoulder.

Through the blur of tears, Elen couldn't focus on Birikti's face as she lifted her head from between her knees. The buckets she had brought to fill with water lay abandoned beside her.

Her friend and neighbor leaned over her, her face pinched tight. The buckets were still rolling from where she had dropped them moments before.

Whenever she could, Elen coordinated her daily trips to the well with Birikti, her window to the outside world. Her friend's family dabbled in trade and, in addition to the extra teff Ghebrekidan gave them, often took what they grew to Adwa for sale.

Unlike Elen, Birikti occasionally left the village to travel with her father and came back with stories of black roads as smooth as eggshells but hard like stone, about throngs of people fighting for walking space on the streets, and of marketplaces with food stalls stretched out as far as the eye could see.

Elen let the tales of Birikti's big-town adventures fill her imagination in their daily walks to get water. She hung on to each detail, wishing she was there, untethered to a dismal future.

"I am so sorry," Birikti said after Elen recounted Tsehay's conversation with her parents.

Elen's shoulders shook, and her tears flowed more freely under Birikti's concerned gaze.

Birikti moved her hand around Elen's shoulders and pulled her into a side hug. They hunched into each other, their worn dresses merging as their knees pressed close together in a single, intertwined silhouette against the orange glow of the sunset.

Shhh! The wind rustled through the leaves above them, then quieted, as if listening to their conversation and sympathizing with the distraught teen. Elen's sobbing soliloquy eventually fizzled into silence.

"Hey—I have an idea." The sudden animation in Birikti's voice startled Elen, but she kept her head down. Birikti always had ideas. "I have been thinking about it for a while." She glanced down at the gobabub that disappeared into the folds of Elen's dress.

"Listen! This problem is not going away; we know that. No, wait, listen—" She stopped Elen from covering her face again. "As soon as I get my monthlies, they are coming for me too. Let's run away to Asmara together! I have been setting money aside. Every time we go into Adwa, I pocket a little. I have eight birr, which is enough for our bus tickets. That will get us to Tsehay's house—she will not turn us away."

Birikti's words flooded out, leaving no space for Elen to respond or process. She leaned in conspiratorially and glanced sideways, even though they were alone in the clearing by the well.

"The bus leaves from Adwa to Asmara in a few days," Birikti said, straightening up and gesturing toward the sunset and the eucalyptus trees, their leaves swaying in the wind. "Let's leave this place and make a life for ourselves, just like Tsehay."

Elen dragged the hem of her dress to wipe her nose.

Asmara, Eritrea. A different country, a new start.

A sliver of hope sprouted at the thought. Birikti's words merged with Tsehay's stories, quickening Elen's pulse with the promise of a new beginning.

"You mean, just leave?" Stepping beyond those trees and leaving everything behind felt absurd, as if she were considering stepping off the world's edge. How was she supposed to survive in a whole other country? The idea seemed ludicrous, yet a flicker of possibility lingered.

Elen's eyes rose to the path meandering away from them through the flat field until it disappeared around the clump of eucalyptus trees she stared at so much. She turned back to Birikti.

"Yes!" Birikti said, each vigorous nod of her head growing the bud of hope welling in Elen's chest. "I heard Mama and Baba talking about the bus leaving on Thursday morning. We can catch it and find your Aunt Tsehay. She will be in Asmara by then. She has to take us in. She is on your side."

Elen knew even Birikti had never gone further than Adwa town, but the certainty in her voice cast Elen's doubts aside.

I don't have to get married! I can live in the city!

"I don't have any money to—"

"Never mind that!" Birikti put her hand up. "I have enough money to get us both to Asmara. God will help us from there." She glanced at the sky, and they both touched their fingers to their foreheads and chests three times in prayer.

"Once we arrive, we will have to figure out how to find your aunt's house. I am sure we can do it. I heard those city Eritreans are helpful to villagers."

It certainly sounded better than her father's plan for her life. The sun sank into an amber glow as they continued their conversation. Eventually, they got up, pumped water into their buckets, and headed back home. Elen reached the hut just as the burnt-orange sky faded into the night's blue-gray.

A way out.

She stepped into the dark interior of the hut, where her siblings had already rolled out the cowhide mat for the night. Elen watched as Selas stoked the fire on the small charcoal stove. Its glow illuminated her mother's worn face and cast a sphere of heat that warded off the early-evening chill. Sweat shone on Selas's forehead and cheeks.

"What took you so long?" Selas spoke without looking up.

Elen studied the curve of her mother's back, the sharp bumps of her shoulder blades and spine protruding beneath her thin dress. Each spindly muscle in her arms contracted as she fanned the flames with the menbedbedi, the fan's edges frayed from years of use.

I'm sorry, Mama, I have to do it.

At Elen's silence, Selas looked up from the fire. Elen spun away before she betrayed herself.

I am leaving.

***

Elen's light slumber evaporated in the crisp silence of the pre-dawn hours. The Asmara-bound bus was leaving at 7:00 a.m., about the time it was fully light. Elen needed to learn how Birikti got all the information or how she identified one hour from the other. She smiled in the dark, grateful for her friend giving her a way out.

She lifted her head slightly to assess the quiet hut.

Good. Everyone is still asleep.

Elen kept her body still in the semi-darkness, lifting her head slightly higher to get a clear view of her parents. Satisfied that Ghebrekidan and Selas were fast asleep, she laid her head back down and stared up at the mud ceiling, blinking herself awake. Her hand brushed her cheek, kneading the warm, pulsing sores. Her mother constantly chided her not to touch them, but how could she resist? She curled her fingers away from her face and rubbed the sores' moisture on her dress. Her feet brushed against the gobagub she had discarded the night before, replaying the conversation she overheard.

I have agreed to this deal. We have already made arrangements. What would people say?

She clenched her jaw at the thought of her thirteen years ending in that necklace, and whispered quiet prayers for protection, absorbing the smells and soft sounds of her family around her.

Time to go. Birikti was waiting.

Elen silently slid from her sleeping spot on the mud floor and carefully placed the thick, shared gabi over Solomon's splayed legs. He slept longer if he kept warm. She grabbed the small cloth bag she stashed behind one of the big pots the night before. Then her fingers found her rubber sandals at the hut's entrance. She pinned them under one arm and pushed the wooden door open with the other. Mouthing a quiet goodbye to her sleeping family, she slipped outside.

Elen stepped into the yard, taking shallow breaths of the chilly morning air. The compacted mud was cold under her bare feet, sending shivers up her torso. She quickly tugged on her rubber sandals, barely noticing her big toes touching the ground over the worn rubber. Moving lightly, she unhinged the gate and slipped out. The rooster perched on top of the wall remained silent in the soft pre-dawn light, and she nodded her thanks in his direction. His habit of crowing late would be to her advantage this morning.

Her parents would assume her empty sleeping space meant she went to fetch water and would think nothing of her absence.

I hope.

The eucalyptus trees bordering their family compound appeared sooner than she anticipated. She brushed her fingers around their smooth trunks, glanced back at the hut—its thatched roof the only thing visible behind the wall enclosure—and silently bid her home farewell.

Birikti was already by the well, pacing.

"Come on!" Birikti urged ahead of her as she wrapped the thin cotton fabric of her netsela tightly around her head.

Elen scrambled to keep up as Birikti, familiar with the winding paths, navigated swiftly through the plots of arid farmland.

The rooster would be waking everyone up soon.

Her father's bull stood patiently beside the old patched-up plow at the side of the hut, ready to don his harness at full light and begin his routine churning of the dry earth.

The three goats, huddled together for warmth, waited with udders full of milk that she would not help to empty today. Ghebrekidan would have just enough time to eat a quick bowl of injera fit-fit that Selas prepared before leading his beloved bull to begin the day's work.

They wouldn't miss her for a while. Alem was only eight and not strong enough to carry the full water buckets, so she swept the mud compound around their hut and fed the goats, the cow, and the few chickens they had running around.

With each step that widened the distance from her home, her strides growing heavier, she imagined the scene when they realized she was gone.

Worry, anger, then panic. In that order. Mama would be beside herself, and Baba would be figuring out how to keep the disappearance quiet from the village until he could bring her back. The thought immediately quickened her step.

I have to do this. We have no excuse for being this far from home.

Elen focused on Birikti's netsela flapping ahead of her as her friend nimbly made her way through the brightening landscape. The cover of semi-darkness would not last long.

Elen followed close behind, carefully stepping around sharp stones. They needed to be as far away from Adi Nefas as possible before anyone they knew saw them.

By the time they reached the outskirts of Adwa, the warm rays of the early-morning sun had dissipated the fog and dried the dew clinging to the scattered brown blades of grass. The open fields and the whispering eucalyptus leaves gave way to small, haphazard shacks lining the road, which morphed into a steady pattern of building after building.

In the bustle of central Adwa, the town pulsated around her. Hundreds of people, more than Elen had ever seen in her entire life, swarmed in and out of the buildings and roads like ants in a disturbed nest. She gripped Birikti's arm and followed her lead as they burrowed deeper into the crowds, melting into the cityscape unnoticed.

The hairs on the nape of her neck rose at the immersion into the crush of bodies and the constant murmur of voices. Acutely aware of the ugly protrusions on her face, she drew her cotton netsela over her head, wrapping it tighter around her face and leaving only her eyes visible.

Her overhanging toes lingered on the unrelenting paved roads, taking in the rough texture of the black tar. The sheer number of people and cars and the speed at which everything and everyone moved spun her head.

Each fingertip explored the solid walls of each building, much more compact and sturdy than the walls of their family home. Ghebrekidan had to continuously fortify it by pasting wet mud mixed with cow dung to patch cracks. These walls had no flakes, no holes, or mud.

How did they make this?

After passing the fifth building, Elen forgot where she was and stood transfixed, studying the gray surface of what she would later learn were cement walls. She would have stayed longer if it weren't for Birikti's hurried pull on her elbow.

"Elen! If we stay here any longer, we will miss the bus." The novelty of life in Adwa town had worn off for Birikti long ago. She linked her arm firmly through Elen's, jerking her forward through the streams of people. She kept pulling every time she sensed Elen making another stop.

"We need to keep moving. There won't be another bus for a week, and our parents will never let us out of their sight if we miss this one."

Elen had to agree with that. Catching this bus was their only chance.

Sidewalks and roads swerved and swelled with donkeys and mules laden with sacks of grain stacked high.

Crack! Whips urged them along in an unorchestrated symphony. Each snap kept the beasts of burden trotting forward, some defecating mid-stride as they complied. The smell of their excrement was the only familiar thing Elen could latch on to.

Hawkers yelled their wares in sing-song voices while harried passersby flowed in both directions, some stopping to bargain at the stalls on the roadside.

The girls pushed through the crowded street to the huge bus. Elen refocused on its rectangular form, which loomed tall and stationary in contrast to the hustle and bustle around it.

A man stood on the roof of the bus. His muscles rippled under his sweat-drenched T-shirt as he caught sacks and bags hauled up from his counterpart below, out of Elen's view.

"It's as big as our house," she breathed into Birikti's ear. The bus was a giant metal case, with windows high above them. "We are going to ride in that?" Elen clung to Birikti's elbow tighter as they squeezed through people milling around several smaller buses parked in the lot. The bus's wheels stood taller than the young children playing tag.

"Yes." Birikti kept her eyes forward. "This is one of the big ones. They take people and things for sale from here to Asmara. I have seen this bus many times but never been inside," Birikiti breathlessly whispered in Elen's ear. "We are doing this, Elen!"

She flashed a wide grin for the first time this morning.

"We will be in so much trouble."

Elen's response killed the smile. "We will be at Tsehay's house soon enough," Birikti reassured her, then pulled her forward.

Elen let Birikti's self-assured tone calm her. *Breathe!*

The man on the roof secured all the bags and sacks with rope, bending low to fasten the knots. Though the early-morning still clung to the coolness of the night, sweat dripped from his brow.

"Asmara! Asmara! Leaving for Asmara!" A deep, throaty voice emanated from the bus's entrance and boomed over the chaotic bustle. The conductor's voice rose like a beacon above the bleating of goats and the shouts of traders, guiding the girls through the chaos.

Elen returned the pincer grip on Birikti's arm and followed the line of people snaking into the two-toned bus. A strange calm washed over her as she touched the cool metal and traced her fingers on the tire almost above her waist. The tires were the same texture as her sandals, rock solid and taut against her hand.

Freedom.

She pushed away thoughts of the shame she was bringing to her family by coming this far and the disgrace that would follow when they discovered what she had done. They would have to speak with the family they had made arrangements with and probably lie about her being unwell to buy time until they figured out what she had done.

They would eventually narrow her options and find her at Tsehay's—assuming she made it there. She would be as good as an orphan when she refused to return. Cut off and disowned, she would be on her own.

I am willing to pay the price. I have Tsehay on my side.

"God provides His angels when you need them the most," Selas often told her children, especially when their stomachs ached with hunger. "We must always trust in Him. He tries us as silver is tried in the fire until it comes out a brilliant metal." She would often quote her favorite psalm and kiss the silver necklace with the cross she always wore.

Mama is right, Elen thought; the calm in her core grew, keeping her grounded and firm in her decision. *God sent His angel to me.*

They were now at the front of the queue, and she kept her prayer going as Birikti held out the eight birr notes as they approached the conductor.

Elen clenched her fists at her sides, taking liberties with the words of the Lord's Prayer, and steadied herself.

"The conductor has the power to refuse entry," Birikti told her as they waited in line. Let's hope he doesn't notice we are here without our parents."

Elen forced her breathing to slow down. "Your faith must always remain strong no matter what," her mother always said though Elen knew running away from her family obligations was not what her mother had in mind.

If it is Your will, let it be so.

Elen focused on her prayer, and her eyes lowered to the stairs and onto the bus. "Our Lord always sees us through," she said.

The conductor eyed the money in Birikti's outstretched hand, lifting his eyebrows in question. His eyes darted between the cash and the two girls standing behind it, then scanned behind them for accompanying family members.

Faith will see me through. May Your will be done.

He opened his mouth as if to question them but then seemed to change his mind halfway through a deep breath.

He grabbed the wad of crumpled one-birr notes and handed Birikti two paper tickets.

"Asmara! Leaving for Asmara!" His voice boomed over their heads as Birikti gripped Elen's hand and pulled her onto the bus.

Elen gathered her knee-length dress up with her free hand and heaved herself onto the first step with Birikti's help. Her toes registered the cold, beveled metal as she scaled the following two steps and hoisted herself inside.

She traced her hands over the cloth seats and followed Birikti to the back. The high-pitched voices of women chatting filled her ears, and the unfamiliar cold of the metallic floor pressed against her thin sandals. When they got to an empty row of two, Birikti stepped aside, allowing Elen to lower herself into a seat by the window, then settled in beside her.

"This bus needs to move soon," Birikti said wide-eyed as she searched past Elen through the window. "They'll know we're gone by now."

Elen imagined her father materializing in the crowd, gobagub in hand, ready to drag her back home. She shrank further into her seat and leaned her head against the metal bar of the window.

The yells announcing the bus's departure stopped now that the bus was full. Gossip, laughter, babies, and squawking chickens in cages in the back filled the tight space around them.

Elen gripped Birikti's arm at the loud grunt of the engine turning on, vibrating the bus awake. The forward momentum of the bus lurching into gear wedged into the depths of her stomach as it veered onto the main road, clearing a path in the sea of people on the streets.

The vibration of the seat solidified the life-changing decision she had just made. The buildings blurred until the urbanscape relented to the open countryside. Elen's eyes roved over the plowed fields and the ever-present eucalyptus trees, which stood solid, their erect, dignified forms steady while everything else blurred in her vision.

May Your will be done.

She focused on each tree as it passed, one after another, moving further from her home and closer to freedom.

Her family would be confused when they found her buckets. Alem would eventually uncover them hidden behind the goat stall when she went to feed the goats. She imagined Alem rushing to tell their parents.

Her parents would worry, and Elen knew that worry would turn into anger when they discovered what she had done.

Her absence meant the loss of their daughter and her dowry, an income they needed to feed the family.

She had put them in a difficult place; they might never forgive her. She hoped they would eventually understand why she made this choice.

I am in a difficult place too. Elen tightened her lips at the thought of her impending wedding.

"I hope Solomon, Alem, and Semaynesh will be okay. I just left them behind," she finally spoke to Birikti more than an hour after their journey started.

"They will be fine," her friend replied. "Right now, we have other things to worry about."

Elen turned back to the window framing the monotony of the brown flat landscape speeding by.

Am I making their lives worse by leaving?

She hadn't considered the impact of her absence on her siblings. Alem and Solomon were still young, and Alem had some time before talks about her marriage began.

Once I make a new life, I will get her out before that happens.

4

Asmara, 1957

Girmai trudged through the bustling streets of Asmara for hours, the city's vibrant hum a stark contrast to his desolation. His back and torso ached from the officers' kicks, while his mind remained numb from his loss. The cold engulfed him as dusk descended into night, seeping through his gabi and thin T-shirt and hooking into his bones.

Exhausted but determined, Girmai pushed forward, one foot in front of the other. He clenched his jaw to stop his teeth from chattering, renewing his resolve to face the place he refused to consider for the past year.

It was his last resort.

The faint street lamps did nothing to illuminate the looming silhouette of his uncle's sweater factory. This part of town, reserved for factories and warehouses, lay on the outskirts of Asmara, deserted in every direction Girmai looked. The foreboding cement walls and darkened windows muted the hum of the machines inside.

For months, he stayed far from this place, determined not to reach out to family after leaving home and abandoning his responsibilities. He wanted to make it on his own. But now, with his last stockpile of bananas gone, he had no more options.

There is no going back to the village, Girmai thought, tightening his jaw.

He lifted the knocker on the metal door and banged a few times, then stepped back, waiting with a mix of dread and faint hope. Moments later, the heavy door's hinges whined open, revealing his cousin's face.

"Girmai!" Dawit stepped back in surprise, as an awkward silence hung between them. Girmai's cousin, a wealthy urban city boy clad in imported clothes, stood in stark contrast to Girmai. Dawit's father, Russom, owned a chain that dominated the Addis Ababa and Asmara knitwear markets. Like Isaac, Russom prioritized education, and used his profits to send his son to the best private schools in the city.

As he grew older, Dawit took on more responsibilities in the family sweater factory and dutifully followed the expectation that he would take over the thriving business one day.

"It's been a long time," Dawit finally managed to say. His throat bobbed under his beard as he swallowed uncomfortably.

Girmai and Dawit had often met at family weddings, baptisms, and funerals. Despite their differences in class and lifestyle, they bonded over their mutual distaste for small talk. The last time Girmai had seen Dawit was at his father's funeral.

"Kemey kenikha, Dawit?" How have you been? Girmai said, looking up at his cousin standing half in and half out of the elevated factory entrance. Girmai uncrossed his arms and balled his fists behind his back to mask his despair, wincing at the pain of his swollen bruises.

Girmai could imagine how he appeared through his affluent cousin's eyes: matted hair, a torn T-shirt and pants, and his father's gabi, which was more brown than white. He read the unspoken assumptions playing out on Dawit's face—

Isaac's son went rogue—he must have gone mad. He abandoned his duties at home and disappeared, never to be heard from again. How irresponsible is that? Imagine—he just left Zaid with the kids! How are they supposed to survive without a man in the house? Who will till the field and gather the harvest? Who does such a thing?

"Ti'imukha alo mish do? Life is treating you well, isn't it?" Girmai broke the silence with a line they often heard at family gatherings, one they took pleasure in mocking.

Dawit broke out in a smile, the tension dissipating from his face. "You look so much better than me! What are you talking about?" They both chuckled, and in that moment Girmai forgot the past year's trials, feeling once again like a boy living in the comfort of his father's love. Their laughter faded into silence, and the worry lines reappeared on Dawit's face.

"I need your help," Girmai said. "I need somewhere to sleep while I collect myself and figure out how to make things work. I have a plan; I just need time."

Girmai braced himself against Dawit's uncertainty and continued, "I have nowhere else to go, please. I just need time. If I had any other options, I would be there now."

Dawit's eyes flickered with indecision. Girmai knew the burden of taking in a runaway would be heavy. The weight of family expectations pressed on both of them, and Dawit's father would not want to jeopardize his family ties by appearing to encourage Girmai's abandonment of his duties at home.

"I will keep a low profile; I just need a place to stay at night," Girmai repeated, scratching a fresh bug bite on his arm. The evening chill had worked its way to his core. Dawit stood silent and still, clearly conflicted.

"I can leave before the sun rises," Girmai continued, holding his breath, steeling himself for the rejection he had often heard.

"Come in," Dawit said, stepping aside. He waited for Girmai to climb the two steps and enter. The door whined shut as noisily as it had opened, competing with the drum of the machines inside.

"I'm switching my duties over to the night manager in half an hour," Dawit said, motioning for Girmai to follow him inside. "I'll let him know you'll be here for the night." He paused and turned back to Girmai. "For however many nights you need."

"Thank you, Dawit. I appreciate this so much," Girmai said. Relief softened his body, allowing him to feel the exhaustion he had kept at bay. He followed Dawit down the hall and into the expanse of the factory room, where row after row of gleaming metal knitwear machines whirred and kicked under fluorescent lights brighter than any light Girmai had ever seen. With synchronized movements, the machines lowered beautiful knits into long baskets on the floor beneath them.

"Baba will probably not like our arrangement, so we need to handle this carefully," Dawit said, raising his voice over the machine noise. He led Girmai through the rows and stopped at the entrance of a small alcove at the back of the room.

"Hopefully, this mattress will keep you comfortable," he said, looking at Girmai apologetically as if he wanted to offer better. "We set it up for night managers, but no one should be sleeping during the night shift. If you come in around this time, I'll let you in so you have a place to rest."

"Thank you," Girmai murmured. He looked away quickly, blinking hard as his throat tightened.

Dawit put a hand on his shoulder. "You will be okay, cousin," he said. "I know you will." He pursed his lips and put his hand in his pocket.

"I better get going; I must hand over the next shift information to the night manager. I'll make sure he knows you're here."

Girmai stood in the corner and watched Dawit weave through the machines, greeting the three technicians on his way out. He pointed in Girmai's direction, and they all glanced over, nodding in understanding.

Girmai bowed to them in greeting and stood in the corner, drawing his gabi tight around his shoulders. The adrenalin from the earlier chase, the encounter with the officers, and the exhaustion from the long walk seeped out of him as he listened to the hum of the machines. He stood there, watching the technicians change the yarn and punch buttons on the top of the metal casings.

Though bone-tired, his fascination intensified as he watched the men move from one machine to another. Hour after hour, they clicked here and turned a knob there. Metallic poles held up yarn that spun in continuous motion.

Every so often, a man would replace it with another and press more buttons. Row after row, the machines complied, producing brilliant, intricate, patterned fabrics.

Years later, reflecting on this night, Girmai recognized it as the moment that radically changed the course of his life.

He hardly slept that night and many nights after, watching and learning, studying every part of each machine until they felt like an extension of his own hands.

"You are such a clever boy. You need an education to have something better than this village life." His father's words propelled him from one day to the next. Each daybreak, he picked up where he left off. Borrowing again to hawk on the streets, he kept one eye out for municipal officers while perfecting his sales tactics. Night after night, he returned to the factory. He watched, listened, and learned how the machines worked, shadowing the workers until he mastered every design and program they had in production.

He asked countless questions, urging the weary night-shift workers to explain everything they knew about knitwear. He peered over their shoulders anytime a technician opened the machines for fine-tuning, studying the innards of each one.

Days turned into months as Girmai lived and breathed every idiosyncrasy of the machines, mastering the art of knitwear production. His hands became adept at navigating the intricacies of sweater-making until creating those beautiful pieces of fabric became an innate part of him.

"You deserve more than what this village offers." His father's words replaced the recurring memories of his death and Zaid's hatred.

"Knowledge—that's what will make you great."

5

Etege Menen hospital, Asmara, 1962

Elen followed Tsehay's instructions and entered the hospital alone, transfixed by the shiny, mirror-like floors dotted with white gleams from the bright lights above. Rows of matching chairs lined one side of the room. At the center, a woman sat behind a large desk.

"This is where we part for now," Tsehay had said a few minutes earlier. They had stopped at a deserted corner several blocks from the hospital, facing a row of closed cafés with their shutters down. Tsehay placed her hands on Elen's shoulders and bent to meet her eyes.

"We can't risk being seen together. Someone might recognize me if I get closer to the hospital," Tsehay said in a low, fluid tone, familiar with giving such instructions.

Elen studied her aunt's face, trying to distract herself from the hammering in her chest.

"It will work out, ajokhi, don't worry," Tsehay assured her. "Just stick to the plan. I'll take care of you when you get back." She pointed down the street. "Walk straight for five more blocks, then ask for directions to Etege Menen hospital. Remember the route so you can find your way back."

As Birikti had predicted, they navigated Asmara the day before and found Tsehay's place by nightfall. She took them in immediately.

"Your family will come looking for you soon. You must go to the hospital first thing in the morning to get that treated before they take you home."

“I don’t want to go home,” Elen said, clutching Birikti’s hand, who nodded in agreement.

“Let’s take care of one thing at a time,” Tsehay replied. “You need to make sure that thing doesn’t kill you.” She pointed at Elen’s swollen face with her red-painted finger.

“How do you know they will help me, Aunty?” Elen asked after dinner. “What if they chase me away or ask for money? I have nothing.”

Tsehay shook her head. “The Comboni sisters run the children’s part of the hospital,” she said, spooning more shiro sauce onto the plate of injera and motioning the girls to eat.

“The nuns get people from Italy to send money to help as many kids as they can. They won’t turn you away, especially if they think you’re alone.”

Tsehay was right about everything.

Elen pushed the hospital door open and saw a man talking to a woman behind a desk. The door creaked as she opened it wider to step inside, catching the man’s attention. He turned and walked toward her immediately. Elen let the door close behind her and stood there, trying desperately to understand as the man spoke to her in an unfamiliar language.

He was unlike anyone Elen had ever seen; his complexion was devoid of color, like that of a newborn before seeing sunlight. His hair fell in large curls as if weighed down by water, even though it was completely dry, unlike the erect, proudly combed afros of village boys.

The air inside the hospital was sharp, devoid of Adi Nefas’s rich, earthy scents. People moved quickly in different directions behind the man, their white coats blending into the bright, orderly space.

He repeated the question, but she still didn’t understand and stared at him.

“Where is your family?” he finally switched to Tigrinya, a language she understood.

She didn’t reply, but her expression showed she understood.

He straightened up and spoke again. "Do you have anyone to take care of you?"

She shook her head, unable to meet his eyes and lie. He inched closer, examining her wound from different angles.

"Do you speak Amharic?"

She shook her head again, the only safe response.

Elen had never spoken anything but Tigrinya. She had heard of Amharic, the main language in Addis Ababa, but it was far from her life.

"Well, that has to change." He waved to the woman behind the desk until he caught her attention. "Call Sister Enatye. I'm taking her to Room 2 for an examination," he said, pointing at Elen.

"Come with me," he waved Elen over. He took white gloves from a small bag in his coat and wiggled his fingers into them until they fit snugly.

He held up his gloved hands as he walked into the examination room. Elen followed him into the small white space with two chairs, a small wooden table, and a high bed.

"Sit." He gestured at the black chair, then examined her face. The overpowering smell of his gloves made her stomach roll. It took all her energy not to pinch her nose as he nudged the swelling on her cheek. He reached for a cotton swab and dabbed away the moisture.

"My name is Gabriele," the man continued in Tigrinya. "Hopefully, you can let your family know you're here. We have treated many children and will help you, but your family must be worried."

He spoke with the familiarity of someone accustomed to receiving stray children.

Elen didn't trust herself to speak.

"Sometimes you learn more by being quiet and observing," her mother used to say when teaching her to make injera and maximize their cooking ingredients. "Many answers will come if you keep your ears and eyes open."

Silence seemed perfect now.

"Lucky for you, there's money to support your treatment," he told her. "Dr. Giribi is an excellent doctor. He will fix your face."

She watched Gabriele leave the room and lowered her eyes when he turned to her in the doorway.

"Wait here. Sister Enatye will come and tell you what to do next. Your face is badly infected; it needs to be looked at right away."

After what seemed like an eternity under the bright lights, Sister Enatye, the head nun and caretaker of the children in Ward C, stepped in to greet Elen. Her grandmotherly demeanor instantly dispelled Elen's tension.

"We will take care of you, gualey," she spoke in Tigrinya, her eyebrows arching as she examined Elen's cheek. "You're lucky we just had a bed freed up. Come with me."

Elen followed obediently through the stark hospital hallways. The tiles radiated cold sterility through her thin sandals, slapping with each step.

"You can't let anyone know you have family," Tsehay warned Elen moments after she had said a tearful goodbye to Birikti. "They will make us pay for your treatment or may refuse to help you altogether. We can't afford that. They may offer you a place to stay in return for work. Make yourself useful. When they think your wound has healed, they will talk about moving you to a children's home since you're still underage. That's when you return to me—don't let them transfer you, or I will never find you."

During their pre-dawn walk to the hospital, Elen committed everything Tsehay said to memory. She noted all the landmarks and street corners Tsehay pointed out that would guide her back home.

"Dr. Giribi will be by soon," the nun told her when they reached a room with a row of beds, each occupied by children with various ailments. "I'll see that you get a change of clothes. You can wash after your checkup."

The old Italian doctor, who smelled as pungent as Gabriele's gloves, began what would be a four-month regimen of surgeries, cauterizing sessions, and constant poking and prodding to treat the stubborn infection.

In exchange, Elen threw herself into washing laundry, sanitizing medical equipment, and cleaning outpatient rooms as Tsehay instructed. She worked hard on any task Gabriele or Sister Enatye assigned to her between Dr. Giribi's visits, taking on more than was asked of her and learning as much as she could.

Out of habit, she listened for birds every morning, but their sounds didn't penetrate the concrete walls. No roosters crowd, no cows mooed, no goats bleated their impatience for breakfast. Rolling carts, click-clacking shoes, and beeping machines drowned out any outside noise.

She only allowed herself to miss her siblings in the pre-dawn silence of the children's ward. She had no idea if her parents had come for her or what Tsehay would say to them if they did. She knew her mother would not leave the home, so it had to be Ghebrekidan who took the bus all the way here to bring his daughter back and fulfill his obligations to her husband-to-be's family.

Weighed down by the guilt of being unable to say goodbye, she often thought about Solomon, Alem, and Semaynesh, wondering if they were confused.

Do they miss me at all?

The last hugs she gave Birikti seemed like a lifetime ago. Elen missed her aunt's voice.

Four months was a long time for a thirteen-year-old to be away from everything familiar but, strange as it was to live in this concrete hospital, she got used to it quickly. The pace of her daily chores wasn't too different from what she did at Adi Nefas.

Rubbing the sleep from her eyes now, she ran through her daily tasks and had the complete list in her head by the time she finished washing her face.

Boil water for sterilization.

Check on the senior patients down the hall.

Empty the bedpans.

Check in with Gabriele. Be on time for morning rounds.

Gabriele took everything seriously—from meticulous timekeeping to medical intern duties under the esteemed Dr. Giribi to supervising Elen. She didn't know anyone who paid as much attention to time as Gabriele. She could never figure out why he insisted she learn Amharic or why he took so much time to teach her to match the punctuality of the hospital clocks.

Time was a difficult concept for a village girl who navigated through her days based on the shadows of the eucalyptus trees on their family plot.

Elen cleaned patient rooms after Gabriele and Dr. Giribi's morning rounds. She followed Gabriele when Dr. Giribi moved on to other areas of the hospital, listening and absorbing his constant chatter.

"I am training to be a great doctor," he told her. "Great doctors pay attention to details."

Gabriele's connections through his Italian father paved the way for medical training in Italy, and his Ethiopian roots on his mother's side brought him back to put his skills into practice.

Watch closely and listen. Your eyes and ears will tell you everything you need to know. Her mother's advice proved useful. Elen absorbed it all.

During Dr. Giribi's painful visits, Gabriele translated and eased her fears at seeing the sharp operating tools the doctor seemed to love. At first, Gabriele mixed Tigrinya and Amharic as he translated the fast-talking doctor's Italian.

Though a fluent Tigrinya speaker, Gabriele soon insisted on talking to her only in Amharic. "You know the Emperor has declared Amharic the official language now," he often reminded her. "You need to learn it quickly. You won't last long in this city without it."

After four months of treatments and Amharic lessons, she was conversant, and under Dr. Giribi's insistent attention, her face had lost almost all signs of the infection. The last round of bandages was due to be removed soon.

She replayed the route back to Tsehay in her mind every night before she fell asleep.

Tsehay told the girls how she made her first fortune by selling her special suwa, the best homemade brew in town. She used the money saved from that business to buy properties all over the city and now mostly lived off the rent.

"Even though this world isn't friendly to women, you can always find opportunities and use them," Tsehay told the wide-eyed girls over the spicy doro wat dinner with fresh injera the night they arrived. You have to know how to handle people to succeed. Once you take care of your face, I will teach you everything you need to know when the time comes. Your lives will be complicated, but you can do great things, just like I did," she said.

It will be hard to leave this soft bed, Elen replayed the conversation as she brushed her fingers over the soft sheets in the children's ward.

Burrowing deeper into her bed, she stretched her fingers again to soak in the sensation of the cotton sheets for a few more minutes before getting up to start her morning chores. Most of the children in the other beds still slept, their bodies motionless mounds of white in the two rows of beds.

So many came and went. It was hard to keep track.

An unfamiliar buzz of activity, faint but distinct, came from down the hallway, startling her out of her reverie.

She peeked over her sheets, craning her neck toward the hall. Voices and people rushing back and forth filtered through the doors.

What's happening?

She threw her blanket aside, grabbed her netsela at the foot of her bed, and wrapped it around her shoulders as she sprinted barefoot through the double doors to the main hallway.

"What's going on?" Elen asked a cleaner who was mopping a section of the floor with frantic zeal.

"The Emperor is on his way for a visit now!" She bent to wring the mop into a bucket of soapy water. Her rushed movements flung droplets of suds in a spiral pattern on the ceramic tiles.

"Go tidy up your area!" The woman waved Elen away. She extended her mop and scrubbed, leaving swirls of soapy trails on the floor.

Emperor Haile Selassie?

After a few seconds of processing what the woman meant, Elen needed no more prompting and hurried back to bed.

Nurses streamed in right after her. The early-morning surprise visit injected urgency into their movements as they tucked in loose sheets and inspected the cleanliness of the ward.

"Stay in your beds and behave," a nurse warned the children. Some barely heard her, sleep still weighing down their eyelids.

"You are so lucky—you will get to meet the Emperor!" one of them said as the troop of nurses disappeared through the double doors as quickly as they had entered. With their exit, the air grew heavy, and anticipation anchored the children to their beds.

The obedient exhibit was ready.

The nurses' footsteps faded into silence as they took positions at their stations down the hall. Through the glass section of the double doors, Elen glimpsed a nurse patting down curls under her white cap before smoothing her starched uniform.

"Did you know they named this hospital after his wife?"

Elen turned toward the tiny voice and locked eyes with a newly arrived waif of a girl. A row of stitches hugged her half-shaved head, curving from her forehead toward her left ear. She had been in the hospital for three days, and this was the first time Elen heard her speak. The girl's voice trailed off seconds before the ward's double doors swung open.

In a few movements, Elen brought the sheets higher to her chin so only her bandaged cheek and eyes were visible.

Emperor Haile Selassie.

Elen never considered him a person. He was a concept, a picture on the wall, a voice on the radio. His Highness, the Lion of Judah, a descendant of King Solomon, ordained by God to rule Ethiopia.

Gabriele told her how Eritrea was part of Ethiopia. The Emperor said it was so, and what he said was blessed by God. Sometimes, when Gabriele was deep in political debate in the break room, she learned more through eavesdropping than she ever could by asking busy adults who had no time to talk to a sickly looking thirteen-year-old.

"That shifta Idris Awate thinks he can get His Highness's attention by shooting at a police station like he did last year," he would scoff to any colleague who would listen. "He is nothing but a rogue bandit. Doesn't he know he and his ruffians are mere mosquitos on the back of an elephant?"

"Gabriele, don't be ridiculous," someone would reply. "Eritrea has never belonged to Ethiopia. We have our constitution and government—we don't belong to anyone but ourselves. His Highness, as you call him," the voice was sarcastic, "will regret not listening to the people."

Elen didn't know what government or constitution meant or what people the man was referring to, but she loved the idea of fiercely wanting freedom, just as she did when she left the village traditions behind. It came at a big sacrifice, but the more she lived her own life in Eritrea, the more she felt it was worth it.

This was the place Tsehay moved to and became successful and independent. It was the place where Elen found healing. Eritrea was her new home, where people refused to accept oppression.

"Agh! You don't know what you're talking about!" Gabriele's exasperation had risen to a high pitch and cut into her thoughts. Elen would peek through the doorway and make out the curve of Gabriele's back, arched forward as he gestured to his colleague, his four fingers rigidly pointing as if he were about to slap him.

"His Highness belongs to a long line of kings that has ruled for thousands of years. We are talking about biblical times here. Why would anyone even think of opposing that? Are you trying to bring curses and misfortune to us all? You'd better watch yourself!"

"A smart man like you shouldn't be such a fool." Elen caught the diminishing patience in his colleague's voice. "How is an educated man like you so naive? We are the mighty ones. "He can't subjugate Eritrea for long, believe me."

"Our Emperor knows what is right," Gabriele would retort with conviction. "He is the Chosen One who continues a three-thousand-year-old monarchy. He succeeded many divine leaders, including Emperor Menelik, who defeated colonizers and anyone else who dared defy centuries of tradition. Any Eritrean opposition doesn't stand a chance against his God-given power."

He sounded so much like Elen's father.

Elen thought of those conversations. She often puzzled over how Gabriele juggled his Italian and Ethiopian identities, but she put her ruminations on hold as a large group filled the ward entrance.

The Mighty One is here.

She didn't have to wait long to adjust her expectations of the man she envisioned as larger than life. The compact figure entered their ward. He seemed tiny in the center of the entourage floating around him. They moved in unison with every motion he made, like migrating birds following their leader.

They stopped a few beds down. Dr. Giribi's voice rose from the silent crowd as he gestured toward the invalid. When he finished, Dr. Giribi replaced the clipboard at the foot of the bed and led the imperial crowd around it.

The tidal wave settled around the next patient.

At the end of each of Dr. Giribi's speeches, the royal hand flipped back to take something from a faceless attendant, then deposited it near the child's head. The wave moved closer to Elen.

She retracted her neck into her sheets as the Emperor stopped beside her. His entourage surrounded her bed, their eyes on her bandaged face. Proximity did nothing to increase his stature. She could only muster enough courage to bring her eyes up to his chest.

Shiny medals on his brown lapel sparkled with each movement as he leaned over her bed to examine her face. Keeping her head still, she moved her view up to his beard, a perfectly manicured frame around his chin.

Dr. Giribi kept talking from the other side of the bed. His fingers pointed at her large bandages, his gestures conveying his frustration with her obstinate medical condition and his inevitable triumph over it.

Gabriele stood proudly beside the Emperor and relayed Amharic translations as Dr. Giribi talked. She focused on his voice, her hands clenched tightly under the covers. She sensed rather than saw the imperial smile break on the Emperor's face as Dr. Giribi finished speaking.

As before, His Highness's compact hand shot out, reaching behind him as it had at the other beds. Someone swiftly filled his palm with something, which he placed on the pillow inches from her head.

Money.

The acrid smell of the five birr notes filled her nostrils as the crowd parted for him to float out of the room, following Dr. Giribi's streaming monologue. They left behind a vacuum of silence and the pungent smell of wealth beside her.

6

Asmara, 1958

Bits of dried blood clung to angry welts on Girmai's arm where he had scratched the night before. The thin mattress did nothing to soften the uneven cement floor. Girmai sat up cross-legged in the semi-dark of the tiny room, the raw flea bites trailing up his arms and legs. Foam flakes from the worn mattress stuck to his thick hair, now pressed flat on the side he had slept on.

He stopped scratching to pinch and pull his hair into neatness without a mirror or comb to organize his afro.

Berhane, still asleep, lay curled up in his corner of their tiny space. A scruffy, street-savvy hawker like Girmai, he shared the cost of the room they had just started renting. With the extra income he managed to scrounge through his street hustle, Girmai could finally get off the streets.

Girmai had spent his nights in the sweater factory for months until his uncle found out. As Dawit had predicted, his father was enraged that he used the factory as a home, especially after the scandal Girmai created with his departure from the village.

"This can't work," he had told Girmai after reprimanding Dawit. "You need another place to stay."

I got what I needed from that place, anyway.

During his nights at the factory, the bored technicians were happy to slack off and let him do their work, which he took every opportunity to do.

He did it well.

I have almost enough to rent a sweater machine, Girmai thought. Just a little more, and he would be ready to make his own sweaters.

Girmai stretched to shake off the sleep. He slapped an itch on his neck and murmured gratitude to the almost empty red can of insect repellent beside him. It cost him every birr of his week's earnings, but it was worth the price.

He had sprayed most of its contents around the room, and dead bugs lay scattered as evidence of its power. It relieved the boys from the persistent fleas that lived deep in their mattresses and feasted on them as they lay exhausted from a day of hustling.

Fleas or no fleas, having a place of his own was the greatest achievement of his young life. The pile of T-shirts, chewing gum, and sunglasses Girmai prepped for sale lay by his feet. A plastic tarp underneath protected them from the small stones and dust on the floor.

He'd gotten good at selling. He designed a mobile display of hangers strung together with twine to show off his T-shirts. Girmai studied high-traffic spots throughout the city to find the best places to sell. He avoided areas the municipality spotlighted and worked in the outskirts near the Edaga Hamus market, Geza Banda, and Abashawl—his neighborhood.

His sales savings were slowly growing—five birr here, ten there. He made enough to stay in the shared space with Berhane and put a little aside, but he needed to sell all the items on the floor so he could rent a knitwear machine and make his own designs.

That won't happen today.

Day two of the countrywide labor-union strikes had emptied the usually bustling Asmara. The eerily quiet streets produced no buyers. All his regular customers were sitting at home in protest.

He rubbed another scab on the back of his neck. If what Berhane said was true, their chances of earning anything in the next few days were slim.

Berhane had told Girmai all the details when he first heard about the strike. "It will last for three days. Shops and businesses will be closed. Everyone will stay home. Students are leading protests, too. The labor unions think this protest will make the Ethiopians listen."

"But I see so many more soldiers around now," Girmai had said, dismayed at the potential interruption of his business. "It doesn't sound like they are here to talk."

Berhane and Girmai had gone to sleep the night before with empty stomachs and heads full of worry. Hunger gnawed at him now as he stretched again and yawned.

Their small room was on the fringes of Abashawl, a neighborhood of sprawling makeshift mud and metal structures standing one after the other, with little thought for beauty or function other than providing basic shelter.

Italian colonialists pushed Eritreans out of the city center as they built Asmara, their little Rome. No running water or infrastructure existed in the expanding slum. Mud paths zigzagged around jutting stones and ditches, making nighttime walking hazardous or, at the very least, unsanitary, dotted as they were with the occasional pile of excrement.

Girmai didn't care. He had a roof over his head and a dream of the freedom wealth brought. Once he had saved enough to rent a knitwear machine, he would sell what he had made to people in his neighborhood and make enough money to get out of there. The plan was solid, except for this strike.

He froze mid-stretch at the sound of quick footsteps outside. He yanked on his pants and stooped to shake Berhane awake. "Something is happening. I'm going to check." Girmai didn't wait for him to respond.

The metal sheet that served as their door hung on a rusty hinge. It squeaked when Girmai lifted and pushed it open. He barely hooked it before stepping back as several people rushed past him.

"What's going on?" he asked no one in particular as he followed the flow of people.

"Shobero!" a grim-faced old man muttered through clenched teeth, not breaking his stride. Girmai recognized the bastardized Italian word "sciopero."

Strike.

Steam flowed from nostrils and mouths in the crisp morning air. A few murmurs occasionally broke the rushed silence. Girmai followed the crowd, snaking a path out of his tiny street.

The line of people kept a brisk pace as they streamed over the steep hill, heading toward Kidisti Mariam church. They stopped in a condensed, hushed mass at the vast square before the church. Girmai hung back at the edge, just within sight of the broad steps.

He craned his neck over the people murmuring prayers that reverberated among the crowd and glimpsed a row of women standing at the foot of the steps. Colorful blindfolds covering their eyes contrasted with the white of the netsela over their heads and shoulders.

The crowd mimicked the stillness of the church's two tall towers. Only lips moved in unified prayer. Placards with slogans and demands for freedom and autonomy stood high and still.

Feeling the tension, Girmai pressed forward to see better. The women each held a lighted candle high, swaying in prayer.

"Asfaha ordered extra military and police presence throughout the city. He sent his henchmen to do the dirty work," two men were talking beside him.

Girmai knew that name—Asfaha Woldemikael, Eritrea's newly appointed Chief Executive, and Emperor Haile Selassie's yes-man. Girmai heard people complain about him and his violent repression of rebellion.

"Asfaha has broken down many protections for the labor union and allowed many large business deals to migrate to Addis Ababa," the man in a brown suit beside him said as if responding to Girmai's ruminations. His eyes were trained on the top of the steps. "The proceeds go straight into the Emperor's pocket, of course."

"What are the women doing up there?" Girmai asked him.

The man turned to Girmai in surprise, incredulous that he didn't know.

"It is symbolic." Before Girmai could ask what that meant, the man continued, "They blindfolded themselves to send a message to our traitor of a leader who bows to the Emperor's demands instead of watching out for his people's interests.

"Haile Selassie doesn't care for us. Asfaha needs to know that our people are oppressed and cast aside so the Emperor can profit off our backs. The Tigrayans and Amhara are taking away all our businesses and economy, and our so-called leaders are doing nothing about it."

The smoke from burning incense on the steps rose in soft curls above the women's heads. Girmai was no longer at the edge of the crowd. Multitudes of others filed in and sandwiched him tightly in quiet dissent.

"We are tired of these Ethiopians and their cronies. They need to go back and leave us in peace," the man wagged his finger above his head, the movement shaking through his whole body.

Girmai felt his money-making scheme evaporate at the sight of the growing crowd. He, too, began to pray, trying to dispel the dread rising in him as he remembered a story his father told years ago.

"Why does Aboy Kudus not have a leg and an arm?" he had asked his father when he accompanied him to the neighboring village to visit the distant uncle on his deathbed.

As long as he had known him, Aboy Kudus sat outside his hut, cane in hand, hardly moving due to the difficulty of getting around with a missing leg and arm.

Often sullen and distant, most of the children in the village were afraid of him and kept their distance. He usually stared into the distance, glassy-eyed, as if yearning to let go of this life and be released into the next. He lived many years that way until an incurable illness finally gave him his wish.

"Our people have suffered so much," Girmai's father had said as they followed the well-worn path to Aboy Kudus's house to pay their final respects while the old man was still alive.

"Before the battle of Adwa in 1896, long before I was born," his father continued, "we all used to be one people. We ate the same food, dressed the same way, and had the same traditions—even now, nothing separates us except our history.

"When the Italians took over Eritrea, that wasn't enough for them. They wanted to occupy Ethiopia too. The Italians thought they would be more successful if they recruited our people to fight with them."

"Aboy Kudus was a soldier?" Girmai asked.

"Yes," his father replied. "Emperor Menelik was ruling at the time, and he and his army waited for the Italians and their Eritrean conscripts above the Adwa valley, which they had to cross to get into Tigrayan territory. With the advantage of their elevation and cunning battle skills, the Italian army was no match for them.

"Menelik and his army showed the Eritreans they had captured no mercy. The Emperor was so angry that they would dare fight against him that he gave orders to have the right hands and left feet of more than eight hundred Eritreans cut off. Many died from all the blood they lost."

Girmai had to stop walking then to take in all this information.

"But, Baba," he croaked, a lump forming in his throat as the thought of what Aboy Kudus had gone through solidified in his imagination. The questions tumbled out in his confusion. "Weren't they forced to fight? They didn't have a choice, right? Why did the Ethiopians do that to them?"

"That is the ugly truth of war, my son," his father sighed, wrapping his arms around a tearful Girmai. "The line that separates our people into two countries was first formed from that battle. We in Eritrea continued to suffer under Italian colonization while Ethiopia fended them off, creating a different historical trajectory. This division planted roots of hatred and polarity that will probably outlive us."

"But why did the Tigrayans have to cut off his leg and hand?" Girmai said, still stuck on the cruelty of the Emperor's decision. "They had already won the battle. They didn't have to do that to people who had no choice."

"He was incensed seeing our people fighting on the white man's side," his father replied. "He wanted to punish them so badly that others would refuse to join the Italians. We have been cruel to our own for sure, but our colonizers have split our people up in ways we may never heal from."

Baba was right, Girmai thought, as sirens from multiple directions pierced the calm of the gathering. *I'm beginning to understand what he was talking about.*

The wails crescendoed with the appearance of green military trucks screeching to a halt at the edge of the crowd. Soldiers streamed out, some not waiting for the trucks to come to a complete stop.

A group with Kalashnikovs slung over their shoulders came up behind where Girmai stood. The barrels of the guns pointing high above their heads bobbed up and down as they shoved people aside and headed to the steps.

Girmai and several others around him lost their balance and fell on each other. The soldiers formed a solid circle around a man in the middle.

In full regalia, the uniformed man walked confidently within the vacuum of the circle of armed guards. Girmai scrambled back up and helped the man in the brown suit stand. Others disentangled themselves and struggled to find a foothold.

Girmai looked up in time to see the armed group scale the steps past the praying women.

Once he reached the top, the uniformed man turned and pushed his chest out. He surveyed the crowd. His eyes hovered just above the silent people facing him, still and expectant, holding placards with handwritten messages of "Free Eritrea!" and "We Want Our Country Back!" high above their heads.

The man in the brown suit grasped his head with both hands, his elbow pressing against Girmai's ear. "Why are they calling armed guards to a peaceful gathering?"

The panic in the man's whisper raised the hairs on Girmai's arms. "Maybe they just want to show us how strong they are," Girmai said. He was used to threats from uniformed people. "I'm sure he will just give a speech and leave."

"That is National Police Commander Tedla Ogbit," the man

in the brown suit whispered to his friend beside him as if Girmai hadn't spoken. "Why is he here?" He rocked back and forth on the balls of his feet now, his elbow brushing Girmai's ear.

"By the authority given to me by His Highness Emperor Haile Selassie, I order everyone here to leave immediately!" The Commander's voice boomed from the top of the stairs, pausing the prayers and incantations.

Tendrils of the threat extended menacingly all the way to where Girmai stood. The women in the front adjusted their blindfolds up to their foreheads and looked up at him.

"I command you all to leave. Now!"

No one moved. A sea of Eritrean bodies stood in quiet defiance.

The women at the front resumed their invocations louder than before, sending back ripples of prayers throughout the square. The Commander pursed his lips and gave a slight nod to the soldiers on either side of him.

They simultaneously pulled the rifles off their shoulders and flooded down the stairs. They swung their rifle butts in every direction, crashing into the women and shoving them to the ground. White-clad bodies crumbled from the force and disappeared from view. Screams spread like wildfire.

The soldiers kept their stride. They stepped on and over the women while swinging their rifles like a farmer chopping down bushes in his path. They hit this way and that, pushing into the crowd.

Commander Ogbit watched his orders play out.

"Free Eritrea!"

The man in the brown suit startled Girmai. His jacket flapped, revealing a pudgy midriff. His fist punched toward the sky and moved in synch with the bouncing placards as people backed up from the batons. The chants intensified.

"Freedom from oppression! Workers have a voice! Free Eritrea!"

The energy pulsed even as the soldiers pushed on. Tedla Ogbit's face darkened as he glared down from the top of the church steps.

Then he raised his hand.

Whizz! Canisters shot up in an arc and crashed into the middle of the crowd. White clouds rose and spread. The soldiers paused long enough to pull on masks, then pressed forward again.

Chants turned into coughs. Before Girmai could catch his breath, a rapid succession of gunshots rang through the smoke. Everyone clawed at each other to get away.

Girmai turned to run. Out of the din of screams, the sound of a man's head cracking when it hit the ground emerged from the surrounding chaos and stopped Girmai cold. The man in the brown suit was on the ground.

Coughing, Girmai pulled his shirt over his nose, crouched low, and hunched his back to stiffen it against the stampede.

The man lay motionless, his body in an unnatural heap.

"Ato! Ato! Mister, get up! We have to leave. It's dangerous here!"

Why isn't he moving?

The smoke lodged in Girmai's throat and stung his eyes. Coughing through the fumes, he could hardly see through his tears. A multitude of feet stepped on them both, knocking Girmai over several times. He regained his balance and shook the man's inert body.

The man lay face down, his brown suit blending into the dirt between the cobblestones. He didn't move no matter how hard Girmai shook him.

Girmai braced against the stampede of feet and tumbling bodies. He put a hand under the man's heavy shoulders and heaved to turn him over with a strength he didn't know he possessed. A scream stuck in his throat when he saw the gaping hole in the man's chest, just above his round belly.

A flower-shaped bloodstain spread across his white shirt. Blood oozed onto his jacket and pooled on the ground around them. The man stared upwards, eyes vacant, mouth open as if he had stopped speaking mid-sentence.

People ran over and around them, spreading bloody footprints in all directions as they stepped on the widening pool of blood.

It's too late.

He straightened up in time to see masked soldiers a few feet away. Shots rang in the air around the square even as soldiers beat body after body with batons.

Girmai scrambled away, coughing and spitting out the burning particles of the white gas cloud that stung his eyes and throat. He managed only a few unsteady steps before something slammed into his shoulder, knocking him to the ground. He struggled to get up and spat out dirt stuck to his lips. Just as he got onto his knees, two men stepped up on either side of him and dragged him into the back of an open truck. They kept shoving more and more people in until they ran out of space.

"A few days in jail should set you all straight," he heard before he blacked out.

7

Asmara, 1962

Boiling pots of water intensified the heat in the laundry room, spreading clouds of disinfected, humid air that lingered on everything. Elen finished folding the last sheet and walked over to the sterilization pots. In the far corner, a few women were scrubbing sheets in large basins.

"That batch of syringes is ready to come out," said Sister Enatye, sitting by the window and tilting a white bed sheet to the sunlight as she stitched a rip.

"I'll get them, Sister," Elen said. "I hope you're not straining your eyes too much. I can finish fixing the sheets after I take these syringes upstairs."

"Oh, don't worry, my dear," Sister Enatye replied, her smile deepening the V-shaped lines from her eyes to her chin. "I need to keep my skills sharp!"

Elen smiled back, washed her hands thoroughly, and grabbed the metal tongs. With the dexterity of a trained professional, she maneuvered the glass syringe cases out of the water, placing them in a neat line on a sterilized metal tray.

Enatye squinted, struggling to thread the needle. Elen set the tray down and walked over to her.

"Here," Elen said, "I can at least do this part."

Enatye watched Elen thread the needle, then rearranged the sheet pooled around her on the floor. "I know there's another tear here somewhere. Thank you, my dear."

Her creased eyes crinkled again as Elen handed the threaded needle back. “What would I ever do without you?”

“Sister! You always give me too much credit,” Elen said with genuine humility, holding Sister Enatye’s weather-beaten hand and giving her a slight bow. “I learned everything I know from you.”

“You certainly did not. Praise be to God!” the old woman laughed, raising her palms skyward as Elen returned to the syringes. “But compliments will get you everywhere.”

“May God be praised,” Elen murmured. She owed this woman her life.

Elen poured hot water into a basin full of sheets on the floor, then reached for the tray to take it to the third floor. An influx of patients urgently needed the syringes.

As she walked, she recalled the first time Nurse Mariam, now tending to patients on the upper floors, patiently showed her how to sterilize equipment. “These tools can save lives, Elen,” she had said. “Your attention to detail makes a difference.”

Elen ran the sterilization process so efficiently that Nurse Mariam no longer had to supervise her.

“I’ll be right back,” Elen said, covering the syringes with a clean cloth, and pushed the door open with her back.

She delivered them safely and was back a few minutes later to start scrubbing a new pile of white sheets.

“You’ve learned to care for people so quickly,” Sister Enatye continued as if Elen had never left the room. “You’re a natural caretaker with a healing touch, and you are truly a blessing to us, Elen. I hope you can continue working here after you settle into your new home. You have the makings of a great nurse.”

“New home?” Elen stopped scrubbing and looked up at Sister Enatye.

“Once they believe your wound has healed, they’ll discuss moving you to a children’s home, since you’re still underage. That’s when you leave and come back to me—don’t let them transfer you, or I’ll never find you.”

The idea of relocation overshadowed Sister Enatye’s compliment.

“I’m happy I secured a wonderful place for you at our children’s home, not far from here. I’m not sure what happened to your family, but they would have contacted you by now if you had relatives.”

Sister Enatye didn’t pause for Elen to confirm or deny; she’d stopped asking a while back, knowing Elen was tight-lipped about her past.

“Anyhow, living in a proper home will be better than being here,” she gestured around her. “We’ve set up a good school with everything you need. You can learn to read and write and make something of yourself.”

She smiled broadly at Elen, who stood still, hands half emersed in the sudsy bucket.

“I’d love for you to continue working here. Maybe after school you can work a few days a week.” Enatye’s benevolent smile remained as she returned to sewing.

“Thank you, Sister,” Elen replied, bowing, and returned to scrubbing.

Her new life had started here at Etege Menen hospital. They took her in like an adopted daughter, cleaned her up, gave her a hospital bed, fed her, and taught her how to care for others as she healed.

She even attended Catholic services on Sundays. Despite her discomfort with the unfamiliar customs far removed from her Orthodox Christian upbringing, she recognized God in that place.

A melancholic weight grew in her gut as Elen scrubbed the sheets. She began a prayer of gratitude as she thought about what she needed to do next.

She thanked God for this place that took in a poor village girl and Sister Enatye’s constant companionship and maternal love. For the nurses she shadowed who taught her the art of ministering to the sick through their medical knowledge and being good listeners. They taught her the power of finding joy in unlikely places and, most importantly, relying on the power of prayer.

She gave thanks for Gabriele, who taught her a new language and how to tell time, and for Dr. Giribi, who healed her and gave her a second chance at life.

This place was the haven she sought when she thought she had no control over her future.

She allowed her eyes to roam around the room as she completed one task after another—more barrels in the endless cycle of cleaning and washing, more used syringes ready for sterilization, soiled bedsheets to be washed, and bedpans to be cleaned and delivered to the rooms upstairs.

"You've been so generous to me, Sister. Thank you." She bowed again in deference to the elderly nun.

She ached at the sight of the older woman's warm smile.

I'm about to break her heart.

The bandage on Elen's cheek was now a superficial covering. Multiple surgeries and treatments had finally turned Dr. Giribi's frown into a satisfied appraisal of the healing skin. "It has been an interesting case study; we've learned a lot from you, young lady!" he exclaimed. Elen didn't think she could teach anyone anything, much less this distinguished doctor, but she didn't contradict him.

A week ago, Dr. Giribi had removed the bandages to reveal tender but smooth skin beneath her eye. Gabriele held up a mirror, and she marveled at her unblemished face.

"I'm so grateful to you, doctor," she had said in Amharic, bowing to them both.

My time here is done.

***

Elen dressed in the semi-dark without the birds signaling the start of the day. The wall clock told her she had twenty minutes before the nurses' shift change. The sheets were clean, all her chores from the day before were complete.

Now was the only window of time she could leave unnoticed.

She patted the five birr notes deep in her dress pocket and wrapped her netsela tightly around her head and shoulders. Guilt at leaving Sister Enatye and Gabriele without saying goodbye slowed her movement from the children's ward toward the hallway.

As dawn broke, the hallway filled with the organized chaos of nurses coming in and their counterparts signing off.

Elen quietly followed the exit signs, grateful for the predictability of the hospital routines. Other than the nurses' chatter, it was relatively quiet, and no one paid attention to Elen as she made her way down the hall.

She slipped out a side door of the hospital, gently shutting it behind her. Four months after walking into the hospital, she walked out healed, confident, and ready to move on to the next step of her new life.

Her departure was unlike the desperate escape from Adi Nefas. Back then, her focus had been solely on getting out without being caught. As she walked into the crisp morning air, her emotions swung between doubt and guilt.

I should have said goodbye, she thought, her heart heavy. *What kind of person leaves without a word?*

She imagined Sister Enatye's kind eyes filled with worry and Gabriele calling for her, never getting a response. The thought almost made her turn back.

But if I return, can I ever leave? She shook her head, knowing the answer was the same as it had been in Adi Nefas.

She paused and turned to take one last look at the hospital's silhouette framed against the dawn.

No, I must move forward, Elen thought. *I can repay their kindness by building a new life with the skills they taught me.*

She retraced her steps to Tsehay's house. Breathing in deeply, she let the chill flow through her. With each breath, she remembered the warmth of the hospital: Sister Enatye's smile as she stitched a tear in a sheet, Gabriele's patient guidance as he taught her new Amharic words, and Dr. Giribi's satisfaction at her recovery.

She focused on the landmarks Tsehay had pointed out, her pulse quickening as she walked faster and closer to her aunt's home. By the time she reached Tsehay's street, the tugs of regret for leaving Gabriele, the nuns, nurses, and doctors who had cared for her so well weakened their pull on her.

"You must come back here. It's the only way I can help you. It's the only way to make a life for yourself."

The hard heels of her shoes, one of many donations to the hospital, echoed on the empty sidewalks as she closed this chapter of her life.

***

Birikti was not there when Elen returned.

"They took her home," Tsehay said, her voice low and emotional after their tearful reunion. She hugged Elen again and motioned for her to sit on the couch.

"Look at you!" she exclaimed, touching Elen's smooth cheek. She fumbled in her pockets, grabbed a tissue, and blew her nose. "It's completely gone, and I swear you've grown taller too!" She smiled through her tears.

"Yes, Aunty," Elen said. "I'm so grateful for your help. I learned a lot at the hospital and could never have done it without your advice."

Tsehay's face softened. "I checked in on you whenever I could. I needed to make sure you were alright."

Elen's eyes widened in surprise. "I didn't see you, Aunty. Not once."

A mysterious smile played on Tsehay's lips. "I was there, Elen. I've been keeping tabs on you the whole time. I'm just glad you're back."

Elen hugged her aunt with gratitude and relief. "Thank you for watching over me," she said.

"I wish I could have done the same for Birikti," her aunt said and sighed heavily. "It was good you left when you did. Soon after the hospital took you in, I sent a message to the village to let your parents know you were alright. Both your fathers came, and we had a terrible argument. I asked them to let her stay with me for a while, but her father was so angry he began fighting with Ghebrekidan. Your father then blamed him for your escape, saying if he hadn't taken Birikti to Adwa with him, she would never have known to take the bus.

"He told him that he was to blame for your disappearance. Birikti's father took her and left immediately. She was crying and screaming—it was horrible. She resisted, but he had also come with two of his cousins. She was powerless to stop them. I was too."

Tsehay wiped her tears. "There was nothing I could do."

Elen's heart ached for her friend. "She saved me. Now I'm here, and she's back to everything I ran away from."

Elen clenched her fists, desperation mixing with her sorrow. "Will she be able to come back?" she asked her aunt, searching her face for any sign of hope.

"I'm afraid not," Tsehay said, her vivacious aura dimmed. "I haven't returned to Adi Nefas since I last saw you there. Even if I went, I doubt anyone would let me near her." She leaned back on the couch. "She will most likely marry as soon as her monthlies appear. They'll keep her under lock and key until then."

"What about my family?" Elen asked, almost afraid to know.

"When he was here, your father demanded that I bring you back from wherever I had taken you," Tsehay said, blowing her nose into the tissue again. "On that one, I stood my ground. I told him I didn't know where you went for treatment, and I refused to let you go without getting the medical help you needed. He was not happy with me."

"He came to take me back," Elen spoke her thoughts out loud.

"Yes. Your father sends me messages every week asking about your whereabouts. The man you were supposed to marry got impatient, and his family made big demands. I told him I would let him know once you healed."

Elen, alarmed, opened her mouth to protest, but her aunt held up her palm. "Don't worry, I won't. The man's family found him another bride, but unfortunately, your parents owe a debt for backing out of the agreement."

Elen buried her head in her hands and let her grief pour out. "I will find a way to pay them back," she said.

"Your mother also made me promise I would let her know when you got back." She took a deep breath. "We need to be prepared for her visit."

"Even Mama taking a trip here will not convince me to go back,"

Elen said, straightening up. "I love my family, but I will never return. This is my home now."

"I know," Tsehay said, "but you'll have to help your family understand, and that won't be easy."

8

Rome, 1973

The austere stone lion heads at the base of the obelisk were frozen, mouths agape in a perpetual, silent roar. Girmai had scouted the area a few days earlier to make sure he arrived at the correct meeting place.

Monumento ai Caduti di Dogali—a Monument to the Fallen of Dogali.

A monument to the defeated, more like it, Girmai thought as he gazed up at its starred peak. Light moss clung to the names of Italian soldiers who had lost their lives in another defeat to the Ethiopian army a year after their loss in the Battle of Adwa.

Girmai shrugged, tightened his leather jacket, and shook his head at the monument's irony.

Where are the names of the Eritreans who were forced to fight, and lost their lives? he thought, barely able to look at the obelisk as he remembered Aboy Kudus and his missing limbs. Every time he came to Italy, he struggled to contain his frustration.

Who commemorates those who lost their land so the Italians could replicate their beloved Rome in Asmara? What of those who served as housemaids, errand boys, gardeners, and street cleaners while forbidden from their own land's main streets after dark?

Girmai swallowed his bitterness and glanced across the street, checking for any sign he was being followed. He decided to walk around the block again, just in case.

He briskly sidestepped harried commuters, glancing around

every few seconds. He had just left the knitwear expo a few blocks away, where the exhibit of his latest sweater designs was a big hit. He'd signed on more investors and ordered machine parts to be shipped back to Asmara.

He had come a long way in fifteen years—from street boy to one of the city's more affluent businessmen. He had the street smarts, the drive, and the aversion to hunger that fueled his business ventures.

Expo 69 Enterprises Inc.—named after the place and the year it went international. His exhibit at that expo catapulted him to purchasing deals beyond Asmara.

The first transformation of the sweater-production business from a one-man show to mass production clicked into place after an Italian knitwear factory in Addis Ababa hired him after seeing his samples.

The job allowed him to save the money he needed to start his small factory in Asmara. Single-digit orders from his tiny shack in Geza Banda multiplied into hundreds, then thousands.

Now, he had customers in Sudan and Ethiopia, and he was branching out to Kenya. He produced and sold volumes of original sweater designs, reinvesting the profits to purchase state-of-the-art machinery and train his employees. The exponential growth fulfilled every dream he had as a young homeless boy.

He hoped this exhibit in Rome would expand his sales to Europe.

First things first, Girmai thought as the meeting place came back into view.

Obelisco Dogali, near Termini Station. 5:00 p.m.

He quickened his pace and thought of his family back in Asmara.

Girmai first met Helen at their engagement ceremony in a crowded Geza Banda house. By then, he had moved out of his tiny shared room in Abashawul and lived in a middle-class Geza Banda neighborhood.

Helen was a good woman. His older half-brothers and her relatives took care of the logistics and presented them to each other as a perfect match. She fulfilled her end of the bargain as the dutiful wife. She bore him four healthy children who filled the house with joy, lighting the empty crevices of Girmai's soul.

His children knew nothing of the suffering that defined his younger days. Girmai vowed to always give them the life they deserved. Yonas, the eldest and most thoughtful, was now eight and took his responsibilities seriously. Samuel, the calm one, never rushed for any reason. Rahwa, the spitting image of her mother, had bright eyes that shone with a love of life. Alexander, barely one, was most content in Helen's arms.

Baba would be proud.

The hunger and deprivation that plagued Girmai in his teens manifested in his need to provide abundance for his family. Every night he would open the pantry, the sight of stacked shelves calming the lingering dread from his teenage years of hunger and want. As his business expanded, he moved his family into a prestigious house in Sentata Otto, an elite formerly Italian neighborhood.

He took great satisfaction in living in a house like the one the municipality officers had kicked him out of as a street boy.

The more successful Girmai became, the worse the political situation in Asmara and Addis Ababa grew. The labor-union protest that had turned violent at Kidisti Mariam church had been Girmai's first experience with resistance, and his response to it was just the beginning.

When Girmai first arrived in Asmara, Eritrea was in a federation under Ethiopia.

Italy had lost its rights to the colony. Instead of granting Eritrea independence, the United Nations decided Emperor Haile Selassie should rule it in a ten-year federation meant to end in 1962.

That was ten years too long for the Eritreans.

In 1961, when Girmai first rented his knitwear space and began production, revolutionary leader Hamid Idris Awate fired the shots that triggered a nationwide war against the Ethiopian Federation and Emperor Haile Selassie's iron-fisted rule.

By 1962, members of the Eritrean Assembly—either coerced or bribed—voted to dissolve the federation. The Emperor decided Eritrea was a province of Ethiopia despite the widespread desire for an independent state.

His father had been right in his predictions all those years ago.

The fissure between Eritreans and Ethiopians created by the Italians in the last century had widened so much that even Girmai agreed Eritrea's historical trajectory had diverged too far from Ethiopia's for them to be considered one people.

"You can be an instrumental member of the freedom movement," a nameless ELF contact told him during a family gathering Girmai attended.

That's all Girmai needed to hear to join the Eritrean Liberation Front. He was all in. He organized medication delivery and monitored and reported on the movements of high-ranking Ethiopian military officials—anything he could do to support the freedom movement.

By the time Girmai launched Expo 69, the pinnacle of his knitwear business, he had received orders for sweaters faster than he could produce them. With over sixty employees, his factory functioned at full capacity and continually expanded to meet demand.

Girmai learned more subtle ways to resist authorities and avoid repercussions. Money spoke a universal language, so he used it to make the necessary connections with people in power to make things go his way.

The Eritrean Liberation Front jumpstarted a clandestine movement to remove the Emperor's hold on Eritrea, but the ELF imploded just as it seemed to gain traction in the resistance. Deep disagreements, formed along tribal lines, tore the movement apart. One commander would declare himself the leader, only to be unceremoniously eliminated by a shot to the head or a knife to the back.

We have a common enemy. It is insane to fight with each other. Girmai could no longer be a part of it. *But I can't stop fighting.*

Pigeons scattered as Girmai approached, then settled back

around the lion-head statues and on the steps, resuming their rhythmic pecking at cracks in the cobblestones.

A bitter taste filled his mouth at the memory of clouds of tear gas and the sound of the man's head cracking on the pavement during the strike at Kidisti Mariam.

He made a small sign of the cross, remembering all those jailed with him that day. He had been released because of his age, but many remained in jail.

Who knows what happened to them, Girmai thought. *This is not the world my children will grow up in.*

The stillness of a solitary figure sitting on the concrete steps behind a newspaper contrasted with the bustling crowd around him. The paper partly obscured the man's face, but Girmai recognized Asefaw Kidane from one of the secret meetings he'd attended in Asmara.

Asefaw folded down a corner of the newspaper, tucked it under his arm, and rose. He extended a thick palm toward Girmai and gripped his hand in a tight handshake.

"You are a persistent man." His tone was warm despite the abruptness of his words. "I trust your exhibition went well?"

"Yes, very well, thank you." Girmai nodded to Asefaw's back. He had already turned to walk down the stairs without waiting for a response.

Asefaw was a senior member of the newly formed Eritrean People's Liberation Front (EPLF), a separate solution to the self-destructing ELF. A group Girmai wanted to join because of what he'd heard Woldeab say on the radio several times. The man he was finally going to meet.

"We must stand against any kind of oppression," Woldeab had said in one of the speeches Girmai memorized. "Whether it be from the European or the African, we cannot be confined by the subjugation of others."

The six assassination attempts on Woldeab Woldemariam made it impossible for him to live in Eritrea. Kissing the ground as he left the country, he withdrew to his secluded hideout in Rome, where he continued writing, publishing, and advocating for Eritrea's independence.

It had taken Girmai many meetings and months of waiting to arrange this connection with the man nicknamed the Father of the Eritrean Revolution. A man who built a workers union when no one else dared, who challenged the colonial power, who spoke of freedom with such conviction that he made people believe in the inevitablity of a free Eritrea.

"Come, he is waiting for you," Asefaw said over his shoulder.

Girmai followed him on a circuitous route, which suited him just fine. It gave him time to think about the upcoming meeting. It was a risk to be seen with Woldeab; he was a wanted man.

"We are not too far," Asefaw said.

They turned onto a narrow street leading to a corner pastry shop. Its huge front window yawned tall and wide as if to inhale as much light as possible. Climbing plants by the entryway gave off a vineyard feel. However, the smell of roasting coffee and the grunting espresso machine quickly corrected that impression.

Weaving past small circular tables sprinkled around the room, Asefaw led Girmai through narrow glass double doors to a quiet outdoor area in the back, a surprising shift from the warmth and chatter inside. Woldeab's compact figure sat at a table near the tendrils of climbers stuck to the wall. He adjusted his round glasses and began to rise.

"No, please don't get up, sit, please!" Girmai bent low in deference, cupping Woldeab's outstretched hand with both of his own. "I've been looking for you for a long time, Baba Woldeab." He waited for Woldeab to settle, then sat across the table.

"I have heard of your good work," Girmai said.

"Thank you," Woldeab replied, a smile stretched across his lips.

"I know you have very little time, and I hope to learn from you." Girmai leaned forward, getting right to it. "What can I do?"

Woldeab put his cappuccino down. The steam deposited a foggy cloud on his glasses, and his left eye peered through it.

"First, you need to be informed," he said as he removed his

glasses, rubbed the opaque moisture off with the corner of his shirt, then placed them back on his nose in a smooth, deliberate movement.

"Make sure you have as much information as you can. That is the first step. You will not last long if you don't understand why you are fighting."

His voice was low, with a slight whistle. Asefaw leaned back in his seat, his eyes bouncing from one man to another. "Second, think of yourself as an Eritrean more than anything else. Unity is key. You are not a highlander, or a Christian, or a businessman. Your family is your country. Your country is your life. You are Eritrean first."

As Woldeab continued to speak, Girmai absorbed the weight of his words, feeling his own purpose crystalizing. Clarity opened his mind for the first time in years.

"You need to understand the risk of what you are committing yourself to. Once you join this fight with us, you can't walk away. Your involvement in anything related to the liberation movement could cost you everything, including your life. Are you prepared to do that?"

Girmai sat still and let Woldeab's words sink in. The memory of the man in the brown suit morphed into the bodies of his children, their heads cracking one by one on the sidewalk, their blood spreading a dark stain on the road, their deaths going unnoticed beneath the bloody footprints of soldiers' boots.

"Yes, I am prepared."

9

Asmara, 1974

The woman in the mirror bore no signs of the Adi Nefas runaway she once was, except for the faint scar on her cheek. Elen's red lipstick caught the light as she flicked her hair back and reached for the copper kohl container.

Leaning close to the mirror, she lined each eye with a practiced sweep, the black kohl brightening the white of her eyes. Her floor-length dress hugged her frame, its braided neckline plunging in a subtle spiral pattern.

She crossed her legs and slipped on a stack of gold bangles, followed by rings, and topped off the look with round gold earrings embedded with matching blood-red stones. Satisfied, she took a deep breath.

Almost ready.

"Mama?" Aman, her six-year-old son, pushed the bedroom door open and walked in, his legs still heavy from sleep.

"Good morning, my sweet," she replied.

Aman stretched his arms for his daily dose of love. Careful not to brush her painted lips against him, she scooped him up, embraced him, and breathed the soft scent of soap from his bath.

"Kemey hadirka?" She held him tight. "Did you sleep okay?"

He burrowed into her shoulder in response while Faven, Elen's rambunctious three-year-old daughter, waddled across the room as fast as her legs could carry her, determined not to let her brother get all the attention.

Elen's sister Alem leaned against the doorway and smiled as Faven fought Aman for a place on their mother's lap. "It's good they woke up before you left for work."

Elen's blow-dried hair cascaded over her daughter's face, giving Faven the perfect opportunity to pull it.

"Hey, young lady!" Elen said, shaking her head so that more of her hair covered Faven, who giggled. "Come up here, you silly little one."

Elen swiveled, shifted Aman under one arm, and scooped Faven up to her lap with the other in smooth, practiced motions.

"What would I do without you?" she asked Alem over Faven's soft curls.

Elen blinked back a wave of emotion and pulled her children tighter against her. Alem was the spitting image of their mother. A mother she hadn't seen for eleven years.

* * *

Two weeks after her release from the hospital, Elen was still riding the wave of euphoria at being free, healed and independent in the city until Selas had appeared unannounced at Tsehay's. Her father must have thought her mother's presence had a higher chance of success at discreetly bringing their wayward daughter back home to set their family finances back on track.

Emboldened by all the prospects of her new life, Elen resolved to be unmoved by any argument her mother might pose but wavered at the sight of her mother. Her eyes were sunk deep into their sockets and new worry lines etched prominent tracks on her forehead and fanned out from the corner of each eye.

Though her mother embraced her and Elen clung back, the rift between them was more significant than either could articulate.

"You look well," Selas had said as she unwound from their hug and sat on Tsehay's couch.

"Thank you, Mama," Elen said, settling beside her.

Tsehay sat at a distance in a chair by the dining-room table, ready to intervene whenever needed, as they had discussed before Selas arrived.

"Thanks be to God," Selas murmured under her breath, her response to most things in her life.

Elen bowed and remained silent, knowing what was coming next.

"You left us in a bad situation," Selas told her.

"I'm sorry, Mama." Elen lowered her eyes, but she was determined to stand firm. This conversation would not end with her going back to the village.

"The fine is heavy," Selas continued, her voice more potent, as if taking Elen's silence as consent. "Our family cannot bear it, and we live in shame."

"I can change that in time," Elen responded, glancing at her aunt, who was nodding encouragingly out of Selas's line of vision. "Tsehay helped me find work in a restaurant. I just started the job, but as soon as I have enough money, I will send it to you so you can pay the fine. Maybe one day I can even support you so you don't have to work so hard."

Selas's eyes clouded, She pivoted to Tsehay, then cast Elen an incredulous look before pursing her lips and composing herself.

"I can help you all from here," Elen continued, her mother's silence encouraging her. "My salary will be good, and in time, it will be bigger than any dowry you could have gotten for me, and I can help support everyone at home." She hoped repeating that fact would help it sink in.

Selas's jaw muscles twitched, her eyes now trained on a spot on the floor.

Just as Elen wondered if she heard her, Selas spoke. "You have to fulfill your obligations," she said, in the same tone she used to admonish Tsehay half a year before. "Your father knows your treatment is complete. Despite this shame on our family, another man has agreed to move forward with a marriage. Thanks be to God." She looked up, raised her palms, then clasped them back together.

Heat rose in Elen's gut. Her mother was supposed to be her defender, shielding her from all the bad things in the world. Instead, here she was, trying to force her back into bondage.

"He is from a village further than the first one," Selas continued, now facing Elen. "He is a respectable man and he has agreed to take you. You will be happy with him, and your union will restore our family name. I can tell you all about him on our way home. We will leave tomorrow."

Elen erupted into an angry tirade, the details of which would forever overshadow all memories of her mother.

"I will be dead before I let that happen!" she finished through clenched teeth. "You will find me hanging from a tree by my neck the minute I set foot in that village. Either let me be, or you will have no daughter."

Selas returned to the village alone and, as she promised, Elen started sending a little money back home every month, hoping it would make amends, but she got no response until a phone call from her father months later.

"Your mother is very sick and asking for you." Ghebrekidan's voice crackled through the phone.

"What happened? Is she okay?" Elen asked, half-suspecting this was another ruse to lure her back to arranged marriage bondage.

"You should come home," her father said flatly. "She is asking for you. That's all I can say."

"Usually, things are serious if you get a call like that," Tsehay said after Elen hung up.

"What if they are just saying this to get me back?" Elen replied. "Then some man will strap me on a donkey and take me away, and that will be the end of my story. I feel like I just started living. I can't leave now."

Tsehay had asked a favor of her friend Awash, who immediately gave Elen a job at Awash Restaurant. It was only a ten-minute walk from home, and Elen quickly settled into the routine as she had done in the hospital.

She was just getting into city living. Having never waitressed before, she had mimicked the other waitresses when they talked and laughed with customers, encouraging them to buy more. Now, she could hold her own.

She was learning to read and write through a tutor Tsehay brought home for her once a week. Another friend, another favor.

Going back now would be the death of all that freedom, a regression into the black hole of eternal wifely servitude.

"It must be serious if your father walked to Adwa to give you this message."

"True," Elen replied. Usually, he would send one of her cousins or Solomon to make the call. "But remember how badly our last conversation went?" Elen said. "She hates me. Why would she want to see me after all this time?"

"Don't worry," Tsehay reassured her. "I will come get you if you don't call me or aren't back in a few days."

With Tsehay's reassurances as her lifeline, Elen took a bus back the following day and began her walk down the road from Adwa to the village. The path wasn't wide enough for cars. She was grateful for the time to rehearse what she would say to apologize and begin to repair her relationship with her mother.

The shift in her childhood home hit her as soon as she reached the clump of eucalyptus trees at the edge of the family plot. Ghebrekidan's bull stood unharnessed beside the stationary plow under the shade of the lone tree despite it being mid-morning, the height of the workday.

Something is wrong, Elen thought. Ghebrekidan never stopped farming.

She rushed through the field to the wall that enclosed the family compound.

In contrast to the emptiness of the fields, netsela-clad people filled the hut's outdoor enclosure filling every space, squatting or sitting cross-legged on the floor. Some silent, others wailed incoherently.

Ghebrekidan, Selas, and Elen's siblings were nowhere to be seen.

People parted to let her through, and she quickly followed the opening path into her childhood home.

Ghebrekidan's hunched profile on a low stool slowly came into view as her eyes adjusted to the hut's interior darkness.

"Ah! My daughter, you are here," he croaked, barely lifting his head. "Come sit down, my dear. We need to tell you something."

What he said next came to her in broken pieces. "Your mother is dead … the baby had still been kicking as life left her body … died right there … in the kitchen … the same place you were born … we buried her already … couldn't wait … nothing we could do …"

Her father spoke in jerky phrases, much of which was garbled by the time it reached Elen's ears.

"But you told me she called for me," Elen almost choked on her tears.

"It is God's will."

"Was she alive when you called?"

"No," her father replied, putting his head in his hands, "but I couldn't think of any other way to get you here so you could hear this news from me and mourn with your family."

"I didn't even know she was pregnant."

"She was with child when she came to see you," her father said, his voice heavy with grief. "We didn't know it at the time. I am sorry. Please stay with us."

Solomon, Alem, and Semaynesh appeared beside her, but Elen barely registered their presence.

Either let me be, or you will have no daughter.

Those were the last words her mother heard her say. Now she had no more words.

Elen was unaware of how long it took her to get up, free herself from her siblings' mournful embraces, and walk out of the house.

She couldn't be there anymore, not one more minute.

Alem, Solomon, and Semaynesh followed and clung to her. Neither their voices nor their pulling could break the rigidity the shock had locked her body into.

One foot after the other, she moved out through the low doorway of her family home, past the mourners, past the field, past the bull and the eucalyptus trees, and into the afternoon bus back to Asmara.

* * *

Eleven years and it still hurt to remember it.

"You okay?" Alem asked, unfolding her arms.

"Yes," Elen smiled at the younger version of their mother and loosened her grip on her children. "You just look so much like Mama today."

The mention of their mother brought a sheen to Alem's eyes. "You look exactly like her too," she said.

"Twins!" they said simultaneously and laughed.

Faven wiggled in her lap. Elen followed Selas's advice and said a quick prayer of gratitude for Alem and that Ghebrekidan accepted Elen's request to have Alem come to the city to help her with the children.

After Elen abandoned village traditions and Ghebrekidan failed to present her for a second marriage arrangement, all the families with eligible sons were reluctant to enter into agreements with him for any of his daughters. This reputation spared Alem.

Several years of measly harvests after Selas's death, a second marriage, and another child on the way softened his decision to let Alem go to Asmara to stay with Elen.

Elen pushed away her guilt with money she sent home monthly, and showered Alem and the kids with as many luxuries as she could afford.

Alem got her through two failed relationships. Yacob was the first. He had walked into Elen's life when she was still an impressionable young woman but several years and experiences away from the naive village girl she was when she left Adi Nefas.

A regular at the restaurant, Yacob was an older man with a quiet elegance and kind eyes who pulled her into a sense of comfort and security, everything she had imagined a relationship could be. His slow smile and eagerness to focus on nothing but her were rewards she eventually allowed herself.

As promised, Tsehay showed her how to live independently, which rules of society could be bent, which to handle delicately, and which to ignore entirely. "Everyone wants something from you at all times," Tsehay had warned. "The key to keeping your freedom is remembering that and always being a step ahead. Watch and learn how people behave and carefully listen to what they say. Identify what they want and adapt, and you will always have the upper hand."

Elen fiercely held on to her independence and remained uninterested in marriage. Yacob didn't bring it up, and it worked perfectly for her. They settled into comfortable routines in their agreeable relationship until Elen got pregnant.

Overjoyed at the prospect of being a father, Yacob unintentionally revealed he was married to a woman who couldn't have children—a woman he had no intention of leaving. Elen cut off the relationship.

It's a blessing in disguise, Elen reassured herself. *I would never spend the rest of my life with him anyway. I don't need any man's help to raise my child, reputation be damned.*

Elen hatched a plan she hoped would benefit them both. She moved out of Tsehay's house. That is when she began working on convincing her father to let Alem come to the city to live with her as she raised her child.

"One less mouth to feed," Ghebrekidan had said, only half joking, when he finally agreed.

Elen worked, and Alem helped her raise Aman with Yacob, who visited regularly until his job moved him to Keren shortly after Aman's first birthday. The hour-and-a-half drive north of Asmara cemented the separation.

She let him visit his son as often as he liked over the years, much to Negassi's consternation.

Negassi, Faven's father, was as different from Yacob as one could be. She met him a year after Yacob moved to Keren. His electric personality swept her off her feet until she discovered his volatility. His alcohol-induced fits of jealous rage surfaced just after Faven's first birthday when Elen decided to go back to work.

Stop working now.

I will take care of you.

I am the father of your child.

Marry me.

You must take care of me.

I don't like the way you look at other men.

I don't like the way other men look at you.

Stay home.

Marry me.

You are mine.

"I'm sorry," Negassi would say when his inebriated fists left deep bruises all over her.

Elen was grateful that he had spared her face. *Less explaining to do.*

The groups of people scattered around the restaurant one morning were too far to hear but close enough that he couldn't make a scene.

Elen was stepping back from the bar counter when Negassi's long, bony fingers wrapped tight around her arm so fast she couldn't move. He pulled her toward him, the stale tinge of alcohol still wafting from him.

"I just love you so much. I am sorry, okay?" His eyes searched her face. "I don't remember much of what happened, but I know I hurt you. Will you forgive me? I will make things right, I promise. Just give me one more chance."

She couldn't keep a love that came with fists. She hadn't run away from her family to be a prisoner of volatility and fear.

She remained silent and rigid, waiting for him to let go of her. He didn't.

"No. Not now. Not ever," Elen said, the steel in her tone loosened his grip. "We are done."

Negassi's sober self accepted defeat, though he continued to approach her over the years whenever he had the chance, hoping she would change her mind.

***

I am done with all that. I can take care of my family myself, Elen thought as she reflected on the faces framed by the dresser mirror. *Alem and the kids are all the family I need.*

Elen shook off her melancholy and looked at her sister leaning against the door frame. Though Alem had moved in with Elen years before, the city hadn't changed her much. Unlike Elen, she shied away from the ever-evolving European fashion trends, braided her hair in traditional cornrows, and wore simple dresses.

With her netsela draped respectably over her head, Alem often hid her radiant smile behind her hands, just as their mother had taught them decent, respectable girls should do.

My children will have the best of both of us, Elen thought as she smiled at how wildly different they were. *I will always be here for them, no matter what,* she promised herself often, though she knew that promises were fragile things with no guarantee that one could truly keep them.

Elen left as Alem, Faven, and Aman settled down for breakfast. She braced herself with a deep inhale before stepping out onto the sidewalk.

As she had for the past several months, she walked the most populated route to the restaurant, hoping to avoid the attention of the soldiers who seemed to multiply on the streets these days. She'd draped a heavy gabi around her head and shoulders for the walk. The less attention she got, the better. Elen quickened her pace, weaving through the more crowded streets and main avenues.

She stepped through the Awash restaurant entrance and stretched her neck to release the tension built up in her shoulders. Grateful she didn't have to ward off groping hands or unveiled demands for access to her body this time, she fingered the ring she had on her left hand, one that fabricated a story of a husband to ward off horny soldiers.

The chatter of the morning crowd calmed her as she made her way to the bar counter, stopping several times to greet regular patrons nursing steaming cappuccinos and macchiatos. She passed the cash register and poked her head into the cramped inner office to check on Awash.

"How is Tsehay doing?" Awash asked her before even glancing up, the radio behind him droning unfamiliar, military-sanctioned music instead of the urban hits that usually filled the airwaves at this time of day.

"She's okay," Elen said, feeling the weight of the untruth. "She gets more tired each day but she's eating, which is a good sign."

The ethereal Tsehay, Elen's lifeline who taught her everything she could about navigating life, was now bedridden; it was only a matter of time before the cancer claimed her. She coughed more with each passing day, a mere shadow of her former self. Elen didn't understand how a woman as vibrant as Tsehay could deteriorate so fast.

"I will see her again on my way home today," Elen said. "She likes your croissants, so I'll take her one."

Her head was still craned into Awash's office when the song on the radio faded into silence.

"Come." He motioned her to the chair before him. He turned up the volume on the radio. "They are about to make an announcement."

Elen closed the door behind her and sat down. "About what?" she asked.

He pointed at the radio and put a finger to his lips just as a scratchy voice began to speak.

"We bring you this special announcement from the Provisional Military Council."

The Derg.

"On this day, November 24, 1974, we confirm that executions of several corrupt former cabinet ministers and government officials took place yesterday. Before their execution, they were held on charges of corruption and have now paid for their crimes. They will no longer taint our society with their unscrupulous divide-and-rule policies. This cleansing of feudalistic leaders who purported to support the people but only served themselves will give power back to the people. Those not executed will face a military tribunal for their crimes."

"Besma'am! Oh God!" Awash said, holding his head. "What is happening, Elen? They were supposed to stand trial. What is happening?"

The radio usually offered limited information. Elen got most of the news from conversations she overheard at the restaurant like what areas soldiers patrolled the most, the next location for a demonstration, the arrests, the violence, and the disappearances that followed.

This broadcast was the first announcement of its kind.

Emperor Haile Selassie's biggest mistake, one that made the Derg possible, had been to ignore the devastation of the famine that took the lives of so many, especially in places like Adi Nefas, where one fickle rainy season was the cliff drop to starvation.

Those who didn't have someone like Elen supplementing their meager harvests wasted away on parched land perpetually deprived of rain, with no other way to replenish their teff stockpiles.

Meanwhile, the Emperor had built shiny hospitals and state-of-the-art universities that few could afford to go to.

More companies in Asmara migrated to Addis Ababa. The joblessness and hunger escalated to a boiling frenzy of rage.

The Emperor's government either ignored students' street protests or quickly squashed them as they had with the labor-union protests more than a decade before.

Nothing budged until January when a small group of hungry soldiers in Negele Borana, a barren military outpost in Southern Ethiopia, became the spark that lit the point of no return for Ethiopia and Eritrea.

Incensed after discovering their supervisors were hoarding food and water while they went days without eating, the soldiers tied them up and ate full meals for the first time in months.

Elated with the success of their little rebellion, they broadcast their triumph on the radio, which inspired other units across Ethiopia to revolt en masse. The Emperor's soldiers turned their allegiance to the Provisional Military Council, a mysterious group of high-ranking soldiers who called themselves the Derg—The Committee.

They kept their identities hidden behind their promises of "from the people for the people" as they silently took over, cementing their control in a swift and bloodless coup.

Elen hadn't heard about the Emperor's removal until she saw the newspaper with a large picture of him being led out of his palace and into a beat-up Volkswagen.

As of today, September 12, His Imperial Majesty Haile Selassie has been deposed from office. Elen had gotten her hands on the *New York Times* after one of the regulars brought it to the restaurant and translated for her.

Shops were open, buses were running normally, and a good-natured populace appeared to greet the Emperor's overthrow with joy, the newspaper article said. *For example, a waiter at the city's Hilton Hotel said, "This is great. I'm very pleased about it. Things will change for the better now."*

It was November now, and no one knew what happened to the Emperor.

At first, both Asmara and what she heard of Addis Ababa seemed to rest in a suspended hope. The Derg's slogans of "Ethiopia first," "Land to the peasants," and "Democracy and Equality to all" spread fast.

Elen caught snippets of conversations in the restaurant:

"Now we will have a better chance of eating."

"The Derg have risen from the people. Enough of elite aristocracy!"

"Good riddance. We can finally get that meat the Emperor imported for his dog."

"We will have our jobs back. Our economy will thrive!"

"Eritrea can finally be free of Ethiopia. The Derg is not interested in us."

The tanks that had swiftly descended into Addis Ababa, probably in anticipation of demonstrations at the Emperor's removal, were instead decorated with flowers.

The masses greeted the soldiers with *Ethiopia First* stickers on their uniforms with joy and gratitude, anticipating the end of their hunger.

In the months that followed, the Emperor's disappearance didn't bring any change. Optimism turned sour. Opposition groups began asking questions and shifted the political tides. Demonstrators vocalized their opposition to the swift takeover and turned up on the streets, only for the army to quickly silence them.

"Did you hear about the students they killed?"

"They shot them at the funeral!"

"Slaughtered like sheep!"

"Those were probably the same soldiers who killed the friend they gathered to bury."

"They said they would make things better for us, but they are worse than the Emperor."

Static filled the silence in Awash's office before the announcer resumed. He continued dryly, detached from the life-changing words he delivered to the country.

"Former Prime Minister Endelkachew Makonnen and former Chairman of the Derg, Major General Aman Andom, are also dead. Following are the names of all who were executed yesterday. Families of these individuals should not try to locate the deceased."

Elen and Awash sat stock-still as the announcer read the names of all sixty former government officials loyal to the Emperor, now probably buried together in a mass grave.

The music came back on when he finished reading the list, closing the announcement.

"Aman Andom," Awash said, cradling his head as he bent to face the floor. "Our last hope for peaceful independence from Ethiopia."

Elen had long before gotten her resident papers from Asmara, which identified her as an Eritrean.

Where do I belong? she thought silently. *What are my children? How am I going to keep them safe? Which side is better for them?*

"Imagine what the Derg is going to do to us Eritreans if they can do that to their own leader."

10

Asmara, 1975

"You'll have to take a break at some point!" Berhane exclaimed, plonking himself into one of the two chairs facing Girmai's desk. "Come on, just for a quick coffee." Girmai's old roommate draped his bony figure loosely over the chair.

Girmai's office lay between his bustling main street sweater shop and knitwear factory in the back. He had designed it as a quiet workspace close enough to manage both ends.

With so many employees depending on him, Girmai had little patience for wasting time and didn't plan to socialize anytime soon. Everyone knew not to disturb him when he shut his door, but Berhane, predating Girmai's successful businessman phase and structured rules, felt entitled to ignore Girmai's irritation.

"You have all day to get to this." Berhane waved at the stack of invoices.

Girmai set his pen down and leaned back in his chair. "I have too much to get through," he said, crossing his arms. "The trucks leave for Addis tomorrow. They've rotated the guards at the checkpoints again. With everything changing so fast, I need to make sure all of them get through."

Orders continued to stream in for his bold colors, collared casual knits, formal knitwear, and unique sweater cuts. He had recently opened a children's wear shop across the street and was working on further expansions.

"I don't have time," Girmai insisted, gesturing at the desk.

“Listen,” Berhane said, “Kifle has a job coming up and won't be around for a while. There is plenty of time for all this when you get back.”

Girmai had met Kifle months after he and Berhane began sharing the small room in Abashawul. Over the years, Kifle built a trucking business that delivered produce nationwide. He knew the language and cost of getting through Derg checkpoints.

Berhane sold the latest fashionable watches just down the street from Girmai's sweater shop, so they stayed close. Their friendship, born from the days of fighting off constant hunger, had deepened over time. Even after achieving financial security, their shared survival instincts and steadfast loyalty remained constant.

With his focus on the receipts and ledger now broken, Girmai's resolve faltered. He knew his friend wouldn't budge until he relented.

“It would be good to get together to discuss the latest news in the *Vanguard*,” Berhane continued, mouthing the illegal magazine name.

Girmai had returned from his meeting in Rome two years before with a renewed sense of purpose and a copy of the first edition of the *Vanguard*, a magazine that documented the widespread killings, arrests, and changing Derg policies in more detail than he had ever seen before. Risking arrest or worse, Girmai had hidden it in the inside pocket of his jacket, moving it undetected through the airport checkpoints. He sneaked in every edition he could get his hands on since then and buried them deep in Biet Giorgis forest, where he, Kifle, and Berhane would read them. Berhane's mention of the magazine instantly took Girmai back to his initiation meeting into the EPLF two years ago.

* * *

“A funeral will take place in Quazen next Thursday,” Asefaw had said when they parted outside the café in Rome, after their meeting with Woldeab. He would not tell Girmai any more than that. “Plan to be there.”

Girmai waited for more than an hour among the mourners gathered in the village for the funeral before Asefaw appeared.

"I'm glad you made it."

Asefaw's voice, so close to his ear, startled him. Girmai did a double take, adjusting to the complete makeover before him. Gone were the soft Italian loafers and the clean-cut jacket of the Rome meeting. Instead, Asefaw wore an old T-shirt loosely tucked into oversized pants held up with a frayed rope for a belt. A thin gabi draped over his shoulders finished the look—standard-issue village wear.

Girmai caught a faint outline of what he thought might be a gun tucked into Asefaw's waist beneath the loose-fitting clothes.

They moved out of hearing range of the funeralgoers. Just as Girmai squatted beside Asefaw at the base of a tree, two men appeared as swiftly and unannounced as Asefaw, flanking them. Both had the same dusty, disheveled look that blended seamlessly into the village-scape.

"Welcome to the EPLF," Asefaw said. "This is Daniel Kebib, your field partner. He will work with you on all your assignments. He is in and out of the city often and is your direct line of communication with our fighters in the field. Memhir Yemane is our operations coordinator."

They didn't ask Girmai questions. He suspected the EPLF had already vetted him and probably knew everything there was to know.

"It is safer that you and Memhir are never in direct contact. He will supply all the information you need through Daniel."

"You are an asset to our operations in Asmara," Memhir said. Girmai recognized him as the pharmacist several blocks west of the cathedral downtown.

"We need access to medicine, money for food, and weapons," Daniel continued, his lips barely moving. "People like you are our lifeline. We will win this war together."

"Our strength lies in our people," Memhir agreed. "We have cells all over the city that serve different purposes. Daniel and I focus on transferring information and goods through checkpoints.

"Other fedayeen cells have begun to plan missions to eliminate high-ranking Derg officials, conduct sabotage operations, and monitor the movement of Derg troops so we can plan attacks in the field.

"Given your key position in this city, you will not be involved in those operations." He shook his head slightly to silence Girmai's questions.

"You are uniquely positioned to get Derg officials on your side," he said, shifting closer to Girmai. "Gain their trust. Gather what information you can from them and relay that back to us.

"You will need to recruit people you can trust with sensitive information to help you. We may have a few meetings like this to move things forward. Funerals here are a good cover."

A wail from one of the mourners cut into the conversation. The priest's incantations rose as four men shoveled dirt into the grave. Girmai understood the reason for this unusual meeting place. Unlike the streets of Asmara, there were no soldiers in sight at this village funeral.

"As few people as possible must know about your work with us, so choose your people wisely."

Girmai thought of his friends right away. *There isn't anyone I trust more than Berhane and Kifle.*

"If we need to arrange a meeting with you, we will give you a time and a place we know is secure," Memhir added. "The only way into those meetings is a code word—d'rar leyti. Tonight's dinner.

"We have systems in place to get that word to you. The code changes daily, so if someone doesn't know it or uses the word from the previous day, the cell is compromised, and you need to stop and let Daniel know right away."

"The *Vanguard* magazine is a good way to educate people about what's happening around us," Daniel said. "Keep it in a safe place. It could get you killed."

Two days after that meeting, Girmai drove Kifle and Berhane into Biet Giorgis forest with the magazine hidden under his seat. The small nature sanctuary hugged the outskirts of Asmara and was the perfect cover. He revealed the magazine once they reached a secluded spot.

The black ink of the title contrasted deeply against the red cover of the illegal publication, making all the letters appear to levitate.

Berhane and Kifle spoke at the same time. "This could get us arrested," Berhane breathed. "How did you get this into the country?" Kifle's eyes roved wildly over the page, not expecting an answer.

Girmai remembered Woldeab's words as he turned to the first page. *To make a difference, educate yourselves so we can be united in our fight against our common enemy. Use this to learn from the past so you can heal the future. Only by learning through our successes and mistakes can we pave a path forward.*

They read about fractures in the ELF's revolutionary movement, where Eritreans fought each other for power while the Emperor took advantage of their fragmentation to maintain control. They learned about the Derg's coup and the massacres that continued.

Unlike their initial public declaration of executions, these more recent killings went unannounced. The deeper they delved into the magazine, the more they understood the scale of the Derg's agenda of rule by force.

They read about the birth of a new rebel movement that rose out of the ashes of the divisions that crippled the ELF. The Eritrean People's Liberation Front erased lines of gender, religion, and ethnicity to create one unified body with one agenda—Eritrean independence.

"The EPLF is what we need to be free," Girmai told his friends. "We can finally make a difference."

They read until the flashlight was a distinct beam of light in the darkening forest, then covered the magazine with a stone at the base of a tree to return to later.

***

Girmai now looked at Berhane across his desk. It would be good to see Kifle. He knew their friend had his finger on the pulse of the city and probably had something new to share.

"Okay," Girmai pushed his chair back. "Half an hour, then I need to get back." He grabbed his brown leather jacket from the coat hanger and power-walked out of the office without glancing back to see if Berhane was following.

"I'll be back soon," Girmai told Araya, his store manager, who was talking to a customer at the far end of the shop.

"No problem," Araya replied with a wave as Berhane caught up to Girmai at the front of the store.

They stepped out into the sunlight. Girmai squinted as the glare momentarily blinded him. A group of soldiers walked toward them on the opposite side of the street.

Girmai and Berhane fell silent as the gap between them and the soldiers narrowed. *Too young to be carrying Kalashnikovs, too young to hold the power to take lives,* Girmai thought.

"They are everywhere," Berhane said once the soldiers were out of earshot. Tension wiped the joviality from his face, and he forcefully shoved his hands into his jacket pockets.

"Did you hear the Derg controls the grain flow now?" he continued. "No trader can move their goods without paying hefty bribes."

"It's affecting my supply chain too," Girmai agreed. "Why do you think I needed to work today?" he said, pursing his lips.

"They even regulate the flour mills so people can't get their teff ground without paying a fee," Berhane said, raising his palms in frustration as if Girmai hadn't spoken. He quickly put them back in his pockets. "If they don't destroy the mills first, that is. How can we do business if we can't trade freely?"

Girmai waited until they rounded the corner before he spoke. "We will have to figure out how to get around this."

Though he had left his office begrudgingly, he was grateful Berhane had dragged him out. The walk could help clear his mind and allow him to focus on what he needed to do.

The Derg had divided neighborhoods into wards called kebeles, installing their own administrators to govern each one. In the cities, kebele lines mostly followed existing neighborhoods, but they expanded into larger areas in the countryside. Prices were rising everywhere, and crossing kebele lines was particularly costly. These administrators, the Derg's eyes and ears on the ground, were loyal to the regime but didn't shy away from profiting from their positions. Many demanded their cut for anything that functioned within their jurisdictions and they had the authority to collaborate with soldiers to weed out traitors as they saw fit—constant reminders of the regime's pervasive reach.

Girmai and Berhane walked silently for a few blocks until Berhane caught sight of Kifle. Kifle's hand shot up in greeting, and he ambled over to them from across the street. His oversized clothes hung loosely over his thin frame. The men fell naturally into the traditional embrace, knocking shoulders several times.

"It's been a long time!" Girmai beamed at Kifle. It seemed like an eternity since they had met in the forest.

"It is always a long time whenever I deprive you of my presence," Kifle joked, wiggling his eyebrows. Unlike Girmai and Berhane, Kifle was away for chunks of time, driving containers of goods up and down the country and into Ethiopia before the recent roadblocks stifled the flow. He spent more time in the city now, waiting for several stages of kebele official approvals to allow him to pass through the checkpoints.

Girmai did his part to open some roadblocks, but this only worked until they rotated the soldiers on duty, which they did more frequently recently.

Girmai and Kifle coordinated the transportation of supplies for the EPLF. Payments to Derg soldiers on duty kept the searches superficial, and well-hidden undercarriage compartments on Kifle's trucks remained concealed from even the most discerning eyes.

Kifle led them around a corner, keeping his chatter buoyant as he asked Girmai about his kids and jokingly poked fun at Berhane's faded suit jacket. He had a way of easing tension.

It is a good time for a break, Girmai repeated to himself, rolling the rigidity out of his shoulders as he walked.

The red-on-white Awash Café and Restaurant sign was visible from blocks away. The prominent letters occupied the whole breadth of the top of the window. The vast, almost floor-to-ceiling windows revealed the animated discussions of the patrons inside.

Kifle swung the glass door open, laughing loudly at Berhane's joke. Girmai hadn't heard it, his mind back on the work he had left behind.

Still chuckling, Kifle stepped into the restaurant. Berhane smoothly cut in right after and held the door open for Girmai. The restaurant was several degrees warmer than the breezy street outside.

As Kifle looked around for a free table, Girmai rolled his shoulders again, willing the tension out of them. He untied the leather straps that held his coat closed, shrugged it off, and draped it over his arm before scanning the room.

His eyes froze when they landed on her. She seemed to float around the tables as she moved toward them. The woman flashed Kifle a brilliant smile as she leaned in to tap his cheek with hers in the traditional greeting. She said something to Kifle, but Girmai couldn't hear it through the drumming in his ears.

One tap—he saw her entire face, her eyes momentarily closing in synchronicity with her cheek lightly touching Kifle's. She pursed her full lips to make the motion of a kiss. Her face disappeared to the other side of Kifle's head for another tap. A waterfall of thick curls bounced off her shoulder to fill the gap where her face had been seconds before. Her face came into view again for the third and final cheek tap.

The woman motioned for Kifle to follow her as she led them to an empty table. Her hips swayed, flicking her long dress from side to side in a gentle motion. The sleeveless cut accentuated the deep brown of her arms, a striking contrast to the brightly colored patterns on the dress.

She stopped at a table by the window and extended her arm toward it. Her gold bangles danced noisily with the motion. Three chairs around the table were angled toward each other, all strategically placed to give each occupant a view of the street through the large windows.

"I know you like this spot, Kifle," she said, her bright red lips stretching across the white of her teeth.

Girmai was captivated by how freely she smiled, as if nothing bothered her. He walked around the table, acutely aware of her slight step back to give him room to get to the chair. As he passed her, his lungs filled with her soft, rosy scent. He inhaled it in until his head spun. He had to sit down.

He blinked rapidly to clear his head and focused on Kifle.

"You may already know Berhane," Kifle said to her, pointing at him. "He has been here several times before."

Berhane stood and shook her hand.

"And this is my friend Girmai," Kifle said, gesturing in Girmai's direction.

Her dark eyes, kohl-lined, turned to him as he stood transfixed by the bare arm she extended, palm open.

When he took her hand, the hairs on his arms and neck rose. His eyes watered. He couldn't look away. He covered her hand with both of his, breath catching as he took in every detail: how the whites of her eyes contrasted with the kohl, her smooth brown skin, a faint silvery scar under her eye that creased with her effortless smile.

Girmai's gaze locked with hers and she held it. A fierce need to know everything about her flooded him. He held her palm with a rising desperation to make the moment last.

Who is she? How have I not seen her before?

"Nice to meet you," she said, her velvety voice rising gently above the restaurant's white noise. "I'm Elen."

11

A few minutes before, Elen's ears had pricked at the voice that cut through the restaurant's white noise.

"They're going to get them all. The bastards!"

She stood still behind the cash register, keeping her eyes cast downward. The restaurant's L-shaped floor plan offered a small alcove hidden from view, where the voice had originated. Elen couldn't see the speaker from her spot.

Usually, during the mid-afternoon lull, streets, restaurants and coffee shops usually emptied, hosting just a few patrons here and there as everyone headed home for a quick siesta. Shops closed for lunch and even soldiers took respite from their routine harassment before everything reopened again for the afternoon shift.

Elen used this time to tune out the few scattered conversations and focus on tallying up the earnings. Her thoughts drifted from Aman and Faven to the safest route home and methodically went through her ever-growing to-do list. It was the perfect time of day to find calm.

But what she just heard evaporated whatever complacency she had felt moments before.

Who is going to get whom?

Elen cocked her ear to catch whatever else they said. She could see Akberet, who had served that table, now taking orders from a couple near the window.

People had become more guarded with their words, but she had developed a knack for blending into the background and catching even the slightest whispers of information. That was the only way to gauge how bad things were.

"I heard they are hiding out in Gejeret," the voice continued, barely audible. "They have been watching that area for a while."

That was close to where she lived. It took all her energy not to lean toward them more than she already was.

Something bad's about to happen.

"I think they might be EPLF fedayeen," the man said. "It is only a matter of time before the Derg find them and destroy the entire place." He lowered his voice. "Soldiers have already arrested so many suspects, but those people in Gejeret don't seem to care. They keep helping the rebels."

Elen had heard about the fedayeen and knew of several EPLF safe houses across the city. The EPLF trained these elite fighters in assassination, theft, and sabotage. They perfected disguises and could work undercover, undetected for months.

The fedayeen often moved in and out of the city unnoticed. After completing missions—stealing money or weapons, intercepting medication or food—they would vanish into EPLF-friendly homes until it was safe to leave.

Elen had sharpened her hearing at home as she did at Awash. Everyone stayed home after dark. She listened for cars roaming the deserted streets. She and Alem taught Aman and Faven to keep quiet, fearful of the Tor Serawi—the Derg security officers and their dreaded strangulation teams.

Investigations after coordinated attacks usually involved violent banging on doors followed by intensive searches that often ended with arrests and detainment in undisclosed locations.

Despite the danger, safe houses were plentiful across the city, with Asmara residents hiding EPLF members from even the most watchful kebele officials.

Elen suspected many Awash patrons were Derg supporters, though no one openly showed their allegiance.

Awash's home served as a safe house, and Tsehay's did, too, until her illness prevented her from helping. Elen had not yet offered her tiny place but wanted to. She couldn't stand the constant fear and the feeling that she was doing nothing about it.

"We can't just sit by and let them do what they want to us and our country," she had told Alem when her naturally cautious sister reminded her to be careful. "This is our home. God is with us always. We must do the right thing, if not for ourselves, for Faven and Aman."

The voice around the corner pulled her back to the present.

"I hope those fighters get out in time, or it won't be good for them or anyone caught with them," the first man said.

The hairs on Elen's neck stood on end. If someone got caught in a safe house, an entire neighborhood would suffer the consequences.

Who are they with?

"How do you know all this?" another voice interjected.

"I overheard it in the changing room at the end of my shift. The Colonel mentioned an ambush." A chair scraped against the floor as she imagined he moved closer to his friend. "He ordered more guns from surrounding outposts. I think they're planning to get them tonight."

God have mercy!

A thin sheen of sweat broke across her skin. If there was a raid, everyone within a kilometer of the house would be in danger.

For the past few months, Elen and her neighbors stopped turning on lights at night. Lights attracted soldiers patrolling the streets, eager for a catch. She and Alem used candles and entertained the children quietly until bedtime, hoping the tightly drawn curtains would protect them from unwanted attention.

Successful fedayeen operations often triggered rampages, though the Tor Serawi seemed to choose which houses to search at random. Searches meant open drawers, broken belongings, and residents taken to interrogation facilities. If they found anything suspicious, the soldiers would comb houses within a few-block radius. If residents were lucky, they stayed alive in their upturned homes.

Who do I warn?

Elen slowed her breath and moved closer to the corner to try to see the men. It would be helpful to know who they were.

"Apparently, six men went into that area yesterday," the voice continued. "Someone reported that to the Colonel, and then he ordered more guns. They suspect these men are connected to Commander Negassi's death last week. The Colonel is planning to—"

The restaurant's main glass door flew open. Three men stepped inside, the one's deep-throated laughter severing any chance of hearing the rest of the conversation.

Irritated, Elen replayed what she had heard so she wouldn't forget. *Safe house in Gejeret … six men, probably fedayeen … retaliation for Negassi's death … weapons ordered … raid planned tonight …*

The men paused at the entrance and surveyed the room for a table. She smiled despite herself when she recognized Kifle. It had been a while since she saw him. A long-time customer, Kifle's visits for his double cappuccinos were as unpredictable as the rainy seasons. He came to Awash whenever he was in town, and she'd grown fond of him and his boisterous demeanor.

This is good timing. Kifle might know what to do. She knew she could trust him with this information.

Before she could move to greet Kifle, movement behind him caught her eye. One of the men with Kifle was removing his brown leather coat, its exaggerated lapels flapping. Elen barely blinked, her gaze fixed on his every movement.

She sensed lithe energy in him, like that of a runner poised just before the starting whistle. His eyes darted around the room, a half-smile on his lips at something his friend had said.

The man's movements were fluid and effortless as he walked, like water flowing over river rocks. His jacket hung carelessly over his arm. He exuded a quiet confidence that made Elen's breath catch.

"Everything okay?"

Elen jumped as Akberet poked her with an elbow, a cuppuccino in one hand and a worried frown wrinkling her forehead.

Elen blinked, her kohl suddenly heavy around her eyes. She

plastered on a smile and willed herself to move. "Yes!" she said as she placed papers into a drawer and shut it, then she walked around the counter and began weaving through the tables until she reached the trio.

"Kifle! How nice to see you!" she smiled at her friend. He reminded her so much of her brother Solomon.

She offered her cheek in greeting, and he leaned forward to reciprocate. "Why do you abandon us like this, my brother? Do you not miss us?" she said. Their cheeks connected three times.

"Elen, haftey, my sister! If work didn't drag me away, you know I would eat breakfast, lunch, and dinner here!"

Elen relaxed into the familiar banter. Kifle's body shielded the other two men from her as he continued to hold her hand.

"I see you are not missing me at all." He smiled and gestured at the people around the room.

"You know we can't live without you, my brother," Elen said lightly. "It's you who insists on leaving for months, then you forget your friends here. Come, let me show you to your seats."

Elen's back tingled at the thought of the man behind her. Her bracelets jingled as she gestured to a table by the window. She seated them diagonally opposite the cash register, somewhere she could observe without being seen.

She stepped aside to let them weave through and settle into their seats. It took all of her energy not to look at the stranger.

Kifle's voice came back into focus. "These are my friends. You may know Berhane; he has been here before," Kifle said. "We go way back … he has a shop down the road … sells watches … close friend …"

"Nice to meet you." Elen bowed as she shook Berhane's hand, catching only half his words.

Kifle pointed to the other man. Elen turned slowly to him, silently celebrating that he sat where she'd hoped he would. She willed her trembling fingers to steady themselves.

"This is my long-time friend, Girmai," Kifle said.

The man rose from his chair and gently wrapped both his hands around hers. The handshake felt familiar, yet thrillingly new. A warm charge shot through her arm and settled deep in her core.

She fixed her expression into a pleasant mask, hoping her face didn't betray her as she looked up and held his gaze.

He held her hand longer than was necessary, and she let him. She smiled wider and gave his hand a soft squeeze.

"Nice to meet you. I'm Elen."

***

A week had passed since Elen had first laid eyes on Girmai. He hadn't returned, and sometimes she thought she had dreamed him up. She was back at her usual spot behind the counter, her gaze fixed on the doorway, willing Girmai to show up again.

She had replayed a scenario countless times over the past week. The anticipation of him stepping through those doors was almost unbearable, but she couldn't help but crave it.

She was grateful she had put her confused emotions aside long enough that day to pull Kifle aside to tell him what she'd overheard. Girmai and Berhane had gone ahead and were outside chatting as they waited for Kifle. "Unfortunately, I didn't see who the men were before they left."

"You did well, Elen, haftey," Kifle had assured her. "I'm sure it will be okay."

"I hope so."

As the moon hung in the sky that night, Elen lay in bed, her mind racing with conflicting emotions. Part of her was relieved that the children were quiet and asleep, but another part was on edge. She tried to quiet her thoughts, but they kept her awake well into the night.

The only sounds had been the occasional rumbling of an army truck passing by. She prayed that the quiet meant the fighters had made it out safely. It didn't matter who they were or what they were fighting for; all that mattered was that no lives were lost. Elen inhaled sharply to bring herself back to the present. The restaurant was abuzz with activity, leaving Elen little time to daydream.

"Can you make sure those four in the corner get their second beers?" she asked Akberet, pointing to a group of older men, each leaning in to hear each other better.

"Ishi," Akberet said. "I will get it to them immediately. Is it okay if I take a quick break after that? I haven't gone to the bathroom in ages!"

"Of course," Elen laughed. "I don't know why you wait until the very end. I will cover for you, don't worry."

Elen allowed herself one more look at the busy street beyond the window. She froze.

Girmai's lean frame cast a long shadow on the glass as he approached the entrance. Despite his brisk pace, his confident stride exuded ease. The sunlight danced off his fitted leather jacket, highlighting every contour.

Just as he did last time, he paused once he stepped inside, shrugged off his jacket, and looked around. His lips curled into a smile beneath his thick mustache when he saw Elen.

He reached the counter in a few quick steps. His proximity muted the laughter and chatter from the other diners. The clinking of silverware and glasses faded into the background even more as he lowered himself onto one of the high bar stools.

"Selam, Elen, how are you?" he said.

She wondered if he smiled often and who he smiled at, feeling a pang of yearning at the thought.

They didn't shake hands this time. Elen didn't trust herself and kept her hands glued to the counter's edge. Girmai crossed his arms, resting his elbows on the counter, and leaned forward. His eyes didn't leave her face.

"Selam, Girmai," she said and cleared her throat to steady her voice. "So nice to see you here again. What can I get you?"

His eyes dropped to her lips as she spoke. The sensuality of the motion set the pit of her stomach on fire. She instinctively placed her hand above her collarbone, over her pulse that hammered through her bare neck. She regretted wearing the dress with a revealing neckline today.

"Just a club soda, thank you." His smile stretched wider.

His eyes were on her as she poured him a glass.

I can't let fleeting emotions distract me, Elen thought. Doing so would only complicate her already complicated life. She needed to be vigilant.

She slowly placed the glass and half-empty bottle in front of him, embarrassed by the warmth radiating from her flushed cheeks.

Girmai kept looking at her over the rim of the glass as he downed most of his drink.

She shifted her gaze.

There was no time or space for Elen to lust after a man. She had been doing well on her own, finally free from the toxicity of the relationship with Negassi. His recent time in jail for drunken driving solidified her decision to cut ties with him. She was settling into a safe, platonic routine with Yacob; balancing her work and home life while keeping Alem and the kids safe took all her energy.

"How is Kifle?" she said, keeping her voice light. "Please tell him not to disappear like he did last time. We enjoy his company over here."

"That is what I came to talk to you about."

Girmai's face was suddenly serious. His eyes scanned the restaurant. No one was within earshot. Most customers sat several meters away.

His voice lowered when he spoke next. "You saved them all."

"What?" she said. "Saved who?"

"The men at the safe house."

He emptied the rest of the bottle into the glass before looking up at her again.

"Kifle told us what you overheard, and we got them out. Soldiers came in a few hours after they left. You saved them."

Elen stifled her relief as she processed what Girmai was telling her. *They got away, and no one got hurt. Thanks be to God!*

"Kifle told me how perceptive you are," Girmai continued. "He says you have a way of making others feel at ease, so they naturally open up to you, that you are skilled at reading people."

"This is a busy place," Elen said with a smile. "When you are around as many people as I am every day, it's easy to understand how different people think."

Girmai looked at her as if considering what to say next, then took another sip of his drink. "How much do you know about the Derg?" he asked.

The question took her by surprise. It was rare for anyone to ask her opinion. She had listened and observed enough in the restaurant to know this was not a safe subject to discuss openly. She glanced around to make sure they were out of everyone's earshot before responding.

She decided to be frank with him. "I heard they got rid of the Emperor. I think he is probably dead. I heard they executed most of his officers. They claim they are all about giving power back to the people."

"Do you believe that?"

She didn't hesitate. "No."

Her guard was down, something she never allowed, but something about Girmai put her at ease, and trust came easily.

"Neither do I," he said.

Silence stretched between them as Girmai finished his drink, carefully setting the empty glass on the counter before meeting her gaze again.

"What if there was a way to do something about it?" he asked, his eyes flickering down to her lips. Heat flared through her again.

How insane that I have so little control over myself.

She squeezed the counter's edge to stabilize herself and direct her energy anywhere but on him.

"I'd do what I could," she replied finally. "We all have to, don't we?"

"Yes." Girmai held her gaze. "Maybe we can work together on that."

"How?"

"Keep listening and observing as you have been. Let me know if you hear anything interesting or potentially important."

"That's all?" she asked. Elen thought he meant doing something more dangerous.

"That will mean more than you know."

Part 2

12

Asmara, 1975

"Mama?" Aman tugged on Elen's dress, shifting the sisal grocery basket off her shoulder. "Are you almost done?"

The afternoon sun bore down on them, making Elen question her decision to bring her seven-year-old son to Edaga Hamus market. She squinted against the brightness, saw his pleading eyes and the beads of sweat glistening on his forehead.

"We won't be long, Aman, wedey." She grasped his chin, kissed his damp forehead, and wiped off the smudge of lipstick.

Elen knew the market's noises and smells overwhelmed him. Usually, she wouldn't bring either of the kids, but Alem had come to run errands with her, and she didn't want to leave Aman at home alone, though he was content in his own company.

Unlike Aman, Elen loved the vibrancy of Edaga Hamus. Even though it was over a decade after she first set foot in the market, it never failed to remind her of her arrival in Asmara—her face oozing with infection but her heart full of hope.

The market was life's essence with all the vendor negotiations, corn sizzling on coal fires, vibrant vegetables, and stalls brimming with berbere and spices.

"We just need a few more vegetables and some shiro," she said. "Look, Aunty Alem already has many things we need. It won't take long."

Aman followed her finger skeptically. A few stalls away, Alem stood with Faven, fast asleep on her back, inspecting tomatoes. A young girl bagged onions for another customer, assuring Alem she had the market's finest tomatoes and didn't need to go elsewhere.

Elen patted her son's head and led him to Kudusan's spice stall. She set the basket by her feet and bowed to the old lady.

"I hope you are well, Mama Kudusan," Elen said.

The old woman's face erupted into a wrinkled smile. "Elen, haftey, I am well now that I have seen you!" Her front teeth jutted out, keeping her lips from fully closing. "Look at that handsome boy!" she said, smiling at Aman. She adjusted herself on the upturned bucket she used as a chair. "How could he have grown so much? What a blessing!"

"Thanks be to God," Elen responded, smiling at her patient son.

"What can I pack for you today?" the old lady gestured around. "You've come at a good time. Everything is fresh!"

Ground and unground grains, shaped into cones, rose symmetrically from each sack's folded edges—mustard, beans, berbere, shiro, and more beckoned.

"That's why I came straight to you, Mama Kudusan," Elen said. "You always have the best."

Kudusan beamed.

"A half kilo of shiro, please."

"Only half a kilo? That won't last you long!" Kudusan said, smacking her lips. "Why not take a kilo or two? You never know when you'll run out!"

Kudusan placed a paper bag on the scale, brought one of the sacks with the bright orange powder closer, and spooned some out.

Elen inhaled the shiro, already tasting the evening's dinner they would have with the fresh injera Alem had made before they left the house.

"Oh, thank you, Mama Kudusan," Elen said, waving her hand. "That's too much for now. It's just the four of us, and these kids eat like birds. I'd rather come back for a fresh batch once we finish this."

"May God light your way back," the old woman said. "Always a blessing to see you."

Kudusan's weathered hand trembled as she focused on the task at hand. Though her movements were slow and methodical, shiro dusted off onto the scale as she spooned more powder into the bag.

Elen had been coming to Mama Kudusan for years. She resigned herself to the wait. It was worth it. Kudusan's shiro was the best.

She gave Aman a sympathetic look as he leaned on her. She moved him into her shadow and let her thoughts wander to her recent investment.

By happenstance, she heard about a bar's quick sale from a woman needing to move to Addis. Her rush to move made the price affordable. Elen used all her savings for a down payment on the bar and the small apartment that came with it.

"I will miss you," Awash had said when she shared the news.

"I will miss you too, but you'll be fine," she had replied, her heart aching for her mentor. "I won't be far, and we can visit often."

The back apartment had enough space for all of them. Elen worried less about the curfew now since she only needed to walk to the back after she closed the bar door. Alem and the kids used a separate entrance on the building's other side.

"It's safer for everyone this way," she had said to Awash.

Awash had reluctantly agreed to the logic of her plan. He was protective of her and had known her since she was a naive young village teen. "But you are the heart of this place. Will you manage on your own?"

"I will be fine, thanks to you and everything you have taught me," Elen had told him. "You are like a father to me, and I will forever be in your debt."

Awash had waved her away and wiped his eyes. "And you are my daughter."

Elen smiled at the memories and let her gaze wander over the stalls. She stopped at a half-torn poster behind Kudusan's shoulder. It hung from a pillar supporting the tarp over the stall. She could make out the faded imprint of the Emperor's chin and medals; someone had ripped the rest of his face off.

The Emperor is gone.

The radio report she and Awash heard announcing the elimination of the Emperor's officials, now called the Black Saturday executions, was over a year ago. That was just the beginning. Despite the initial hope of freedom and wealth that the Derg promised, independence never came.

Just as they took over Ethiopia, the Derg held onto Haile Selassie's claim on Eritrea and continued to treat it as a rebellious Ethiopian province. Derg militia unleashed fury on any sign of dissent, especially in the villages they suspected of harboring ELF or EPLF rebels.

Elen heard Girmai's voice played back to her from their last conversation a few weeks before.

"Counterrevolutionaries, that's the new word for people who ask questions," Girmai had said. "Elen, the scale of what's happening is unbelievable." Girmai had sipped on his usual soda water, his voice somber.

"After every one of our successful missions, the Derg retaliates with a brutality that is a hundred times worse than anything we have endured before. Many times, they target people that don't have anything to do with the missions."

She knew bits and pieces about the liberation forces' operations. They came into the city to take what they needed to sustain the fighters in the field and found refuge in homes that sympathized with the cause. They did the same in nearby villages, until they reached their base of operations high in the mountains spread over different parts of the country.

They took medicine, food, money, and weapons with them to keep the fight against the Derg going. The networks in the cities and villages were growing, and the scale of the operations grew with them.

"Derg soldiers are burning villages and massacring innocent civilians everywhere," Girmai had continued, quietly seething. "Women, children, the elderly, entire families—none are spared. Those who are lucky and survive are leaving everything they know to end up north, in Sudan, some even further. We are trying to help the survivors with the supplies we collect, but the needs are great."

Elen had clenched her fists under the counter. "I know," she had said softly. "Aboy Yonathan, Aman's grandfather, barely escaped with his life in Himbirti."

When Aman's grandfather miraculously got to Asmara a few weeks before, she had visited him at Yacob's house.

"The soldiers came and just shot everyone," Yonathan had cried. "I heard them coming up the hill and hid behind a rock so they didn't see me, thanks be to God, but I could do nothing but watch them kill everyone and take all our teff. They even threw a grenade into the mill, so we can't use it anymore. We have lost everything!"

Rage and fear tightened her chest as she listened to his story. Did she come all the way here to create a new life just to have irrational soldiers snuff it out?

I need to make a change, Elen had thought. *I need to be part of something bigger.*

She knew it was only a matter of time before they would face the same horrors. She couldn't just sit by and let that happen. *God lights the path for us to follow. That path won't always be easy, but if it is for the good of others, it is the right one.*

Elen had reached out and clasped the old man's trembling hands in hers as he spoke.

"They said it was because we helped the ELF," Yonathan had said. "So many died, Elen! So many! They are erasing us all."

"Their sacrifices will not be in vain, Aboy Yonathan," she had said, her voice steady and resolute. "We will get justice, and freedom. I pray that we and our children will live without fear one day."

"May God hear your prayer, Elen, haftey," the old man had said, wiping his tears.

"Himbirti is one of so many places," Girmai had said when she told him about her conversation. "Ona, Weki-Duba, She'ib—villages that have been peaceful for centuries are now being obliterated. The Derg suspected these villages of sheltering fighters, so they went there and killed everyone."

The worst was in Weki-Duba, she'd heard from a conversation between some patrons. The village, just six kilometers north of Asmara, was the target of infuriated Derg soldiers who accused the villagers of helping the liberation fighters get away. They rounded everyone they could up in a church and started shooting, then went on a rampage to other villages.

"They came back with tanks to make sure they finished the job," she'd heard the week before as she lingered close enough to listen to a conversation in the bar. "Those people can't even have a proper funeral. Too many of them died. There's no one alive left to bury them."

Some survived by playing dead. Hospitals were over capacity, with patients suffering from days-old injuries. Tears welled up in her eyes every time she thought about it.

How do we stop this? Elen couldn't let her children grow up in fear. *We have to do something.*

Girmai's jaws had clenched. "They think this will stop the resistance, but their cruelty only fuels our determination. Every atrocity, every crime only strengthens our resolve to fight."

"May God help us," Elen had agreed.

No help was coming from anywhere else. All the major foreign embassies shuttled their people out of the country, and the few foreigners who drank at the bar regularly dwindled to nothing. One by one, they got on one-way flights out. If there were any left, she didn't see them.

"The foreigners here watch and say a few things in newspapers here and there, but they don't get involved," Girmai had said bitterly as if reading her mind. "It doesn't matter. We will fight for ourselves. The more they try to suppress us, the stronger we get. We will overcome this."

"I'll do whatever it takes," she had vowed.

What she could do for now was listen and gather information. "Everyone always wants something," her aunt would say. Though Tsehay was now forever at peace from the pain of cancer that ravaged her body, the memory of her weaved into everything Elen did.

"Watch how people behave and listen to what they say. Everything is important, and knowing how to use what you learn is key to gaining the upper hand," Tsehay would say. "Identify what they want and adapt."

In many ways, Elen was glad Tsehay wasn't around to see what was happening. Her aunt taught her well, but she was all about surviving urban life, not war.

Elen's bar was now up and running, and though many regulars were neighborhood people, plain-clothes Derg officials often filled the seats.

Her birthplace gave her an advantage. They relaxed once they knew she was from Tigray. Ethiopian by birth, she was considered "one of them." She didn't refute that. Neither did she counteract those who felt she was Eritrean.

Perhaps I am everything and nothing.

Elen kept quiet and listened. The Derg officials who came to get their daily drinks didn't even bother to talk low.

Stupid people. Do they think they can face our army?

We will take the land. We don't need the people.

… get rid of every single one of them.

Traitors.

She mentioned everything she heard to Girmai, including names, dates, places, and even things she didn't think were important.

"It's very helpful," he would say every time she finished. "Even the smallest piece of information can save lives."

Girmai had finished his drink and rose from the high bar stool. "There's a meeting in a few weeks," he had said, sliding a folded paper across the counter. "There's much more to share than we can talk about here."

Girmai took a step toward the door. "I look forward to seeing you there."

Elen had quickly slipped the piece of paper into her dress pocket and nodded.

***

Elen moved closer to the shade of Kudusan's stall umbrella and dabbed sweat off her forehead. "Almost done, Aman, shikor," she said.

It had been a few weeks since she last saw Girmai. He told her he would travel, so she didn't expect to see him.

The meeting was in two days. Elen regurgitated the address she had memorized. *I'll see him soon.* Her breath stuttered at the thought of the meeting, the first time she would see him outside the bar.

She forced aside the memory of his eyes flickering to her mouth whenever they spoke.

No distractions! I need to focus. She couldn't afford to let her attention waver. There were too many things to think about now. She had her children and her sister to protect.

I need to keep them safe, Elen told herself. *I'm not starting another relationship.*

Elen put her arm around Aman as weary relief settled in. She was glad she had moved her family.

As the Derg's violence escalated, divisions between Eritreans and Ethiopians widened. Everyone suspected each other of being informants. Walking on the streets was becoming increasingly dangerous, especially with temperamental armed patrols with full authority to do anything they wanted. The sunset curfew was strictly enforced, and Elen was constantly alert.

She looked away from the torn poster to Kudusan, still spooning shiro into the bag.

"How are you doing with all these changes, Mama Kudusan?" she asked, nodding toward the poster.

Kudusan's half-smile faded. She stopped scooping and looked up at Elen as if carefully considering her words.

"It's not going well, I'll be honest," she sighed. "Who knows what's really happening. The soldiers are young and their youth makes them careless with their weapons. One started shooting here in the market the other day!" She pointed beyond where Alem stood.

"You know what the rest did?" she asked, shiro spoon suspended. "They laughed, as if people running for their lives was a joke. I don't know what to do, Elen, haftey. May God help us all. We're living in tough times."

Elen nodded, squeezed Aman's shoulder, and turned to watch

Alem selecting the last of the tomatoes, an ache of affection settling in her.

Thank goodness she's here, Elen thought. *We're stronger together.*

Kudusan fell silent. The bag was almost full.

From the corner of her eye, Elen noticed a figure move toward her and stop next to her basket. Elen grabbed Aman's hand and moved him aside to make space for the woman.

"Oh, hello, Halawit," she said, forcing her voice to brighten to greet her neighbor from a few doors down the street. "How are you today?"

Dread settled as soon as the words left Elen's lips. Halawit, older and stoic, had never been warm toward Elen. Her face was a permanent mask of disapproval. She often verbalized her opinions on Elen's perceived transgressions—the provocative dresses, makeup, uncovered and unbraided hair, and husbandless family.

Elen braced herself for the usual monologue about the sanctity of marriage and how a woman needed a husband. What purpose did an unmarried woman have?

This would not be pleasant.

A customer came to the other side of Kudusan's stall. The old woman got distracted as she greeted her and suspended Elen's shiro-bagging as she exchanged pleasantries.

Nowhere to go now. Elen sighed.

"It's time for you to go back to where you came from," Halawit hissed, her lips pulled tight against yellowed teeth. The steel in her tone sliced through the market's noise and startled Elen. This was harsh, even for Halawit.

Kudusan, oblivious to the confrontation, continued to chat with the other woman browsing spices.

Elen expected a lecture, but Halawit's unveiled animosity threw her off guard. Aman's eyes grew wide, and Elen pulled him behind her. She kept her expression even, controlling the aggravation pounding at her temples.

Help me through this, Lord, Elen said a silent prayer. *I must not speak in anger.*

She turned her back to Halawit.

Elen was relieved as Kudusan rolled down the paper bag's edges to seal the shiro.

"Did you hear me, you filthy Ethiopian?" Halawit growled behind her. "You're a disgrace, opening a bar and catering to the filth while they kill us every day." She edged closer. "Do they come to you to celebrate killing us and our children?"

Not in front of my child. This has to stop.

"Why do you speak to me like this?" Elen spun to face her. "You don't know me."

"You Ethiopians are all the same," Halawit said, seeming to take energy from Elen's attention. "Always taking what doesn't belong to you. Scum, that's what you are." Her lips turned down, nostrils flared. "Do you think your Derg ruffians will rule us? Never."

"What have I done to you?" Elen asked, genuinely shocked. "How can you accuse me of things that have nothing to do with me?"

"Oh, I know you!" Halawit retorted. "Living in sin with your fatherless children!"

Elen pushed Aman further behind her as Halawit's spittle landed on her arm.

"Go back to where you came from. You hear me, agame?"

The insult reserved for Ethiopians from Tigray made Elen flinch.

"Our country doesn't belong to your kind!" Halawit continued. "It never has, and it never will!"

Elen thought of the Derg soldiers in her bar, imagining what that must look like to someone like Halawit.

I am trying to fight back, don't you see? she wanted to tell her. *It hurts every day to see them drinking and laughing, knowing they've hurt and killed people. I am doing what I can to help.*

She heard Girmai's voice in her head. *You may suffer for what you choose to do. Everyone will judge you, but stay vigilant. Everything you do counts. We will win this fight by working together.*

"What's going on?" Alem walked up beside Elen with Faven still asleep on her back.

Seething, Elen turned away from Halawit to Kudusan, quickly handed her some coins, then put the shiro bag into her basket.

"Thank you, Mama Kudusan," she said, keeping her tone even.

Elen slung the basket over her shoulder, took Aman's hand, and held him protectively behind her as she stepped toward Halawit.

"This is my home, just as it is yours," Elen said coldly.

Halawit stepped back, startled by Elen's proximity. Her eyes widened, her nostrils still flaring. Elen moved closer, holding her stare until Halawit's wavered and flicked away.

"This is my home as much as yours," she repeated, moving even closer until she could smell Halawit's body odor. "I am not going anywhere. You don't know me; you've never known me. Don't speak to me like that again, especially in front of my children. Do you hear me?"

Elen yanked Aman's hand and lifted him almost off the ground. She pulled him away before Halawit could respond. Alem darted after her, glancing sideways at Halawit.

"Mama, what did that woman mean?" Aman asked, his voice small.

Elen barely heard him through the drumming in her ears. She couldn't slow down, even though her pace was too fast for his little legs.

"Mama?"

"She doesn't know what she's talking about," she snapped. "Ignore her."

Elen didn't slow down until she cleared the marketplace. She needed to think.

It wasn't up to Halawit or anyone else to say where she belonged. This was her home. She wanted to believe Girmai that freedom would come as long as she stayed steadfast in the mission. Keeping them thinking she was on their side made their tongues loose, and that made it easier to collect information.

If keeping a persona of being on the Derg's side would help the fight, so be it.

13

Elen pushed through the beaded curtain at the butcher shop's entrance. Hooks on either side of the wall held the blue metal doors open. A tall young woman stood behind the counter.

"I'd like eight chicken drumsticks," Elen said, skipping the customary greetings.

The gleaming white floor and countertops contrasted starkly with the red of the meat hanging on hooks behind the woman. Her hands rested on the glass counter above various cuts of meat on display. She adjusted her apron and waved away a lone fly buzzing between them.

"How do you want the drumsticks?" The woman's expression was unreadable.

"Skinned."

Satisfied with the code words, the woman nodded, walked to the counter's far side, lifted the flap, and motioned for Elen to enter. She led Elen through the back of the store into the dark hallway of an adjoining apartment building.

They passed numbered doors as they walked.

Smart, Elen thought. *No one will have seen me enter through the main entrance on the other side.*

Elen blinked to adjust to the dark as she calculated how much time she had to beat the curfew after this meeting.

Just two weeks before, she had watched a young boy die only a few minutes past curfew. His body had spun when the bullets first hit him, like the ballerinas she had seen on TV. The bullets that followed sliced through his chest, making his body convulse as if he were a piece of paper caught in the wind.

The shooting had continued even after he hit the ground. It stopped when a red halo of blood framed the boy's body and expanded beyond his head. His body lay still, twisted at an unnatural angle.

Elen had stood hidden in the darkness of the closed bar when the soldiers came into view. One soldier nudged the boy's body with his boot.

No movement.

The soldier had said something to the other, then stepped over the boy, leaving a trail of dark footprints that faded around the corner.

Hopefully this meeting will be quick, Elen thought nervously. *I need to be home on time.*

At the end of the hall, the woman opened a door, gestured for Elen to enter, then quickly closed it behind her.

"Be prepared for a lot of information," Girmai had said when he gave her the note with the address. "Just listen and process it. It's easy to get overwhelmed."

Overwhelmed was the word. Elen hadn't slept well since that shooting. The boy's body on the ground haunted her and merged into nightmares. Sometimes she dreamt of the dead Emperor—his severed head floating above her, his face missing like on the poster at the market, his dismembered hand waving the five birr in her face.

"The Emperor no longer has authority over the people of Ethiopia," the radio announcer had promised in that first broadcast she and Awash listened to. "We will break down the oppressive feudal system and return the land to the people."

What they gave the people were rape, mass shootings, unexplained detentions … None of the promised reforms.

What if I get caught?

Elen banished the thought with her mother's words. *If it is for the good of others, it is worth doing. God is with me.*

She stepped into a small living room full of more books than she had ever seen. Kifle sat on a leather couch near tightly drawn curtains, likely covering a street-facing window.

Kifle smiled and stood when he saw her. Beside him, a heavyset man pushed his thick glasses up his nose and rose with him.

"Welcome, Elen!" Kifle tapped her cheeks with his. "I'm glad you made it. Come, sit. Petros, this is Elen." Kifle put his hand on her shoulder. "Elen, Petros is a professor at the university."

"Ah, Elen! I have heard about you." Petros moved in for the three-cheek tap, and Elen responded, his warmth dissipating some of her nervousness.

"Wonderful to meet you, Ato Petros," Elen said. The scholarly décor of the house made sense now.

Petros motioned for her and Kifle to sit on the couch. "Just call me Petros," he chided. "Don't make me feel old! Come, let's have some tea and himbasha."

She lowered herself onto the edge of the couch. A glass table in the living room held a tray of teacups and a thermos. Triangles of sliced himbasha lay stacked in neat columns on a miniature mesob.

Petros poured tea and gestured for them to take some himbasha.

"How are your classes going?" Kifle asked between sips. "I heard the Derg is planning to cut university funding."

"One good thing I can say about the Emperor is that he kept schools open," Petros sighed. "That backfired when students got smarter than he could handle. Most people in control now have little or no education. In fact, they are working to dismantle schools. They've sent thousands of high-school students in Addis Ababa to villages for a so-called reeducation program. They want to separate the educated to diffuse our power. The Derg knows the youth are a catalyst for change."

Petros reached for a piece of himbasha. "I have lost so many students," he continued. "If they're not conscripted, they run off to join the fighting. Those who support the Derg are more radicalized than ever. Everyone is a suspect."

They sat in silence until the door swung open and a woman

with large silver hoop earrings walked in. Her tight beige skirt stretched across her hips as she bent to place her bag on the floor by the doorway. She straightened and headed toward them, heels clacking on the wood floor. All three rose to greet her.

"Nigisti, haftey! What a pleasure to see you again!" Petros enveloped her in a hug, forgoing traditional greetings.

"Petros, old man!" she said, her deep, raspy smoker's voice vibrating. "It's been too long. Those students are keeping you busy, eh?"

"You know it!" he smiled and turned to introduce her.

"Kifle, Elen, please meet my dear friend Nigisti. She's a former student and one of the most intelligent women I know."

"You mean one of the most intelligent *people* you know," she said, wiggling her eyebrows.

"Yes! The most intelligent of anyone!" Petros laughed and gave a ceremonial bow.

Elen smiled and poured Nigisti some tea as they settled. She liked her already.

They bantered about Petros's courses and Nigisti's job until the door opened again. This time, Girmai filled the doorway. His movements were fast and purposeful, as if he had many things to do and not enough time. His hair was shorter than before, his thick mustache tapered perfectly to frame his mouth. Elen's pulse quickened.

Berhane and two men followed him in. They looked as nervous as she felt. The older man's slight slouch suggested he sat over stacks of papers in an office all day. The younger man, possibly a student, had long, wild hair fighting itself for space. His eyes darted around, lingering on her for a moment before continuing to survey the room.

Girmai reached them in a few swift strides. He grabbed Kifle's hand, and they knocked on each other's shoulders in greeting. Then Girmai moved around Kifle to Elen, leaving the others to the customary greetings.

She rose as he took her hand. He leaned in for a three-cheek tap. The proximity of his cheek pushed everything from her mind. This time there was no bar counter between them.

"How are you?" he whispered in her ear as their cheeks touched. His warm breath sent tingles down her neck.

"Fine, thank you," she managed. "How are you?"

He came around for the second tap. "Doing well."

Both her ears burned. Girmai still held her hand, and she felt both safe and exhilarated.

On the third tap, his face lingered against hers a moment longer than it needed to.

It took all her energy to pull away. "It's nice to see you again," she continued.

She looked away to see Nigisti watching them with a knowing smile. The heat rose to her face as she lowered her eyes.

"Shall we sit at the table?" Kifle gestured toward the dining table.

Girmai let go of her hand and followed him. Elen clasped her hands to stop the shaking and followed the group. Nigisti hung back and moved toward Elen. She tapped her left ring finger and looked pointedly at Girmai's back. "That will get complicated fast," she whispered. "Believe me, I know." Her smile slowly reached her eyes.

He is married? Elen was surprised. *How had I not noticed that before?*

Elen didn't have time to respond to Nigisti or process her reaction to the news.

We have a strictly working relationship, Elen assured herself. They had met many times and kept their conversations brief, always in the public space of her bar, she made a mental note to keep it that way.

Chairs scraped as they all took their seats. Girmai pointed to an empty seat beside him and raised his eyebrows at Elen. All the other chairs were taken so she lowered herself into the chair and struggled to clear her mind.

"Thank you for coming today." Girmai looked around, suddenly serious. "Normally, we wouldn't meet in a group, and this is the last time we will all be together." He took a deep breath. "We must prepare for tough times ahead. General Aman Andom is gone, and our hope of a peaceful transition to independence was buried with him.

He leaned forward. "I won't lie to you. It will be dangerous. The possibility of arrest increases as our work intensifies. Derg troops and officials can and will act on their suspicions with force.

"You must protect your knowledge and educate others. Over the next few months, you will be called on to do different tasks. Follow the instructions exactly. Be vigilant, and don't draw attention to yourself."

Elen turned slightly to look at him, trying to digest the magnitude of what she was stepping into.

"Our sources say the Derg has assigned a colonel named Zenebe to oversee operations in Asmara and nearby towns. Unlike others before him, Zenebe has had many wins on the battlefield that have revived his troops' morale. They respect and listen to him, and his popularity has energized them. This is bad news for us. But he could be a significant asset if we get him on our side. We must do what we can to make him our ally."

Girmai leaned back. "We will use dirar leyti, as you did today, to access information and messages and identify allies.

"Remember, only trusted confidants within the underground cell network will know the day's code word. Those giving an old or incorrect one are likely enemy spies—be careful, there are plenty of those around."

Girmai gave Berhane an almost imperceptible nod.

"The opportunity to access Zenebe might come sooner than we think. He likes drinking and women," Berhane said, glancing at Nigisti. "It will take some strategy to lower his guard and reduce his security."

Elen searched Nigisti's face for any signs of trepidation at the hint she should start a relationship with Zenebe, but Nigisti simply nodded as if considering a bank transaction.

"Zenebe could be a useful contact in the city as more of our people are interrogated and imprisoned," Berhane continued. "One phone call from him can stop that. It may take months to soften him up. Your bar will be key in this operation, Elen. Between you and Nigisti, we can make this work."

Nigisti lifted her chin in acknowledgment and snuffed out her cigarette. "I'll do my best."

Elen didn't trust herself to speak.

Berhane turned to the young man whose eyes darted around the room. "We need to monitor his movements in the city at all times. Girmai and I will be your main contacts."

"Okay," the man said. The muscles in his forearms jumped as he crossed his arms.

Berhane turned to the older man. "Kifle is your contact. You will also monitor Zenebe. Observe who he meets and where he goes, and find patterns in his routines. Others will monitor him outside of Asmara."

A contemplative silence fell as Girmai reached down to the side of his chair for a bag Elen hadn't noticed.

"There's news from the front lines." He pulled out a magazine.

The *Vanguard*.

He and Kifle took turns reading the one copy. Elen soaked up the news: women fighters in the field alongside men digging trenches, setting up makeshift hospitals and schools, providing medical treatment.

Doctors, mechanics, engineers, and teachers were using their skills to build communities in liberated areas with unmatched survival skills. They used the natural contours of the desert to carve out bomb shelters and underground hospitals. The articles extolled the EPLF's determination to erase all lines that separated people: gender, ethnicity, and religion all took a back seat to the collective Eritrean identity.

Through their stories Elen realized that she was part of something bigger. Pride replaced her fear and anger for the first time in a long time. She was no longer a bystander, scrambling to survive. She wasn't an outsider. She was a fighter, just like those women in the field.

Girmai closed the magazine and tucked it into the bag. Everyone needed to get home before curfew. Chairs scraped as they all rose and headed to the door.

"Elen." She was in the living room when she heard her name. The others' small talk faded into indistinct mumblings as Girmai came close.

"Looks like your business is going well," Girmai said. She searched his face for the judgment she saw in Halawit's but found none.

"It's God's will," she said, bowing slightly.

He took her hand as he had the first time they met. "Thank you for all you do. I appreciate you taking the risk."

When he let go of her hand, she felt the hard edges of a note he left behind and pocketed it without looking at it.

Later, in the quiet of the night, she unfolded it under candlelight. Beneath his phone number, she traced her finger on the words he had written.

I am with you—always.

14

Four men sat at their usual table across the room. One spoke in a steady stream while the others, eyes bloodshot from either lack of sleep or too much drink, barely listened. The calmer they were, the better the chances Elen could close the bar without a fight breaking out.

Most of her customers were Derg supporters, and many were armed. The off-duty soldiers were obvious, but she could also identify those in plain clothes sent to root out counterrevolutionaries. Occasionally, an EPLF scout would enter, blend in, and leave without drinking much. She spotted them instantly.

This usually signaled a mission was underway. Violent raids would follow. Unlucky suspects, taken from their homes in the dead of night, would return as mere shadows after days of torture.

Many never returned home at all.

One of the four slouched on his chair, sleep taking over, but Elen knew he would wake up in a few minutes and be angry to find his beer bottle empty. Elen grabbed one out of the fridge and walked over to the table with it. She quietly placed it in front of him. The rest barely noticed as they kept their half-closed eyes trained on the one that was still talking.

No one bothered Elen, since the Derg's higher-ups frequented the bar. She used all the customer-service skills she had learned at Awash to put them at ease: an enthusiastic welcome here, a joke there, and a continuous supply of booze.

Since the meeting behind the butcher shop, Girmai had convinced Elen to install a telephone in the bar. She looked at it now and wished she could call Girmai whenever she felt like it, but that would be foolish, and foolish got people killed.

She called only when the room was empty. Sometimes she had news to share; other times, she simply enjoyed hearing his voice and learning about his business and travels. He was intelligent and witty, always finding a way to make her laugh—a rarity, given the balancing act that was her life.

"It's getting harder to get supplies," she had told him once. "They get upset when we run out of drinks."

"I will help you with that," he had said. "We need you to keep them coming in so you can gain their trust. You'll get even busier when they know they have a place that won't run dry."

Girmai was right. The bar grew more crowded each evening, with curfew enforcers lingering longer than the rest. Bar Elen had gained a reputation for being well stocked and a place to unwind, and she maintained the act of the perfect host.

Afternoon phone calls with Girmai during the after-lunch siesta when the bar was empty had become a vital part of her routine. Each conversation charged her with adrenalin, and she was torn between the thrill of hearing his voice and the gnawing fear of getting caught and risking her family's safety.

She lived for those stolen moments. It was the only time of day when she let her guard down. She didn't have to be strong, cute, or pretend to be enthusiastic and welcoming to people she hated. She could just be herself.

Elen hired Tigist right after the official opening, and Akberet had followed her from the restaurant when Awash retired soon after Elen had left.

"It's time for me to rest now," he had told her. "Take care of Akberet, and keep yourself safe."

The three of them had barely managed to keep up with the orders.

She had mentioned this to Solomon once when he called from

Adwa, and he begged her to let him come help. "There's nothing for me in this village, Elen," her brother had said. "We can help the family more if we work together. I'll be of more use to you and Baba if I work with you rather than sit here waiting to pass the time during this dry spell. We can't get a big enough harvest to feed the family, and supplies are dwindling fast. Baba relies on what you send every month."

With three more children from his new marriage, their father could not refuse the extra support.

Solomon had always been energetic and a quick learner. As soon as he got to Asmara, Elen had enrolled him at Comboni High School to continue the limited education the village school had provided. She planned for him to attend classes during the day and work at the bar in the afternoon.

"I will take care of him, Baba," she had promised. "When he finishes school, he'll have many more job opportunities, and we can help the family more."

The school situation shifted daily. "Attend" was a loose term for how often Solomon went to school. He was supposed to be in his last year of high school but had just received a few weeks of classes since coming to Asmara. Derg nighttime rampages and bodies left in the streets as examples kept schools closed for days. Derg soldiers posted throughout the city waited to arrest family members searching for loved ones or showing signs of mourning. The recent influx of soldiers contracted to control Asmara were barely adults, and most were illiterate.

Much to Elen's dismay, her dream of Solomon getting a solid education seemed increasingly unlikely. The universities in Asmara and Addis had been closed for months, and attendees disappeared, either arrested, killed, or bussed to villages for "reconditioning," as the radio announcements stated.

Not going to class didn't bother Solomon as much as it did Elen. Once he arrived in Asmara, he focused on learning the bar's inner workings, becoming semi-oblivious to the horrors outside.

"Keep that table happy," Elen told her brother, nodding toward the four men. This group had caused problems before and got impatient if they had to wait for their drinks. They rarely paid their bill, leaving her feeling lucky if they did.

"This is for them," Solomon said, taking the St. George Amber beer bottles from the fridge under the bar counter. Elen reached for clean glasses on the shelf behind her.

Solomon stacked the tray with bottles and glasses.

"I don't like the look of that guy at the corner table," Solomon said as he placed the last beer on the tray. "As usual, he hasn't said a word since he came in."

She didn't need to look to know who he meant. Though in plain clothes, the man was clearly a Derg army officer. He was quiet; even as others drank their rationality away, he stayed sober. The few times Elen saw him drink, he became even quieter, which scared her the most. It was as if he were sizing up everyone and filing the information away.

"We'll have to be careful," Elen agreed. "Do you want me to—"

"Elen!" A familiar voice interrupted her offer to take the drinks.

Mebrahtu, a regular customer, slid onto a bar stool and flashed her a smile. "Why am I not surprised this place is full?"

"We're here to serve!" Elen said, as brightly as she could, plastering on a big smile.

Mebrahtu was not one to be trusted. He smiled and acted like a friend, but she knew he had gotten many people arrested. He worked as an accountant at the downtown bank, and rumors spread that he got rewards for passing information about colleagues who then disappeared into Derg interrogation centers. He walked with an air of a man who didn't fear for his life.

"You want the usual?" Elen asked, reaching into the fridge for a cold beer.

"Of course!" he said, grinning as he adjusted himself on the bar stool. "You always know what I need."

"That's what I'm here for," she said, sliding the open bottle to him.

Guilt muted Mebrahtu's voice, and her throat tightened as she watched Solomon weave through the crowded bar, the beer bottles balanced precariously on the tray.

Mebrahtu droned on as she held her breath. The men snatched the beers from the tray, barely giving Solomon time to set it down. He placed the glasses in front of each man with a steady hand and tucked the tray under his arm, then moved to another table where a group of young men had just settled. He pulled out his notepad, his face a mask of concentration as he prepared to take their orders.

Akberet walked back toward Elen with an empty tray, exhaustion lining her face. Elen knew what was bothering her. "Ajokhi, Akberet," Elen said reassuringly. She glanced at Tigist, who was taking orders from people at the far end of the room, her face pinched as she tried to memorize them.

"I'll be right back with your orders," Elen heard her say.

Unlike Tigist, a more traditional netsela-wearing older woman, Akberet struggled with unwanted advances from all directions. A bar wasn't the safest place for a twenty-year-old to work. Elen had hoped to replicate her experience at Awash Restaurant for Akberet, but the bar's volatile atmosphere was far different for a young, attractive woman.

"It's almost time to close," Elen said. "Solomon and I can handle the rest. You and Tigist should get going before curfew."

"Thank you, Elen." Akberet didn't resist the offer. "I'm afraid that one with the hat will follow me. He's been aggressive today."

Akberet kept her back to him as she spoke and busied herself at the sink. Elen glanced at the table and confirmed the soldier's eyes were on her. She knew that look.

"He keeps touching me every time I pass by and says he's made plans for us to meet later." She brushed the back of her hand across her eyes. "I don't know what to do if he finds me alone."

"I'll go distract him," Elen said without missing a beat. She smiled, waved to a table of men, and gestured for them to drink more. "Take the back exit and use the apartment door to leave. Slip out when you can; make sure he doesn't see you leaving."

Akberet nodded, about to say something, but shouting from the room's far end startled them both.

"YOU THINK YOU'RE SMART, EH?" the voice boomed, slicing through the room. All eyes turned towards the young soldier towering over Solomon, whose face had gone pale.

Solomon stood frozen, his notepad clenched in his trembling fingers. The tray, no longer secure under his arm, slipped and clattered to the floor, the sound sharp and jarring against the sudden silence. The soldier stepped forward, his sneer deepening as he jabbed a finger into Solomon's chest.

"What are you? A student?" he spat. "What are you writing, eh?" The soldier's words slurred, then he slapped the notepad out of Solomon's hand. It fluttered down near the fallen tray. "You're writing this down to tell your counterrevolutionary buddies about us, right?"

He jabbed at Solomon's chest with his finger so hard, his back arched at the pressure. The man pulled back his jacket, revealing a gun in its holster.

"Sorry, sir," Solomon said meekly. The trumpet in the Ethio-jazz piece played eerily into the silence over the room.

"Go!" Elen nudged Akberet toward the back door. "I'll take care of this."

Steady, Solomon, don't aggravate him. She needed to defuse the situation quickly.

"I don't even go to school, sir," Solomon continued, shrinking into a compliant boy. "I was just writing your order to get it right, that's all. Please let me serve you drinks." He bowed and pressed his palms below the soldier's arm on his chest.

Elen glanced at the quiet officer at the other table, startled to find his eyes focused steadily on her. Though his face was expressionless, she sensed he was waiting to see her reaction.

Before she could move toward Solomon, the bar's door swung open, drawing every eye to the entrance.

Nigisti stepped in first, each movement deliberate and graceful. Her tight pants clung perfectly to her, the high waist and flared bottoms emphasizing her every curve. Her silk shirt caught the dim light as she glided forward, shimmering with each step.

She paused, scanning the room with a practiced gaze while she held the door open. Colonel Zenebe followed her in, his two bodyguards close behind him, making all the soldiers stand at attention.

Elen walked around the counter to welcome them, grateful for the distraction. Solomon scrambled to pick up the tray and notebook before returning to his spot behind the counter.

"Nigisti, Colonel! How nice to see you both! Welcome!" Elen said, feeling the officer's eyes still on her. Nigisti acknowledged Elen with a small smile. With the certainty of an endless supply of drinks, Zenebe brought her here often. Girmai was right on every count.

Zenebe nodded to the soldiers and motioned for them to sit, easing the tension in the room. "Elen, haftey! It has been a long day. We are ready for drinks!"

Solomon was safely behind the counter, a half-smile plastered on his face. The only sign of his anxiety was the tremor in his fingers as he placed a few glasses in the sink.

"I have your usual spot ready," Elen said, smiling. The act was on. She turned her back to the weight of the officer's stare, hoping she passed whatever test he had set for her.

Bar Elen had an alcove similar to the one in Awash Restaurant, with a deeper recessed room that offered more seclusion from the rest of the bar. She always left it free for Zenebe.

"I'll get your drinks right away," she said as they settled into their space.

Zenebe leaned in and reached for Nigisti before she even sat down. The bodyguards positioned themselves at the alcove entrance, their backs to the couple.

Elen would serve them herself. Her stomach churned at the sight of Solomon hunched over the sink, scrubbing dishes with a determined but weary motion.

She stepped closer and squeezed Solomon's arm reassuringly. His warm, solid skin beneath her fingers was a stark contrast to her cold fear.

Elen gritted her teeth at the memory of Girmai telling her about Petros's death. She had to lock herself in the bathroom to cry when she heard the news during one of their daily calls.

"He insisted on teaching Eritrean history and taught all his courses in Tigrinya," Girmai had told her. "It was his act of defiance, I suppose. Some of his students were probably Derg collaborators planted to watch him. He got into an argument with one of them, and the next thing we knew, he was strangled to death with a piano wire in his home. We have lost a great educator, a great man."

"Are we all just suspended on the edges of minutes, swinging from one to the next like monkeys on branches?" she had cried into the phone. "What are we left with when all our branches are cut?"

"We find new trees," Girmai had said. "We have no choice but to keep going, or everything he did would have been for nothing."

In just moments, Solomon's life had been suspended at the whim of drunken soldiers. *It could have been him.* She mouthed a silent prayer. *Please be with us, Lord.* He could have been safe in the village, she scolded herself. I have made a big mistake.

She would talk about it with him later. Maybe she could convince him to go back home until things quieted down.

Elen mixed a gin and tonic for Zenebe and brought a cold Amber for Nigisti, returning to the alcove with a tray.

With his arm around her waist, Zenebe pulled Nigisti close and nuzzled her neck, burying his face in her afro. Her friend's face was flushed and less composed than when she first came in, as if her personality detached from her body. The unbuttoned top of her shirt revealed glimpses of her bra. Nigisti took a long drag from her cigarette, the subtle shake in her free hand betraying her unease. She let him kiss her.

When Elen set the drinks on the table, Zenebe pulled away long enough to grab his glass. The cigarette was still between Nigisti's fingers when she wiped smeared lipstick from her lip with the base of her palm before reaching for the beer.

So calm and collected, Elen thought, unable to imagine the strength it took to maintain this level of pretense.

"Ah!" Zenebe took a swig of his drink and smacked his lips. "Just what I needed after a long day's work!" He kept one possessive arm around Nigisti.

The women locked eyes. Nigisti blinked to dissipate the tears their quick connection triggered. Her nostrils flared with the effort.

"Of course, Colonel!" Elen's gaze lingered on Nigisti, hoping she felt the silent reassurance. "It's our pleasure. Enjoy, and let me know if you need anything."

Nigisti looked away, her jaw clenched. She relaxed it long enough to take another drag from her cigarette.

"We need to keep the Colonel happy for a while," Girmai had told her months ago.

"How long?"

"As long as it takes," he replied.

15

Early-morning light filtered through the transparent corrugated skylight, casting a soft glow on the cluttered garage. The hum of Welde's tools and the scent of engine oil filled the air.

Seven-fifteen. It was almost time.

"Are you done yet?" Girmai asked, glancing at his watch with a furrowed brow. "Daniel will be here soon."

Daniel, Girmai's EPLF field counterpart, was big on punctuality. Lives depended on it, and for this particular mission they needed every minute to get ahead of the morning rush hour.

"Almost done," Welde mumbled, the flashlight wedged between his teeth, garbling his words as he worked beneath the blue Opel Kadett. Girmai lowered himself onto a stool and nodded, even though the mechanic couldn't see him.

An extended jack elevated the Opel several inches off the ground. "Just making sure it can hold the weight," Welde added.

Metal clinked on metal as Welde reinforced the concealed undercarriage compartment, which now held a newly acquired batch of Kalashnikovs, the largest they'd ever handled.

Hundreds of Eritreans were killed since the Derg declared martial law in the beginning of the year. In response, the underground resistance grew in cities and towns all over the country. Each life lost to Derg violence pulled more people, like Elen, into the cause. The EPLF fighters in the field depended on underground city networks for information, food, money, medicine, and anything else they could get—including weapons.

Everyone contributed what they could. A mechanic like Welde was essential. When EPLF recruits gathered enough supplies, he modified the transport vehicles, creating hidden compartments beneath seats, behind dashboards, and inside trunks. Every inch of space mattered.

The previous evening, disguised as Derg soldiers, a team of fedayeen had stolen the guns from a Derg army base and delivered them to Welde before going into hiding. A different team smuggled the Derg soldier who'd led them to the stash out of the city.

Girmai and Daniel had to move the guns to EPLF contacts close to a checkpoint leading out of the city before Derg officials realized they were missing. They would then take them to EPLF safe zones.

Sometimes, Girmai delegated delivery jobs to trusted recruits. But this one was too risky; he had to do it himself. Girmai knew the city streets well and, as a well-established resident of Asmara, would raise less suspicion.

Daniel entered and left the city when needed, often in various disguises. Girmai marveled at how Daniel managed to evade detection so consistently.

For this mission, they decided on an extra layer of caution. Daniel would ride with Girmai and take over after reaching their contact at the checkpoint. Girmai would then walk back to work before all his employees arrived.

Depending on how frequently they used the vehicle, Welde regularly switched license plates, adapted different cars to fit the mission's nature, or worked on a major overhaul.

As Welde worked, Girmai smiled at the thought of seeing Elen afterward.

"Sounds like you two are getting close," Daniel had warned when Girmai told him about their daily phone calls. "She is a valuable asset. It's good she trusts you and that you have established effective communication. Taking your relationship beyond what it is now will risk too much."

"We just work together, nothing more," Girmai had said to Daniel, trying to convince himself more than anything, though he heard the lie in his voice. He wouldn't allow himself to go beyond fantasies. The fantasy where the Derg didn't exist and the biggest problem they would both have was planning where and when to meet just to enjoy each other's company.

Sometimes, his dreams took him back in time to a world where they met each other before they had relationships with anyone else, where it would be simple to just be with her long enough to let something between them grow.

When he invited her to that recruitment meeting behind the butcher shop, he knew she would be an asset to the liberation cause. She was witty and sharp, and nothing passed her notice.

She went beyond his expectations in every sense of the word and proved to be an exceptional informant with whom he was completely at ease. She had a way of doing that with people.

She even had Colonel Zenebe at her fingertips and convinced him she was his ally. Her being from Tigray helped, but her art was how she managed to get him to let his guard down and made him feel comfortable at Bar Elen. When he went to her bar, he came with only two bodyguards rather than the usual four he used for any other business.

Elen created that atmosphere for anyone who came into her bar. When they drank, their tongues loosened, and the information she gathered informed multiple successful operations. The snippets of conversations Elen relayed to him often revealed potential threats and opportunities to relieve the Derg of supplies the liberation forces desperately needed.

All that while, she laughed and joked around, making them feel at home. She was beyond suspicion. For now, at least.

She's brilliant, Girmai thought. Despite what they risked by being in touch daily, he eagerly anticipated the next time he would hear her voice, his daily solace. He imagined her on the other end of the line, bangles clinking on her wrists as she moved. As she told him about the events of the previous evening, he visualized her pouring drinks, mingling with customers, and laughing at just the right moments.

He pictured her shoulders and hips moving as she danced to the latest music she had blasting on the LP while working behind the counter, her long hair bouncing off her shoulders and face.

He would give anything to brush her hair away from her kohl-lined eyes and see the full depth of her gaze.

The stool creaked as he straightened up and stretched. *That can't happen,* he thought. *She's in enough danger as it is.* He took a deep breath and gave himself a pep talk. *I'm a married man. Helen is a good woman—she always puts her family's needs before her own. She deserves a faithful husband. I will do my best to be one.*

"Okay, I think I got it," Welde said.

"Good, let's go," Girmai replied, pushing aside the nagging thought that he should never have involved Elen in EPLF operations. It didn't take much to get arrested or killed these days.

Three quick knocks on the back door startled them. Girmai waited for Welde to roll out from under the car and nod, confirming that it was okay for Girmai to open the door.

Welde folded a cloth over the scattered tools, pumped the jack, and lowered the car by the time Girmai got to the door.

By the time Girmai reached the door, four more knocks had sounded. He checked the floor for incriminating tools, then knocked once in response.

"Daniel." The familiar voice filtered in muffled from the other side.

Girmai unlatched the door, opened it enough for Daniel to enter, then shut it behind him. He secured the latches and followed Daniel to the far end of the garage, where Welde stood.

"We've loaded everything into the undercarriage compartment," Welde said, rubbing stubborn oil stains from his fingers. "I double-checked to make sure it can carry the weight."

"Our contact will wait just before the Beit Gheorghis checkpoint at eight o'clock," Daniel said, spreading a city map on the worktable. "The goods must be at the checkpoint just before the guard switch. If you drive, we're less likely to be stopped within the city."

Both men looked at Girmai, who wore one of his finer blazers for the task. His carefully constructed status as a wealthy business owner who supported the Derg warded off questions and random stops.

"We'll switch here, right before the stadium," Daniel said, pointing at an intersection on the map. "I'll take the car from there to meet our contact and get through the checkpoint. You'll walk back to work along this route." He pointed to a narrow street on the map, then shifted on his feet.

"I'll offload the stash and take it to the field. Our contact will return the car and park it four blocks from Bar Elen here," he pointed at another intersection. "To avoid compromising this garage, you'll need to pick up the keys from her as close to curfew as possible and return the car here. Fewer people will be out then."

"Got it." Girmai allowed himself to visualize seeing Elen for a fraction of a second. "What's plan B?" They had to take Beheware Avenue. The usual congestion on that main road could slow them down.

"There is no plan B," Welde said. "They haven't noticed the guns are gone yet. This stash needs to be out of the city before they do. Tonight's raids will be bad either way, and we won't know where they will decide to search. We all must go home early and hope for the best."

* * *

"What the—" Girmai cursed under his breath and gripped the steering wheel when they reached the Beheware Avenue intersection. They had been on the road for less than ten minutes when traffic reached a standstill. The lights were not working.

A man in a police uniform stood at the intersection directing traffic. His gray hair peeking out in tufts on the sides of his head and his stooped neck gave away his age.

Damnit!

At his signal, several cars inched forward. Girmai moved close to the car in front of him and hoped to make it through the intersection quickly.

As Girmai approached the crossroads, the police officer's hand shot up, signaling him to stop. He waved the drivers on the intersecting street forward with his other hand.

"We are going to be out of time," Girmai told Daniel, looking at all the cars. "We can't miss the handover. I am going for it."

Before Daniel could say anything, Girmai sped through the intersection, ignoring the policeman's shouts to stop. He stared straight ahead and hoped to go around the cars ahead once he crossed over.

Traffic on the other side ground to a stop in both directions.

He had nowhere to go.

The police officer's reflection filled the rearview mirror. The man abandoned his post and moved toward them fast as the traffic flowed behind him.

"Get out, go now!" Girmai urged Daniel. "I'll see you at the meeting point. If I'm more than ten minutes late, just leave."

Daniel nodded, slid out of the passenger side, walked through the line of cars, and disappeared around the corner. Girmai noticed the officer glance at Daniel for a split second before refocusing on him.

The man slammed his hand on the car and leaned into Girmai's window. Girmai stared out at the emptying road the cars ahead left behind.

Think!

Any search would ruin everything Girmai had built for years. Everything the EPLF trusted him with.

"What the hell do you think you are doing?" the man screamed. "Didn't you see me telling you to stop?" He knocked hard on the glass of Girmai's window, just above the circle of fog from his breath.

White stubble poked out of the man's cheeks and chin. Girmai rolled down the window, letting in the stale smell of sweat and old injera.

"I told you to stop, and you keep driving?" the policeman said, narrowing his eyes. "You rich guys think you can do anything you want, eh?"

"Sorry, Ato, I am late for an appointment," Girmai started. "I didn't see you had told me to stop. I was just following the car ahead of me, which has now moved, as you can see, and the road is clear. Please let me get going. I'm so late," he said, hoping his voice sounded sincere enough.

Cars now rolled past them freely. Girmai tried to gauge his chances of making a run for it.

"The only place you are going is to the police station with me," The policeman said.

This car is not going into any police station.

"I'm charging you for disobeying direct orders from a police officer," the man continued. He straightened up and almost ran the few steps it took to get around the front of the car. He was in the passenger seat before Girmai could say another word.

"Drive to the police station now," he said, shutting the door. "Today is the day you learn your rich man's lesson," he said as he half-turned and pointed a finger at Girmai. "I am here because I have the authority to be. It is me in charge, not you. When I say stop, you stop. When you don't, you learn what happens. Drive now!"

That can't happen. Girmai gripped the wheel and tried to think fast.

The police would search the car the minute it entered the station. Once they caught Girmai, everything he had built—his business, family, and fight for liberation—would end.

"Please, can't we sort this out?" Girmai pleaded. He softened his tone and hoped the man would calm down. "I am very late for my appointment. Don't you know me? My name is Girmai. I am sure you have heard of my sweater factory, Expo 69. It is just there around the corner."

Girmai let go of the wheel and clasped his hands together. "I would be happy to gift you my finest sweaters so you can forgive my mistake. That is all it was. I apologize for what I did, but I have to go. I have a business meeting I cannot miss. I made such a small mistake. Look—traffic is moving now."

Girmai pointed at the road ahead for emphasis.

"Who the hell do you think you are?" the police officer's cheeks flamed. "Didn't you hear what I said? We are going to the police station now!" Spittle launched out of his mouth and landed on the dashboard, Girmai's arm, and face.

"Ato, I deeply respect you and the work that you do, but I have to go to my meeting," Girmai said again, desperation lodged in his throat.

He put the car into gear and drove—not to the police station.

He veered the car around the corner Daniel had disappeared into, then headed back through the streets of Geza Banda, away from the meeting point.

"What the hell are you doing?" the policeman's voice cracked mid-scream. "I said drive to the police station! Where are you going?" The man grabbed the steering wheel and the car swerved, narrowly missing a few pedestrians about to cross the road.

Girmai desperately held on to the wheel and kept his foot on the gas. There was no way he would go to the police station. He struggled to maintain control of the wheel while pleading with the man.

"Please, I just need to get to my appointment," he repeated. "Let me go there. I am in a hurry, I don't have time to go to the station. What can I do to sort this out with you? Please!"

The officer was sweating now, his vein-lined hands still glued to the wheel. Girmai held on, too, his feet on the gas pedal.

"I am the police!" he shrieked. "I told you to drive to the station now!"

He lifted his foot over the gear lever to step on the brakes, but Girmai fought back, raising his knee to prevent access. The tight car swerved again as the men wrestled for control.

Girmai's panic reached a crescendo at the sound of a siren behind them. It got louder, then wailed past as a motorbike swerved ahead and stopped in front of the car, forcing Girmai to slam on the brake and stop inches from the motorbike and the gun pointing at him.

I am finished, he thought.

The officer's helmet gleamed in the sunlight as he maneuvered his motorcycle to a complete stop. With a quick flick of his leg, he dismounted and closed the distance between them, keeping his pistol trained on the windshield of the Opel.

Girmai gripped the wheel tighter. His foot, still on the brake, shook with tension. He stared straight ahead as the tall officer approached his side of the car. The engine was still running.

The pistol barrel inched into Girmai's half-open window so close Girmai could smell the metal.

He relaxed his grip on the wheel and raised his hands in surrender.

16

"The traffic on Beheware Avenue was deadlocked," Girmai told Elen later that afternoon at Bar Elen. The morning's close encounter kept him tense all day. "I thought I was dead for sure!"

Elen's eyebrows raised slighty above her widened eyes in response but she said nothing.

"It worked out eventually," Girmai reassured her. "The flow loosened as soon as Habteab came to help with the congestion."

Sergeant Habteab, the officer on the bike, was from Girmai's village, Zurbien, and one of his early recruits. Girmai had supported his family after Habteab's father died, and had encouraged him to join the police force, which, at the time, had paid well.

Habteab's stellar record earned him trust among the Derg ranks, allowing him to operate as an EPLF spy undetected.

That relationship saved his life.

Habteab convinced the police officer to let Girmai go. The old man reluctantly got out of the car in a huff, and Girmai gave them both money to "get themselves some tea," as everyone called such an exchange.

Habteab had no idea what Girmai had in the car. The less he knew, the better.

"That must have been a great inconvenience," Elen said, glancing over his shoulder. It was right before the early evening crowd came in. "Hopefully you don't have any more driving to do for a while?" she added.

"Yes," he replied. "I will be doing less driving for a while."

Girmai was here to pick up the car keys, as planned. A simple task. Elen would hand them to him; he would take them and leave.

But Girmai could not bring himself to leave. Seeing Elen felt like a rebirth after what he thought was the end.

The bangles on her right wrist clinked as she wiped the counter, then reached behind a stack of glasses. Her fingers brushed against Girmai's as she slid the Opel's key toward him. The warmth of her fingers lingered on his skin long after she pulled away.

Cool down, Girmai, he chided himself as he slipped the key into his pocket.

"We all have to slow down for a while," he said. He looked to make sure no one was within listening range and spoke fast. "The night raids will begin once they discover what's missing. They may already be planning them. Lock up as early as you can and stay quiet tonight."

Her hands moved swiftly, pouring his drink as if he hadn't spoken. Plain tonic with lemon. The clinking of her bangles complemented the Amharic music playing on her LP.

She leaned a fraction closer, slid the glass to him, and gave him a small smile. Her eyes met his as he inhaled her rosy scent. The combination was enough to drive him mad. Behind him, Bar Elen hummed quietly, oblivious to the electricity between them. Her carefully curated music selection infused the place with a rich, inviting ambiance.

She broke the connection when she turned to the record player to increase the volume. Contrary to her usual loose curls, she'd styled her hair into a high bun, accentuating the elegant curve of her neck and the grace of her bare arms. Her long dress brushed the floor, creating the illusion that she was floating, a vision that filled him with a sense of power and purpose. He didn't know where it came from and didn't care. He needed to hold on to that feeling before returning to the duplicity of his life.

As he lifted his glass, he noticed a piece of paper beneath it. Elen raised her eyebrows a fraction and looked away.

When did she put that there?

"Something I heard earlier," she said, with a small nod in the direction of the note.

He slipped the paper into his jacket pocket and took a swig. The fizzy bitterness of the lemon burned down his throat. During one of their phone calls, he mentioned that he didn't drink alcohol during the day to stay sharp. She remembered. Her flawless attention to detail intoxicated him.

"Can I have two more of the gin and tonics?" Akberet asked as she came around the counter. Hello, Ato Girmai!" she beamed at him. "It has been a long time!"

"Selam, Akberet," he replied. "Work has been busy. What can we do but keep going, right?"

"For sure!" she laughed, and went to the fridge.

Elen prepped the drinks, placed them on the tray, and waited until Akberet was out of earshot. "I'm so glad you made it back," she said, her eyes meeting his. "It's getting risky here too," she said, smiling and waving at a customer who walked past them to the bathroom. "Solomon almost got shot the other day for writing in his notepad."

"Being literate is dangerous these days," Girmai said, shaking his head. "I'm glad he's okay."

"For now," Elen said, her face falling for a beat before she inhaled and plastered on a semi-smile. "There's one guy who comes here often. He makes me more nervous than the Colonel."

Her shoulders shook in an involuntary shudder as she continued. "I heard some soldiers call him Ashagirie. Do you know anything about him?"

Girmai froze. *That's not good news.*

"Stay away from him," Girmai warned. "He was recently assigned here. He has a reputation for being unpredictable. They sent him to get things under control here. Try to stay off his radar."

"It might be too late for that," Elen replied. "He comes here occasionally and just stares at everyone and everything. It's creepy."

"Our sources in Addis say Ashagirie has open orders to arrest whomever he wants and extract information however he sees fit," Girmai said as he took another sip. "Those he interrogates rarely make it out in one piece—if at all."

Elen tensed but kept her hands busy.

"Please be very careful when he is around."

Elen glanced toward her brother. "What should I do if Ashagirie sets his eyes on Solomon? He already got heat the other day with that notepad business, and that man was around to see it. I don't know how to keep him safe anymore."

"You need him here to give you all the support you can get," Girmai assured her. "Unfortunately, it will get worse before it gets better. The Derg loyalists are controlling kebeles everywhere, even the villages. Some kebeles have informants pretending to be anti-Derg, hoping to infiltrate our networks. All are drunk with the power the Derg promises them."

"That's nothing new," Elen said. "Everyone is a suspect for the wrong reasons. I heard someone was arrested the other day for some obscure crime, only to find out he had insulted the kebele officer when they had been high-school classmates. How do we fight something like that?"

"There's no rationality in anything they are doing right now," Girmai said. "They've sent people like Ashagirie to extract information from those who informants identify. Killers like him have proved their brutality on the battlefield and now have unlimited authority in major cities and towns to squash what they call counterrevolutionaries. All we can do is survive, one day at a time."

He paused as Akberet approached the counter to pick up the drinks.

Elen nodded toward Akberet when she was out of earshot. "There's one soldier who's relentless with her," she said, concern tingeing her voice. He corners her every time he sees her. I worry about her every time she leaves for home."

It's too late to back out now.

"Have her leave before the heavy drinking starts, while it's still light outside," he said. The euphoria from the success of the day's mission dissipated as he considered the danger he was in. "You need to look after yourself."

"I'll be fine," she said, waving dismissively. "But tell me more about Ashagirie. What do I need to know?"

"He oversees multiple kebeles and zones and brought in his crew from Addis. He's running a new interrogation operation in Karchele. They've converted the jail into torture chambers. His specialty is information extraction, often to the death. He's already gotten his hands on some of our people. The few who returned are barely alive, and what they say about their experiences are not to be believed."

He took a deep breath, thinking of ways to protect Elen. She was safe as long as Colonel Zenebe was around.

Ashagirie must know the Colonel has a soft spot for her, Girmai thought grimly. *But Zenebe won't be with us much longer.* The elimination plan was already in the works.

"As far as we can tell, Colonel Zenebe is the only person Ashagirie reports to. Zenebe is preoccupied with battles on the front lines and doesn't concern himself with Ashagirie's operations. He just wants Asmara to be his oasis when he returns.

"Zenebe handpicked Ashagirie to maintain order here and avoid dealing with day-to-day issues. We must keep the Colonel happy and use his protection while we can."

"Zenebe came in with Nigisti again the other day," Elen said. "He seems quite smitten. I'm worried about her."

"Nigisti will be okay. She's tough."

What we do is the price we pay for freedom. He hoped they'd all live to see that day.

"Zenebe is back in Asmara now, but not for long," Girmai said. "He's going to Gash Barka soon, probably to launch an offensive to counter EPLF's recent advances. Nigisti will be safe as long as he's happy. Keep him on your side as you've been doing. I've also had a couple of good meetings with the Colonel."

Elen gave him a quick sideways glance but said nothing.

"Luckily, we can buy the things he likes," he said, firming his tone. “We need to ride this as long as it lasts. Once he’s gone, only Ashagirie is left, and he’s unpredictable.”

“Once he is gone?” She arched her eyebrows in question, then rearranged her expression as more people entered the bar. She waved them in with a big smile.

“Don’t raise his suspicion under any circumstances,” Girmai said as she turned back to him, still smiling. “The less he knows about you, the better.”

“Understood,” she said with a nod.

“Okay then,” he said. “I better get going.” He still needed to take the car to the garage. He drained his glass, slowly tearing his eyes away from Elen as she moved to the music.

“Take care,” Elen said. She moved over to the record player and browsed her collection of LPs.

Girmai reached into his pocket, left some notes on the counter beside his glass, and headed toward the bar door.

He locked eyes with the man entering.

Ashagirie.

The man’s blank stare rested on Girmai, then slowly moved to Elen, who was switching one LP with another.

Shit. Girmai continued walking toward the door as calmly as he could.

Ashagirie’s group stepped aside when Girmai reached the door. He bowed slightly in greeting as he walked past them.

It took all his energy not to look back.

17

Rat-tat-tat! Distant gunshots burst in rapid succession, lasting almost a full minute.

Elen blew out the lone candle, her heart pounding in the sudden darkness. The silence that followed was even more ominous.

It was going to be a long night.

"We must stay quiet," Elen whispered to Solomon and Alem, her voice too loud in the tiny living room. The kids were still asleep.

"Remember," Elen whispered into the darkness, stilling their movements. "We just need to survive the night. Okay?"

"Okay," Solomon and Alem whispered back in unison.

They must have discovered the guns are missing, Elen thought as she recalled the metallic, slightly acidic smell that followed Ashagirie as he lowered himself onto the stool Girmai had just vacated earlier that afternoon.

"Good afternoon!" Elen had forced brightness into her voice and tried to ignore the unsettling feeling pinpricking all over her.

"What can I get you to drink?"

"I will have whatever he just had."

Elen's eyes followed the direction of his finger through the window to Girmai's receding silhouette disappearing around the corner.

"Who?" she asked.

"He was sitting right here," Ashagirie had said, one eyebrow slightly raised.

"Oh," Elen had frowned and pretended to think. "I think he had a gin and tonic." She had flashed him what she hoped was a confident smile.

"I will get that for you right away," she had said when he nodded and waved away the two men shadowing him. They retreated to the closest empty table.

Elen had forced fluidity into her stiff hands while his eyes followed her every movement. "Here you go!" she had said, a lot chirpier than she meant to sound. Enthusiasm worked well to disarm her customers.

Don't overdo it. Elen had reminded herself and cleared her throat.

"I hope you enjoy it. Let me know if there is anything else I can get for you." She had started to move away as she glanced beyond him to the most crowded sections of the bar, hoping to busy herself somewhere else.

"You know what I find interesting?" His words had anchored her in place.

"I'm sorry, what did you say? Ato … what do you prefer I call you?"

Keep as much distance as you can from him. Girmai had warned her, but there was no way of getting out of this one without raising his suspicion.

But this might work to my advantage.

She had stepped back and stood directly in front of him, steadying the quiver in her chin and resisting the urge to flare her nostrils as she looked up at him.

"Call me Ashagirie." He had finally put his hand down and circled his fingers around the glass before him.

The ends of his thick mustache had held on to residual drops of liquid following his thirsty gulp of the drink she had poured. He had brought his hand up to scratch just below his chin, jutting his lower jaw out to give his darkened fingernails more access to the itch. The motion had exposed dark dots on his neck that looked like they had resisted an attempted scrubbing.

Is that blood?

"Ato Ashagirie, I am so glad you are here. Welcome once again to Bar Elen!" she had smiled. "I hope you have had a good time here and we have served you well?"

"Yes." He had waved at her dismissively as he lifted the glass to his lips and smacked them after he swallowed. "I was just saying I find it interesting that your bar is so popular. You seem to be unaffected by the problems around Asmara."

"Problems?" she had said innocently.

The blank stare returned. Elen had let the silence between them continue for as long as he wanted. She knew how to play this game.

The door opened again. Elen's heart had sunk seeing the soldier who lusted after Akberet among the men who stepped in.

"Welcome!" she had said to them. "Come, sit, and we will be right with you."

Ashagirie had continued watching her as she gestured toward the empty chairs at the center of the room. Out of the corner of her eye, she had seen Akberet stiffen at the sight of the man. She composed herself quickly and caught a bottle just about to tip over.

Keep your cool, Akberet.

With her attention divided, Elen had barely heard Ashagirie talking to her. She had forced herself to focus back on him.

"I am curious. How does someone like you become so well established in Asmara?"

There it is, Elen thought. *He's digging for information. Does he mean me as an Ethiopian? As a woman? As a villager?*

She had lowered her hand under the counter so he wouldn't see her dig her fingernails into her palm. "I left Adi Nefas as a young girl for medical treatment, then started working soon after." She lifted her other hand and pointed at the faint scar on her cheek. The truthfulness of her words had eased her tension a little. "I loved the city life so much I never returned to the village. I saved for many years to get this place."

No need to rehearse the truth. Now, on to the fiction.

"I enjoy talking with people, especially my Ethiopian brothers."

She had motioned to the crowd of customers behind him and emphasized brothers, hoping he would feel some kind of kinship with her.

"Indeed. And your brothers also enjoy talking with you."

"I am so glad about that." Pretending not to notice his sarcasm, she had put her palms together in gratitude, and prayed he didn't see the flush on her cheeks.

"If it weren't for these nuisance counterrevolutionaries causing us problems, life here would be perfect," he had said, his eyes searching her face. "They are everywhere. Maybe some are here now."

He had swiveled slowly in his stool, gave a slight nod to the entrance, then turned back to her. "Maybe they are here, drinking your drinks, talking with our brothers." His finger lifted slowly and pointed to the crowded bar behind him.

"I hope not!" she had managed, swallowing the thick saliva that filled her mouth. "I can't understand why they are agitating the peace. I hope they come to their senses and we rise to the great Ethiopian nation we were always meant to be."

His face had brightened slightly, a rabid look flickering through his eyes.

Elen had resisted the urge to fan herself in the hot bar.

Ashagirie had pulled his shirt sleeves up his arms. The wild expression on his face didn't change. Purple scratches zigzagged across both arms—raised welts traced up and under his shirt. Despite the heat, a shiver ran through Elen's body at the sight of them.

He watched her glance at them and flexed. It looked like someone desperate to get away had left their mark on him.

"We will be great when we eliminate all the counterrevolutionary rats." He had caressed the welts on his right arm with a finger as he opened and closed his fist. His eyes glazed over, a glimpse of pleasure sweeping over them. "One by one if we have to."

***

Survive the night.

She shuddered to think of Ashagirie coming to her home in

the middle of the night. Nothing would stop him if he decided he wanted to do that.

"Interrogations are worse the first night they catch you," Girmai had told her during one of their phone calls. "They know chances of finding more suspects decrease with each passing day. They are fast and aggressive to extract names before curfew lifts. We commit to not giving up names for at least three nights if we can bear the pain."

A silence had hung between them as each held onto the receiver.

"One night gives the rest enough time to find out what happened and escape. Everyone has different levels of pain tolerance. Sometimes, the torture is too much, and our people confess. We just ask for time. The Derg's techniques are getting more sophisticated—pulling fingernails, pouring hot oil, beatings, electrocutions ..."

Elen shook her head in the dark and refused to imagine these things happening to her. She had to compartmentalize.

If it is for the good of others, it is worth doing. Elen repeated her mother's words in her thoughts like a mantra until her breathing steadied. She would fall apart if she let herself imagine the consequences of her choices.

"That's why your recruits shouldn't know each other," Girmai had told her. "Then they don't have names to give. Your name may be the first they reveal as a recruiter, so be careful who you recruit. If you suspect danger, let me know right away."

She had chosen her people wisely: Solomon, Alem, and Gennet, the seamstress from a few stores down who tailored most of Elen's dresses. She and Gennet got along the instant they met, bonding over fashion and the latest designs. Elen had the ideas, and Gennet had the talent to make them into the most beautiful dresses.

Nigisti knew who she was, but Elen couldn't imagine the crafty woman divulging anything.

She, Solomon, and Alem read the newsletters about the liberation movement Girmai provided by candlelight, soaking in the EPLF's successes. Every word filled them with purpose. Elen was grateful for her strong memory. She replayed the stories in her mind long after they got rid of each edition. *If it is for others, it's worth doing.*

Delivering the newsletters to Gennet added risk. Elen hid them in the seam of her dress. Gennet's talent for sewing hidden pockets meant that all of Elen's dresses served multiple purposes.

"If ever you get caught, we'll know," Girmai had reassured her. "We'll use our network to get you released. Just hang on and don't answer questions until we can get to you."

Remembering their conversation made her shudder. The scratches on Ashagirie's arms were recent—signs of a desperate clawing for life. He seemed proud of them.

Something is wrong with that man.

Ashagirie had left the bar without incident, but she couldn't shake the feeling that he was on to her. Worse, he may have seen Girmai with her. They had been so careful until now.

Let's hope we survive the night.

Elen listened to Solomon and Alem shuffle to their rooms.

Tat! Tat! Tat! The shots sounded closer.

Besma'am welmenfes kidus. In the name of the Father, Son, and Holy Spirit ... she prayed as she felt her way through the dark living room to where her children slept. Her arm rested on Aman's back, her palm on Faven's shoulder. She didn't know whether to be sad or relieved that they were so used to gunfire they didn't even stir.

Elen repeated the lines until the words calmed her, and the gunfire receded. The silence amplified the children's rhythmic breathing, making her thoughts wander to Nigisti.

"Did you know I have a son?" Nigisti had revealed this during their first Sunday coffee date in Elen's living room soon after the recruitment meeting behind the butcher shop.

The obligatory coffee invitation had morphed into an instant connection, and Elen insisted Nigisti's son, Haben, join them every Sunday. The bar was closed then, giving everyone a chance to be together.

They had stayed inside and let the children play together in the tight living room. The sounds and smells of coffee beans cracking over the small charcoal stove gave them the illusion of normalcy they desperately needed.

Nigisti was a single mother. Beneath her nonchalance simmered a determination to fight back since her partner's disappearance after a nighttime raid. Her acceptance of his likely death bubbled into intense hatred for those responsible—for the necks strangled with piano wire, the nighttime raids and disappearances, and the death of a father who would never see his child grow up.

"One day he was with me; the next he was gone," she had told Elen, holding the rim of her coffee cup as it steamed in her face. She had reached into her bag for a cigarette, a habit to relieve anxiety. The kids' laughter reminded her where she was. She put it back and took another sip of coffee.

"When the EPLF approached me and said I could be instrumental in this fight, I didn't hesitate. Pretending to enjoy being with Zenebe is hard. With every smile, every touch, every disgusting lie I tell him, I avenge my love's death. Seeing them pay will be the greatest victory of my life." Her lips curled, revealing the slight unevenness of her teeth.

"Colonel Zenebe. He's the big one," she said, grief darkening the circles under her eyes. "He's given all the wrong people the power to do as they wish. So our people disappear, die, fade away, and no one notices or cares. We have to believe our sacrifices won't be for nothing, Elen. What you and Girmai have is special. Who knows how long you will have it?"

Elen had needed a moment to adjust to the change of subject.

"I recognized something between you the first time I saw you together. It's been, what, about a year now?" Nigisti asked, taking another sip of the hot coffee.

"You both resist your truth, but a connection like this is rare, especially in such times," Nigisti continued. "Our reality is that we are all on borrowed time. We could die or lose our loved ones, and all we will have left are our regrets if we don't do everything we can to make sure we don't have any." She raised her eyebrows pointedly at Elen.

Nigisti's words had unearthed a longing for Girmai that overwhelmed Elen, but she didn't trust herself to talk. Not a day passed without her thinking of him and yearning for him. She committed every moment they had together to memory, storing it for later and replaying the images when she was alone.

What insanity is it to feel attracted to someone in times like these?

"I'm going to leave this place soon," Nigisti had continued, her tone changing abruptly. "It's time to end this dangerous game we are playing. They have decided."

"Doesn't that mean ...?"

"Yes. Zenebe is not long for this world." She clenched her jaws. "Once the operation is complete, all this will change. He's protecting you, Elen. No one will harass you while he's around, but who knows what will happen after. You need to make a plan for yourself and your kids."

The conversation had shifted from her attraction to Girmai to imminent danger so quickly Elen barely had time to process it all.

There is no space and time for love in this place, she thought, keeping her hand over her children as another round of gunfire sounded in the distance.

She stayed in that position until light filtered through the curtains in the early morning.

* * *

They had made it to the morning alive.

Alem prepared breakfast in the kitchen, and Solomon was already in the bar helping Akberet set up. The children were still asleep.

Elen locked the door to her room and went straight to the radio beside the children's framed pictures on the large credenza. She lowered the volume before turning the tuner knob.

Derg technicians constantly prowled the FM airwaves, blocking EPLF broadcasts. Sometimes, the EPLF quickly changed the frequency and distributed new numbers; other times, it took days to reestablish.

Her fingers delicately twisted the radio dial to the frequency she had memorized. She closed her eyes and got close, listening for the subtle changes in sound through the soft crackle of static.

Solomon and Alem didn't know about the broadcasts. *The less they know, the better.*

Finally, a voice emerged from the speaker, cutting through the white noise. Elen lowered the volume even more and glued her ear to the radio.

"Welcome to Dimsti Hafash, broadcasting from the hills of Nacfa. We thank you for your efforts to liberate our country. Freedom will be ours.

"Awet N' Hafash! Victory to the masses!

"In today's news, we confirm several successful operations conducted in Asmara this week. Thanks to the diligence and dedication of our committed members, we acquired funds, much-needed medication, and weapons from various points in the city that continue to sustain our liberation movement.

"Thanks to every one of you, we walk closer to freedom. The Russians recently supplied the Derg with Kalashnikovs, tanks, and various other weapons. Instead of being used to kill us, we will use them to liberate us.

"We also relieved the Derg of several tanks they were transporting to the Gash Barka region.

"Victory is ours!

"We commend our brothers and sisters in Asmara for their bravery and sacrifices. It will not be for nothing. We are together in this.

"Awet N' Hafash!

"Along with our victories, we must acknowledge our sacrifices. The Derg retaliates with senseless acts, and we continue to endure their anger and brutality. This week, more than twenty students lost their lives through strangulation. Multiple people took bullets near Cinema Dante and in Geza Banda and Gejeret.

"Their crime? They looked like counterrevolutionaries. The Derg believe displaying the bodies of our brothers and sisters on the streets will make us fearful and obedient. They think fear will stop our fight for what is rightfully ours.

"Don't let their threats discourage you or weaken your resolve. Thanks to our solidarity, we have made advances on several fronts throughout the country, and it is in solidarity that we will walk together to freedom.

"In related news, we received timely tips in Asmara, and more than twenty of our fighters moved from safe houses in Arbate Asmara before a Derg raid began in the early morning. All escaped and are now in EPLF territory—"

Static cut off the reporter's voice.

Elen leaned her head against the radio.

They found it. Derg technicians must have intercepted the EPLF broadcast. To get more news, she'd have to wait until they set up another frequency.

Thanks be to God, Elen thought, grateful she had time to pass the note to Girmai before Ashagirie walked in. *He must have acted quickly.*

She had scribbled disconnected words she caught in conversations, put the note under Girmai's glass, and hoped he would make sense of them.

Arbate Asmara. Move out.

The validation of her role clashed with the precariousness of her situation. She lived in two conflicting realities resting on a carefully crafted facade and was acutely aware of how easily her world could come crashing down.

Elen turned the radio dial to another frequency and switched it off. She uncurled her legs, lay flat on the floor, and let herself feel the exhaustion in her bones.

18

Elen tickled Faven until she laughed so hard she ran out of breath. As Elen loosened her grip, Faven launched out of her arms and darted around the living room.

"Silly child," Alem laughed over Faven's giggles. She shook the menkeskesh to roast the raw coffee beans over the small charcoal stove. "Be careful, gualey! Don't come near this fire, or you'll get burned," she warned.

Nothing gave Elen more joy than just being around them. Faven's untainted innocence and pure joy were infectious, lifting everyone's spirits wherever she went. Aman's calm nature balanced her energy.

Elen worried about him. He kept to himself most of the time, and she knew he absorbed much of what was happening around them. Today, though, he seemed content a few feet from her, focused on drawing a car.

Delicious-smelling white smoke from roasting coffee beans curled into the streaks of sunlight streaming through the window. Elen sighed in gratitude for the daylight. She still had an hour until opening time.

Solomon had gone into the bar to set up for the evening crowd, a job she had to do before he moved to Asmara. "Thank God Solomon is here," she said to Alem, moving to the corner of the couch to be closer to her. "I go back and forth between regretting he is here and being so grateful; I can't decide." She shook her head.

"He can take care of himself," Alem said. She poured the black-ened beans into the bottom half of the stone grinder and began pounding them. "He is a mischief maker. He knows how to make trouble and work his way around it. Just like that little one," she jerked her head toward Faven, who was sneaking up on Aman.

"Gotcha!" Faven pounced on him, making him push the pencil diagonally across his sketch.

"Hey!" Aman said, looking at the long line scarring his drawing. "I was just about to finish that!"

"Sorry," Faven said with a pout, her eyes filling with tears. The only thing she was sensitive to was her brother.

Elen watched her son recognize his sister's look and soften.

"It's fine," he told his sister. "Want to draw with me?"

Faven nodded vigorously, sat down beside him, and dragged a marker across her forehead.

Aman burst out laughing, a rare, melodic sound that was music to Elen's ears. He was usually so serious.

Faven's face brightened, happy to have brought that out in her brother.

Elen looked forward to her afternoon coffee and times with Alem and the kids before the hours of pretense she had to undergo all evening. She was dressed and ready for work but sunk deeper into the couch. She was going to linger here as long as possible.

"Elen?" The living-room door opened after a quick knock, and Akberet poked her head through. "Sorry to bother you, but Mebrahtu wants to see you."

"What? Why is he here?" Elen asked, inwardly groaning at the thought of talking to that leech of a man. "Hadn't you locked the door? We're still closed for a while."

"He saw me through the window while I was sweeping and knocked," Akberet said, only half her body visible through the doorway. "How could I ignore him?

She shrugged in apology and for a moment Elen felt a sharp pang of jealousy at Akberet's ignorance of the tensions around them. Other than evading the amorous soldier, she kept her head down, oblivious to the massive undertones in the bar.

Ignorance is a blessing, Elen thought, uncurling her legs with a sigh.

Knowing what Mebrahtu had done, she didn't want to spend her last hour talking to him.

"He's ignored two EPLF warnings," Girmai had told her in one of their phone conversations. "It's a matter of time now."

The first EPLF warning, delivered on a white slip of paper, gave the recipient time to make different choices and prove allegiance to the liberation movement.

If the recipient ignored the second warning on blue paper, they would receive the final one on a red note. By then, it would be too late.

"We've traced many disappearances and interrogations back to Mebrahtu," Girmai had said. "He's accumulated wealth and power at the expense of his subordinates, many of whom were innocent of the crimes he accused them of."

Mebrahtu had become a supervisor and rose to the ranks in the Derg's kebele system. He took bribes, blackmailed and threatened whoever he could to get money and status, and reported incriminating information to many within his kebele. They disappeared soon after with no opportunity to refute accusations.

He is bad news, Elen thought, her gaze moving from Akberet to her children, now both drawing at her feet. *What does he want with me?*

Mebrahtu always had an ulterior motive.

"Mama, don't go!" Faven abandoned the markers and wrapped her pudgy arms around her neck. Elen hugged her back and watched Aman quietly draw in his notebook. She knew he was listening.

"I have to go to work, baby," she said into Faven's fresh braids.

Faven's wail started before Elen finished her sentence.

"Don't cry, my baby, I'll be back soon, okay?" She gently pried Faven's hands from her neck. "Ajokhi, my daughter, don't be sad. Look how well you are drawing!"

They both looked down at the scribbles on Faven's paper. "I hope you finish it so I can hang it up in my room."

"No, in my room!" Faven demanded despite herself.

"Okay, my sweet," Elen said with a smile, "we will hang it up beside your bed, but that means it has to be really good, okay?"

"Okay, Mama."

Elen sat her down beside Aman, gave him a little squeeze, kissed him on top of his head, and walked away.

"She will be back soon," she heard Alem telling the kids as she closed the living-room door behind her.

Elen walked through the residential area and adjoining hallway and entered the bar from the back entrance. Solomon was bent over invoices on the far side of the register and gave her a quick nod as his eyes darted in Mebrahtu's direction.

Mebrahtu straightened up on the bar stool as she stepped in. The bright orange of the bottled Fanta Solomon must have served him looked out of place in Mebrahtu's hand.

"Elen, haftey!" He stood and extended his hand. A small white piece of gauze was taped to the bottom of his jaw, under his ear. Their cheeks touched in greeting, more gingerly on the bandaged side.

"I see my brother has sorted you out with a drink," Elen replied, sounding more enthusiastic than she felt as she walked around to the other side of the counter. "It's been weeks since we last saw you. I hope everything is okay?"

"Ah, because of this!" He tapped the bandage, a stiff smile stretching across his face. "I had a minor operation. It's healing now."

Lord, give me patience, she thought. *Why is he here?*

"I know how that is!" she said lightheartedly. "May God heal you. How is work? And your family? I trust you're all okay?"

He launched into an enthusiastic response, talking about his daughter's beauty and his wife's demands for more jewelry. Elen laughed at the right moments and nodded to commiserate with his problems.

Mebrahtu was a talker but never sought her out like this. His guard came down when he drank, and she had plenty of snippets to pass on to Girmai.

Akberet unlocked the entrance door, signaling the post-siesta opening time. Customers would start coming in soon. Not wanting to interrupt Mebrahtu, Akberet pointed at her mouth, signaling she would eat. "I'll be right back," she said.

Elen nodded. "Take your time. Solomon and I can cover for a while. It's still early." She turned back to Mebrahtu, who continued to talk, oblivious to Elen's diverted attention.

The front glass door opened moments after Akberet slipped out the back. A man in a faded brown bomber jacket and casual slacks entered and scanned the room. His eyes stopped at Mebrahtu, and then he continued walking and sat down at a table in the furthest corner of the room.

This can't be good. Ignoring the dread settling heavy in her stomach, Elen kept her face placid while her mind raced. She had never seen the man in the bomber jacket before but knew a fedayeen when she saw one.

Solomon walked over to serve the man.

"Anyway, Elen," Mebrahtu said, his tone changing. "I have to ask you something."

There it was—the real reason Mebrahtu was here.

"Sure, what can I do for you?" She kept the man in sight as Solomon returned, pulling out a bottle of Ambo sparkling water and setting it on a tray.

"You know Colonel Zenebe, right?" Mebrahtu asked, leaning in after Solomon had walked away.

"Yes, he comes here sometimes," she said carefully. Solomon was making his way back to return the tray.

She watched the man from the corner of her eye and saw him nod quickly to someone outside, beyond her line of sight.

The moments unraveled in a surreal blend of lightning speed and suspended time as the glass entrance door inched open behind Mebrahtu. Elen saw the gun barrel first, its black tip contrasting with the white door frame. It inched deeper into the room until the hand holding it came into view. Three fingers wrapped tightly around the handle, one on the trigger, the barrel aimed at Mebrahtu's back.

"It would be great if you could help me get an introduc—"

Bang! Bang! Bang! Bang!

The man in the corner was up and halfway through the bar by the time the bullets hit.

Elen dived under the counter.

She heard a thud and the sound of a chair falling. She scrambled over the floor between the vodka, rum, and gin boxes. Her knees caught on her long dress, ripping it as she crawled around the foot of the counter.

Elen screamed at the sight of blood spreading under the fallen chair and pooling around Solomon's inert foot. She crawled to him, knowing the fedayeen was long gone.

Thick, dark blood oozed from Mebrahtu's body as he lay on his stomach a few feet away. The whites of his eyes rolled back in their sockets seemed to be the only part of his body not soaked in blood.

Three red circles expanded toward each other across the back of his white shirt.

I heard four shots, she thought frantically.

"Solomon! Solomon!"

Her brother lay motionless.

She put her hand on Solomon's arm.

"Solomon! Wake up, please!" It took a few moments before she noticed the moist warmth on her palms and turned them over to look.

Blood.

19

Girmai needed to see Elen. Their usual phone call wasn't going to be enough today. He reached for the phone and exhaled when she picked up on the fourth ring.

"I'll be there in fifteen minutes," Girmai said into the phone instead of his usual greeting.

Her silence on the other end lasted a beat, long enough for him to think he had made a mistake.

It's too soon.

"Come through the back door," Elen replied, a slight tremor in her voice. "I will leave it unlocked and wait for you at the bar. Lock it behind you when you come in."

Girmai's heels clicked against the sidewalk in a rapid staccato, his breaths coming in quick, shallow bursts. He weaved through the empty streets, his eyes fixed ahead. His muscles burned as he doubled back and wove around blocks just in case, but he saw no one follow.

He slipped in through the back door to her home, bypassed the entrance, and made his way to the bar.

He saw black and paused by the entrance, waiting for his eyes to adjust to the darkened room. A tall floor lamp cast a yellow glow that didn't quite reach the far corners of Bar Elen. The closed metal roller shutters let in tiny slivers of light through the links that held the rollers together.

It took a moment to spot her perched on one of the bar stools, her hair loose and a thin netsela draped haphazardly over her shoulders.

She stood to greet him. "Nice to see you, Girmai," she said, a half-smile brightening her face as she stretched out her hand and turned her cheek to touch his. "Come, sit."

Girmai lowered himself onto a stool beside her. "I'm so glad to see you."

She chewed on her bottom lip and looked down, her nostrils flaring, and Girmai fought the urge to touch the faint shadows under her eyes.

Daniel told him what happened hours after the shooting, and Girmai barely slept or worked until he could call her.

"Solomon got one in the arm," Daniel had said when he called. "That wasn't meant to happen."

"He what?" Girmai had been in his office when he got the call about the mission.

"Hold on," he told Daniel and shut both doors to his office. "They did that at Bar Elen?" he spluttered. "You promised me she would always be safe from any mission!"

He was glad Daniel hadn't been in the room with him. That wouldn't have ended well.

"She is fine, and he'll be fine," Daniel said. "We had been following Mebrahtu for a while, and that's when the opportunity presented itself. It had to be done. When the bullet hit Solomon, he hit his head on the counter on the way down and lost consciousness for a while. He'll live." Daniel didn't seem too concerned.

"It actually worked out well," he continued before Girmai could say anything else. "They're above suspicion since he was a casualty of the operation, and Elen was convincing in her panic."

"I'm sure nothing about how she reacted was an act," Girmai said, rubbing his forehead. "You promised me, Daniel. This can't happen again."

"Alright," his partner said. "But you know we can't promise anything these days. We are fighting a war."

Elen took a deep breath and half stood. "Can I get you something to drink?"

Girmai's hand moved on its own, his fingers brushing her wrist before gently closing around it. The contact triggered a shiver that quickened his pulse.

"No, sit," he said, his voice thick. "I need to hear how you are doing."

She paused, her eyes meeting his, then nodded and sat down on the bar stool again.

"The soldiers arrived soon after the shooting," she said. "They took Solomon and me to Karchele and told us we were under arrest. A doctor there saw to Solomon's wound. The bullet went straight through, and, thanks be to God, he is alive and will be well."

"Did they—" He hesitated. *Do I want to know?*

He had looked for signs of torture when he'd first arrived.

"No," she said, understanding exactly what he was asking her. "Solomon's bandage was barely on when they took us to separate rooms. Different interrogators asked me many questions: Was he a regular customer? Was there anyone in the bar before the incident? What did I see after it all happened?"

"What did you say?" Girmai held his breath.

"I just said I don't know. Yes, Mebrahtu was a regular, but I didn't know him that well." Elen looked up at him. "I didn't tell him about the fedayeen who came in and gave the man outside the signal to shoot."

"God!" Girmai rubbed his eyes.

"Several hours in," Elen continued, "an officer called Habteab came in and told us we were free to go. He took the time to tell me his name, so I figured he was with us."

Girmai let out a breath he hadn't realized he'd been holding. "Yes, he is with us."

That's why Daniel was so calm, Girmai realized. *He'd already planned to have Habteab ready at the prison.*

"Ashagirie came just as we were leaving," she continued. "He stopped Habteab and talked to him for a while before we could leave. I couldn't hear what they were saying and …" Her voice trailed off as she wiped her eyes.

"Solomon was in so much pain," she sniffed. "He could have died."

"But he didn't," Girmai said and inched closer. "Ajokhi, Elen. He didn't die. We must believe that we will be okay and put our minds in that space every minute of the day; otherwise, we won't make it."

She nodded and looked at her hands. She brushed away a tear before it got to her chin.

"It's unfortunate this happened here, Elen," he said. "They saw an opportunity and took it."

"From what you told me about Ashagirie, it seems odd that he just let us go," she said, changing the subject.

"We are working on neutralizing him," Girmai said. "I mean to get him on our side," he quickly added when her eyes widened. "Ashagirie can be bought."

"He accepted money from one of our contacts recently," Girmai said, repeating what Daniel had told him. "We'll have him working for us in no time."

"Maybe he let us go because he wants to watch us," Elen said. "I don't trust that man."

"That could be," Girmai agreed. "Either way, Habteab convinced him there was no way you could have shot Mebrahtu due to the trajectory of the bullets that hit him and Solomon. They also found no murder weapon."

"How do you—" She shook her head and stopped herself. "The less I know, the better, right?"

"Right."

Girmai didn't want to spend any more time thinking about Ashagirie. He was here with Elen now, and that's what mattered.

Elen shifted on the bar stool. They were only a few feet from the crime scene, already cleaned and disinfected after the police investigation. All signs of the assassination were gone.

Girmai planted his elbow on the counter and rested his chin in his hand.

"I had to come here in person to see that you are okay," he said, "and to let you know I will be more involved in anything planned around this place. You are important to us, to me."

She smiled for the first time and started to say something when indistinct conversation from outside filtered inside in a muffled murmur. They locked eyes and froze. Shadows moved across the small slats, briefly casting dark shapes across the length of the bar.

Girmai's muscles tensed, even though he knew no one could see inside. They both listened intently until the footsteps and voices faded.

"Thank goodness we don't need to work today," Elen said, glancing at the locked entrance. "It's good to have some time just to be." She fiddled with the edge of her netsela.

Girmai could make out the floral pattern of her dress through the thin white cloth that flowed over her legs to the floor. He felt a pang of guilt, knowing the danger he put her in. *It could have been her with a bullet hole.* He shook his head free of the thought.

"I can't lose you," he said, the words slipping out before he could stop them.

She looked up, her eyes wide with surprise and something else. "You've always been there for me," she said softly. "Even when you shouldn't have been."

He had to touch her. His hand inched closer to hers, slowly and tentatively. When Elen didn't move hers away, he moved closer. His fingertips shook when he touched her. The sensation traveled up his arm, heating his whole body. He covered her hand with his, keeping his eyes locked on her face.

"I won't let anything happen to you," he repeated, a promise and a plea.

She held his gaze.

He leaned forward. Elen's eyelids fluttered as she inched toward him. Her rosy perfume heightened every sensation in his body. She closed her eyes, inches from his face, and only her lips filled his vision.

This is where I belong.

"It's hard for me to explain what I feel for you," he whispered, moving back from her just enough to talk. "I've never felt this way about anyone." He kissed her forehead and weaved his fingers through her hair.

"Me too." Her raspy voice held an invitation in its cracks.

The moment they connected, the pent-up longing and frustration flowed out of him. All his self-control, the person he needed to be in his duplicitous life, and the constant micro-decisions he had to make while people died around him, working both ends of the fight—growing his business and working as a spy—were gone. The pretense was crushing him, a fact he didn't allow himself to acknowledge, and now the release of it all was intoxicating.

He brought her closer to him and held her tighter as if to store as much of this sensation before he had to let her go.

"We're closed for the rest of the day and have time before curfew," she whispered, her breath hot on his lips. "Stay with me."

20

Girmai inhaled the crisp morning air deeply, appreciating the sharpness in his lungs as the cool breeze swept through the Seicento's open window. The leather seats still held the lingering scent of the cleaner Welde had used the day before, a sterile smell that reminded him of hospital wards—of lives hanging by a thread. He leaned back, closed his eyes, and allowed the previous afternoon's events to replay. His arms held the memory of her.

Focus.

They had a big job today, and he couldn't afford any mistakes. The money they planned to get was desperately needed. The reports of increased injuries from aerial attacks and ambushes in the villages were growing more alarming by the day. EPLF field doctors were running out of medical supplies and food. Every minute counted.

This will save lives.

The plan was simple, at least on paper. Teklai, a janitor at the telecommunications building, came in early every morning to clean. As the building custodian, the old man had an hour alone in the area behind the main lobby where the cash registers and the safe were located.

A seasoned EPLF recruit working as a bank employee had access to the safe keys. He told Daniel everything they needed to know—routines, supervisors, the safe's location, and the best time to empty the registers.

Though Daniel had voiced his doubts about working with the old janitor, Teklai was in an ideal position to get the money out. "He seems jumpy and nervous," Daniel had warned Girmai during the planning. "It's too much responsibility for him."

"He's our only option," Girmai had said, more to himself than to Daniel. "We have to risk it."

They added duplicate safe keys to the already bulky keychain Teklai carried.

After unlocking the safe and stuffing a garbage bag with as much birr as it could hold, he would deposit it by the curb with the other bags awaiting collection.

Daniel would wait at the corner of the building, pick up the money, and bring it to Girmai in the car diagonally across the street.

Just as with the guns, they would drive the bag to a waiting EPLF member, who would take it to the field.

They had meticulously mapped out the route and timed it to pass the checkpoint when the soldiers they'd bribed were stationed there. Girmai calculated that he had enough time to return the Seicento to Welde and still open the sweater shop by 8 a.m.

I hope he doesn't panic.

Girmai sat up at the sight of movement—Teklai was unlocking the entrance doors from the inside. He had parked close enough for Daniel to walk over yet far enough to avoid suspicion.

Daniel remained still, hidden from the janitor's line of vision. At Girmai's slight nod, he edged forward and peered around the wall, ready to grab the bag.

The door opened with a creak that seemed unnaturally loud in the stillness of the morning. Teklai emerged unsteadily with his fingers laced tight around the knot of a large black bag; his thin arms trembled against its weight. The man's eyes darted nervously, his hunched shoulders a clear sign that he was on the verge of breaking.

Girmai wrapped his fingers around the key in the ignition, his heart hammering in his chest. He was ready to move as soon as Daniel picked the bag up.

Just as he was about to turn the key, Girmai's fingers froze. The bank door opened again, revealing a bulky man in a guard uniform.

"Hey!" The deep voice cut through the morning air. "What's that?"

Teklai froze, his eyes wide. Girmai recognized panic washing over the old man, his frail body betraying him.

Girmai shook his head at Daniel, who quickly retreated, disappearing around the corner. The plan had failed, and there was nothing more they could do.

A U-turn would draw too much attention. Girmai turned the key and eased the Seicento forward, forcing himself to remain calm as he merged onto the empty road. He drove past the two men, the old man's hands still gripping the bag like a lifeline.

Don't look back.

But he did. Against his better judgment, Girmai glanced back. His eyes locked onto Teklai's in that split second, and he saw recognition in the janitor's widened eyes. The guard yanked the bag from Teklai's frozen hands and untied the knot.

Girmai rounded the corner by the time Teklai lay crumpled on the sidewalk from the force of the baton on his back. He gritted his teeth, his grip tightening on the steering wheel as he drove on, trying to suppress the guilt gnawing at his insides.

Keep to the routine.

Girmai walked straight to his main sweater shop, as he did every morning.

They'll be interrogating him soon.

The beatings and torture only stopped when the victim produced names—any names. Teklai would probably cave soon.

One glance was all it took.

Girmai walked to the empty factory in the back. He removed his alternate identification papers hidden beneath the ironing sheet of knitting machine number 62. The machine was used daily, but he had disconnected the heating sheet to hide the documents in plain sight.

He looked at the papers, then shoved them back into the hiding place. Leaving now would admit guilt and negate everything he'd built. He couldn't go.

He walked back to his office and dialed.

Daniel, already back at the safe house, picked up on the first ring.

"I'll reach out to Habteab to get to the Colonel," he said before Girmai could ask. "He's planning to leave the city soon. Hopefully, we can get to him before he does—just in case."

We can only hope.

"We can't compromise Habteab's position with us," Girmai said. "We need him."

"He can work through other contacts to get to him, so don't worry," Daniel reassured him. "You have made the Colonel very comfortable, and he will want to preserve that if it comes to it."

"Alright," Girmai said, taking a deep breath. "I'll call you from home after curfew to check in."

Girmai hung up and headed to his children's apparel shop across the street. The shop's floor-to-ceiling windows allowed him to see everything happening on the street to the end of the block.

He stayed there all morning with two of his staff, talking to customers and rearranging the displays while he watched and waited.

At noon, just as his tension began to ease, a soldier drove a military truck up the street and parked outside his main shop. Two soldiers got out of the back doors and entered.

Damnit!

Moments later, they came out and spoke to someone in the car, who stepped out with two more soldiers. Girmai spotted Teklai in the middle. A soldier's uniform replaced his cleaner's overalls, and he wore a cap pulled low over his forehead to hide his face.

Girmai stood still behind a display case, watching as the group headed his way. Teklai's awkward gait and nervous fidgeting betrayed his poor attempt at a disguise.

Teklai had bargained Girmai's life for his own, taking the easiest route: finger-pointing to stay alive and avoid violent interrogation. Girmai couldn't blame him. *This fight isn't for everyone.*

Wiping his hands on his pants, Girmai leaned against the display to steady himself and waited as the group moved in unison.

Four soldiers filled the store's width. "Girmai Issac?" one of the men said, stepped forward. "You're coming with us."

***

Former Expo 69 Exhibition Center.

Girmai had been to these showgrounds several times to exhibit his sweaters. He'd reserve the biggest booth possible and went all out on his displays. That was before the Derg converted it into a prison and interrogation center.

"Why were you trying to steal money from the telecommunications building?"

Girmai's protests that they had the wrong man fell on deaf ears. The swift journey to the expo grounds ended with him sitting in this old wooden chair.

"Don't even try to deny it. A witness identified you." The soldier leaned in close, his breath hot and rancid on Girmai's face.

Girmai looked away from the scratches and stains covering almost every inch of the table in front of him. The unpainted concrete walls seemed to press the air around him, tightening his chest every time he inhaled the stifling scent.

Five soldiers crowded around him, stagnating the air even more.

"Why would I want to steal any money?" Girmai kept his tone even and calm despite the rising dread. "I'm a successful business owner. I don't need to steal from anyone. Ask anyone about me. Whoever gave you my name wants to use these false accusations to take what I've built."

"Tie him up!" The soldier had no patience. "We won't waste time coddling you."

They descended on him with hurricane speed. The first blow to his head knocked him off the chair, sending him sprawling onto the bare cement. The rough texture scraped against his sweaty cheek as a hand grabbed his hair and yanked him up while heavy boots slammed into his ribs, driving the air from his lungs.

Girmai barely managed a shallow breath before another kick sent him careering across the floor. The pain was sharp, hot, searing through his side.

Disconnect. Girmai forced his mind to separate from his body, focusing on anything but the agony.

The men, indistinct blurs in his vision, blended into one another. Fists and boots rained down on him until he couldn't tell them apart. His left eye swelled shut while he blinked his right rapidly, trying to clear the blood blurring his vision.

Two pairs of hands straightened him to a seated position on the floor. Girmai braced against the searing pain in his ribcage, stiffening his torso to dull the sharp sting.

A broken rib.

Two men held him while another soldier shoved a thick wooden pole behind his bent knees. Another yanked Girmai's hands under the pole, around his ankles, and tied them over his feet so he was bound into a tight ball.

Number eight.

He'd heard of this torture method.

As the two men moved to each side of the pole, another swung his fist into Girmai's face, landing a blow below his right eye.

Girmai forced himself to dissociate. *Just survive. Separate mind from body, it's the only way.*

Steely fingers forced a moist, vomit-soaked rag into his mouth. Girmai gagged as it was pushed deeper toward his throat. He struggled against the rope on his wrists, but each movement made it dig deeper into his skin.

Elen. He focused on the memory of her voice and let his body go slack. He closed his eyes and withdrew into the vision of her as she was at the bar that day after the shooting. Wispy, sun-kissed curls framed her face as they pushed against the confines of her netsela. Her smile shone on him now, dulling the pain.

"What if all this just disappeared, and it was just the two of us?" Her voice was so clear in his mind.

Was that just yesterday?

"I would never leave this moment if I could," he had told her.

The next two punches landed. Girmai didn't feel them.

Elen. He focused on her face, those eyes, those lips—he kissed her again and again.

Someone was removing his shoes and then his socks. He lay still on his back, his legs already numb from the wooden pole wedged under his knees. His hands were losing feeling too.

A scuffle, then a dragging noise, pulled him out of his meditation. He opened his eyes in time to see a table he hadn't noticed before being moved next to the one he had just been sitting in front of. They left a gap between the tables.

His neck snapped back as two men lifted the pole and Girmai with it. They dropped each end between the tables, suspending his body so it swung like a pendulum by his knees. The burn on his wrists intensified with each swing.

"Please!"

The word didn't escape the rag shoved in his mouth.

"You'll talk eventually."

All movement paused as one of them spoke. Girmai tried to lift his head, but gravity won. He let it hang and stared at the soldiers' boots upside down.

Girmai braced himself for what was coming next. He saw the top of the whip almost touch the ceiling as the soldier on the other side raised it and snapped it down on the soles of his feet. The rag absorbed his screams and forced him to swallow his vomit. The soles of his feet tore and bled with each strike. Again and again.

He closed his eyes.

"All we have are moments, Elen," he had told her between kisses. "We have to live for these moments."

Whip!

"This is the best moment of my life," she'd told him.

Whip!

"Me too," he said, as her hands had wrapped tightly around him.

Whip!

"We're here for each other, no matter what."

The whipping paused. The rag came out. Girmai's jaw throbbed as he smacked his dry tongue against the roof of his mouth.

"I'll talk," he said. "I'll tell you anything you want," his voice cracked. "Please, let me down first. I can't talk like this!"

A pause.

He inhaled sharply as two pairs of hands lifted both ends of the pole and then dropped him onto the floor. His ribcage rattled.

They untied the ropes around his feet, slid the pole out from under his knees, and lifted him by his armpits, shoving him back onto the chair. His hands, still tied, rested limp on his lap. Girmai gingerly stretched his feet to minimize contact between his bleeding soles and the cold, grainy floor. He rolled his tongue around his mouth to get rid of the taste of vomit.

He had to buy time. Daniel would have heard of his arrest by now. Hopefully, they'd have activated the release plan.

"Well, talk." The icy tone pierced the thick air.

"My name is Girmai Issac," he managed. It was hard to talk through the pain in his jaw. "I own two shops and a sweater factory. You may know them. In fact, I named my sweater shop after this Expo Center. Anyone you ask will tell you I am a patriot. Look into my history. You'll find many things to protect our city from counterrevolutionaries."

The men looked at each other, then back at him.

"I don't know why I'm here. Whoever gave you my name just wants my money. Look at my clothes, my watch, my shoes. Do you think someone like me needs to steal money?"

Their silence gave him some hope.

"Ask anyone," he continued, his head spinning. He sat straighter to resist the urge to vomit. "Like I said, everything I've done to support the Derg is clear. I don't know why someone would say I stole …" He was rambling now.

"Liar!" The blow to his temple launched him off the chair. He fell on his side, the chair clattering behind him. His feet were bloody lumps beneath him.

The soldier's boot creaked beside Girmai's head. "Get him up!"

Hands hoisted Girmai up again while another put the chair back upright.

"Tie him to the chair. He's wasting our time."

"Please …" Girmai began as the door behind him flew open.

"What is this?" Colonel Zenebe walked in and planted himself before Girmai, his brows furrowed. All the men stood at attention.

They did it. Girmai allowed himself an exhale.

"This man was trying to steal money, sir." The man's tone turned deferential so quickly that Girmai looked to see if it was the same person talking. "A witness identified him in this morning's incident at the telecommunications building."

The Colonel faced him, shoulders straight, hands on his hips. His authority was unquestionable.

"I take it you have proof? Was he caught with the money? Was he in the building?" Colonel Zenebe had yet to look at Girmai.

The man hesitated. "No, but we have the man who gave us the information. He saw him driving near the building at the time of the incident. No other reason he would have been there so early in the morning."

"So, no proof other than he was driving by." The Colonel regarded his subordinate coolly.

Girmai blinked through the blood. He couldn't see where the other officers were.

"Do you know who this is?" Zenebe pointed at Girmai, though his eyes never left the interrogator. "This is Girmai Issac. He's our ally and a valued member of our community. Unless you have proof that he's stolen something, you won't continue this line of questioning."

Zenebe turned to look at Girmai.

"But—"

"Leave him with me."

After a slight hesitation, the men filed out of the room.

Every part of Girmai's body hurt. He strained to hold his head up as the room spun around him.

"How did you get into this mess?" the Colonel said, lowering himself into a chair across the table from Girmai. He leaned back and crossed an ankle over a knee. Both men looked quietly at each other.

"It was a misunderstanding," Girmai managed. "I don't know what they're accusing me of."

Girmai could see the conflict in Zenebe's eyes as he stared at him. The Colonel was probably thinking of how to keep the money stream that Girmai provided intact.

"I can arrange your release, but the paperwork will take some time. You'll have to wait here until then."

Zenebe scraped the chair back and left the room.

Moments later, the five soldiers returned. No one spoke as they walked Girmai across a narrow outdoor path, then shoved him into a small empty room. He crashed to the floor, in too much pain to do anything but stay still.

"Let's see if your luck lasts in here," the lead soldier said as he slammed the door shut, enveloping Girmai in darkness.

21

The normality of the morning cast doubt on the reality of her time with him just a day ago. Alem boiled water for tea, Solomon settled in front of a plate of frittata, Faven played tug-of-war with their adopted street cat's tail, and Aman reviewed his homework one last time before school.

Their stolen moments were borrowed, fleeting slivers of time that never belonged to them. It was as if the most monumental transformation in Elen's life hadn't happened. Life just moved forward, and she had to move with it. She made herself tea and sat down beside Solomon.

Alem fussed over him as she did with the children, her voice a constant stream of instructions and reminders. "Here, why don't you move this way?" she said. "Look, if I move this chair here and angle the table like this, you don't have to lean over your hand so much." Tea sloshed over teacups as she dragged the table.

"I'm fine. I can do it," Solomon said, sending a piece of scrambled egg flying off his fork as he waved her away. "See?"

Faven and Solomon laughed as he exaggerated the difficulty of the task and let most of the food drop back onto the plate as he tried to maneuver his fork to his mouth with his left hand.

"You are sillier than the kids," Alem said, rolling her eyes.

"Speaking of kids," Elen said. "It's time to get those teeth of yours brushed. Off you go."

Solomon finished his food and got up. "I'll check in with Akberet to see if she needs help setting up," he said, heading to the front door.

"I am sure she is fine," Alem said to his back. "Can't you just sit and rest?"

Solomon gave her a thumbs-up without turning around and disappeared through the door. He was not one to sit still for too long.

"Is he allergic to taking care of himself or what?" Alem said, shaking her head.

"Must be," Elen chuckled. "I don't think anyone can make him rest; that would kill him for sure."

They settled into a comfortable silence before Alem turned to face her, eyes sparkling.

"I have some news," Alem began, adjusting her netsela over her head. "Melak and I have been talking, and he is thinking about us moving to Addis after the wedding."

Elen was caught off guard. "Move to Addis?" she repeated.

Elen had encouraged the budding relationship and was genuinely happy for her sister. Melak, her husband-to-be, was an honest, thoughtful, hardworking man, and his love for Alem was obvious.

Their small, family-only wedding ceremony was happening that weekend, and Elen couldn't be happier for her sister. She had no doubt Alem would do well with him anywhere, but the thought of her sister living so far away filled her with a sense of dread she couldn't shake.

She tried to match Alem's enthusiasm, but her time with Girmai, Solomon's brush with death, and all the increasing tension in the bar threw her off track. The feel of Girmai's arms around her was still fresh in her mind. How liberating it must be to just love and be loved openly and not worry so much.

Melak will keep her safer than I can here, Elen admitted to herself. *That's what matters.*

Alem continued talking, oblivious to Elen's inner turmoil. "Melak told me he found us a place close to his work. His commission to oversee the construction of a large office building is the biggest job he has ever gotten." Her smile faltered as she searched Elen's face.

"Wow," Elen replied, the right words not quite coming out fast enough. "That sounds like a great plan, but we will miss you."

How do I protect her from such a distance?

Alem reached out to squeeze her hand. "Don't worry, Elen. It's not like we'll never see each other. You'll visit us, and I'll come back to see you whenever I can. Melak said there's a shop with a phone close to the house, so we can talk as often as we like."

She loved her sister's optimism. Elen nodded, forcing herself to return Alem's reassuring grip. "I know. It's just … I'm going to miss you."

"I'll miss you too, but this is the start of something good, right?" Alem said, her voice tilting at the last word. "Isn't that what you always tell me, to take joy wherever we can find it?"

Elen's smile grew. "Absolutely," she replied. "You must always soak in the joy whenever it comes to you. I am really happy for you, Alem."

Back in her room, Elen closed the door and looked around. No signs of him remained. He had broken the rules they had made when they first started working together, that they would not meet in person and risk someone seeing them together. He shouldn't have come, and he couldn't stay. He had to return to his family, his work, and his life. She caught the faint smell of him lingering on her pillow and buried her face in it.

A joy I can't have.

Inhaling his scent again, she thought of him in this space, his arm around her, his body spooning hers as they faced the heavy curtain she'd drawn against the window.

"Where do we go from here? There's no future for us." She hadn't wanted the moment to end.

"We can't think that way," he'd said. "We have each other right now. People are dying around us every day without the chance to feel what we're feeling." He'd wrapped his arms around her tighter. "Let's live in this moment and not taint it by worrying about a future we can't control."

All we have are moments.

She put the pillow down and gently laid the bed cover over it.

It was time to get ready—lots of things to do today.

Her first stop was Gennet's house, followed by the Edaga Hamus market for vegetables before opening the bar in the afternoon.

Elen put on the long green chiffon dress that Gennet had perfectly integrated with layers. The tiny inseam on the hem, large enough to slip in a folded newsletter, was imperceptible. Even Elen had to fumble to find it. Once dressed, she slid open the false bottom of her dresser drawer, extracted a newsletter, folded it in half, and slid it into the seam. She had received this latest edition right before all the chaos of the Mebrahtu incident and needed to get it to Gennet.

The delivery was long overdue.

This new publication was their window into the revolution. Produced in the field by the EPLF using stolen typewriters and printing presses, it was called *Sedici*—sixteen, representing the sixteen kilometers remaining before they took over Asmara.

They just have to hold on a little longer. Victory was in sight.

Whenever they got their copy, Elen, Alem, and Solomon would pour over it under candlelight. Elen marveled at the pictures portraying women in liberated areas dancing regally, unreserved pride shining on their faces. Men in their long, flowing traditional jalabiya wielded swords, showing off their jumping skills as they leaped several feet.

What freedom! A far cry from their lives in Asmara. Who has the luxury to dance here?

Solomon had smiled at the article "Youth Carry the Revolutionary Torch."

"Yes!" he'd said, smacking his thigh. "That's absolutely right. It's up to us young people to win this!"

They all stared at pictures of Derg soldiers standing on the roofs of tanks or in the middle of the battlefield, hands up in fearful resignation in front of EPLF fighters surrounding them. None looked a day over twenty.

They read about children born in liberated areas, sons and daughters of liberation fighters. They learned in makeshift schools with underground bomb shelters.

Everyone—boys and girls — learned to read and write. They shared chores equally, so no one sacrificed study time. When they were old enough, literacy and political lessons went hand in hand with military training. They learned the art of stealth warfare and weapon maintenance.

The girls staring back at them from the newsletter pages wore canvas shorts and matching shirts. Their unencumbered afros burst out in a defiant statement of liberation. Some looked the same age Elen had been when she ran away from home.

The newsletter showed how donations from the cities and collections from abroad provided resources for food, schools, hospitals, and recreation in the field.

"Self-reliance is our way of life!" an EPLF teacher had said in the article. "Our power lies in unity."

"Awet N' Hafash!" it declared on almost every other page. Victory to the masses!

"We need to stay informed. That way, we know why we do what we do," she had told Alem and Solomon as she fed pieces of her newsletter into the hot coals while shaking the coffee beans to roast over the fire. There could be no trace of it in the house. She absentmindedly thought of the other copies she had distributed, hoping their readers were doing the same. "Knowing about all the successes in the field gives us strength and hope. That's our weapon."

It was time to continue that work.

"I'll just get a few things from the market," she told Alem on her way out. "Make enough injera for dinner tonight. I'm sure Kudusan will have some fresh shiro ready for me. We can have that for dinner."

"Be careful," Alem replied, as she always did whenever Elen left home.

"I will," Elen said. "I'll be fine, don't worry."

Strangely, Elen didn't feel scared. Perhaps being with Girmai had emboldened her, or maybe surviving the shooting had acclimatized her to danger.

The weight of the newsletter in the seam of her dress rested against her foot.

"We can't worry about a future we can't control," Girmai had told her.

Time to go.

Elen tightened her netsela around her shoulders as she left through the back gate. It was hotter than she expected. The midday sun warmed her as she adjusted her netsela to cover herself.

Despite her bravado with Alem and the peace she had felt moments before, a familiar uneasiness crept up her chest now that she was out in the open.

She picked up her pace. The muted, faint outline of leaves on the chiffon material deviated from the usual bright outfits Gennet made for her. Elen had also bypassed her kohl and jewelry routine this morning—no need to draw attention to herself out here.

The severe ponytail she had combed her hair into now felt too tight, pulling at her temples. The thin foam of her worn flip-flops did nothing to soften her tread on the sidewalk. Flashes of her red toes peeked out from underneath the dress.

I should have worn closed shoes.

She reached the top of La Fontana, paused, and scanned the surrounding area as she listened to the calm flow of the water cascading down the fountain steps.

No sign that anyone had followed her. The midday heat bounced off the pavement, distorting her view of the few people walking in the distance.

All the shops were closed for lunch; everyone had wisely escaped the unsparing sun, which made this the safest time to make the delivery when even the soldiers were too hot to harass people.

"Train your mind," Girmai had told her once, his voice from her initial recruitment meeting clear in her memory. "You'll constantly feel doubt and fear, especially when you see the extent of the Derg's brutality. The only way to get through any challenging task is to train your mind to think of something else you love—think of freedom. Think of us living in that freedom. Go to the place in your mind that gives you courage."

She thought of him now in the silence of the streets leading to Gennet's house.

Were we together just yesterday?

The broad avenues narrowed into modest streets, where sidewalks swelled to allow tree roots to break through. Elen's steps faltered at a familiar corner.

The bloodstains were still there.

A week before, Gennet had told her about the three bodies that lay strewn around the lamppost on that corner—two men and a woman.

"They looked so young," she had said. "The woman was in her pajamas, and blood completely covered the upper half of her body. Two men lay beside her. They had all been shot."

"Soldiers were watching from a distance, so I kept walking," Gennet had said, wiping her tears. Derg soldiers arrested anyone who mourned over bodies lying on the streets, accusing them of being rebel sympathizers.

"Why are you crying over this counterrevolutionary filth, eh?" they would say. "You must be one yourself. Get in the truck!"

They would squeeze more bodies into jam-packed prisons and interrogation centers and charge victims' families a bullet tax for the Derg's expense of the ones they killed. Bodies left on the streets served as a warning of consequences, with signs pinned to their chests: DEATH TO ALL COUNTERREVOLUTIONARIES!

"It's good you kept walking," Elen had told her. "You need to keep yourself safe. It frustrates them that they can't stifle the revolution. They want us to be afraid when we see our brothers and sisters killed and disrespected."

"You should be careful too, Elen," Gennet had replied. "None of us are safe."

"I'll be okay." Elen had sighed at the lie she told so well. "Don't worry about me."

Elen walked faster. Gennet's house was just a few blocks away. She had recently moved her sewing equipment into her home since she wasn't earning enough to pay the rent for her tailor shop. Her customers showed up there randomly, sometimes to drop off clothes for minor fixes but other times for fittings, which could occupy her for more than an hour. In that case, it would be impossible to give her the newsletter.

The black metal gate separating Gennet's house from the street was wide open. Elen hesitated before she walked through.

Something didn't feel right. Gennet left her gate unlocked but never ajar like this.

Elen's unease intensified with each step up the narrow path to the front entrance.

The door also stood open, and the usually upbeat, chaotic interior was silent.

"Gennet?"

Elen stepped through. Her hand shot up to her mouth to stifle a scream.

All the furniture in the house lay in broken heaps, stuffing from the chairs pulled out and strewn across the floor. Pieces of Gennet's prized glass coffee table lay in shards, and her sewing table was upside down in the middle as if thrown on top.

Drawers lay open, their contents haphazardly scattered. Black bits of coffee grounds spilled from a broken jebena, the clay coffee pot Gennet loved. Pieces of ceramic coffee cups were scattered as far as the living-room entrance.

A clock on the floor kept ticking despite multiple cracks on its face, the sound magnified in Elen's ears.

Oh, Gennet!

Elen turned and walked away quickly.

* * *

"What happened?"

Elen ignored Solomon in the hallway leading up to the apartment and walked directly to the phone in the bar, her heart racing. With trembling fingers, she dialed Girmai's number, each unanswered ring amplifying the fear that knotted in her stomach.

Where was he? He would usually answer by now. The silence on the other end felt like a chasm opening beneath her feet.

Come on, Girmai, I really need you to pick up today.

Just as she was about to hang up, an unfamiliar voice caught her off guard.

"Hello?"

Elen's pulse quickened. Who was this? No one but Girmai had ever answered the phone.

"Hello, men kibil?" the voice repeated.

"Selam," she managed to say. "Men kibil?" she asked, keeping her tone steady.

"This is Araya," the man said. "Men kibil?" he asked again.

Araya. Girmai had mentioned him; he was the shop manager and was trustworthy and dependable. But why was he answering the phone?

"I was hoping to speak with Girmai." She injected a note of casualness into her voice, though her insides churned with dread. "Is he close by?"

The pause on the other end stretched uncomfortably long. Elen opened her mouth to tell him a fabricated story about who she was but thought the better of it. She leaned into the silence and pressed the phone closer to her ear until he spoke again.

"They arrested him earlier today," Paulos finally said, his tone subdued.

Elen's world tilted. *Arrested?*

"What? What happened? Where is he?" Her voice came out sharper than intended, fear slicing through her composure.

"Who is this again?" Araya asked, suspicion in his voice.

She hung up, her breath hitching in her throat. Without meeting Solomon's questioning stare, she hurried to her room, every step a desperate attempt to hold herself together. She pulled the newsletter from the seam of her dress and shoved it back into the drawer's false bottom, her hands shaking.

Where is he? Why was he arrested?

She blinked hard, her hands clenched into tight fists. Her

breathing slowed, each inhale deliberate, as she willed her mind to steady and push away the panic threatening to drown her. Then, a memory of the tiny roll of paper she'd hidden behind her mirror surfaced.

Daniel. Girmai's backup plan.

"Only call him if it is an emergency and you can't reach me," Girmai had told her when he handed her the note with a phone number. "This is your option when you have no other options."

Elen unrolled the paper, the numbers blurred by the tears she refused to let fall.

Elen rushed back to the phone in the bar, her fingers fumbling on the rotary dial.

Damnit. Elen clicked on the receiver and started again.

Solomon edged closer, concern etched on his face. "Elen, what is happening?"

She waved him away, her focus singular.

Finally, she got the number right. A voice came through on the first ring.

"Hello?"

She almost dropped the phone in relief.

"This is Elen." She steadied herself. It could be a Derg soldier on the other end, but she had to take the risk. "I was told I could call this number to find out the offer for the lunch specials."

In the silence that followed, she kept her mouth open to beg and plead in case her code was incorrect. That is what Girmai told her to say after she called this number, but things could have changed.

"This is Daniel."

It worked. She allowed herself a small, shaky smile, remembering how she'd laughed at Girmai when he told her what to say.

"My lunch appointment was canceled today, and I just discovered one of my friends is gone." She rushed through, hoping he would understand what she was saying.

"Girmai went to Mai Chelot today." His tone was brisk.

Mai Chelot, a natural spring believed to have holy water, was the code name for prison.

"What?" she said aloud. "How did that happen? Is someone helping him?"

"Yes," Daniel continued, his words clipped. "We are working on it."

Elen gripped the phone tighter until her fingers went numb.

"He will be back soon."

She wanted to believe in the certainty in his voice but couldn't shake the dread.

"What is your friend's name?" Daniel asked.

"Gennet, the tailor, lives just a few blocks from me. I don't know where she is, but I was just at her house. It's … messy," she said, the words faltering at the horror of what she'd seen.

"Do you know if they found anything?"

"I don't know," Elen replied. She gripped the phone even tighter.

"We will look for her and tell you what we find out," Daniel said. "I have to leave soon, so you won't be able to reach me here. I'll send you new information on how to contact me."

"What about Girmai?" her voice cracked, desperation seeping through.

"I'll let you know when I have news."

***

Elen had started burning the tiny bits of Gennet's newsletter too soon. The coffee beans Elen roasted over the charcoal fire were still green. The sharp smell of raw beans did nothing to hide the scent of burning paper. She shook the beans in the kesh kesh pan, her hands moving mechanically.

EPLF writers risked their lives to write those words in underground bunkers, words that hid inside burlap vegetable sacks snuck past checkpoints on donkeys' backs, and slid into the false bottoms of beer crates to get to Elen. They hid in the folds of her skirt as she carried copies of the newsletters past drunk soldiers and into other homes where they could continue to give strength.

Those stories had to continue to live in her. She couldn't burn them without reading them first.

She savored every precious story of EPLF victories all over the country. She traced her fingers over every paragraph that told her of the schools that had been built for hundreds of children, both girls and boys, of communities bound by collective suffering that worked and supported one another. There were so many children, so many orphans, and there was hope, adults to care for them despite heavy bombings and attacks.

They persevered just like Elen was going to have to do now.

The flames curled around the title of an article "Women Are the Backbone of Our Fight". Elen watched it until all the words curled, then disintegrated into black ash.

"I thought we already destroyed it," Solomon said, watching the flames dance in the small brazier.

It had been almost a week since the phone call with Daniel, and there was still no word about Gennet or Girmai. The silence gnawed at Elen, leaving her feeling hollow and brittle.

"This one is not ours." Her voice was flat, drained of emotion. She had yet to speak about Gennet or Girmai to anyone, and deflected all of Solomon's questions after the call. The less he knew, the better.

Keeping herself functioning through the tidal wave of customers and suppressing her emotions had taken all her energy, leaving nothing for explanations or reassurances.

"It isn't?" Solomon's curiosity was piqued, but he didn't press.

"It will definitely be safer for Alem if she moves to Addis now," she said, her eyes fixed on the coffee beans, darkening as they roasted. The white smoke finally rose, signaling the right time to shove the last bits of the newsletter into the fire.

"Seriously?" Solomon's voice pitched higher in surprise. He had never been in favor of the siblings splitting up.

Elen's thoughts drifted back to Gennet's ransacked house, the violent reality of their lives. *I can't lose her too.*

"Yes," she said.

The coffee beans now gleamed black, and the flames consumed the last of the newsletter. It had been hard to find enough time to burn Gennet's copy. Elen saved it in what she now knew was unreasonable hope that her friend would come back. What were the chances after a week?

Elen spread the beans around a circular sisal fan to cool down, her movements deliberate and methodical.

"Things will not get any better here," she told her brother. "Melak is a good man. They will live in a quiet neighborhood in Addis, and she will be much safer with him than here with us." She shook her head, her mind heavy with the burden of decisions she had to make. "Once she leaves, we will figure out how to get you out too."

"I am not going anywhere." Solomon's voice was firm, and at that moment, Elen recognized their father's quiet resolve in him. "I don't have anywhere else I want to be. This is not how we will live forever, Elen. I know things will change for the better; we are doing something about it, and we are not the only ones. People all over the city and the country are fighting like we are, and we will eventually succeed. I know it."

Elen turned to him, hearing the conviction in his voice. *How does he still believe in a better future?*

"You seem like you have had much on your mind these past few days. Tell me what's going on."

And so she did. It all came tumbling out—her love for Girmai, what happened with Gennet, Girmai's disappearance. Naming everything she'd kept bottled up over the past week brought a strange sense of relief, like finally releasing a breath she'd been holding.

"I am still waiting to hear from Daniel. I don't know what's going on with Girmai or Gennet."

"We have to keep faith that it will be okay," Solomon said, his calm voice a balm to her frayed nerves. "Let's worry when we have reason to. Wait for Daniel to contact you and, in the meantime, stay strong in hope."

It was impossible to feel hope, but Solomon was right. Hope was exactly what she must force herself to feel.

22

Former Expo Exhibit Center, Asmara, 1975

How many months has it been? Girmai's eyes roamed around the dark cell, haunted by memories of his exhibits at the trade shows in this very place. The once bustling buildings stood quiet now. Prison cells now replaced the vibrant exhibit stalls the expo grounds used to be known for. Vigorous weeds took over the winding cobbled walkways, claiming every crevice and crack available.

The angle of the sun's rays filtering through the small window hinted at midmorning. He shifted on the floor to sit closer to the beam of light. The thin ray hit a spot right above his head, and in just another hour, he would briefly enjoy the sunlight on his face before it disappeared again. The tight space made the perfect isolation chamber. The room was big enough to let him stand and stretch, with a space to pace just a few steps.

All we have are moments.

His beard had grown so much over the past weeks … *months*? It covered the lower part of his face, a wild and unkempt mass that he barely recognized. Sweat had hardened into crusty flakes in his neck that constantly itched.

He didn't get his shoes back after they beat him. The soles of his feet healed in hardened, calloused ridges over the torn skin. He still wore the clothes they had arrested him in. Hunger and filth were all too familiar.

At least there were no fleas. A small mercy, one of the few he allowed himself to acknowledge.

Other than the guards walking him to the pit latrine by an outer wall, he saw no one, though he knew the grounds were full of prisoners.

Dried blood splatters marked a wall at the far end of the prison, clearly visible even from a distance.

The execution site.

The screams of the hundreds of victims went unheard beyond the high compound walls. Several rooms around the compound served as detention chambers, just like his.

Moans filtered through high windows as he walked past. Sleep deprivation was one of the torture methods. The more desperate screams reached a crescendo in the middle of the night, though reused rags quickly muffled them soon after they escaped the victims' mouths.

Every day, he relived his own interrogation, his body breaking under the impact of their boots, the whip descending on his bare feet, the punches to his face. He replayed the events of the heist over and over.

Things might have been different if I had parked further down or waited a few more seconds before driving off. The what-ifs were the worst. Things he could not change. The weight of regret mingled with the ever-present fear.

His mind often rested on thoughts of Elen. She brought him to the light and drew him back from the tipping point he constantly teetered over in his isolation. Her smile, her face, her voice, how she felt in his arms that afternoon—he saved those memories for the darkest hours.

Sitting in the patch of sunlight, his mind roamed to his family at home, the children playing outside. Helen, ever observant, quietly watching over them.

They haven't killed me yet. Someone is working to get me out. Daniel will come through. He clung to hope, fragile as it was. *It's a long time to wait.*

A vibration at the door startled him as keys rattled against each other outside the door. Girmai struggled to sit up, his legs splayed out in front of him. They usually came twice daily to let him out to the bathroom, once in the morning and once at dusk. If Girmai needed to go in between, he had a bucket in the tiny room that he emptied when they let him out.

The doorway opened, the profile of a thin soldier filling it. The sudden abundance of light forced Girmai to squint and shield his face with his arm.

"Get up," the voice ordered. "You are leaving."

They haven't killed me yet.

***

Daniel was waiting for him in an unfamiliar car when Girmai hobbled through the Expo Center gates.

"It's been a while," Daniel said after a long embrace.

"How long is a while?" Girmai asked, his arms bent in a weak fold around his friend's shoulders.

"Four months," Daniel replied as he led Girmai to the car and opened the door for him. "Unfortunately, we didn't get to Zenebe in time to avoid your interrogation. Once he saw how much money was coming his way, he came to you fast. Then he got called to Gash Barka to lead an offensive before he finished the paperwork to release you. He is back in town and sent it over after we nudged him."

Girmai closed his eyes and rested his head on the headrest while Daniel walked around to the driver's side. The smell of himself in the car made his nose wrinkle.

"Someone will have to clean everything in here," Girmai said, looking at his bare feet and unrecognizable clothes.

They both chuckled. "I'm glad to have you back," Daniel said. "You made it."

Thank you … is what Girmai wanted to say but he could only nod.

"Hey, let's not get too mushy here," Daniel said, turning the car on. "You are not off the hook yet, that stink won't get you far."

Girmai laughed. "That's for sure!"

Daniel drove slowly as Girmai talked fast, telling him everything he could remember about the prison—the layout, schedules, security. He felt like he barely said anything when Daniel pulled up to Girmai's house and shifted the gear into park but kept the engine going.

"I'll bring the guys over later for a proper debrief this afternoon," Daniel said. "They need to hear this."

"Did you tell Elen I am out?" Girmai asked, pushing the door open.

"Yes." Daniel managed a tight smile. "I told her I would pick you up after Zenebe confirmed your release. She has been waiting to hear the news."

"Thank you, brother." His voice cracked and he cleared it. "I do have much more to tell you."

"Will be back soon when you are smelling better!"

Girmai rolled his eyes and slammed the door in mock anger before walking through the gate of his home as Daniel drove off.

Helen's wide eyes and hand over her mouth told him everything he needed to know about how bad he looked.

"Praise be to God, praise be to God!" Her ululations rang in his ear as she embraced him. Girmai winced at the pressure of her hug. His ribcage seemed to have healed, although it was still sore when he moved in certain positions. "Daniel told me he would be bringing you; we have hot water and I already prepared clean clothes on the bed for you. Come, take a shower. I am so sorry, Girmai. We are so thankful you are back home. We missed you so much."

"Thank you, Helen. It's so good to be home." The words scratched their way though his emotions as she led him to the bathroom.

***

He stood in the shower and let the most beautiful sensation of the hot water spraying his face take over. He reveled in the stream as he scrubbed away the months of grime and dirt. He closed his eyes as the water cleared his mind and ran through all the information he had cataloged from his time at the Expo showgrounds.

Four guards patrol the inside perimeter, two on the tower overlooking the street, and one by the gate. All spaces with lockable doors served as prison cells. Judging by the screams from some bigger rooms, interrogators probably used them for questioning. The splattering of blood on the furthest wall by the open show booth center marked the execution site. Mass graves most likely lined the inside of the outer wall.

Not many people who went in walked out of that prison.

Girmai turned off the shower when the brown water turned clear, trailed past his feet, and circled into the drain.

Elen, I need to see her.

Girmai walked into his living room, shaved and clean, looking more like his pre-prison self. Helen kept a meticulous household. Everything was exactly where it belonged. He turned to the sound of the kids playing in the front yard.

It must be Saturday.

"I told the kids to play outside until you got settled." Helen came in behind him and gestured toward the couches. "Sit, I will get you some breakfast. They will come in soon."

He shrugged away pangs of guilt. "Thank you, Helen." He gingerly lowered himself into his favorite armchair opposite the huge L-shaped couch in the center of the living room.

Helen placed a plate of eggs frittata with diced tomato, onion, and chili peppers in front of him just as his eyes drooped and his head nodded to his chest. She disappeared back into the kitchen and returned with a steaming cup of shahi. The tea, in a short transparent glass, steamed with the aroma of ginger, cardamom, and cloves. It instantly relaxed him.

She is so good to me.

As Helen predicted, all the kids came streaming in when he was halfway into his frittata. They crowded around him on the couch, their shrieks of delight a salve to the trauma of the past few months.

"Kids, be careful," Helen gently said to them as they tumbled over each other to get closer to him.

"I'm so happy to see you all!" Girmai cried. Small arms circled his neck and torso, and Rahwa almost knocked over the breakfast set on the side table by his chair.

“Baba, why was your work trip so long?” Rahwa asked, wrapping her arms around his neck in a hug. Girmai and Helen exchanged glances.

“Sometimes it takes a long time to finish work,” he said. “I don’t understand how all of you got so big, eh?” he asked. “Stand back. Let me take a look at you.”

Yonas, Samuel, and Rahwa stood straight, each with identical grins and puffed-out chests. Alexander stayed on the couch and refused to leave Girmai’s side.

He would not burden Helen or any of them with the horror he’d been through. “Everyone has grown at least a meter!” he raised his hand in exaggeration. “What have you been eating?”

Girmai lifted his fork, gave each of them a taste of his frittata, and laughed at their delight at the big bites. They eventually peeled off to continue playing outside once they got their fill of hugging him. Helen closed the front door and came back into the living room.

“Here, let’s keep you warm,” Helen said, covering him with a gabi. “I am sure you need some rest.” She squeezed his shoulder gently, took the tray of plates, and closed the door behind her.

His eyelids got heavier in the silence of the living room as the food, the tea, and the sounds of the kids’ voices outside placated him on the soft chair.

“He will have more energy later.” The fog of his exhaustion muted her voice. “Stay outside and play.”

***

Daniel was on the couch across from him when he opened his eyes again. He shook his head to orient himself to the moment. He wiped sleep from his eyes and sat up straighter in his armchair. “What time is it?”

“Almost two o’clock,” Daniel said. “You’ve been asleep for a while. Kifle and Memhir Yemane will be here soon.”

Girmai smiled and pushed himself up on the chair. “It’ll be great to see Memhir, and it won’t be so bad to see Kifle’s ugly face too.”

Daniel’s smile met his own. “You will probably have many more visitors once word gets out that you are back. Everyone is looking for something to celebrate."

"I think it's time for some Areki," Daniel continued. "What do you say to that?"

"I say you read my mind!" A nice stiff drink could kick-start him out of this daze.

Girmai only noticed the transparent bottle of Areki and the small shot glasses around it as Daniel reached for it.

The front door opened as Daniel poured them a shot of the strong-smelling liquor. Berhane, Kifle, and Memhir Yemane streamed in, and their voices filled the room.

"Berhane too? Ah, my brother, nice to see you!" Girmai grinned as he got up to greet them. The men settled down on the couches around Girmai, and each grabbed a shot.

"So, Girmai," Memhir Yemane said, wiping his mouth with the back of his hand, "you survived the Expo. That is no small feat. What can you tell us?"

They were all familiar with the layout, so he filled in the details of everything he could remember.

"It would be tough to do a rescue mission there," Memhir mused.

"Very," Girmai agreed.

"It's a miracle you are out," Memhir replied.

"All thanks to you," Girmai said.

"Well, it's time to raise a toast to that!" Daniel poured another round.

"To freedom!" Berhane said.

"Awet N' Hafash!" they all said in unison, each grimacing as the shots went down.

"The wheels are in motion for the big operation. Our big friend's time has come," Memhir said.

"The Colonel?" Girmai already knew the answer.

Memhir jerked his head in confirmation. "It will probably be within the next few months, maybe more. It was good Zenebe got you out. He is useful for that kind of thing, but his strategic offenses cost us too many lives in the field. We need to stop him."

Girmai thought about the relative safety Elen had under Zenebe's umbrella of protection. Once he was gone, they didn't have anyone with his clout to get them out of tight situations. The fragility of everything in their lives hit him again. He swallowed another shot, enjoying how the alcohol burned its way down his throat and dulled the alarm at the thought of Elen going through what he just experienced.

I have to see her soon.

Word of Girmai's release had spread fast. Throughout the day, neighbors, friends, cousins—everyone and anyone—streamed in from the neighborhood and beyond. Some passed by for a quick hug and greeting, and others sat and chatted. Helping hands brought in more chairs. As was tradition, visitors came in carrying either food or drink, which was quickly shared, giving the gathering a festive feel.

The room emptied in the late afternoon until it was just the four men again.

Flushed and jubilant with drink, Berhane got up to pour a final round when a knock at the entrance door made Girmai sigh inwardly. He was hoping to just be with his friends. One of the children walked out of the kitchen to open the door.

Berhane was back on the couch when Colonel Zenebe stepped into the room. His eyes roamed around the room, then he settled on Girmai.

"Ah! Girmai!" He weaved through empty chairs to get to Girmai, who stood up to greet him. Two men in full military uniform followed Zenebe into the house and stood by the entrance to the living room. The door remained open. Their lapels showed they were majors.

Girmai glanced at Memhir. He couldn't read his expression.

The space suddenly felt too small. Girmai saw Memhir's hand fall beside his knee.

He has a gun on him, damnit, Girmai cursed inwardly. He guessed it was probably tied to his shin. No doubt the others were armed too.

Zenebe's own pistol prominently sat in his belt holster.

Girmai reminded himself that Zenebe had yet to meet any of the men and would not know who they were. All negotiations were made through Habteab and others like him spread throughout the Derg ranks.

"It is great to see you out!" Zenebe walked over, and Girmai clasped his hand. He laid a palm on Girmai's shoulder.

They must have paid him a lot of money for him to make time for a home visit.

"Please sit!" Girmai motioned to a space on the oversized couch between him and Berhane. "It is wonderful to see you again! How have you been? Meet my cousins."

Berhane politely got up and turned to the majors. "Please make yourselves comfortable here." He gestured toward the empty chairs and invited them to sit.

Zenebe nodded at each man as Girmai introduced them quickly. He decided to use their real names and hoped Zenebe was not paying too close attention. Berhane was already serving drinks and gave each man a shot of Areki.

"This is quite a house you have here." Zenebe said, greed coating his expression. He threw back his shot with an "ahhh" after he swallowed.

Just then Alexander waddled into the room. Girmai's precocious son was too young to show fear and old enough to love attention. He especially loved visitors, who always doted on him. The others knew better than to interfere with grown-up conversations.

"Who do we have here?" Zenebe leaned down and picked Alexander up until his bare feet dangled in the air. The Colonel eventually placed him on his lap opposite his pistol. He pinched one of Alexander's cheeks playfully.

"Are you going to grow up to be a bandit or a soldier, eh?" Zenebe's eyes rose and flickered to each man in the room. Girmai saw Memhir's hand twitch. He shook his head at him imperceptibly.

There won't be a gunfight in my house.

Alexander held up his hand to Zenebe's face, touching his mustache.

"A soldier like you!" he said.

Zenebe laughed, then let him slide down his lap. Girmai breathed again as Alexander left through the front door to join the others outside.

After the requisite small talk about the weather and predictions of a successful rainy season, Memhir made motions to leave.

"Well!" he said, slapping his thigh. He made a show of draining his glass. "Girmai, it was great to see you. We will have to get going now."

All the men stood up and said their goodbyes. Zenebe and the majors watched their every move as they filed out of the room. Girmai's ears tuned in to the sound of cars driving away.

"Looks like you have a lot of friends," Zenebe said, his expression hard to read.

"My most important friend is you, Colonel!" Girmai said jovially, hoping to break the tension.

"Indeed. I value our friendship too." He drew out the word "friendship", then got up suddenly. One of the majors almost knocked the side table over when he rose with the Colonel. Both stood at attention.

Zenebe adjusted his holster. "Here's to our continued friendship."

Before Girmai could grab his glass, Zenebe tipped his head up, gulped the shot, and slammed the glass on the table.

He stumbled a little on his way around the couches. One of the majors put a hand out to support him, then thought better of it. They followed him to the front door.

"I will be seeing you soon, Girmai," he said. "Don't wander off too far."

23

Asmara, April 1977

Girmai burrowed his nose into her hair, pulling her close. Elen smelled of roasted coffee beans and the familiar sweet fragrance he could never quite name.

Two years of stolen moments.

The months in prison brought the fleeting precariousness of life into focus with painful clarity. The thought of dying without having experienced her love terrified him more than any Derg soldier ever could.

He savored the weight of her head on his bent arm, and stayed still as he tried not to wake her. He imagined the door to her room a seal against the world, giving him permission to feel everything that was impossible to give space to on the other side of it.

How could he not love her? How could he not want to lose himself in her embrace, if only for these stolen moments that made his life bearable?

"You will always have me," he had said, wiping away her tears at their reunion. He had meant it then. As the days expanded into years, the promise became both a comfort and a burden, a vow he wasn't sure he could keep.

Time spent with her was a salve to a wound he didn't know he had. He carved out paths to moments like this one with meticulous planning and constant vigilance.

A dampness spreading on his arm startled him and he pulled back and lifted himself slightly on the pillow to see her face.

"What's wrong?"

She sniffed and pulled the sheet to dab at her eyes.

"Did you see his speech?" she said, her voice barely rising from under the sheet. She refused to say the Derg leader's name; he never used it in her presence either.

"The one they keep replaying on TV," she continued. "He will have us all killed, just like they killed Gennet. Who will be left when this is all over?" Her voice trailed off as she wiped her tears again.

Girmai lay his head back and tightened his grip on her waist. He knew exactly what she meant. The Derg chairman had stood before a silent crowd in Revolution Square in Addis, smashing bottles of red liquid as he promised a Red Terror.

It had begun.

"Gennet is still alive, Elen," Girmai said, softening his voice to take the pain away from hers.

"Is she?" Elen said, bitterness sharpening her tone. She shifted to rub her eyes. "Can you even call the state she is in alive?" Elen's friend had returned a shell of her former self after the raid. Girmai didn't need to ask what happened to her; he understood her state of catatonia.

"She never talks about it," Elen continued. "She barely talks at all."

She turned to the wall. "I don't think she gave my name, or they'd be here. I'm afraid to even think of what must have happened to her." Her voice cracked.

"She's a fighter and will pull through," he started, though even he didn't believe the empty optimism in his words. He knew Elen blamed herself.

"I don't see how this will ever end." She spoke the statement as a question, her voice breaking at the upward inflection. "None of us can be sure of anything these days."

All we have are moments. He held her tighter.

"We can be firm in our belief that what we are fighting for is right and just," he said, reverting to what she called his "rebel speak." He went on talking, despite feeling her head shake softly in the crook of his arm. "Hope is the one thing we cannot let them have, Elen."

"The raids are happening every night now," she interrupted. "I hear them all around us banging on doors, taking people. Every night, we just wait for our turn."

It pained him to hear the tremor in her voice. He held her tight, wishing he could do more to protect her.

"Now that they have given the kebele leaders guns and the authority to be their revolutionary defense squads," she said, dragging the sheet across her eyes again, "they don't even wait for after curfew. They come to the bar just to harass everyone. Many times, they drink and leave without paying. I heard that some of them are settling childhood feuds and taking advantage of the dead by stealing their property. Nothing to do with the revolution at all."

Girmai released his hold on her waist and held her hand mid-wipe. He brought it to his mouth and kissed it several times. "Stay strong, my love," he murmured into it for lack of any concrete promise he could give. "I will do what I can to protect you."

But can I keep that promise? The thought gnawed at him. Solomon still lived with her, which brought Girmai some comfort, although he was hardly in the apartment as he took over more of the day-to-day running of the bar. Alem was in Addis Ababa with Melak. Hopefully, her husband would continue to keep her safe. He knew that brought Elen a small measure of peace.

"Did you hear about the declaration going around telling people to turn themselves in?"

"Yes." Girmai gritted his teeth. "People are actually walking into kebele offices. I don't know what they expect. After the first round of torture they'll tell them anything, even lies."

"That is exactly what I'm afraid of," Elen said, turning to him. "Our work is getting too risky, for you more than anyone. If Zenebe even suspects anything ..."

He didn't tell her how close things had gotten. Zenebe stayed quiet and useful as long as the money kept flowing. The bribes spared many from the inside of a torture cell and, so far, it was enough to keep Elen safe.

But for how much longer?

When the money was right, even Ashagirie fulfilled requests for leniency. Girmai sent funds in every direction he could, but too many still died under torture. He couldn't save them all.

There was more bad news.

"Some Derg soldiers caught one of our people with some stolen jewelry," Girmai said. "He gave up Halawit's name. Do you remember her?"

"Of course," Elen pursed her lips. "I do my best to avoid her, especially after she humiliated me in front of Aman."

"Well," Girmai continued, "someone tipped them off, and they found the jewelry and other stolen items in her house. She is now in Haz Haz prison."

"That is unfortunate," Elen said genuinely. "I wouldn't wish that on anyone. Will she get a trial?"

"Maybe. Who knows with these people."

"I know she won't give my name for sure because she is so convinced I am a Derg supporter," Elen said with a bitter laugh. "At least Alem is far enough from here that she will be safe if anything happens to me. I feel better that she is with Melak, though things are worsening in Addis too."

"He is a good man," Girmai agreed, not acknowledging the latter part of her sentence. The Red Terror campaigns in Addis were in full force, but his contacts kept an eye on Alem.

Girmai had investigated Melak as soon as Alem had expressed interest. All the information about him showed an honest, hard-working man focused on his construction business. His building projects kept going despite the chaos around the city. Alem would be safe with him.

"What do we do, Girmai?" Elen was crying again.

"We continue to fight and trust that liberation will be ours," Girmai said with all the conviction he felt as he wound his arms around her tighter. "What choice do we have but to do everything we can to be free of the fear of being grabbed in the middle of the night or killed on the street, free of drunk soldiers with the autonomy to rape our daughters, free to live, work, and feel joy, free of wondering if each night is the night we will die. If not for us, for our children. They need a future with hope. Maybe that can be true for us, too, if we are lucky."

But what if we don't make it? The thought slipped through his mind before he could push it away.

Elen nodded. "In the meantime," she said, "we love each other as much as we can."

24

Gejeret, Asmara, December 1977

The curtains were drawn tight, shutting out any crack of daylight in the small living room. Six men, silent and tense, were studying the papers spread across the battered wooden dining table.

Two and a half years of cultivating contacts on the inside of the Ethiopian Commercial Bank led to this moment. The iron was hot now. Time to strike.

The safe house was hidden behind a bougainvillea-lined wall on the outskirts of Gejeret. They'd arranged for the elderly owner to be gone well before their arrival, so she could truthfully claim ignorance if anyone questioned her. They spent the afternoon combing through every detail of the operation.

The dim lamp flickered in the corner of the room illuminating Seyoum at the far end of the table, shoulders hunched, hands shaking as he fingered the edge of a forged identification card. A senior analyst at the bank, he had moved money for the EPLF for over a year without raising suspicion. Girmai had recruited him after the Derg took his parents in a night raid, two outspoken educators marked as counterrevolutionaries.

Since then, Seyoum understood what Girmai already knew. Direct confrontation was suicide; meticulous sabotage was the only way. With no foreign aid, the EPLF had become masters of self-reliance and learned to survive off what they could take from the Derg. Now they needed money for food, medicine, and schools for displaced children. Seyoum was their way in.

Watching Seyoum's fingers shake, Girmai remembered their conversation days earlier when he conviced him that the timing was right for this final operation. One that would change his life forever.

"If we are successful," Girmai had said to Seyoum after he told him the date and location of this meeting, "this will sustain our brothers and sisters in the field and bring us closer to independence. All our loved ones will not have suffered in vain."

"Let's go through everything again so we all clearly understand what needs to be done," Girmai now insisted, pointing at the identification cards in front of each man. Daniel picked his up and examined it.

The stakes were too high to leave anything to chance. Failure meant not just a prison sentence but an almost certain death. They needed to account for every second of the timeline and plan alternatives for everything that could go wrong.

"The timing of each part is essential for us to pull this off. One mistake and we lose eveything."

Seyoum's hands trembled as he clasped them together and looked around the table at Girmai, Daniel, Kifle, Berhane, and Memhir Yemane.

Girmai softened, remembering the first time Seyoum told him details of his parents' disappearance. Education was dangerous. His father a teacher, and his mother the school secretary. The Derg nighttime home raid ended in their disappearance, and Seyoum never heard from them again.

He constantly fought the memories of his own imprisonment—the stale air, endless silence, pain. He gave Seyoum a reassuring nod, hoping it would be enough.

Seyoum cleared his throat. "Today, Andom and I transferred money into the four accounts that Daniel, Kifle, Berhane, and Memhir opened yesterday."

It had taken a year for Seyoum to recruit a second ally, Andom, a young teller whose quiet compliance hid deep trauma. He had watched Derg soldiers beat his father to a pulp and throw him into the back of a military truck for a one-way trip to a detention center.

"Collectively, they now hold four hundred and twenty thousand birr," Seyoum continued. "We need to act fast to withdraw it before anyone notices."

Each man nodded in silence.

"Okay," Girmai said, remembering Teklai, the wildcard janitor who gave away the last operation. "No signs anyone is suspicious?"

"Not yet," Seyoum replied. "Each of you will have to go over the next few days. Use the identification cards and withdraw no more than twenty-five thousand birr at a time."

He glanced around and wrapped his fingers around a cup half filled with cold tea.

"The bank is busiest in the early afternoons and mid-mornings, so aim for those times. The more crowded it is, the less attention you'll draw."

"Andom is ready," Seyoum added. "He'll handle the withdrawals when you come in. Don't go to any other teller."

Seyoum reached for the teacup and wiped the ring it left on the table with his sleeve.

The stakes are too high for the man's nerves to crack now, Girmai thought as he watched him warily.

"We should have it all out by December third at the latest," Seyoum said, swallowing hard. "That will conclude the operation from my end."

Girmai gave him a tight smile as Seyoum set the cup back down and clasped his hands.

"After each withdrawal, I'll collect the money from each of you and take it to Bet Gheorghis forest," Girmai added, giving Seyoum another appreciative nod. "Once we have it all, Daniel and Kifle will move the bags out of the city. Our contacts at the checkpoints are informed and in place."

"Can you really assure our safety?" Seyoum's voice broke as he asked the question for the fifth time that afternoon. "It might take a day or two, but once they notice the money is missing, they'll trace it back to Andom and me." He cleared his throat before he continued. "Neither of us has anyone left here, so they'll have no one to interrogate to get to us, so at least there's that," he said as if to assure the group of his commitment.

"A car will pick you up at the end of the day on the third," Girmai reassured him. "Just leave as you normally do. We will get you out safely."

As Girmai spoke, he visualized the people this money would reach, the displaced, the orphaned, the starving. For once, their suffering might ease.

What we are doing means something.

Just as quickly as his exhilaration rose, a shadow crept over the elation. The wall clock ticked its steady reminder of the inevitability of the moment when luck would run out.

There's always that thing called chance.

***

Over the next few days, exactly as planned, each man went to the bank like any other customer. Andom nodded them through, registered their cards and handed over bundles of birr with barely a second glance. They each walked past the guards unnoticed, the money tucked into old briefcases.

By December third, the team emptied the Ethiopian Commercial Bank of four hundred and twenty thousand birr. The branch shut down for four days as chaos spread inside its walls and Derg investigation units roamed the streets day and night, looking for the perpetrators of the largest bank heist in its history.

As Seyoum had predicted, his name came up during the investigation. By the time the Derg attack units came looking, he and Andom were long past city checkpoints, smuggled through by guards who'd been bought off weeks before.

It had been four days, but Girmai knew the danger wasn't over. After the botched telecommunications heist, he left nothing to chance. He had tied every loose end and there was nothing that could lead to him, yet every noise, every knock kept him on edge.

He knew Derg agents would keep retracing every step, every

signature, and every withdrawal until they found something, but the four men had already vanished along with Seyoum and Andom.

The sirens quieted down by the fifth day.

Everything had gone according to plan, but as always, Girmai couldn't shake the lingering doubt—*Was it too perfect? Too good to be true?*

Memories of 1975 haunted him. The slight glance over the shoulder. Timing off by seconds. Those were the things that got people killed.

Since his release, Girmai knew hundreds of others who suffered the same. There were thousands more whom no one would ever know about. Their stories were buried in mass graves.

That's why we need to continue this work.

But then he thought of Elen. The gift of her in his life was like stepping out of a storm and toward the warmth of a fire. With her, the noise in his head quieted. She grounded him in ways nothing else could. Loving her was reckless. Dangerous. Being with her kept him from unraveling. Right now, that was the only place he wanted to be.

"That's a lot of money to carry," he told Elen six days after the operation ended. "Several trips of hauling those bags into the forest has built up my muscles," he joked, flexing his biceps in the soft light of her room.

"You are a crafty one, aren't you?" One side of her lips arched in a half-smile.

"Come here, and let me show you how crafty I can be."

He turned the key to lock her bedroom door and pulled her toward him.

25

Asmara, 1978

Elen sat up in bed, waiting for her stomach to settle as she had for the past several days. She tried to ignore the nausea building up in her throat each morning. On some days, it bubbled in the pit of her stomach and rose so fast she barely reached the bathroom. On other days, it lay dormant as if tired of itself.

It was almost time for the broadcast. She swung her legs from the bed and steadied herself. Solomon had probably already gone to the bakery for bread. Fresh bread often worked magic to temper her queasiness.

Bread was a luxury now. Solomon's crack-of-dawn visits often ended with nothing but apologies from the staff. Elen rubbed the sleep from her eyes, put on her robe, and moved to the window. Pale morning light pushed against the curtains, brightening the crack between them just enough for her to navigate the room.

She felt her way along the walls of the dark hall to the living room and the radio on the credenza. She'd moved it from her bedroom so they could listen to the news together. Even if the Derg only spewed propaganda, it was best to be informed.

The station she was about to tune into wasn't the Derg's. The stool creaked as she lowered herself onto it. She turned the volume down, then switched the radio on. Static squealed as she tuned into the numbers she'd memorized for Dimtsi Hafash Radio, the EPLF's banned broadcast.

The radio frequency had come with the latest newsletter, hidden in the false bottom of her drawer.

“Good morning, and welcome to today’s Dimtsi Hafash news, coming to you from the liberated zone of Nacfa. This is an EPLF broadcast brought to you by the people, for the people, and with the people. Awet N’ Hafash!”

Elen swallowed as acid crept up her chest to the base of her throat. The thrill of finding the station did little to stop the nausea. She lowered the volume further and leaned closer to the radio.

“Today we bring you good news from the front lines!” The voice came through the speaker clearly. “Thanks to the bravery of our brothers and sisters, we have held steady on the southern front and repelled the Derg offensive. The Ethiopian aggressors hoped to break through our defense lines, but our strategic positions and united efforts moved us closer to Asmara. Victory of the masses is inevitable. Awet N’ Hafash!”

The news anchor’s voice bubbled through Elen’s pounding headache. She swallowed with effort, saliva thick in her mouth.

“Today we acknowledge and commend the bravery of our brothers and sisters in Asmara.

“A significant leader of the enemy, Colonel Zenebe, and his two bodyguards were eliminated in a stealth operation in Asmara yesterday with no casualties on our side.

“The Colonel is responsible for hundreds if not thousands of deaths. In the years he served as a Derg leader, Zenebe launched several large military offensives, which we pushed back many times. His aggressive tactic of sending large numbers of uninformed and novice soldiers into our defense lines only got thousands of his soldiers killed, wounded, or captured.”

Elen edged closer as the report continued, her ear glued to the speaker.

“Brothers and sisters, no force can stand against a united people. In their retreat, the Derg army abandoned weapons and heavy artillery that foreign countries armed them with. We will use these to take Asmara!”

The announcer’s fervor made Elen forget her physical discomfort for a moment.

"We have surrounded Asmara on all fronts and are certain that independence is within our reach. Stay strong in this fight, brothers and sisters! We are yet another step closer to our freed—"

Static.

Elen rested her head against the edge of the credenza, turned the dial, and switched the radio off. A fleeting warm triumph danced in her chest.

She finally did it. Nigisti must be gone.

Elen closed her eyes and murmured a prayer for her friend's safety.

Her stomach gurgled again. She held her head in her palms and rocked back and forth to quell the nausea.

Freedom was near. The days when they could walk outside without dreading an encounter with Derg soldiers or go to sleep without fearing a knock on the door in the middle of the night—it was all within reach. The EPLF was closing in on Asmara.

Our work means something, Elen repeated to herself.

How many are dead because of Zenebe's strategic offences on the battlefields? Her chest hurt knowing so many lives had ended each time he took those trips to launch offensives. How glad had he been on his return, rewarding himself with the luxuries of the city, including his possession of Nigisti.

He can't hurt anyone now.

She rocked herself gently, imagining the retreating Ethiopian army leaving behind tanks and guns. She saw the EPLF fighters' joy in seizing victory, always watching, always ready for the next move from their trenches and underground hospitals.

She let herself slide briefly into the memory of a trip to Addis with Girmai three months before.

"I have some equipment coming in from Italy," he had told her. "The shipment went through Assab and will arrive in Addis within a few days. I have to travel there to sort out the paperwork. Come with me."

She did. They spent two weeks together in Addis, far from the tension that defined their lives. They built a world of make-believe where they could simply be together, free from the constant weight of worry. They could just be.

"Wouldn't it be amazing if we had a child together?" he had asked her one afternoon as they sipped coffee on the hotel balcony.

She had laughed at the idea. What a ludicrous thing to think about, a child at a time like this, when people were dying all around them.

They'd spent many evenings on that balcony, dreaming and hoping for a life beyond their constant fear. Being with him gave her a peace she had never felt, a sense of belonging and wholeness that anchored her. Despite her misgivings, the idea grew and blossomed.

He recognized the changes in her body before she did, on a quiet afternoon back in Asmara when he visited her. He watched her rub the side of her head with one hand and press down on her stomach with the other.

"Elen?" He stood in the middle of the room, looking at her with a wild expression, then pulled her toward him. He turned her around and embraced her from behind in front of her dresser mirror. She saw then what she had avoided thinking about, his hand gently caressing her stomach as he kissed the back of her neck.

Life was growing inside her.

A life they had created.

They stood that way for what seemed like hours, suspended in the realization of the growing physical manifestation of their love.

"We have something of each other now, Elen," he murmured in her ear. "We will get through this and make it work for our child."

Her initial panic at the thought of bringing another human into this mess of life grew into something else: a fierce protective energy. She felt the magnitude of her love for Girmai grow.

Yes, Elen thought. *We will make it work. We have to.*

Her thoughts returned to the silence of the previous night in the city. Considering Zenebe had died just yesterday, it seemed too quiet.

"Elen!"

She jumped out of her reverie. The strain in Solomon's hoarse whisper as he entered the living room immediately put her on edge. He was halfway across the living room by the time she stood up.

"What happened? Are you okay?"

"There are bodies everywhere!" he said, his face almost gray.

"What do you mean?" She was confused. She'd heard no gunshots. How could there be bodies?

"I …" Solomon paused and caught his breath. "I went to the bakery and saw them. All strangled." His face was in his hands now, the empty cloth bag for bread still on his shoulder. "They are everywhere, Elen, more than I have ever seen! Some of them have those ugly signs with 'Death to counterrevolutionaries' pinned on them. Oh, Elen!"

They embraced each other. Elen had no words.

I was wrong. Zenebe is still hurting us, even in death.

"We should stay inside today," she told him. "It's Sunday anyway. Let's wait it out."

The queasiness in her rose with an intensity she couldn't contain. She let go of Solomon and rushed to the bathroom. An involuntary spasm rolled through her stomach and made her lurch again and again long after it was empty.

* * *

In the weeks that followed Zenebe's death, the spike in killings and arrests decreased only slightly from day to day. The day he died, Derg soldiers found his body half in the car, the rest of him splayed out on the street. The fedayeen had left without a trace. There was no sign of the love interest who had lured him to the spot.

"She got out of town," Girmai told her days later. "Nigisti will be fine."

A different kind of soldier soon filled Asmara's streets—a more bloodthirsty, ruthless kind.

The EPLF had surrounded Asmara, hadn't they? Where were they now?

Elen wanted to close the bar completely, just hunker down and wait for it all to end. But closing the bar for any period outside her usual hours would be highly suspicious, Girmai said. "If you don't open as usual, they will accuse you of having something to do with it. You need to keep things going as you normally do. Ashagirie is directing most of the interrogations, and he is a wild card. He's brought in many new people, and working through them will take time to find trusted allies."

***

Elen was standing at her spot behind the counter where she could see most of the bar—just a few more hours until curfew.

She was telling Akberet to leave so she could get home safely. Submerged as they all were in the unpredictability of everything around them, time was a luxury.

The door swung open to a group of men who streamed in, their pistols visible in their holsters.

"Go now!" Elen said and nudged Akberet, who didn't argue. She untied her apron and slipped out the back door.

Elen turned toward the men and smiled a silent greeting.

The men sat down at two tables, and Solomon went to take their drinks order. Elen took out several bottles of cold Amber beer, anticipating what they might ask for.

"Do you want one or two?" said one of the men.

The tone of his voice—more a threat than a question—made Elen look up. The man was slumped in the chair, looking up at Solomon.

"Excuse me, sir, what do you mean?" Solomon cloaked his voice in meek subservience.

"I said," the man took out his pistol without shifting his body and aimed it at Solomon's head, "do you want one bullet or two?" He bared his teeth.

Those within earshot turned to look. Elen stayed as still as she could behind the counter. The others around the table slouched in disinterest, their expressions uniform in their bored familiarity with this situation.

"Sir, what would be much better than wasting your bullets is me serving you a cool drink." Solomon's voice didn't have so much as a tremor in it. "I know you have come here to relax after working so hard. What can I serve you so you can be happy? I will bring it right away!"

Solomon bent slightly at the waist in a respectful bow, his hands clasped together. The man kept staring at him, but Solomon didn't move. Slowly he lowered the gun and put it back in his holster.

"Beer for all of us," the man said finally.

"Right away." Solomon scampered off toward Elen, who had the beers on a tray before Solomon reached the counter.

Thank God Solomon is not as skittish as Akberet.

Solomon served them quickly, and everyone else at the bar returned to their conversations. He kept working fast to serve all the customers what they ordered, and Elen did her best to keep up with the pace.

She alternated between fanning herself and pressing her hand to her abdomen to quell cycles of nausea. She couldn't go to the bathroom and leave Solomon here alone. She reached for the bread they'd managed to find that morning on a plate beside her, tore off a piece, and chewed on it discreetly.

It helped—a little.

26

Sleep clung to her eyelids. Opening them made little difference; the room was pitch black.

What time is it?

There was a banging at the door, slashing through the silence and shattering Elen's semi-consciousness. Her temples thumped in unison with the blows.

"I said, open the door!"

Elen's eyes flew open; she bolted upright from the couch where she must have fallen asleep.

A search. Here?

Elen touched her fingers to her forehead then clasped both hands to her chest. "God, please be with us," she said.

Solomon hurried into the living room and flicked the switch, flooding the room with harsh light as Elen tied her robe around her waist. She squinted and glanced up at the clock on the wall.

Eleven p.m.

"Stay with the kids!" she whispered, pushing him back as he moved to open the door. "Call Girmai. Tell him soldiers are here. I'll talk to them."

After Zenebe's death and the chaos that followed, Girmai had insisted on installing a phone in her apartment. Elen held her breath until Solomon dragged the phone into the kids' bedroom and closed it.

"Open this door before we knock it down!"

The door rattled with each pounding blow. Elen instinctively covered her head with her scarf as she approached the now vibrating door, her fingers trembling as she turned the key.

Make yourself small, Elen, she told herself. *You can get through this.*

Three uniformed men filled the doorway, their shadows spilling into her home as the hallway light poured in behind them. The first two pushed her aside as they charged in, the third grabbed her by the arm and dragged her to the living room.

"This is where you live, correct?"

"Yes, sir." She kept her eyes down, her voice low, struggling to stay calm.

"Why did you take so long to answer the door? Did you need time to hide something?"

"No, sir." Her voice was barely audible to herself through the roaring in her ears. "I was asleep. I'm sorry."

She immediately regretted her apology. She bit her lip to avoid saying anything else.

"Sit." He pointed to the small stool she used to sit on to listen to Dimtsi Hafash.

Obediently, she lowered herself onto it. Nausea gurgled in her stomach, sending a bitter burn up her throat. She clamped a hand over her mouth, swallowing the acid that threatened to spill out.

"Look inside the rooms," the man barked. "Bring any others here."

No, please. Elen's breath caught in her throat.

A soldier's rough shove propelled Solomon in moments later. Aman and Faven followed, eyes wide, faces pale in the harsh light, too frightened to cry. Elen opened her arms, and they ran to her silently. She moved with them to the couch, holding them close, while Solomon replaced her on the stool.

The soldier who had shoved Solomon stood beside them, his Kalashnikov slung casually over his shoulder. His eyes moved over the room, assessing and calculating.

The other two were already deep in the apartment. Elen winced at the sound of crashing plates and the tinging of metal utensils in the kitchen. In her bedroom, the closet's left door squeaked loudly.

The sounds melded together—breaking, rolling, crashing. Each noise was a punch to her gut, and each crash ripped away the illusion of safety. She tightened her grip on Aman and Faven and waited.

The soldier beside her went straight for the radio. "You won't be needing this, will you?" It wasn't a question.

He yanked the plug from the wall and kicked it toward the window. The radio hit the wall beneath the window with a violent crack.

He moved to the credenza, pulling open each drawer and tossing everything onto the floor. The pile of Elen's carefully curated belongings grew by the second—tablecloths, extra plates, sisal hotplates.

The Lord is with us. We will be okay, she assured herself.

"Aha! Aha! Aha! Look what I found!" a soldier shouted from her bedroom. The words struck her like a blow to the chest—

He emerged into the living room, his wide grin exposing large, yellowed teeth.

His eyes gleamed with triumph, the newsletter held high above his head.

27

Elen clutched the children tighter and lowered her head. She visualized the drawer, how she had put the newsletter back and anticipated when she could finish reading it.

"Traitor!" The man's fist rose and connected with her cheek before she could brace herself. She flew off the couch, crashing to the floor, taking both children down with her.

Aman scrambled to crouch protectively beside his howling sister.

Elen pushed both of them to Solomon, who pulled them close and backed away from the soldier. She stayed on the floor, hugging her knees to her chest. She'd heard enough stories to know he wouldn't stop at one hit.

She could have burned the newsletter the day before. The fire on the charcoal stove had still been on when she finished reading one of the stories. Solomon had left her to get the bar ready for opening time. She had two more stories to read. Instead of burning it as she normally would after she'd read it, she had slipped it back into the drawer. Big mistake.

"I see you at the bar, acting like you're one of us," the soldier said, his voice looming over her. "But you're not. You're a traitor."

He stepped closer, and she curled tighter, his black boots just inches away.

"What else do you have in here?"

Say nothing. Girmai needs time to get away. It wouldn't be long before they connected the dots.

The soldier squatted, bringing his face close to hers.

"Not talking, eh?" he sneered. "We're going to enjoy this."

She kept her eyes on his boots as recognition clicked into place. He was at the bar with the soldier who had threatened to shoot Solomon.

The man straightened up. "Have you been a counterrevolutionary this whole time? You'll talk soon. People like you don't stay quiet for long."

In seconds, he was at the credenza again. Without another word, he ripped out anything he'd missed, then kicked through the mess on the floor. The radio slammed into the wall and came apart in a burst of plastic, metal knobs, and tangles wires

Elen gripped her knees tighter and wiped blood off her lip with her shoulder. Solomon rocked the children and murmured soothing words she couldn't make out as they whimpered at the crashing and banging.

Picture frames came down and got crushed underfoot, glass scattered on the floor and crunched with every step he made.

The sounds of her shattering life echoed from the other rooms—drawers ripped open, furniture smashed. They seemed to search for hours, tearing through every corner until nothing was left to destroy.

"Aklilu! Girmachew!" The soldier's shout made Elen flinch, her heart pounding against her ribs.

"Take this filth to Karchele. Tell Ashagirie what we found here."

Besmam Welmenfes Kudus ... In the name of the Father, the Son, and the Holy Spirit ...

More glass crunched, and two pairs of boots appeared before her. Two hands yanked her up by the armpits. Across the room, the other soldier wrenched Solomon away from the children.

They shoved Elen and Solomon toward the front door, their grips bruising her arms.

"Faven! Aman! Wait for Asefash—she'll come in the morning. If not, go to her house. Stay together!"

"Mama! Mama!"

"It'll be okay, my babies." Elen's voice broke. "You'll be—"

A soldier struck her on the shoulder, sending her crashing into the wall beside the front door.

"Be quiet unless you want me to beat the life out of you and your children!"

Tears blurred her vision as she turned back to them. Faven curled herself into a ball, and Aman scrambled to cover her with his tiny body. Elen moved toward them, but a rifle butt slammed into her. Her netsela, caught under a soldier's boot, slipped off her head and pulled at her neck. Solomon grunted close behind her.

My children!

"Move!"

Rain soaked them in seconds as soon as they stepped outside. Elen couldn't tell which soldier pushed her to a military truck outside, its engine idling. One wheel was on the sidewalk as if the driver hadn't bothered to park straight. Another blow to her back sent her crashing into it.

Rifles butts prodded them to the open back of the truck.

Be with us, Lord, and help us survive the night.

"Get in."

The soldiers loomed like shadows, Kalashnikovs aimed. Elen reached for the first step and hauled herself up. Solomon followed, sitting across from her on the hard benches. The soldiers quickly took their places next to them.

Elen tensed as the truck lurched forward.

Just survive.

28

"Soldiers are here," Solomon said in a barely audible whisper. "Elen told me to call you."

Girmai angled forward in his armchair, elbows on his knees, and pressed the phone harder against his ear.

"Solomon?"

The phone went dead. Even after the prolonged monotone, Girmai couldn't pull it away from his ear. The tone drilled into him.

His mind spun. What was happening at Elen's house? He clutched the phone handle, knuckles tight. Around him, the quiet Setanta Otto Street slept, each home tucked behind bougainvillea, untouched by the chaos he imagined tearing through Elen's.

It will be okay, Girmai assured himself. *Elen is careful. She will be okay. She has to be okay.*

He finally put the phone receiver back in the cradle, picked it up again, and pushed the rotary keys, waiting impatiently for each rotation to complete.

"They are at Elen's house now," he told Daniel, bypassing code words as soon as his partner picked up the phone.

"If they find anything, it is only a matter of time before they connect you to her. Did they find anything?" Daniel asked.

"I don't know—"

"You need to move ... just in case."

Girmai remembered the day he had crossed paths with Ashagirie at Bar Elen. Ashagirie had no way of knowing Girmai was the source of the bribe money he received, and Girmai didn't want to risk facing him.

"We have a safe house we can take you to for now, but I'll have to confirm it's secure." Daniel cleared his throat. "We'll pick you up from the factory. Your house will most likely be a target. Get there at first light. Berhane will pick you up at the corner of Cinema Dante."

"Where am I supposed to go until then?" Girmai asked, looking at the darkness beyond one of the living-room windows. "What if they come here tonight?"

"She'll buy you time," Daniel replied.

His answer sent chills through Girmai.

Oh God, no! What have I done?

"Going out now after curfew is suicide," Daniel continued. "Lie low and stick to the plan."

Helen's light in the master bedroom was still on. Girmai lowered his voice even more. "Daniel, keep my family safe. Please."

"I will do my best. Just make sure there's nothing to find in your house."

Girmai hung up and hurried to his bedroom.

"Helen?"

She was sitting on her side of the bed. She turned from her waist to face him.

"Soon—tomorrow morning or maybe even tonight," Girmai said quickly, "people might come asking for me. Be calm and respectful. If they come during the day, invite them in and offer them tea. Try to keep calm no matter what. They might leave if they don't feel the need to search."

"Search?" Helen stood up and faced him fully. "What reason do they have to come here?"

He shook his head—no time to explain.

"If they come in the morning, tell them I went to work," he continued.

Girmai squatted in front of his closet door, pushed aside the folded sweaters on the second shelf from the bottom, and reached inside the shallow space in the back panel. He pulled a small brown envelope out and carefully put the clothes back.

He picked a warm jacket from a hanger and slid his hands through. "I have to leave now."

"But there's a curfew," Helen said, her eyes wide. "Girmai, can you please tell me what's going on? You are scaring me!" She reached for her robe and fumbled as she put it on.

"If any soldiers come tonight, tell them I didn't come back from work." Girmai turned to face her. He knew he was talking too fast. "Tell them I worked late and slept at the office."

He put the envelope inside his jacket pocket and zipped it up halfway. He put a hand on Helen's shoulder and hoped she could understand the gravity of the situation.

"Don't tell them anything other than what I just said," he said, his voice coming out a lot harsher than he intended.

"You and the children will be safer that way." He moved toward the door. "I have to leave now. I'm sorry."

"But ..."

He hurried out of the room. Helen followed him and tightened her robe as she watched him from their bedroom door.

Girmai paused by the first bedroom, opened the door, and stepped halfway in. The low fluorescent garden light beside the tall exterior wall seeped through the window and rested on the boys in their beds.

Yonas and Samuel were sleeping soundly in their bunk beds. Alexander was laying on a bed beside them on his stomach, snoring softly.

Girmai quickly walked to the next room where Rahwa lay splayed out, deep in sleep.

Life for all of them was about to change. Girmai's jaw clenched to hold back his emotions. *There's no time for that. God willing, I'll come back for all of you. I promise.*

Helen remained by their bedroom door, her arms tight around her torso, her face searching his for answers.

"What's going on, Girmai?"

"I'm so sorry, Helen. For everything." He rested his hand on her tightly crossed arms and felt her trembling. He blinked to fight back tears, realizing what all this meant for her, his family, and Elen.

I did this.

"It will be okay." He tried to sound reassuring. "Remember what I told you about the soldiers. They are not interested in you, so keep calm and do what they say."

"When will we see you again?" Helen's voice was small. Her lips trembled.

"I don't know." It was too late for explanations. His skin crawled at the idea that they could be here any moment.

Helen didn't come after him after he squeezed her arm one last time and speed walked to the living room. The well-oiled door made no sound when he opened it a fraction, slipped through, and closed it behind him. He lingered outside the door, his head against the wood. It took all his effort to peel his hand from the doorknob and walk away.

The rain had eased from the torrent of a half hour before. Girmai zipped his jacket against the cold, circled the house, and headed straight for the bushes in the far corner of the garden. He parted the branches and stepped into a small clearing against the corner of two walls bordering his neighbors' homes.

Just like his father had fashioned parts of the house with mud, Girmai had used a composite of dirt and clay to mold and compact makeshift steps into the corner. Shielded by the bushes, no one ever noticed them. He built the highest step to give him enough boost to scale over the wall and quickly get into his neighbor's compound.

The fragility of this escape route was not lost on him.

He now had to wait until the curfew lifted before he made his next move.

He patted the keys to his office in his pocket to make sure they were still there, withdrew deeper into the shadows of the bushes, and sat on the steps with nothing but empty time in the dark—a dark that forced him to see the enormity of what he was facing.

A family he could no longer be with, Elen in the hands of the Derg, and the uncertain future of his unborn child.

What have I done?

29

"Death is painless."

Ashagirie's breath was hot in her ear. "It will come anyway. Whether it happens now or later is up to you."

Elen took shallow breaths, her panic over the children greater than his immediate threat.

My kids are home alone. What have I done?

"Tell me everything now and make it easy for yourself."

She was sitting on a hard, straight-backed chair in the middle of a small room. With her hands tied to the sides of the chair, she could barely move. She had a glimpse of a small table, now behind her, with wrenches, hammers, wires, and other things she couldn't make out.

The newsletter lay on the table in front of her. In the corner of the room, a man in plain clothes held a pen poised over a notepad, his eyes oscillating between her and Ashagirie.

She hadn't been able to communicate with Solomon in the truck. It was too dark for them to read each other's faces, and the soldiers sitting beside them made it impossible for them to talk. Her shoulders ached where the soldier hit her.

Does Girmai know where I am? Does he know he needs to protect himself?

She tried to bend her torso to protect her stomach, but the ropes didn't let her move far. She had had this life inside her for three months, the life she and Girmai created.

I will keep you safe, baby. I will survive this, and you and I will be with Girmai soon.

The force of Ashagirie's fist on her face disintegrated the image of her baby and the small bud of hope she had conjured up.

"Tell us what you know!"

She opened her eyes to double vision. The pen that hovered above the notepad turned into two, then three, then merged back together, hovering, waiting.

Ashagirie didn't give her much time to recover. His open hand smacked her face. She pulled against the sisal ropes as her head snapped to the side, but her wrists were bound taut. The vision out of her left eye grew hazy in the dim room. It was getting harder to blink.

"Please," she managed, blood in her mouth. "I am pregnant. Please spare me for the sake of my child."

His lips curled back in a feral sneer. Elen remembered the scratches on his arms when she first met him and how he relished showing them to her.

"You're a nasty little whore, aren't you?" He drew his hand back above his head, slapped her again.

She strained against the ropes around her wrists and ankles.

"Isn't it enough that you are a counterrevolutionary, eh? You are carrying one too! It's a wonder that the Colonel trusted people like you. Look where that got him."

Ashagirie sat down on his chair opposite her and slid the newsletter on the table toward her. Its sides curled up around the words "Awet N' Hafash!" Victory to the masses!

"It is up to you whether you and your bastard live through this."

She squeezed her lips tight to quell the rising panic.

Ashagirie nodded to someone out of her line of vision, who came up behind her. She wrinkled her nose at the acrid smell of the cloth he shoved against her lips and moved her head from side to side to keep it from going into her mouth.

The man grabbed a chunk of her hair at the base of her neck. The cloth pressed into her face harder and covered her nose. She couldn't breathe.

“Open your mouth, or your bastard dies now,” Ashagirie shouted.

She relented. The rag pushed into her mouth so deep she could not tell if it was the force or the taste of it that made her gag.

She had heard of this happening. Old socks, bits of gabi, any piece of cloth recycled from one mouth to another through countless interrogations. She braced her tongue against it, hoping to push it out.

“Secure it,” Ashagirie said.

The hands behind her stretched another cloth around her stuffed mouth and tied it in a tight knot at the back of her head.

How many people’s mouths had this rag been in?

“The only way for you to get out of this is to tell us where you got the newsletter.” Ashagirie’s voice was softer now. “Who gave it to you?”

The legs of his chair screeched on the cracked tiled floor as he got up, his face inches from hers.

Nausea bubbled up again, but there was nowhere for it to go. It burned Elen’s throat and pushed against the cloth, only for her to swallow it back down. She responded with grunts and a shake of her head.

The blows came in rapid succession, on her head, her back, her shoulders, her hips. She strained to bend over, anything she could do to shield her abdomen from the hits, but the ropes held steadfast.

Minutes or hours passed. Elen couldn’t tell which direction the blows came from or who was delivering them.

Just …

A boot connected with her arm, and she toppled over to her side.

survive …

Hands pulled her back up again.

the night …

Kicks and punches rained down from every direction. No one was asking questions anymore.

Elen took herself back to her room with Girmai. He lay beside her and spread his palm out over her belly button. "We made something beautiful together. We are bound forever through this child. I love you, Elen," he had whispered to her.

Elen let the words echo in her mind and fill her consciousness. They evaporated when Ashagirie kicked her chair over again. She strained against the sisal rope that bound her wrists and ankles as her head bounded off the floor.

Boots with dirt caked into the treads stepped inches from her face.

"Who gave you the newsletter?"

If only Elen could put her arms around her belly and protect her child.

Their child.

We made something beautiful ...

Her vision blurred. She felt the weight of Girmai's arms around her.

You and I are bound together for life, Elen.

"What else are you hiding?" She pushed Ashagirie's voice further away, retreated into a place he couldn't reach.

A black dot appeared in her vision, then spread until it swallowed her whole.

***

Moans, labored breathing, and what sounded like prayers beside her slowly came into focus. The floor smelled of urine. This was not the interrogation room.

Elen blinked herself awake and winced as she rolled onto her back. The exposed flesh on her arms peeled painfully off the cement floor. Everything hurt.

"You are awake?"

Elen jerked at the sound of the unfamiliar voice. Sweat and the stench of vomit filled her nostrils in the tight cell. She tried to sit up, but each movement sent pain searing through her body. She rolled back to her side and tried to drag herself to a sitting position against the wall, as far away as she could from the voice.

Soft daylight filtered through the slip of a window set high on the wall.

"I'm Zimam," the voice reached out to her again. Elen tried to focus and turned toward the woman. "You are in Karchele. They brought you in here several hours ago. Are you okay?"

What a question to ask! Elen couldn't piece together a response. The woman's features were more distinct now, though it was hard to see from her right eye.

"My name is Zimam," the woman said again as she inched closer. Grains of dislodged cement dug into Elen's skin where her nightgown had ridden up. She grimaced as she pulled it down over her knees.

"Where did you say we are?" Elen managed and stretched her stiff neck.

"You are in Karchele, in Wenjel Mermera. They must expect good information from you; otherwise, you would be dead. Looks like you took quite a beating."

Zimam leaned against the wall beside Elen, and they looked up at the light filtering through the window.

The contours of Zimam's face, partly hidden in the shadows, curved and dipped with cuts, swelling, and healing bruises.

"How long have you been here?"

"I am sure I am about to get transferred," Zimam said , not quite answering the question. "They rounded me up randomly with lots of others. It's been a while since they questioned me. Maybe they have lost interest."

"What did you do?"

"I was at a funeral for some Derg official. They told us to come out into the street to pay our respects. I had just washed my hair and set it with rollers. I didn't have time to take them out before they forced us to go outside for the funeral procession. They said I was disrespectful to the dead for showing up that way, and now here I am. That was three weeks ago."

She raised her palms facing up and seemed to say a prayer to herself. "I was at the wrong place at the wrong time." She shook her head and put her hands together. “I’ll go to trial soon to plead my case. Many others have already gone to Haz Haz prison.”

In a dark corner, a moan rose a few feet away from them. A woman lay on her stomach, her shirt torn and dark with dried streaks of blood up and down her back.

“Her name is Abeba. She is only fifteen. She came in several days ago. They accused her of bombing a meat factory, but she has not said a word about it. Her back is in shreds from all the whipping. Hopefully, they will let her go soon. She’s just a child. May God help us all.”

Several days. A chill rippled through Elen, thinking of a repeat of the night before.

“They usually stop the torture when we lose consciousness,” Zimam continued. She fell silent for a few moments and raised her palms. “Then they wait for the night to take us back out again just as we are about to sleep.” She started to recite a prayer again.

Elen closed her eyes. She couldn’t be sure if the soothing voice or her prayers made her like Zimam instantly.

Elen rubbed her stomach, closed her eyes, and rested her head against the cement wall. “I’m pregnant,” she said, “I can’t tell if my baby is still alive after what they did to me. What they did to us.” Her lip quivered. “I am not sure either one of us will survive this.” She slowly wrapped her arms around herself, straining against the pain of the bruises and open cuts all over her.

“Ajokhi,” Zimam’s voice floated to her as if from a distance. “Prepare yourself for what is coming, but know the Lord doesn’t give you more than you can take. You have the day to rest. They rarely take anyone out during the day. Gather up your energy and be strong. God is with us.”

Elen winced as she shifted her legs. Dried blood on the edges of her underwear scraped her skin every time she moved.

“Maybe it is better this way,” Zimam whispered as an afterthought. “What kind of world is this to bring a baby into?”

Elen floated in and out of consciousness throughout the day and barely noticed the hard bread Zimam put in her hand hours after they first spoke.

"Eat."

Was she imagining her voice?

"Eat, Elen, you are going to need it."

What for?

When she opened her eyes again, the light through the window had darkened to orange.

She let her eyelids close. *My children, I hope someone is taking care of you. Solomon! What have I done? I should have sent him away a long time ago.*

Abeba's soft moans and Zimam's prayers beside her filled the small cell and merged with the desperation rising in her.

Maybe they forgot about me. Could I have convinced them I had nothing to do with the newsletter?

She hadn't said a word throughout the entire beating except to beg for her child's protection.

Girmai will get me out, she assured herself. *They will let me go.*

She drifted off to a dreamless sleep.

30

Asmara, 15 July 1978

Girmai's back and shoulders strained from hours of sitting on the mud steps. The burst of rain at midnight subsided to a drizzle, and the dampness soaked into his bones.

The banging on the gate Girmai expected all night never materialized. He had focused on the main bedroom light until Helen turned it off, and then nothing else separated him from his thoughts.

He grimaced, remembering the advice he gave Elen and all his recruits. They committed to enduring the pain of interrogation for at least a night or two to give their cell members time to get away.

Oh, God! What have I done? I have to get her out. There was no guarantee of protection now that Zenebe was gone.

When the curfew ended at 6 a.m., it was still dark. Girmai glanced at his home through the bushes one last time, then stepped onto the dirt steps and scaled over the wall into his neighbor's garden. It was best for the family that no one saw him leave through his gate.

Deep in his pocket, his office keys gave a muffled jingle as he landed hard on the other side.

Wincing at every squeak, he moved the gate latch back and forth gingerly. It took him longer than usual to pry it open. He wasted no time slipping through once it gave way.

The translucent exposure of the pre-dawn light quickened his pace on the empty streets until he made it to the sweater factory.

He slipped in through the back door and sank into his chair, promising himself just a few minutes of stillness before heading up to the flat roof—his temporary hideout until Berhane came for him later that afternoon.

Any information they tortured out of Elen would become clear in a few hours. *They must have suspected something.*

Girmai pressed his palms into his eyes, trying to steady the sobs wracking his body at the thought of Elen in a Derg interrogation room. He drew a deep breath and wiped his face.

She has to be okay. The baby has to be okay.

The shrill ringing of the phone made Girmai jump in his seat.

He hesitated, then lifted the receiver, quickly setting it back down.

The phone rang again seconds later, and he did the same, much quicker this time. Then it rang again.

He relented and raised it to his ear without saying a word.

"Girmai, this is Daniel. I don't have good news. It's bad."

"What?"

"Ashagirie got to her." Daniel's voice was flat.

Girmai's blood went cold. The last time Daniel sounded like this was when he told Girmai about three prominent EPLF members the Derg had shot dead in an ambush.

"Where is she?"

"Both she and Solomon are in Wenjel Mermera. They are interrogating them separately. As far as we know, neither of them has talked yet. They are going harder on her since it's her house, and Ashagirie knows her from the bar. They aren't bothering with Solomon. He'll get out of it without getting roughed up too much. We haven't gotten any of our people into the cell or in touch with Ashagirie. He was … questioning her for several hours last night."

"Daniel, we have to help her," Girmai said, his head in his free hand, his body heaving with dry sobs. "She is pregnant."

Silence.

"She is in there because of what we asked her to do—what I

asked her to do. Whatever they found, whatever they pinned on her—I did it. Me. We have to get her out. I will give myself up."

"That will not guarantee her release," Daniel said. "If you give yourself up, your presence will confirm that there is information to be extracted and solidify their suspicion she is guilty. Then we lose you both." Daniel cleared his throat. "I will see if Habteab can get there today."

"Daniel, there might be a way to get her out alive and stop the interrogations," he said as a half-formed idea sprang into his mind.

"What are you thinking?"

Girmai collected his thoughts, then exhaled a breath he didn't realize he was holding.

"The only thing they could have found at her place is the newsletter. She doesn't take anything else home. If that is the case, we must pay Ashagirie off so he can leave her alone." His thoughts became more coherent as he spoke. "You have access to the money. Take what you need to make him stop."

The plan made sense as he formed it.

"We need to act fast, Daniel; she won't survive for long and, even with money, Ashagirie won't let her go without some kind of explanation. She will have to give a plausible story."

Girmai became more certain they had found a newsletter as he spoke. She loved reading it so much, and he remembered warning her to get rid of each issue as soon as she could. Maybe she had held on to the one he had given her recently. That's the only thing the Derg could have found in her house.

"What do you suggest?" Daniel asked.

"Tell her to blame me," Girmai said. He spoke faster now. His employees would come into work soon, and he had to leave before they saw him, for their sake and his.

"What?"

"She can pin whatever they have found on me. Say I left it there when I visited. That might get her out of the interrogation. Then we can try to pay our way through a trial if it comes to that."

"If you find out the newsletter got her arrested, she should tell them she can't read. Being a village girl with no record of her having gone to school will give that part of the story credibility."

"If we want to go this route," Daniel said after a long silence, "you can never come back. Once she identifies you, they will conduct a thorough search for you and issue a warrant for your arrest or order of execution. You need to go into hiding today and then leave for the field. You can't take anything you don't already have with you. You need to think this through, Girmai. It doesn't sound like she has said anything yet. If she continues to say nothing, you could continue your work here and—"

"She will probably be dead within the next day or two—if she is lucky," Girmai finished, his voice tight. "Ashagirie likes to drag things out and finish off so no one lives to tell."

Girmai needed to clear his mind so he could think logically. "Can you keep my family safe if we move ahead with this plan?"

"We can make sure of that, yes," Daniel said, sounding confident. "You've done a good job separating them from your work with us. The Derg will search your house and come up clean. Helen knows nothing."

"Okay then, let's do it, " Girmai said after a deep breath.

He closed his eyes and imagined Elen as he had seen her last with her kohl-lined eyes looking up at him.

He rubbed his eyes. "Just make sure Elen gets out and take care of my family."

Daniel exhaled loudly into the phone, the *whoosh* loud in Girmai's ear. "Once Berhane picks you up, hide. We will find a way to get you out of the city. Do you have that ID card we made for you?"

"I do." Girmai patted his jacket pocket where he had put the small brown envelope he had taken from his closet.

Girmai hung up and walked to the back exit of the building. He passed through the factory, tracing his hands along the knitting machines, idle in the darkened room. He locked the door from the outside before entering the narrow alley, pushed aside boxes he had used to hide a ladder. Once he climbed up to the flat roof, he pulled up the ladder after him.

* * *

The sun got hotter on the roof with each passing hour. It bore down on him as its trajectory pulled it higher in the cloudless sky until it was directly above him. He continued to lie still against the three-foot wall bordering the flat roof.

Noon. The hours crawled by.

Helen would have been awake for hours now. She probably gave all the kids breakfast and got them ready for the day. Hopefully, his children were in school. They would come back to a fatherless home.

Maybe one day they will understand. Girmai hoped to be the one to tell them why he took all the risks, why freedom was more important than anything else, and why he sacrificed everything to get it for them.

I will get them all out, he promised. He gritted his teeth to focus his pain somewhere. *If I survive.*

He had always separated everything he did for the EPLF from his home life. He hoped that was enough to keep the Derg at bay. Once they focused on him and Elen, they wouldn't bother Helen. She was never involved.

God laughs at those who make plans.

The familiar rumble of military trucks—two, he guessed—broke through the rhythmic sounds of the weekday bustle.

He lay flatter on the roof as he visualized the soldiers filling the street as they had when they came to arrest him the last time. Girmai stiffened as he heard them talk to one another. They filed into his shop, then into his office, and out through the factory into the alleyway where he had climbed into hiding.

"Where is Girmai? Have you seen him come to work this morning? We just want to ask him some questions," the voices floated up, the tone not aggressive.

Elen hasn't talked.

Girmai inched to the roof's edge to hear as much as he could.

"We haven't seen him since yesterday," Araya answered.

"We need to speak with him. He needs to report to the kebele office as soon as possible."

"I will tell him, sir," Araya said. Girmai could imagine him giving a little bow.

It was too soon for Daniel to have reached Elen with his rescue plan. The soldiers lacked the urgency they would have had if Elen had already told them the story he had thought up earlier that morning.

The rumble of the military trucks faded down the street, and the morning bustle died down with the approaching lunch hour.

Girmai raised his arm to check his watch and kept it there to shield his face from the overhead sun.

The street below grew silent as all the shops closed for lunch.

13:25. It was time.

He slid the ladder down against the wall and descended its rungs quickly, then hid it under the boxes. Following the alley to the end of the block, he walked steadily toward Cinema Impero.

Berhane's car idled on the side street as promised. Girmai slid into the back and temporarily lost his balance as the wheels started rolling even before he closed the door.

"Lay down on the floor. Use the blanket to cover yourself."

Girmai sunk under the stifling heat of the heavy blanket and replayed the events of the last twenty-four hours in his mind. The precariousness of their situation hit him again.

He forced himself not to think of Ashagirie hurting her. He knew she would try to protect him and could not imagine what that was costing her.

The plan has to work.

The car engine shuddered off about twenty-five minutes later. Girmai stayed still, his stiff muscles relaxing only after he heard Berhane's voice.

"Come on, let's go before the girls come home."

Berhane had two daughters in school, so Girmai had to stay hidden from them since they were too young to lie when questioned.

"There's a well out back. You will hide there until we can transfer you. I'm the only one who knows where you are, so don't make any noise. I'll get you some food. Once curfew starts, you can stretch and go to the bathroom."

The mention of food made Girmai's stomach growl. He followed Berhane through the narrow walkway around the house into the backyard.

Berhane led him to the back of the small garden where the well cover lay concealed and heaved open the metal grate.

"This is it for now." He jerked his head downward. "Don't worry; the water is low," Berhane assured him after he saw Girmai's dubious expression as he looked down the dark well.

"Water filled up just a little after the rain last night. You should be alright staying there until we find another solution."

Girmai put a hand on Berhane's shoulder. He wanted to say so much to his friend but could only tighten his grip. His other hand came over his mouth to still the quiver of his chin. "Thank you," he said from beneath his fingers.

Berhane nodded and pursed his lips. He blinked back a film of tears that hooded his eyes.

Girmai let go of Berhane's shoulder and slid down into the dark well, the top of which was a few feet above his head. He groped around to find footholds he could use when it was time to climb back out. Berhane was right. The water only partly soaked his shoes.

"I'll get you something to eat soon." Berhane lowered the cover over the opening and plunged Girmai into darkness.

31

"This will be another long night unless you decide to put an end to all this." Ashagirie pressed his knuckles onto the table, leaning his weight forward until his face was inches from hers. "We are waiting."

They were in a different interrogation room. A table separated her from Ashagirie, but not by much. As the night before, the man with the notebook sat waiting in the corner, his pen hovering over the paper.

The ropes held Elen's ankles to the chair legs and burned her wrists as she strained to pull away from Ashagirie and the familiar nauseating stench rising from the rag on the table.

"Who gave you the newsletter?"

The man who tied her up shifted behind her, his presence a heavy weight against the back of her neck.

"I, I …" Her mouth wouldn't move the way she needed. "I am pregnant. Please, spare me for the sake of the child. Please …"

She jumped when he banged his fist on the table. "You should have thought of that before you got mixed up in things that don't concern you."

Ashagirie leaned in, and Elen recoiled from his hot breath.

"You are a traitor," he snapped, his narrowed eyes inches from her face. He raised a finger. "This is your chance to redeem yourself."

Metal clanged behind her. She had heard of the tools they kept in these rooms—pliers for nails, clamps for nipples, things designed to tear flesh.

I can't think about that. I won't. I made it through the first night. I can make it through the second. Lord, give me strength.

"I knew you were up to no good," Ashagirie drew back, his stare fixed on her. "Dressed like a whore and working all those men up. You played a dangerous game, and now it's caught up with you."

Tools rattled behind her. Ashagirie's eyes flickered.

"I am just a village girl from Adi Nefas," Elen managed. "A mother trying to take care of my children, that's the truth." She hoped the sincerity she put into her voice was believable. "I don't know where the newsletter came from. Please believe me."

The tears streaming down her face were real. She cried for the unborn dream that was the life growing inside her, for the love she had found, then lost. She mourned for her children, who might be orphans soon, and for what? She had too much work left unfinished.

After all these years of fighting and all the risks she took, freedom was not here yet. Now she might never get to see it. She cried for all the people who died, for those who lived as shadows of themselves, for the unspeakable things people did to each other, and for the death that surely was coming for her.

Ashagirie's blank expression frightened her more than anything he'd said. "Please," she said.

"Hmm," he said and pursed his lips. He nodded as his eyes rose to signal the man behind her, who lifted each elbow to wrap something cold and metallic around her arms. The ropes dug into the open wounds on her wrists and she clenched her fists, breathing rapidly to keep from screaming.

"That's copper wire around your arms," Ashagirie said, his voice tight. "Soon, electricity will flow through it. What do you think that will do to your baby?"

Elen closed her eyes. *Breathe!*

"This is a good time to talk," he continued after a long, expectant pause.

Our Father who art in Heaven, hallowed be Thy name. Your kingdom come, Your will be done, on Earth as it is in Heaven. Give us this day our daily bread and forgive us our trespasses as we forgive those who trespass against us—

"Shut up!" His spittle landed on her face.

She hadn't realized she was praying out loud.

The man in the corner raised his eyebrows, his pen still poised. With nothing to write, he let out an exasperated sigh, closed the notepad, and put down his pen.

"Pity that you are making us do this to you and your baby."

Ashagirie stepped forward, grabbed the rag, and smashed it into her face. The sudden movement took her by surprise, and the rag was inside her mouth before she could resist. It went deeper and deeper, then, satisfied that he'd stuffed it in enough, he took a thin cloth, covered her mouth, and tied it at the back of her head.

"We will talk again in a few minutes." He sat down again, his expression blank.

The black of Ashagirie's eyes was the last thing Elen saw before the icy-hot current tore through her like exploding shards of glass. Her body convulsed, her vision blinding white against her tightly closed eyes as her wrists and ankles strained against the ropes.

Her body burned. Hours? Minutes? Seconds? She couldn't tell.

Then it stopped.

"Ready to talk now?"

The man behind her removed the rag and vomit shot out of her and splattered across the table. Even in her daze, she felt a small victory when she saw some of it land on Ashagirie.

"Shit!" He jumped back and looked down at his clothes and shoes.

Ashagirie waited until her retching subsided, then grabbed a fistful of her hair.

She was numb to everything but the burning line above her elbows and the intense heat that radiated between her thumbs, forefingers, and the soles of her feet. Her head lolled lifelessly in his fisted hand.

"How did that feel, hmm?" His face was a blurred dot. "Has that loosened your tongue a little?"

He's killing my baby.

"Who gave you the newsletter? You can stop all this with just one name."

It took all her strength to look up at him. Vomit slid down her chin. She pressed her lips together and opened her mouth, but only a grunt escaped.

Ashagirie let her hair go, and her chin fell to her chest. "You disgust me," he said, lowering himself on his chair. "You go through all this for what?"

Elen was out of breath. Her head felt so heavy. She could only raise it from her chest a few inches before it fell again.

Please, she wanted to say. *Don't kill my baby.*

The only sounds that came out of her mouth were more unintelligible grunts.

"Let's show you what being a traitor feels like." Ashagirie looked up at the man behind her again and nodded.

Elen closed her eyes as a new wave of electric current surged through her until her convulsions toppled the chair.

Then, silence and the smell of burned flesh—her own.

Something within her snapped, something beyond the reach of the electricity or the punches and kicks.

Let go of the fear. Let go of everything. Death is painless.

She'd fought to survive, past the arranged marriage, past the death of her mother and her aunt, past so many other painful moments in her life. She fought now to keep her baby alive, but no three-month-old fetus could survive this. To speak now would make it all for nothing. To speak now would be to kill Girmai, and she wouldn't give Ashagirie that. All she had left was death.

She closed her eyes and saw Girmai's face. *We made something beautiful …*

I'm sorry I couldn't protect you, my baby. I'll see you in Heaven soon, where we can be together without pain, where I can hold you and tell you how much I love you.

* * *

Day four.

Morning light pushed into the cell. Elen blinked herself awake with the realization that the hadn't come for her the night before.

"Come on, we have to go out for a roll call," Zimam said.

The vomit had dried around the neck of her nightgown and halfway down her chest. Elen instinctively felt between her legs. Blood. Her underwear was heavy with it.

"Steady," Zimam said as Elen opened her eyes fully. "I'll help you to the end of the line beside the wall. You can lean on it and rest."

Elen gritted her teeth in pain as Zimam draped her arm around her shoulder. Grateful her cellmate didn't expect her to talk, Elen leaned heavily on her as she limped into the courtyard.

The sun warmed her skin, a temporary distraction from the body aches and crusted underwear that chafed her skin.

I didn't die, but ...

Elen put her hand over her abdomen and pressed her lips to contain the sobs that threatened to launch out of her as women silently streamed out from other cells in the block and lined up in a long, single line.

"I'll go back to help Abeba out," Zimam said. "I'll be right back."

The women obediently stood, waiting to be counted along the length of the narrow outdoor hallway. Guards, clad in the green army uniform of the Derg, stood scattered throughout the courtyard. Some had their Kalashnikovs draped over their shoulders, while others held them at the ready, training them on the women.

The wall was a welcome support after the excruciating walk from the cell. Elen rubbed her thumbs against her fingers. They were still attached to her hands, but neither had any sensation to the touch. Her fingers shook as she tried to spread them out. The burn marks at the base of both forefingers stung. Her blistered wrists swelled to twice their size.

A coarse whisper came from somewhere behind her.

"Girmai is safe."

Startled, she straightened up at the sound of the voice and winced at the searing waves of pain that the quick movement brought. She dared not turn. Without moving her head, her eyes slid toward the closest guard at the far end of the line. He was out of hearing range. Prisoners still streamed out of cells, but no one was close to her yet.

Is this a trap?

She decided not to react. She kept still and faced forward.

The voice behind her spoke again. She sensed him stepping closer.

"No, don't," he said as she was about to turn. "Listen carefully, we don't have much time. Tell the interrogators that the newsletter belongs to Girmai and that you didn't know what it was because you can't read."

Something about the voice was familiar. As ludicrous as his suggestion sounded, Elen wanted to trust him.

"Tell them you never learned to read or write. Tell them your brother helped you to run that part of your bar business and did all the accounting for you," he continued. "Admit to your affair with Girmai and say he must have left the newsletter in your house during one of his visits."

"I won't do that," she said when she finally spoke, moving her lips as little as possible.

"You have to," he said. "Girmai told me to tell you it's the only way to survive."

Her eyes widened as recognition settled. It was Habteab.

"He is safe now and will get out of Asmara," Habteab continued, talking faster now. "Ashagirie will call you in for questioning tonight. His tone will be different. He has been paid off and will stop questioning you. He has to go through the motions and can't let you go without a statement explaining the newsletter. Do everything you can to stay alive. We are with you, Elen. Awet N' Hafash!"

Hearing the EPLF slogan in the middle of the detention center chilled her to her core. The guard doing the roll call got closer.

He escaped?

"What about Solomon?" she asked through clenched teeth. Elen shuddered to think about what they must have done to him.

"He is fine," Habteab quickly responded. "They focused all their energy on you. It will be easier to get him released since the newsletter was in your room, not his. We will make sure he goes back home to the kids. You need to take care of yourself now."

Habteab shifted behind her. "Ashagirie can't let you go without something to report," he repeated, his voice closer. "He will accept your story. Save yourself and your baby."

My baby is probably dead. She winced as she lifted her hand to her belly again.

"Name? Cell number?" The guard was getting closer as he checked the names against the list on his clipboard.

"Do what you can to save yourself and the child," Habteab repeated.

"I … I don't know if the baby survived," she whispered, barely able to hold herself up. "I'm bleeding too much."

Habteab was silent. His boots stepped back out of her line of vision. Zimam got to the line with Abeba seconds before the guard approached them. The young girl struggled to keep her legs moving. Zimam had her arm around her waist.

"Name? Cell number?"

"Elen Ghebrekidan. 36."

With roll call done, the soldier went back to the other end of the line. Two soldiers behind him pointed their rifles at the women one by one to direct them back into their cells.

Elen dared to turn back only after she got to the entrance of her cell. Her eyes landed on Habteab. He stared right at her as if he had been waiting for her to turn. They locked eyes for a few seconds before he raised his eyebrows questioningly.

Girmai is safe. God be with my baby.

She gave him a brief nod, which he returned, then walked away.

***

It was harder to fall asleep with the certainty that the soldiers would come to take her again. They seemed to wait for the most silent hour of the night before they started their extraction. They banged on doors as loudly as they could to shock not only their designated victim of the night but also everyone else in the block who could hear it—torture by sleep deprivation.

Elen shifted from one side to the other to relieve the pressure of the unforgiving floor on her hips.

They had taken Abeba away earlier in the day.

"Hopefully, to get medical attention," Zimam had said. "I will be gone soon too, God willing."

While Elen had been asleep in the afternoon, Zimam had been taken to court for her case to be heard. "One year in Haz Haz prison. Can you believe it? One year in prison for wearing rollers in my hair."

Elen looked at the silhouette of Zimam's body lying on the floor now, fast asleep. She sighed. Their fate was all random, left to the will of the oppressor.

Despite herself, Elen's eyelids got heavy. She lay suspended in a dreamless sleep until boots stomped on the cement hallway and stopped at her cell door. It flew open seconds later.

Please, God, be with me tonight.

"Get up!" said an unfamiliar soldier. He couldn't have been over twenty years old.

Zimam, startled into alertness, shrunk to the other side of the cell. Elen got up as fast as the pain would allow her. She let the two soldiers lead her to the interrogation room.

Please, God, be with Girmai. What she would say tonight was his death sentence.

The torture implements lay where they had been the previous nights. This time, Elen took in the full view of them. Pliers, pincers, and scalpels. The electric conductor box sat in a corner. Her body involuntarily shook at the sight of the copper wires snaking out of it and flowing to the floor.

A soldier shoved her into the chair just as Ashagirie walked into the room. Once the soldier stepped out, Ashagirie closed the door behind him and pulled out a chair across the table from her. His steely gaze never left her face.

They didn't tie her hands to the chair tonight. She wrapped both protectively around her torso.

"Upon further investigation, it seems like we have uncovered the truth." His voice was even and calm, devoid of the spittle-inducing anger of the nights before. "The newsletter is not yours."

Startled at the magnitude of the shift in his demeanor, she just stared at him.

Habteab had been telling the truth.

"No, it is not," she said finally, her voice small and shaky.

"Whose was it?" he asked.

She took a deep breath, and pain sliced through her rib cage.

"Girmai's," she said. No turning back now. "He … he must have left it at my house when he visited me once. I was raised in Adi Nefas village, so I was never taught to read. I didn't know what it was."

"Hmm," he nodded. His chair scraped beneath him as he stood up and left the room. A moment later, the man with the notebook followed him.

"She is ready to talk," Ashagirie said to the man after he had settled into his usual chair, his pen hovering closer to the notepad.

"Tell us everything."

32

Wenjel Mermera, one week after the arrest

"Please help me," Elen whispered to Habteab as she stared ahead; the morning chill hardened all the places she had bled into crusty clumps all over her nightgown and underwear.

She shifted her weight from one foot to the other and winced when the thickened, dried edges rubbed against her raw skin. She rubbed her thumbs and forefingers together. Still no feeling.

The guard taking roll call was still at the far end of the line, beyond hearing range.

"I'm still bleeding."

Habteab shifted closer behind her.

Elen ached for Faven, Aman, and Girmai and swallowed the lump in her throat.

"There is no clinic here," Habteab murmured from behind her. "Wenjel Mermera is only for interrogations and for those awaiting trial and sentencing." His thick beard served as a convenient shield for his lips.

Habteab wasn't always at roll call, but he passed by her a few times on her way to the pit latrine. He always walked straight and stiff, eyes darting as if prepared for an attack.

"They are scheduling a trial date for you," he said in a hoarse whisper as the guard read off names at the far end of the line. Elen stiffened. Trials were a joke here, a show for the Derg to pretend they administered justice.

"I need to go home to my children." She stopped rubbing her thumbs and forefingers and moved her hands to her torso.

She remembered Solomon telling her about Tirhas, a pregnant woman beaten so badly in one of these prisons that her baby died and stayed inside her. The infection that eventually grew took over her body until it killed her.

Elen barely survived the electrocution. *If this child is dead, what is it doing to my body?*

She rubbed her torso again. *I have to believe this baby is still alive. We made something beautiful together. We tried.*

She allowed herself to think of Girmai and give herself a moment free of pain and fear.

"Do you remember the first time we met?" he had asked her in Addis as they sat on the balcony of their hotel room. He had held Elen's hand as they gazed over the city, their feet stretched out on the coffee table. Church bells chimed over the traffic below.

God, he was so handsome!

"How could I forget?" she had smiled. "I could barely focus that day."

"I remember nothing about that afternoon except you. I thought you were the most amazing creature I'd ever seen."

He caressed her cheek. "When Kifle told me about the conversation you overheard that saved all those men, I knew you had to be part of my life."

She squeezed his hand. Light fog crept around the buildings below them, settled around a church steeple, and made it seem like the cross was floating before her.

It felt like fate. For a time, nothing could destroy what they had.

We made something beautiful.

The flutter in Elen's chest quickly gave way to reality.

Her knees buckled. She caught herself leaning against the wall. Did Habteab tell her Girmai was alive just to give her the strength to keep going?

"You might see a doctor after your trial. Not here," Habteab said, bringing her back to the present. "They'll probably transfer you to Haz Haz prison."

The dread of an extended stay hammered in her chest. She

wrapped her arms tight around herself to stem her panic, every breath a struggle.

"I thought the story I gave would be enough for them to let me go," she whispered. "I have to get back to my kids."

"Unfortunately, from what I hear, you will have to serve a sentence," Habteab said. "We're doing our best to make it short, but … it's best to prepare yourself."

How does one prepare for this?

"I'll see if I can get some help for your … condition," he added hurriedly.

The guard inched closer.

"What about Solomon?" she asked, desperate for good news.

"He'll be out soon," Habteab replied. "His case won't go to court. They're no longer interested in him since they have you and are now looking for Girmai."

At least they'll have someone.

I'm so sorry, my babies. If I survive this, I promise to give you a better life.

"Elen Ghebrekidan, 36."

She held herself up as the guard marked her name on the list. Zimam was several women down the line, holding Abeba up. The job preoccupied her completely this morning.

The two women locked eyes, and Zimam gave her a reassuring nod. Black gun barrels followed them as they filed back into their cells.

Elen settled onto the floor and into the seconds, minutes, and hours that merged into each other through a steady rain that began after sunset.

"See that window up there?" Zimam asked.

Elen made out the outline of shards of glass jutting out from the gaping hole as if someone had punched it.

"I heard this used to be a men's cell until some of them tried to escape." She gestured at the window. It was close to the ceiling and too small for any man to pass through. The opening let the rainwater splash in. "Get ready for a wet night."

Elen nodded at how accurately the window represented her life. The chance for freedom was too small, too far out of reach, while the misery poured in.

She wanted to believe that Girmai, Faven, and Aman were listening to the same rain. As she lay down, she let that thought occupy her, and the sound lulled her to sleep.

As Zimam predicted, the rain splattered steadily through the window throughout the night, spreading across the floor. Elen woke up in a shallow pool of water.

The guard revealed the extent of the flooding when he opened the door for the daily count the next morning. When Elen stood up, her clothes clung to her, dripping on the side where she had lain. Ripples spread and clashed with each other as the women got up.

"Use the containers to get the water out," the guard ordered. "Scoop it out, now!"

"I will do it," Zimam said. "You stay with Abeba. I'll help her get over there." She nodded at Elen's usual spot by the wall.

Elen knew Habteab was behind her before he said anything. He slipped a hard pack of pills into her palm.

"Hide it quickly!" he said. "We will both be dead if they see it."

Elen looked around before she tucked it into her bra, then put her hands back down by her sides.

"Take one pill a day."

"What is it?"

"I don't know. I told a doctor about your problem. He said to take it for the bleeding."

"Thank you."

"You should also get a change of clothes later today," he continued.

"Thank you," she said again, but he had gone.

A guard threw her a change of clothes later that day without explanation. She used the damp parts of her nightgown to wipe off dirt and dried blood from her body and kept the pills hidden inside her bra.

At the pit latrine, her fingers shook as she tried to free one from the packet. Though she could move them now, the feeling in her thumbs and forefingers hadn't fully returned.

She tore at the packet with her teeth and finally got one out.

The pill went down her dry throat slowly as she threw the bits of wrapper in the latrine hole before she tucked the rest back in their hiding place.

May God be with me.

***

Four weeks later.

"Case against Elen Ghebrekidan: counterrevolutionary activities through the possession of an illegal publication," Elen's trial was announced. "Evidence of this charge is submitted to the court."

The newsletter was handed to the three judges at the front of the room. They passed it between themselves as a witness came up to the stand.

The soldier who struck her in her living room took the stand first.

"She knew what she was doing," he said resolutely. The newsletter is hers. I saw her face when we found it; she looked guilty. She is a counterrevolutionary. I am certain of that. She had it hidden in her drawer."

Elen sat on a bench next to a meek court-appointed lawyer who seemed more of a showpiece than an actual defender.

The other soldiers in the house that night followed with similar testimonies.

Ashagirie, padded with bribes, countered them with the story she gave him.

"This woman is Ethiopian and a very successful bar owner," he said, his beady eyes shifting from her to the judges. "We couldn't find any evidence she attended school or learned to read or write. Her brother helps her with her business operations. We concluded it cannot be hers, but that of her boyfriend, who visited her often and had access to the drawer."

The silent note taker from the interrogation room took the stand and corroborated Ashagirie's story.

The longer the witnesses spoke, the judges' eyelids drooped with disinterest.

"How do you plead?" the judge in the middle asked when Elen finally got on the stand.

The judge beside him rubbed his forehead and yawned.

"Not guilty, sir," Elen said. She kept her eyes down when she repeated the story she gave Ashagirie.

When she returned to hear the judges' decision the next week, they seemed as unmoved as they had been when she testified.

"Will the defendant, Elen Ghebrekidan, stand for the verdict," the court announcer said.

The lawyer beside her moved faster than she did. He was already on his feet when she scraped her chair back. She winced at its amplified sound in the courtroom.

"We find the defendant, Elen Ghebrekidan, not guilty on the charge of engaging in counterrevolutionary activities," the judge in the middle said as he held up the papers before him.

Before Elen could fully bask in the idea, he continued, "However, it is a crime to have a publication such as this and not report it. We find the defendant, Elen Ghebrekidan, guilty of possessing an illegal publication and sentence her to serve three years in prison."

The judges blurred through her tears as she pressed her lips together to control the panic rising.

Three years?

They didn't waste any time moving on to the next case as guards appeared on either side of her. "You move to Haz Haz tomorrow."

They ushered her out of the courtroom and back into the prison truck.

Three years.

* * *

Elen's belly kept growing despite the rest of her body shrinking. She held her hands around it, bracing against the bumps that almost threw her off her seat on the back of the fast-moving prison truck on her way to Haz Haz prison. Her new home.

Elen didn't know if it was the pills Habteab gave her or her body healing itself, but she stopped bleeding soon after she started taking them.

Dare I hope? But what kind of life am I bringing into this world? She tried not to think about the beatings and electric shocks and what damage they had done to the life inside her.

A railing on the truck bench dug into her back, and she focused on that pain. Anything was better than thinking about the next three years.

She fell back on prayer as the truck made a steep ascent to the prison at the top of the hill.

A guard checked her in at the entrance, and another led her through several hallways while a soldier kept pace behind her, his gun trained on her back. Every once in a while, he prodded her forward with it when she slowed down.

Elen kept both her hands firmly pressed against her torso in case he got violent.

"Sundays are wash days," a guard in front of her said. "Your family may send you a mattress no more than four centimeters thick and sixty centimeters wide. They can also bring a change of clothes you can exchange every Sunday. There are no visits. If they bring anything for you, we will pass it along."

"How can I let them know I'm here?" Elen managed to ask. She stumbled forward after another prod on her back.

"If they come asking for you," he responded dryly, "we will let them know you are here."

Before she could ask any more questions, the guard stopped at a metal door, indistinguishable from the others. A square hole at his eye level opened to a dark void inside.

The guard's tight green uniform stretched over his upper back as he bent to unlock the door. He pulled it open and pushed it back until it was flat against the outer wall.

Elen instinctively pulled back from the putrid odor of the groaning bodies inside. The shaft of light through the door spread into the dimness of the cell to reveal a sea of women packed into every inch of the floor. Some lay on their sides, their noses touching the next person's head, others sat side by side against the wall. Those at the corners, whose feet stretched out, allowed others to drape their legs over an intricate lattice of limbs that made it hard to tell where one ended and the other began.

A few women on the floor closest to the door bent their legs in anticipation of her entry. Their collective movement like clusters of worms dug from the soil, desperately groping past each other to get back to the dark.

Once exposed, the floor of the small space in front of her seemed wet. Elen stepped back, lifting her palm to cover her nose and mouth against the stench.

"Get in!"

The guard's hand slammed into her back between her shoulder blades, knocking the breath out of her as she stumbled in. She tripped on a pair of thin, outstretched feet and flailed her hands in front of her as she went down. Her palms landed on a bony torso.

"Ooowie!" The pain in the woman's shriek stabbed at Elen as she pressed on other body parts to straighten up as fast as she could.

"Sorry!" Elen gasped.

She widened her eyes in the dark and scanned the room frantically as the door slammed shut behind her. The legs that had bent to give her space to walk in stretched out again, encircling her feet in a web of limbs.

She stood still, afraid to move in case she stepped on anyone. She blinked and willed her eyes to adjust faster to the murky dark.

Slowly, faceless shadows turned into women with sharp, bony features, each contorted with pain.

The stench of urine, feces, and vomit filled her nostrils and mouth. It settled in her lungs like thick porridge. She didn't need to look long to find the source. The smell was heaviest near the door, where a bucket sat in the corner. She craned her head around to look and recoiled instantly when she recognized the human waste inside.

Right next to the bucket was the only sliver of unoccupied floor space, enough for one person. She tried to swallow, but her mouth was too dry. She pressed her lips together to control the blood rushing up her chest to her head.

Three years here?

"Elen!"

The voice was so familiar that Elen thought she had imagined it. Her eyes darted desperately around the room and landed on Zimam, who struggled to stand over the woman beside her.

"Oh my God, Elen! They sent you here?" She teetered between a woman consumed by hacking coughs on one side and a more petite woman lying motionless on the other.

"Come, you can take my spot here. I'll go there." She pointed at the space beside the bucket.

Before Elen could respond, another voice rose from the sea of moaning on the floor.

"Suq ilki iske kof beli." Be quiet and sit down.

The steely voice shot over to Zimam from the corner of the room furthest from the waste bucket.

"That's your assigned spot. Sit."

Elen turned to the long finger pointed at her and followed it to the woman it belonged to.

Halawit's face was more haggard than Elen remembered; her netsela didn't quite sit right on her. A shoulder poked through a big tear on one side, and her lips, drawn back in a snarl, made her wide eyes pop out.

Elen remembered that Girmai had told her about Derg soldiers arresting Halawit after they found stolen jewelry in her home.

"Someone on the wrong end of the interrogation tools gave up Halawit's name," Girmai had added later on after her trial. "She gave up so much information but still got a ten-year prison sentence."

Has she been here all this time?

Elen had heard about the many names that had rolled off Halawit's tongue. Her confessions had ricocheted into multiple extra arrests.

"It's fitting your place is right there next to the shit," she spat. She pointed at the bucket. "It's exactly where you belong."

Halawit's belief that Elen was a Derg-loving barista who sidled up to colonels and generals to get favors and live a cushy life clearly hadn't changed; she must still think she was a Derg ally.

How can she still think that, seeing me in here?

The woman glared at Elen, her nose wrinkled and her upper lip pulled back in disdain.

"Can I please exchange places with her?" Zimam still stood, her voice tinged with fear.

Some of the moaning tapered off around them the more they spoke. "Elen was with me in Wenjel Mermera and really suffered there. She is pregnant. Sleeping next to that bucket will make her and the baby sick."

"We have all suffered!" Halawit growled. She inclined her face squarely at Zimam. The women between their feet shifted but stayed quiet. All kept their eyes averted.

"Why didn't you volunteer to switch when you saw others choking with asthma or vomiting their guts out? You didn't ask to change places with them then." Halawit's glare remained on her until Zimam looked at Elen apologetically and started a ripple of movement around her as she sat back down.

"Did she get pregnant for us?" Halawit sneered. "There are no favors here. They put me in charge of maintaining order. Rules are rules. She starts in that spot just like everyone else. When her turn comes to move down the line, she can move." She thrust her finger toward the bucket again.

"I'll be okay," Elen said to Zimam. She didn't want anyone getting into trouble on her behalf.

Lifting one foot over a limb and the other over a torso, Elen carefully stepped over another pair of thin legs by her feet and balanced precariously to reach her spot. The cell fell silent as she moved. She reached the wall, stepped into the narrow space, and slid down slowly.

The bucket was so close that its contents stung her eyes. She only had to move slightly for her arm to touch it. The woman beside her seemed to be unconscious or in a deep sleep.

At least the bleeding stopped.

Elen propped her back against the wall and stretched one leg out, bending the other. She wrapped one arm around her elevated knee and the other around her stomach in case anyone walked over her to get to the bucket. She locked eyes with Halawit, then looked away.

She leaned her head back against the wall and closed her eyes, slipping into the memories of the life she lost as the collective moans of pain slowly came back around her like white noise.

She dreamed of Faven, trying on her platform sandals, and Aman, sitting on her lap for a cuddle. Her mind floated into her living room, and she willed herself to remember the delicious smell of roasting coffee to replace the awful smell beside her. She imagined Alem pounding the black roasted beans on the cylindrical grinder as she laughed about one thing or another before she poured the grinds into the jebena. Elen's favorite clay coffee pot had small crosses etched around its diameter.

She heard her brother and sister's laughter around the small charcoal stove as the thick, black coffee bubbled up, then visualized Alem pouring it into the small finjal for each of them to enjoy.

Elen rubbed her numb forefingers against her thumbs at the memory of the tiny coffee cups. She probably wouldn't be able to hold them anymore. She shrank from the thought and let her mind wander to her room, where she imagined Girmai was waiting. She let herself feel his arms around her, huge and tight, and sank into his embrace.

All we have are moments. Let's make something beautiful.

She saw her closet: all those beautiful dresses, her commode with her kohl and lipstick, and drawers full of jewelry.

Then she saw the drawer.

"Look what I found!"

The soldier's jubilation when he waved the newsletter in front of her cut through her meditation. She squeezed her eyes to distance herself from the sound of the judge banging the mallet.

"... three years ..."

Elen eventually succumbed to exhaustion but kept her knees up and arms wrapped protectively over her stomach. The tiny breeze that filtered through the barred opening above her on the door did nothing to dissipate the stench of the rapidly filling bucket. Through the night, cries of pain traveled through the room as women crawled over each other to get to it. Elen kept her hands and knees wrapped tight as women crawled over her too.

The dark was a small mercy for blocking out what happened beside her, though nothing could shield her from the sounds and smells of the constant retching and release of loose bowels.

Every part of her swollen, bruised body throbbed. She squeezed her eyes shut and lowered her head between her knees to block the feel of droplets landing on her.

33

Asmara, six weeks after the arrest

His disguise as a beles fruit trader was perfect and far removed from Girmai the wealthy entrepreneur. The cactus fruit season was in full swing and traders kept the checkpoints busy, traveling into the city with full baskets and leaving with them empty.

"It will be important for you to look as different as you can," Daniel had said when he smuggled Girmai into the latest safe house a month before.

Derg soldiers had distributed copies of his photo at all major checkpoints out of Asmara. His disguise had to be convincing.

With limited food and constant exercise, Girmai's body had shrunk to a fraction of its former self. His sinewy and taut muscles and his long, unkempt beard completed the new look he needed to escape Asmara.

Every day, Girmai repeated the information he needed to remember as a beles trader. The popular cactus fruit was in season now, and traders across checkpoints were plentiful. He meticulously studied unfamiliar aspects of the trade and was ready to follow through with the plan.

The plan turned out to be endless weeks of hiding while Derg soldiers combed the city looking for him. Daniel arranged for each safe house to have a phone, which was Girmai's sole source of information. He constantly asked about Elen.

"She did as we asked her to during interrogations," Daniel had told him when he was days into hiding in the second safe house.

Though it pained him to hear it, Girmai had listened and held on to every detail.

"And the baby?"

"As far as we know, she is still pregnant, but you know Ashagirie. She went through a lot before we could get to him."

Girmai had dug his nails into his palms to keep himself still.

"We have to get her out, Daniel," Girmai said, releasing his clenched fist and flexing his fingers. He rubbed the red curved lines his nails left on his palm. "We can't leave her in there. She's done so much for us and—"

"We are working on it," Daniel cut him off. "Right now, you are the main concern. There's a substantial reward for anyone with information that leads to you. If they catch you, we are all finished."

"So what now?" Girmai asked

"We leave this afternoon," Daniel said in the usual matter-of-fact tone. "We have a good chance of getting through with the other traders."

Survival now depended on an obedient donkey and the quality of Girmai's act as an experienced cactus-fruit trader. The picture on his new ID card showed him as an emaciated, bearded man. It placed him in a nearby village, and he practiced and perfected the life story he would give if asked.

This is it.

Girmai put one foot in front of the other and focused on what Daniel had taught him about village beles traders.

"Control the donkey with your stick," he had reminded him. "Guide him forward with taps like I showed you. You need to look like you know what you are doing. A disobedient donkey can ruin everything for you. The most important thing is maintaining control at the checkpoint and passing the curve leading into the valley. To be safe, we will need to go through separately and then meet down on the valley floor. I'll go ahead of you. After you pass through, go around the first bend in the road overlooking the valley to your left. A huge egg-shaped stone marks where you should turn onto a dirt path descending into the valley. Follow it, and don't stop until you reach the bottom. Once we meet there, I'll connect you with an EPLF contingent. You'll travel onward with those fighters to Ghinda. I'll go back to Asmara to tie up loose ends."

Girmai's donkey plodded beside him, mirroring his cautious pace. Though the baskets balanced perfectly on each side of the animal's back, Girmai adjusted the straps to double-check their position.

No one had paid attention as he and Daniel walked the donkeys through the city. He scratched his chin, then smoothed his overgrown beard down; the edges of it grazed his chest.

Girmai guessed it was about 3:30 p.m. from the angle of the sun. The dry and intense heat still pervaded despite the cold season. Underneath the thick gabi wrapped around his chest and shoulders, he sweated into the old T-shirt and worn pants Daniel had brought him a few days before. They both hung loose on his now thin frame, and the torn cuffs of his pants dragged on the ground over his dusty rubber sandals.

He kept his eyes on Daniel, a few feet ahead of him, in a similar disguise. They merged with other beles traders and women carrying empty baskets, making their way to the Massawa Road checkpoint.

Let's hope this works.

New soldiers had flooded the city in the past few months, so paying off the soldiers at checkpoints didn't work anymore since they constantly rotated. Girmai hadn't been able to build networks since he had gone into hiding, so disguise was the only way to get through.

When they'd met in the last safe house to finalize the plan, Daniel grinned when he saw Girmai's disheveled hair and unkempt beard. "I will give you this one to match your style," he pointed to one of the donkeys. "He's also the less stubborn one."

The donkeys stayed hidden in the walled compound of the safe house so Girmai could become familiar with them and them to him. The quiet of the outskirts of Asmara helped him think through his next steps as he continued the intense daily exercise routine to prepare for the long journey ahead. The more he thought of Elen, the more pull-ups and sit-ups he did, the more he studied, the more he pushed himself, anything to keep from thinking about how she must be hurting.

This walk was the first time he'd been out in the open since Elen's arrest. His nostrils filled with the thick, earthy scent of tesmi—the ghee he'd rubbed into his overgrown afro—a smell that now clung to him like a second skin. His feet were already raw from where the rubber sandals rubbed against them.

The checkpoint came into view when they rounded a corner. Girmai counted ten armed soldiers in front of long lines of people and cars. The queue of people weaved off the road and onto a dirt path. Some stood with donkeys, and some without.

Daniel's donkey ahead of him started to veer off the dirt path onto the road. With a flick of his walking stick, Daniel steered it until it ambled back onto the path and merged into the line.

They all stood silently, waiting to be let through the entry points. Cars and trucks inched forward, their occupants holding out their identity paperwork to be checked and their vehicles thoroughly searched.

Girmai looked ahead at the two soldiers at the checkpoint bottleneck. One soldier checked identification while the other searched bags and patted down bodies before granting approval to pass through. Two more soldiers stood behind them, guns ready to respond to any disturbance.

Girmai hung back as Daniel joined in and let four people go ahead of him before stepping in. He held the donkey's reins and silently prayed that the animal would not betray him.

Daniel approached the checkpoint, one hand holding onto the donkey and the other his identification card. The soldier roughly grabbed the card and brought it to Daniel's face. His eyes alternated between Daniel and the card several times. The other soldier shook the empty baskets strapped onto his donkey. He felt around underneath them on the donkey's back to search for hidden items. He then turned to Daniel and patted him down—shoulders, armpits, torso, hips, and ankles.

The soldier holding the identification card watched Daniel stand compliant, his head lowered to an angle of deference, arms slightly raised to allow for the search.

The soldier handed the card back and waved him through, his eyes already on the next person.

Several people later, it was Girmai's turn. He flicked the donkey with his stick to prompt it forward and again at the neck to signal it to stop right before they got to where the soldiers stood.

"Identification." The soldier held out his hand.

Girmai's gaze fixed on the soldier's yellowed fingernails, which hovered too long over the card, moving slowly, deliberately, as if weighing the picture against the man before him.

Girmai glanced over his shoulder for a split second. Daniel walked on with his donkey and didn't look back. In a few moments, he disappeared around the bend of a hill.

Girmai did his best to look tired but obedient, as a trader traveling daily would.

The soldier looked at the card again, then up at Girmai's face.

"Where are you coming from?" the soldier asked as he turned the card over.

His eyes moved back and forth as he read the false details about Girmai's place of birth and the village he was from, adjusting his gun strap across his shoulders. Girmai recognized the Northern Ethiopian Tigrayan accent.

He didn't travel far to get this assignment, Girmai thought.

"I just came back from Edaga Hamus market, sir," Girmai said. His tone was polite, and he bowed slightly as he spoke. He used his childhood village accent. "Business is slow these days, but I praise the Lord for the blessing of beles."

Girmai raised his palms and looked skyward as if in prayer. "Praise be to the Lord. Our harvest has been good this year. We give thanks always for the grace of God."

The other soldier felt around the baskets on the donkey, then roughly patted Girmai down as he had done with Daniel.

"I give thanks and praise to God," Grimai continued. "Today, I sold just enough to feed my family. Praise be to—"

“Go, move on,” the soldier said, having lost interest, as he shoved the card into Girmai’s chest, his eyes already on the next person.

Girmai bowed and flicked his donkey. He walked forward in measured steps between the two barrels that marked the end of the checkpoint. His feet, slick with sweat, slid around the insides of his sandals as he made his way around the wide bend Daniel had mentioned and turned at the egg-shaped stone leading to the footpath to the valley.

The mountains before him quivered and shook as tears welled in his eyes, blurring his vision. He saw Elen’s face etched into the open spaces between the distant peaks. She reached out to him, calling.

He saw his children; their voices echoed in the valley.

Baba! Baba, where are you?

Tears streamed down his face unchecked at the enormity of the endless mountainscape before him and the magnitude of what he had left behind. He would have to start all over again.

I’ll come for all of you. Stay strong and wait for me.

Down the hill, he put one foot in front of the other until he stood in the shadow of the valley, where Daniel was waiting.

34

"The Derg just received bomber planes from the US and heavy artillery from the Soviets," Daniel said, pulling back after a quick celebratory embrace. Girmai followed him on the path through the valley.

"They've begun the biggest offensive we've ever seen and are using their weapons as if there is no end to their supply. We were so close and pushed hard, but not enough to get closer to Asmara. Our positions are all compromised and under heavy bombardment now. The attacks this past week ended with massive casualties on our side. EPLF command has sent word to begin a strategic withdrawal."

Girmai stopped to look back to the top of the hill he had just descended from, where he had left his family and Elen.

"What does this mean?" he asked. He wasn't sure he wanted to know the answer.

"We have reports that, in addition to weapons, the Derg has brought in Soviet advisors, Saudi, and South Yemeni troops to strengthen their offensive," Daniel answered. He motioned to Girmai to keep walking.

Girmai followed Daniel, his pace slower with a new heaviness that suddenly weighed his feet down. He didn't intend for this life in exile to be prolonged. He hoped to wait outside the city and then go back as soon as possible.

"They have already begun bombing liberated areas all over the country, especially offensive lines near Asmara," Daniel continued, his back to Girmai as he nimbly side-stepped sharp stones on the path. "The Derg is coming at us with everything they've got."

Around them, the cacti offered little cover from the skies. Girmai looked up for any sign of planes.

"They hit further out," Daniel said as if reading his mind. "We will be okay for a while. Our strongholds sit several kilometers out in almost all directions. I heard planes bombed many of them yesterday. Even with our thirty thousand fighters all armed with Derg weapons, even with enough determination to move the world, we weren't able to sustain our defenses against their bombings and rocket-propelled grenades."

Daniel used the edge of his gabi to wipe sweat from the back of his neck.

"Daniel, I need to get my family out of Asmara," Girmai said. "They won't be safe in the city when the EPLF launches a counteroffensive. I need to help Elen …" His voice trailed off, and he swallowed the lump in his throat. "I need help to get her out too."

"I'm afraid that won't be possible right now," Daniel said. "I didn't want to tell you the extent of the situation until you got out." He kept walking and didn't look back at Girmai.

"The EPLF withdrawal is already underway," Daniel said. "There is no counteroffensive. It will take time to come up with a new military strategy to take over the capital." Daniel pointed. "A ganta is waiting for us up there."

Girmai searched the hillsides for any sign of the squad but saw nothing but cacti and the occasional acacia tree.

"They will take you north. That's the plan we have for now. There's no turning back for a while."

"That is *not* a plan!" Girmai walked up to Daniel and pushed his shoulder so they faced each other. "I left people behind. How am I supposed to get them out if I am so far away? We've been in desperate situations before; we can do it again." Girmai's feet stopped moving as his pulse sped up. "We have to find a way to get them out. I need to go back."

"Hard as it is to understand, our only option is to pull out now and head north so we can regroup," Daniel said, his shoulders slumping with the words. He sounded as if he was trying to convince himself too. "We'll gather our strength and come back with force. Too many of our brothers and sisters have died for us to risk pushing forward and failing now."

Girmai wasn't sure what he had expected once he got beyond the checkpoint, but it certainly wasn't this—a complete withdrawal, with no options to salvage any part of his life. His focus had been on staying alive; now he wondered what he had stayed alive for.

While he was in hiding, all the information he got indicated that victory was imminent. The EPLF was only sixteen kilometers from the city and closing in.

Defeat? Withdrawal? He had not heard anything about that.

How do I get to my family? To Elen?

"Come on," Daniel said, now several paces ahead of him. "We need to keep moving."

Girmai didn't trust himself to talk as he processed the inconceivable news.

"Our people are resilient," Daniel continued when he saw Girmai was back within hearing range. Girmai's donkey had stopped to nibble on something at the base of a cactus fruit. He patted it gently with his stick, and it reluctantly stepped back onto the path and continued forward.

"We've had some victories," Daniel said proudly. "We've confiscated more weapons from the Ethiopians, not to mention captured many of their soldiers. We also got our hands on some tanks with barely fifty kilometers on the odometer. You might see them on the way. Small wins, but victories nonetheless. We will win this war, eventually."

Eventually. What good are tanks and guns if we are withdrawing?

A desperate sense of loss gripped Girmai. The last time he felt this way was when he was a penniless street boy, witnessing his small metal scale being crushed, right before the municipal officer kicked him away from everything he owned, everything he had worked so hard for. The resolute determination he always carried usually fueled his belief that things would turn out fine, but now all he had was a desperate tightness in his chest with each step he took away from his home.

"What are the chances we can come back against all that military power?" His voice merged with the crunch of shifting stones beneath their feet.

"We always come back, Girmai," Daniel said over his shoulder as they passed through a narrow part of the path, overgrown with a patch of thorny bushes.

For a few moments, they made their way silently through a small patch of dense overgrowth, donkeys in tow.

Once they cleared the small thicket, the hills on either side lay silent and seemed devoid of human life. Girmai balled his hands into tight fists to control the conflicting thoughts raging in his mind. He focused on the pain of his nails digging into his palms.

"I can't leave, Daniel," Girmai said again. They walked into the hill's shadow, and his headache shifted to one side of his head, pounding just behind his eye. "I have to stay and get Elen and my family out. If I can't do that, I'll join the fighters here and find my way back in when the time comes." He forced himself to ignore the blisters burning his feet.

Daniel was quiet for a few moments, as if considering Girmai's thoughts. His voice was low and calm when he spoke again.

"With all your contacts and resources in Italy, you will have more of an impact on your family's safety and our liberation movement if you work from the outside. Think about it—"

"Are you telling me to run away, Daniel?" Incredulous, Girmai cut him off. The anger and frustration in his voice echoed around them. "How can you tell me to do that? I have to go back!"

Daniel whirled around, anger flashing in his eyes. "Those soldiers back there will skin you alive if they get their hands on you!" he shouted. "Do you remember the men Zenebe stopped from interrogating you in '75? The head guy is leading the investigation to find you. What do you think they'll do to you when they catch you?

What do you think will happen to Elen and your family when you are dead? All this work we did to save you will be for nothing. Do you hear me? Nothing!" His voice startled the donkey, who skirted around them and joined the other further down the path.

Girmai threw his hands up in exasperation and slapped them against his hips. He clenched his hands around his pants and tugged at them in frustration. "What am I supposed to do, Daniel?" he cried. "How can I leave them all behind?

Daniel took a deep breath and wrapped his gabi around the nape of his neck. "You're not running away," Daniel replied, calmer. He stepped closer to Girmai. "Think of it as working smart. If you leave here in one piece, you can prepare a safe place and get them all out. What use are you dead? That is the risk you take if you go back."

Girmai stared at him, unable to speak.

"We have people still in Asmara that can help you to get them all out," Daniel continued. "Also, think about how much the EPLF needs supplies. You can raise funds and keep our fight alive. There aren't many people who can do that for us on the outside."

They stared silently at each other before Daniel put a hand on Girmai's shoulder. "Come," he said. "Too much has happened today. Let's get to where we need to be before dark."

The low angle of the sun's rays illuminated the mountaintops in the distance and cast long shadows over the valley. Girmai's feet moved autonomously, following Daniel as he veered off the valley path and embarked on a steep ascent.

"The donkeys will be fine here," he told Girmai. Both were nibbling on short bushes. "Come on, it's getting late." He jerked his head toward the top of what seemed like an impossible climb.

Girmai scrambled up after Daniel. He had to drop down on all fours in some spots to lift himself over boulders or squeeze through the prickly cacti.

He was out of breath and dizzy by the time Daniel stopped at a wide, flat clearing several hundred feet above the valley floor. It broke up the angle of the hill. The smooth texture of the small open patch held footprints in the shape of the ubiquitous shida, the plastic sandals the EPLF fighters wore.

Exhausted from the steep climb, Girmai put his hands on his hips and breathed through his mouth to steady his pulse. Only after Daniel stood right next to it did Girmai notice the man-sized hole carved into the side of the incline a few feet from the clearing.

"Ahlan wa sahlan," Daniel said in Arabic. It seemed like he was talking to himself in the semi-dark. "Tonight's dinner is goat," he said loudly.

At those words, men and women in tight-fitting canvas shorts and shirts poured out from crevices all around them. They slapped Daniel on the back in greeting. Their quiet laughter and greetings eased Girmai's cramping muscles.

"Please welcome Wedi Issac," Daniel said, stretching a hand out to Girmai. "He is the one going north with you."

Hands patted Girmai's back in welcome while others knocked shoulders in the traditional greeting.

A ganta was meant to have around fifty soldiers in smaller groups called mesre. Girmai counted only ten of them. *Maybe they have all separated,* he thought, looking out at the mountainscape.

"What about you?" one of them said to Daniel. Girmai strained to distinguish one from the other in the growing darkness. "You heard what's happening, right? We are the last ones remaining. You arrived at the perfect time."

"No, I still have work to do in Asmara," Daniel said. With his back facing Girmai, he didn't get the chance to question him. "My cover is still intact. I'll finish a few projects we have open there. I might join you after that."

They nodded in agreement, a collective nod confirming they needed no further explanation.

Girmai reveled in their company. He listened and watched for as long as his eyes would stay open. Here, he was finally on the other side of the struggle. One he never had the chance to see.

A fire they set up within a stone crevice illuminated the marks of the battles they fought—a missing limb or eye, scars on the neck, arms, or legs, a limp, and more scars—yet they smiled and laughed as they shared food as if this were a regular, conflict-free night.

"We work and learn as one to keep our sanity," one man told Girmai. "Doing normal things helps us feel human," the man continued as he took a long drag of his cigarette. He closed his eyes and held his breath for a few seconds, his chest expanding like an inflated balloon. He then let it go slowly, sending a long stream of smoke from his mouth.

After eating a dinner of tea and dry pieces of bread, they moved into shelters dug into various places on the hillside. Girmai settled into a natural concave inset in the hill. He lay down on his side and faced the entrance. The opening was pitch black and revealed nothing of the endless mountainscape beyond it.

He fell asleep, dreaming of walking endlessly, and woke to an orange dawn as soft morning light filtered into the shelter.

He stretched and headed out toward the clearing where everyone was already up and drinking tea.

"This is where we part ways," Daniel told him once they had eaten. "I'll head back to Asmara this morning. They'll get you to Ghinda. You might join a different group to take you north." He waved at the group of EPLF fighters, then looked back at Girmai. "It's been a privilege to know you and to have worked with you all these years."

Why does this sound like a goodbye? Daniel was not one to be sentimental.

"I know we will continue to do great things," he said before Girmai could respond.

"Remember what I said about how you can make an impact? We need different people to play different roles in this fight. Our success relies on it. Don't lose hope. We will be victorious. Awet N' Hafash!"

The finality of their embrace hit Girmai hard. Daniel was his last tie to Asmara. He stared out into the mountain ranges, then back at Daniel, who had already begun his descent.

Daniel's words constantly reverberated in his mind as he followed the EPLF route from one town to another for several weeks. From Mai Wu'ui to Weki Zagir, they wound their way through Keren and other liberated areas. During the day, they moved through places with enough cover, either in vehicles, which the EPLF acquired from raids on Derg military outposts, or on foot.

When the landscape was bare and open, they hid in dugout shelters during the day and traveled at night to evade the patrolling planes that dropped bombs over liberated towns and villages.

He parted ways with the group as he boarded a stolen army truck heading toward Karora, a town on the Sudanese border. The truck would take him to Suakin, a port city and temporary haven.

"One step backward, two steps forward," an EPLF fighter told him as Girmai climbed onto the truck. "We almost had them and could have pushed on, but we won't callously risk the lives of our people like the Derg does. We need to focus on those steps forward."

Girmai lost count of how many days he spent moving. It was almost dawn when the truck slowed to a stop. He rubbed the sleep from his eyes and looked at the gleaming ocean ahead. Behind them was nothing but the dry, stony landscape, empty and hot.

The driver got out and stretched. "Welcome to Suakin!" he shouted.

***

Girmai pulled himself away from his memories and turned to Kifle as he sat on the sand beside him. The emotional reunion with his long-time friend earlier that morning had been Girmai's solace after being on the run for so long. Kifle had left Asmara more than a year ago after one of his cell members was captured. The inevitability of his arrest spurred an escape plan that became a permanent move to the field. Living and fighting on the front lines made him scrawnier than normal. Weather, hunger, combat, sorrow, and constant vigilance had hardened his once jovial features.

"Isn't this place amazing?" Kifle gestured toward the old Suakin ruins in front of them. "Hundreds of years ago, this was a mighty city. Now look at it. Beautiful even in its state of decay. It's served us well as a base of operations, that's for sure."

Girmai followed Kifle's gesture toward the ancient coral ruins. Hundreds of years of neglect had reduced them to crumbled versions of their former glory.

His gaze trailed back to the anchored boat before them. He studied the chipped red paint and the long rope tied to a partially exposed anchor. The vessel swayed almost imperceptibly, its tiny movements synchronized with the waves.

The tide had risen a few feet since Girmai arrived earlier that morning. Once the anchor lifted, all the boat needed was a little more water, then it would be free. Free to head toward the horizon to freedom, to Elen, to … *everything I've lost.*

"Kifle," Girmai sat up and rubbed his hands together to remove the grains of sand stuck to his palms, "I've ruined everything." He lifted his knees and wrapped his elbows around them.

The weight of Kifle's hand on his shoulder triggered the sting of tears that made the coral ruins shudder and dance before him. The touch was more comforting than anything Girmai had felt during the journey here.

Girmai removed the rubber sandals from his now hardened feet and lowered himself fully onto the sand, just out of reach of the waterline. He winced at the ache in his knees and wiggled his calloused toes.

Solomon's voice came back to him as he sat beside his friend.

"Elen is out there with them now. I'm not sure what will happen. She wanted you to know. Please be careful."

It felt as if years had passed since that night. The words that had saved his life also triggered events that propelled Girmai away from everything he had built and everyone he loved. Here he was now, adrift on this sandy, desolate beach where the low tide lapping against the old fishing boats knew nothing of all he lost.

The sandals he'd first put on as a beles trader were now threadbare and softened, molded to the shape of his feet. Scars from cycles of blisters that grew, popped, and healed on the month-long journey out of Eritrea dotted his ankles and the tops of his toes. He propped himself on his arms and shifted on the pebbles that pierced through his thin pants.

"It's been so long, I don't even know if she is alive and I … I just left her," Girmai said, breaking the silence. He stared out at the Red Sea inlet separating them from Suakin Island.

"You didn't leave her, Girmai," Kifle said. "None of us leave anything. We survive and strategize so we can stay in the fight."

"She would have been safe if I hadn't involved her in this mess," Girmai continued, hearing Kifle's words but not letting them get past his guilt. "She is in prison now because she wanted to protect me, and all I did was leave." He pressed the bottom of his palms to his eyes hard.

"And my kids," he continued, unable to contain his tears, "I just left them with no explanation. What kind of damage will that do to them?"

"You did what you had to do," Kifle told him. "Elen gets to live because you gave up your freedom, your whole life. If she hadn't told them what you told her to, she'd be dead right now, and you know it. You did the right thing."

Kifle shook him by the shoulder. "She is *alive*, Girmai. Believe that. She's a fighter and will get through this just like she did everything else. You didn't make her do anything. Elen knew exactly what she was doing and what she would be sacrificing. We are all doing our best to get the freedom we deserve."

Girmai wanted to believe Kifle, but couldn't absolve himself. "I have to get them all out," he said. "But how?" Around him he saw nothing but the ruins and a few fishermen preparing their nets to go out to sea.

"Once we get to Khartoum, we will find out more," Kifle reassured him. "She's a lot stronger than you think. They all are."

"They tortured her, Kifle." Girmai's voice broke. He wrapped his elbows tighter around his knees and focused on the boat again. "She was pregnant. What are the chances that either of them survived that?"

Girmai turned to Kifle and beat his chest, his fist clenched. "They tortured her before we could get her help, and she endured it because of me. I'm responsible for that. She went through all that to protect me."

"We all knew what we were getting into when we started this fight," Kifle said, grabbing Gimai's fists. "Listen to me! She is in it because, like us, she believes in freedom for our country and, God willing, we will all live to see it and reunite in a free Eritrea. Now you need to focus on building yourself back up. You can only help her, help all of them, if you help yourself first. Start your life again like you have done before."

Girmai grimaced. *Start again.*

Kifle let go of his hands and faced the sea.

"We've taught ourselves about the ways of life from an early age," Kifle continued. "We've restarted from nothing plenty of times in the past. This situation is no different."

Girmai shook his head. This time, though, he wasn't starting entirely from nothing. He had already moved some of his money to Italy. Enough to launch a new plan and figure out what to do.

He could start again. Like this boat, he would find a harbor, a place to rest. When the tide rose for him, he would lift his anchor and make his way back to all those he loved.

"What do they call this boat?" Girmai asked.

Kifle turned to the sound of three fishermen who were squatting in front of another boat several feet away, releasing tangles in the nets spread around them.

"Matha tusami hatha murkab?" Kifle asked them loudly in Arabic.

"They call it 'Hiyab,'" Kifle said after a few seconds of listening to their reply.

"Hiyab," Girmai repeated softly.

Gift.

Savoring the new energy building in his chest, Girmai wiped his eyes.

Past the boat and the crumbling buildings, the horizon and

the sky opened up, limitless before him. He drew energy from the boundless sense of freedom it promised—freedom that had enough space for everyone he loved. His eyes went from the open ocean to the boat. It bobbed as if acknowledging his newfound determination. Then he imagined a baby girl with Elen's eyes and radiant smile.

When next he spoke, it was more to himself than Kifle. "If Elen survives this, and if the baby does too, I want to name her Hiyab."

35

Haz Haz prison, Asmara, January 1979

"Halawit keeps telling everyone that you are a Derg spy planted here to identify counterrevolutionaries," Abeba said. "Such a vile woman!"

Naked, Elen shivered as a cold draft swept through the gap between the ground and the makeshift corrugated-iron sheets that walled off the wash area. She tried to keep still as Abeba scrubbed her back.

Space was tight. Careful not to step near the pit latrine, Elen shifted forward on the concrete slab to give Abeba more space to scrub her lower back. She took shallow breaths, hoping to let in as little of the stench as possible, but the thick odor from the hole seeped into her lungs.

During Elen's fifth week in Haz Haz, two women died. Their deaths had been both quiet and resigned after prolonged suffering in the crowded cell. Incredibly, not long after the clinic staff took the bodies away, they brought in Abeba and another woman.

Following Halawit's pointed finger, Abeba sat down silently next to Elen, while the other woman took her place next to the bucket. Elen made space for them, grateful for the slight reprieve from being so close to the communal toilet.

"Abeba, do you remember me?" Elen had whispered as soon as Halawit's attention shifted away. "I was with you in Wenjel Mermera."

Abeba's eyes widened with recognition, and she reached for Elen's hand, unshed tears brimming her eyes.

"Ajokhi," Elen said softly, squeezing her hand. "I'm with you."

The ally Abeba became to Elen was more than she had expected or hoped for, especially on wash day for their cell. Once a week, the women lined up outside the iron sheet structure built around the pit latrine before they washed. Under the watchful eyes of the guards, they kept conversation to a minimum, using the time to bask in the sun while they waited their turn.

The first woman in line had the unfortunate task of cleaning the bucket before her turn. Halawit selected who would do that job and enjoyed making her choice each week.

"You don't have much time, so I suggest you stop gawking and go," Halawit had told Elen as she pointed at the bucket on her first Sunday in Haz Haz. "Wash it over there, then wash off your filth," she sneered at her. "Although I doubt any amount of washing could clean the kind of filth you are."

Elen chose not to respond to her comments but had to break her silence after looking from the half-full bucket in the corner to the tap across the courtyard. "Where can I find soap to wash it?"

Halawit shook her head and turned to leave, her lips pursed in a half grimace. "No soap here."

Each woman had twenty minutes to wash. Elen would have to walk fifty feet to empty, wash, and fill the bucket at the tap, then carry the water into the metal stall with a pit latrine in the middle that served as a toilet and shower. Then she'd have to work her way around the pit latrine to shower.

That first Sunday, Elen hadn't even bathed. She got as far as dumping the bucket's contents in the pit latrine, then rinsing it with water at the tap as best as she could. Once filled, she tried to lift the bucket, but her numb fingers couldn't grip its weight. Before the bucket left the ground, she spilled most of the murky water as she carried it into the metal enclosure.

She had reached out to close the swinging door when the guard yelled, "Next!" Moments later, another woman burst in and grabbed the bucket.

The following week, she made it a little further in the process—though still nowhere near clean.

Halawit chose someone else to go first in the third week, allowing Elen time to place the bucket in the enclosure. This time, she didn't bother filling it.

Without a change of clothes, she could only wash her underwear and feet. The iron sheets around her caved and shook whenever she leaned on them for support. Her shifting center of gravity made her teeter every time she tried to lift a foot. In the end, she just poured water over her feet and watched it flow over the concrete slab and into the hole of the pit latrine before hearing the guard's familiar call: "Next!"

The following two Sundays were no better. She couldn't get past washing her feet and underwear. She wrung as much water out of her underwear as she could, then took it back to her cell to wait for it to dry. She was afraid to remove the now stained and browning dress Habteab had given her in Wenjel Mermera in case the next woman kicked her out of the stall naked.

She held up the wet underwear to dry, wondering if she was better off without it. She mourned the energetic young woman she had once been, with her choice of clothes, someone to help her do her laundry, and never spending a second thought on how to get a shower.

Elen let herself cry silently for what she had lost, for the children they had separated her from, for the baby that continued to grow inside her, possibly damaged, fatherless, and destined to be born in prison.

She passed the time in the cramped cell, holding her wet underwear in one hand and pumping her fingers with the other. It was strange to see her fingers move without feeling them. She was thankful when, eventually, some sensation returned.

Almak, maharana. Lord have mercy. Let me hold my child, she thought. Then she would pump her fists harder.

Occasionally, the women in the cell would fall silent at the sound of a whistle and explosion in the distance. Elen couldn't discern whether it was gunfire or something more significant. Some days were more intense than others. Some explosions were so close they could feel the ground vibrate beneath them.

Was the EPLF finally taking the city? She dismissed the thought when the explosions and gunfire continued for weeks before dying down.

Visions of Girmai haunted her nights until the sorrow overwhelmed her physical discomfort. She imagined him a prisoner like her, wasting away in the dark somewhere or riddled with bullets or—. The darkness inside the cell, the constant groaning and negotiation for space dulled her senses. All the women struggled to find comfort, whether alleviating pressure on body parts, giving others a chance to stretch, or simply shifting to create more space.

For her first few weeks at Haz Haz, Elen watched women receive packages from their families. The guard called out names, and the fortunate women negotiated their way across bodies to get to the door, dirty clothes in hand, ready for the exchange. Bags were tagged with the prisoner's name and location in the prison.

"How are they getting these packages?" Elen asked one of the women.

"Families bring them," the woman said. "They ask around at all the prisons in the city and, if we are lucky, they find us."

The guards delivered the items at their discretion after a thorough inspection. Elen often wondered if the women got everything their families sent.

The day Abeba arrived had been a day of gifts—distance from the bucket, a new friendship, and her first package. With Zimam transferred to another cell, Abeba was the only person Elen talked to at Haz Haz.

"Elen Ghebrekidan!" a guard had called from the cell entrance hours after Abeba came in. "Delivery."

Elen had struggled to stand that day, her movements slow as she carefully stepped over limbs. It took her a few moments to maneuver the short distance to the open door. Her back and body ached from hours fixed in the same position. Every night, she still slept sitting up to protect her swelling midriff from nighttime visits to the bucket.

The guard's hand rose to his nose as he waited for Elen to come closer.

Several bags lay at his feet. Behind him, another guard stood with a rifle at the ready. He handed her a thin mattress rolled up and tied with twine and a small cloth bag.

Elen had wedged the mattress under her arm and gripped the bag tightly, though it took a few moments to steady her shaking hands.

"Next delivery is in a week. You can exchange your dirty clothes then," the man had said.

"Who sent this?" she had asked, searching the guard's face, hoping for any kind of news.

"I don't know; I just deliver," he had said impatiently, picking up another bag from the pile at his feet. "Get back in."

She had waited until she was back in her spot and on her new mattress before opening the bag.

Elen's heart had skipped a beat as she imagined Girmai sending her the clothes. Just as quickly, the thought had vanished. The parcel had contained her favorite gabi and the two loose-fitting dresses from her closet, three pairs of underwear, and a bar of soap. The rosy scent of her past had fought against the stench of the bucket nearby.

It had to be Solomon. He was the only one who had access to her clothes.

"You will get yours soon," she had told Abeba. "I've been here for over a month, and this is my first package."

"I'm not getting anything," Abeba had said flatly. "My family is all dead."

It was the most Elen had heard her say about herself since the first time she saw her lying on the floor at Wenjel Mermera with her back ripped to shreds.

"Here, take this one," Elen had said as she handed Abeba the smaller of the two dresses. "It won't fit me, anyway," she had lied, patting her belly. "Tomorrow is wash day. We can both change then."

Abeba had stood behind her in line the next day and saw Elen struggling with the bucket.

"Can I help her wash?" she'd asked the guard beside the tap. "She's pregnant and can't do it on her own."

The guard had glanced at Elen, who was hunched over, her fingers clenching and unclenching around the bucket's metal handle as she prepared to lift it.

Abeba had sprung into action even before the guard finished his curt nod. Over the next five months, they had refined their washing ritual into an efficient routine. The shower stall became their weekly opportunity to speak freely, although they kept their conversations in whispers. Abeba told her how Derg soldiers had taken her parents from their home years earlier. She never saw them again. Abeba's much older siblings had already left to join the EPLF. She never saw them again either.

Abeba, without her aunt and caretaker's knowledge, joined a youth group that bombed a meat factory where the Derg routinely stored weapons.

"It burned to a crisp!" Abeba had whispered proudly. "We wreaked havoc where we could and fought the only way we knew how. I don't regret any of it. I did it for my parents. When I get out of here, I will go to the field and keep fighting."

The courts had sentenced Abeba to fifteen years in prison despite the lack of evidence linking her to the bombing. She had confessed to nothing during her beatings, and her interrogators eventually lost interest.

Elen wasn't quite sure how, but Abeba had her finger on the pulse of the prison dynamics. Her keen eyes and ears absorbed everything that went on in the cell.

Elen lowered her head to give Abeba access to scrub her neck and shoulders. The swells and curves of her pregnant body obscured the view of her swollen feet. She was long past being self-conscious. Her arms hung at her sides as she opened and closed her fingers.

"Halawit thinks she is the boss just because they made her the prison monitor," Abeba said, her voice dripping with disgust.

"She says you socialized with Derg generals and colonels and that there is no way you would be here unless it was to spy on us," Abeba continued in a whisper. "Such bullshit!"

Abeba was scrubbing Elen's arms now. Elen closed her eyes and let herself enjoy the rare sensation of being clean. She no longer thought about the murkiness of the water or the angry rash that had spread across her body.

"She makes everyone suspicious of each other," Abeba said, cupping water from the bucket with both hands and splashing it on Elen to rinse the soap off. "The Derg put her in charge of maintaining order with a promise of early release. She's always itching to turn someone in. Who does she think she is?"

Elen couldn't help but smile a little despite Abeba's words. The multiple lashes Abeba had taken on her back had done nothing to dampen her spirit.

Was I like that at her age?

Abeba finished scrubbing Elen's knees and ankles. She poured water over Elen's shoulders to rinse her off.

"It'll be okay," Elen said, struggling to believe her words as she scratched the rash on her arm. "The truth wins eventually."

Abeba used Elen's dirty dress to dry her off, then Elen quickly slipped into a clean dress.

"You need to stay away from her," Elen said. "We all just need to do what we can to get through this."

36

The cell door flew open and slammed into the outer wall, bouncing back toward the guard. He stopped it with his hand but quickly recoiled, bringing his hand to his nose to block the overpowering stench from inside the cell.

"Everyone out!" he shouted, without looking at anyone in particular. Elen quickly counted the days since the last wash day. They weren't due for another one yet.

No one moved.

"Are you all deaf?" He unslung his rifle and aimed it into the room. "I said get outside, all of you!"

The number of bodies packed into the cell made it impossible for everyone to get up simultaneously without falling into someone else. Elen shielded her belly. The rolls and kicks she'd felt over the past few months confirmed the baby was alive; this child was a fighter, defying all the odds.

"Out, all of you. Now!"

Elen couldn't get up fast enough. Panic surged through her as women tripped over each other and into her as they scrambled to stand.

Elen and Abeba had moved a few more places down the line from the bucket, so sleeping wasn't as hazardous as when she first arrived. She still slept sitting up every night, just in case. By her calculations, delivery was a matter of days. The baby sat low in her womb, and she felt the end-of-pregnancy pressure on her back.

She fought against the tide of bodies flowing to the door and scrambled to her knees, hunching over to protect her child. She cried out in pain as feet stepped on her fingers.

"Here," Abeba said.

Elen grasped Abeba's hand, pulling herself up like she was climbing a rope until she was finally upright. She leaned against the wall and waited for the last of the women to go before she started moving.

We've come this far, my little one. A stampede is not how this story ends.

They started walking after the last woman shuffled forward.

Elen hesitated when she reached the doorway, looking back at the bare room. She had never seen it empty. Thin, faded mattresses lay stained and worn all over the floor. The bucket sat in the corner by the door, as it always did.

This is no bigger than my bedroom. How did fifty of us fit in here?

The guard had slung his rifle back on his shoulder and watched them stream out. Armed men in Derg army uniforms stood in a line, rifles aimed.

"Anyone with a sentence of two years and over line up here," the guard said. He pointed at an empty spot in the courtyard close to the pit latrine. "Move. Now!"

Elen glanced at Abeba, whose expression mirrored her fear. The women obediently peeled off and followed the guard's finger to the other side of the courtyard. Elen squeezed Abeba's hand as they walked with the group.

Are they going to kill us?

The baby was especially heavy today. She laced her fingers underneath the bulge to relieve the strain on her back. The swelling in her hands and feet had gotten worse.

"What's happening?" Abeba whispered to no one in particular.

Elen searched Halawit's face for clues as she turned to stand in line. Halawit's forehead was contorted into a frown, her darting eyes revealing her confusion.

Elen scooted her toes further into the flip-flops that barely contained her swollen feet and inched closer to Abeba at the back of the group. She laced her fingers tighter and swayed to calm herself.

What a sight I must be! Is this how I will look when I die?

The vanity in the thought made her almost want to laugh at its absurdity. The quick flutter against her fingers sobered her back up quickly.

God help us.

The shuffling stopped after a few minutes. The other doors in the prison remained shut and silent.

The guard walked over to them. "If you are in this group, you have two minutes to collect your belongings and get into that truck." He pointed at the huge military truck parked close to the prison's entrance. He then turned to the group of women serving less than two years. "You stay here until they finish collecting their things. Abraha, record the names of the ones remaining. I will get the others to the truck."

"Where are we going?" Elen heard a voice behind her as they walked back to the cell.

"Shut up, or I can come over there and shut you up!"

Elen dared not look at who the voices belonged to. She followed Abeba back to pack what little they could. She rolled her mattress and grabbed the bag with extra clothes.

They can't mean to kill us if they are making us collect our things.

Maneuvering around the room was less chaotic without the entire group of women. Each rushed to grab what they could. They filed out, heading to the truck, where armed guards stood.

A guard by the truck supervised each woman's ascent. Elen pinned the rolled-up mattress under her arm, and by the time she reached the truck, her arms shook with the effort of carrying its weight. She set the bag down to adjust it as she waited for the women ahead of her to climb on.

One by one, the women threw their belongings onto the truck bed, hooked their toes into the ladder in the back, then hoisted themselves up. Those who got in stretched their arms down to help others climb up.

Elen stared at the metal rung that was a foothold into the truck.

There's no way I can reach that. Her breath caught in her throat as a fresh wave of panic shuddered through her body.

It was too high. Elen couldn't lift her leg enough to climb in.

"Keep moving!" The butt of a rifle prodded her shoulder.

Two women angled around her. Elen watched as one of them missed the rung multiple times before finally managing to hook on to it. Several arms reached down from the truck to help them up.

Abeba climbed up nimbly without help and then turned to Elen immediately. "Give me your things," she motioned to her. Come on, throw it over. I'll help you."

Elen lifted her threadbare mattress first, then her bag. Abeba grabbed both quickly and shoved them aside.

"You can do it, come," she cast a worried glance at the guard Elen could feel standing behind her.

"Go!" his rifle prodded Elen forward. She was the only one left.

She stretched both hands up. More hands joined Abeba's and wrapped around Elen's arms. They lifted her until she could hook her foot into the first rung. She turned slightly so that the metal of the truck bed scraped her side and not her belly on her way up. She finally found her footing and hoisted herself the rest of the way over.

Elen hadn't yet caught her breath when the truck's metal doors slammed shut. As in the cell, the air was thick with their collective breath, bodies pressed close, legs and limbs overlapping in every direction.

From the darkness, a voice began to pray. "Our Father who art in Heaven, hallowed be Thy name. Your kingdom come, Your will be done ..."

Others joined as the engine revved and jerked the truck forward. Prayers continued for the almost hour-long journey through the city until the truck came to a stop and the engine cut out.

The doors opened to reveal the back of an open cargo plane several feet away. The lowered ramp led to an immense hold, empty except for a few crates and sacks tied down toward the front.

"Get out, all of you!"

Climbing down was easier than getting into the truck. Several rifles pointed at the group as they filed into the plane. The propellers whirred loudly, drowning out any chance of hearing what the guards might be saying.

Several women found spots to sit on the floor along the sides of the plane, holding on to anything tied or bolted down. Elen hobbled toward the front of the aircraft, her side throbbing where the metal of the truck had scraped against it as the women pulled her up. Unable to keep the mattress wedged in the crook of her arm, she let it slip and unfurl on the floor.

Abeba quickly moved it next to a crate and motioned for Elen to sit. Elen lowered herself and held on to the netting anchored to the wall. Another woman was sitting beside her, so Abeba had to find space by Elen's feet.

The ramp moved up and locked them in the dark with a bang. A small overhead lamp and the small windows along the walls gave them enough light to see each other.

Moments later, the plane's acceleration sent all those who hadn't yet found something to hold on to flying towards the back of the plane. Abeba grasped Elen's feet to keep herself from rolling all the way back, and Elen, her arms wrapped around the netting, strained to hold on.

As the plane leveled off, women slowly crawled back toward the front netting and huddled together as the cold set in. Elen wrapped her gabi tighter around herself and draped her legs over Abeba's outstretched ones to anchor her down.

They could barely hold on to each other as turbulence jerked the plane in all directions and they struggled to stay in place whenever the plane banked.

"I heard we are being transferred because the EPLF is planning a prison break," the woman beside Elen spoke. "They wanted all the political prisoners out."

"But where could they be taking us?" another voice asked.

"What about the rest who stayed?" another chimed in.

"God only knows what they plan to do with us."

Halawit held no power here as the voices floated back and forth in the dark. The women let go of the reserve that had kept them quiet in Haz Haz. The uncertainty of what lay ahead loosened their tongues.

This can't be the end. It just can't.

Screams reverberated in the hold as the plane dipped into a descent, throwing everyone up and slamming them back down with each air pocket.

Elen squeezed her eyes shut and held on to the ropes. Abeba scrambled to adjust and gripped Elen's knees to keep from sliding forward.

Elen willed her numb fingers to wrap tighter around the netting and whispered a prayer of gratitude for Abeba beside her.

The wheels screeched on contact with the tarmac, and everything went flying forward again as the brakes hit.

They kept careening forward until the plane slowed to a taxi.

They had landed.

But where?

"Are you okay?" Elen asked Abeba.

"I am fine, you?"

Elen nodded. They looked around as women began rooting around their scattered belongings. Too exhausted to care, Elen laid her head back on the netting.

"You lost your flip-flops," Abeba said as she left Elen's side to join the other women in their search. "I'll find them for you."

The back ramp of the plane slowly groaned open until it hit the ground with a loud clang. A line of armed soldiers stood on either side.

"Get out now!" a voice barked as Abeba helped Elen put her flip-flops onto her swollen feet.

She summoned all the strength she had left to stand.

Abeba had found her bag and handed it to her. There was no time to grab the mattress.

Together, they walked out of the plane into the crisp night.

Above them, illuminated brightly across the top of a multistory building, was a familiar sign: *Bole International Airport. Addis Ababa.*

***

"We can't be going to our deaths, can we?" Abeba asked her. They were in another truck, which had been easier to climb into.

"They probably would have done it in Asmara," Elen replied, forcing more confidence in her voice than she felt.

The women were tossed into each other as the truck bounced on uneven roads. Elen strained her ears for any sound of the city, hoping to hear something familiar but only the silence of curfew reached her. She imagined families huddled together in the dark, hoping the Derg would not choose to pay a visit.

What are we doing in Addis?

Elen's thoughts left the truck and settled on a happy memory of when she was here with Girmai.

Girmai had gone to a business meeting and had left her in the hotel to freshen up. Elen had put all her effort into looking her best as she got ready for dinner. Her eyes were heavy with kohl, the way he liked it. She wore red platform shoes decorated with interwoven crosses. Gold bangles and red-jeweled gold earrings finished the look.

They had visited Alem and her Melak for the first time and shared drinks in their cozy living room before Alem called them to the dinner table, which overlooked a small courtyard. Alem had slaughtered a goat to honor their visit and prepared a feast: a dozen sauces and steaming-hot injera.

Just as he sat down, Girmai remembered he hadn't washed his hands. Always quick in his movements, he had leaped up—only to slam his head on the sharp corner of the window Alem had opened earlier to let in the breeze.

The deep cut bled profusely, throwing everyone into a panic as they rushed to stop the bleeding. When they finally settled back down, Girmai had a large folded towel tied around his head, comically secured with another cloth under his chin.

Their concern had melted into laughter when Girmai, ever the joker, danced around with the towel tied to his head.

"Watch out for that window!" became a catchphrase between them after that.

Elen longed for that ache in her belly that came from laughing so hard. She grabbed Abeba's hand tighter and held on to the memory until the truck stopped.

Elen craned her neck to make out what the voices outside were saying. It sounded like they were exchanging information about transfers from Haz Haz. Gates groaned open ahead of them, and the truck jerked forward.

They drove for several more minutes before the driver hit the brakes, sending everyone tumbling forward once more. Elen fell onto Abeba, who, in turn, crashed into someone else.

The truck doors opened to the biting night air. Elen squinted through the dark, catching only a few scattered lights in the distance. She followed the line of women through a narrow passageway and into what looked like a semicircular courtyard. Tall corrugated-iron sheets stretched along the edges, cutting off the view beyond.

Huts built from a mix of mud and iron sheets dotted one side of the courtyard. The semicircle was completed by rows of doors lining a two-story building.

Elen held onto Abeba's hand as they were herded forward until a guard pointed directly at her.

"You! Follow me." The guard jerked his rifle at Elen impatiently.

Elen kept her vice grip on Abeba's hand and pulled her to come along.

"Not her, just you."

Reluctantly, she let go of Abeba's hand. This was not the moment to resist.

"We will find each other," Abeba called after her as she followed the other line of women. "Ajokhi, everything will be okay. God is with you."

Elen shivered in the cold as she followed the guard through the courtyard. She regretted leaving her mattress behind on the plane. It would have been a small comfort in the nights ahead.

Will Alem know I'm here? Does Solomon know I'm gone?

Elen imagined her brother being turned away at the Haz Haz prison gates. They would give him the line they gave to visitors when their family members had died inside the prison walls: "She won't need this anymore."

Will he think I'm dead?

Elen wiped her eyes as they entered the building—narrow hallways lined with metal doors, each with small openings sealed by hatches. Muffled sounds filtered through the closed doors, and the occasional low moan.

The guard stopped at a door, put a key in the keyhole, and swung it open.

He motioned for Elen to enter. "Welcome to Alem Bekagn prison," he said, his tone laced with sarcasm.

Alem Bekagn.

Elen's heart skipped a beat at the infamous prison's name. The place of no return. The place where those who enter suffer so much they give up on living.

The place that is the end of their world.

37

Asmara to Rome, 1979

Tracking the days was too painful. Every second that ticked, every step took Girmai further away from everything he had allowed himself to love.

A continent away from Elen now, he'd lost count of the days and months since he last saw her.

With every milestone he had passed in his escape from Eritrea, all the cells in his body raged to go back, to do anything other than what he was doing—running away.

Getting to Italy had been fraught with lucky coincidences, secret meetings to arrange fake passes, money exchanges, and constant hiding and moving from a certain death sentence.

Kifle had traveled with him for several weeks, as far as the EPLF truck would take them, about one hundred kilometers inland.

"Abdusalam here will take you to Khartoum," Kifle had told Girmai as he said goodbye beside a deserted shack a few meters from the road, still clouded in dust from the wheels of their truck. "You can trust him."

Parting with Kifle in the barren desert had been harder than Girmai had prepared for. Kifle had saved them both from betraying their emotions when he turned and walked away after a quick shoulder tap without looking back.

Girmai had watched the truck disappear into the mirage that blurred the horizon before he followed Abdusalam to a waiting pickup truck on the side of the road.

“I work at the EPLF office in Khartoum,” Abdusalam had shouted over the rattling parts of the old double-cabin truck bouncing on the rough road in the opposite direction.

Though Abdusalam’s tone had been even and casual, the tension in his movements put Girmai on high alert. They were not safe yet.

“This area can be unpredictable,” Abdusalam admitted when Girmai had pressed him for the truth. His eyes constantly darted from one side of the road to the other. “We need to be careful. Derg collaborators are everywhere and people will do anything for a few birr.”

“Don’t worry,” Abdusalam said, looking back from the front passenger seat, his half-smile unconvincing. “We will get you to Khartoum in one piece.”

The driver had yet to say a word. Girmai nodded and twisted to look through the back window, beyond the sack-filled bed of the pickup truck, to the road that had brought him here.

The wind picked up the dust from the wheels and spread it into an immense cloud that spread up and out behind them.

“They’ll definitely see us coming,” he’d said, pointing his thumb at the cloud.

“Don’t worry,” Abdusalam said again, more for his than for Girmai’s benefit, Girmai had thought.

“We are on a well-used trade route, and the occasional car or truck here is not unusual. It’s the villages and towns we need to worry about. Negotiations won’t work if they catch us. The reward for turning people in is high, and this drought has made people desperate.” He had given Girmai a tight smile.

Hours later, the driver dropped them off at what looked like an abandoned hut about a kilometer from the outskirts of a village. A few triangular pieces of himbasha bread and a bottle of water lay just inside the entrance.

“We have people here,” Abdusalam had explained as he handed him some himbasha.

They spent the night there and hitchhiked from one town to the next. They sometimes stayed in a village for several days until Abdusalam decided it was safe to move on. Girmai never knew what he based his decisions on.

Further and further away.

When they arrived in Khartoum, Abdusalam led him to a shack in the middle of a bustling marketplace.

"You need to register at this EPLF office before I can take you to the safe house," Abdusalam said as he parted the beaded curtain leading into the hut.

The beads reflected the afternoon sun into Girmai's eyes as he walked into the darkened hut.

"Welcome, my brother." A young man seated behind a small table leaned forward, his elbows on a notebook. "God has brought you all this way; we trust in your continued safety."

Girmai thanked him, suppressing the sudden burn of tears.

"Here," the man said as he handed Girmai a pen and turned the notebook to a new page.

Girmai registered his information, confirming his new status as a refugee, and walked back out to Abdusalam.

"You must stay in the safe house," Abdusalam said. "Informants are everywhere. We have had a couple of abductions over the past few weeks."

"Isn't it dangerous to write my name back there, then?" Girmai asked as he followed him through a crowded street.

"They will transfer the information quickly and destroy the evidence," Abdusalam said. "The office will arrange to get your paperwork sorted soon. Once you have that, hopefully everything else will work out."

* * *

"Soon" turned out to be more than four months of waiting to get the life-saving paperwork—his passport, business-ownership papers, and a list of his assets on hand so he would be ready for his visa appointment at the Italian embassy.

Girmai had sat across from the Italian consul, hoping that what he had submitted for his visa application would be enough to get him a ticket to freedom.

"Why are you visiting Italy?" the man had asked, pulling Girmai's passport toward him and flipping through the pages of multiple Italian visas.

Girmai couldn't help but stare at the man's hands hovering over the documents he had submitted. He tried to focus on responding to his questions rather than on how much of his life those papers represented.

He took a deep breath and exhaled, grateful for the EPLF network's ingenuity in getting everything he needed here.

He had wanted so badly to tell the truth.

I am leaving because I can't go back. The Derg will kill me if I do. They will kill me after they've tortured me for all the information I have. Then Elen, my baby—if it is alive—and many others will die too.

I am leaving because I need to get my family out safely. Do you know I just left them behind? Yes, I did, and I just can't leave things this way. I am leaving so I can fix this. I will get them all out and continue fighting for our freedom wherever I am.

Instead, Girmai had cleared his throat and said, "I will meet some of my business contacts in Rome. As you can see, I have been to Italy several times."

"Why are you in Khartoum? This is not where you live, correct?" The man had raised his eyes to look at Girmai over the rim of his glasses, his head still inclined toward the papers.

There it was. The big question: what are you doing here?

Girmai had glanced at the man's hands—softer and more relaxed than his clenched fists under the table. These were the hands of someone who had only ever known comfort.

"I'm thinking of expanding my business to Khartoum," he had lied smoothly. "The information I've gathered tells me it's a great market, but I must meet with my suppliers in Italy to see what can be done to set up a branch here."

The man had put the passport aside and looked through the Expo 69 ownership paperwork Girmai had included in the application. This was proof of his ties to Asmara—proof that he wasn't seeking refuge in Italy like thousands of other Eritreans and Ethiopians.

"How long do you intend to stay?"

"Only a month." Girmai had lied again, this time more confidently. "I should be able to get everything done within that time."

The man had stared at Girmai for a moment as if thinking of what to ask next. With a sharp breath, he'd said, "I will review your case." He tucked all the papers into a folder, placed Girmai's passport on top, and tapped his index finger on it. "Come back in a week."

Girmai returned to the safe house and waited.

An eternity of a week later, he'd stood in front of the secretary at the front desk, steadying his hands as she handed him his passport and papers.

"Have a safe trip," she'd said with a smile.

Visa granted. *Time to leave.*

***

A few days later, he landed in Rome, dropped his bag in his hotel room, and went straight to the refugee center, which he knew provided low-cost services, including limited international phone calls.

"The phone is in the office down the hall," the custodian told Girmai, pointing his crooked finger at the entrance of a crowded room.

"Write your name in the logbook over there, then take a seat," the old man said in Italian. Girmai understood enough Italian from his multiple trips to Italy over the years. "Once you register with the receptionist, she'll tell you how to make your call."

Chairs lined the large reception area of the refugee center three rows deep, from one end of the long room to the other.

"Good luck," the man said. "I hope you get through." The corners of his lips pursed downward with a knowing expression. The quick show of sympathy triggered an unexpected lump in Girmai's throat.

Behind the counter, the frazzled young Italian receptionist stared at a woman on the other side holding a baby. Girmai couldn't tell if it was a girl or a boy as it writhed in its mother's arms and screamed at the top of its lungs. The woman didn't seem to notice her baby's noise as she dabbed at her eyes and spoke rapidly in Arabic.

Girmai headed toward the large logbook on one end of the counter. He wrote his name using the pen tied to the book with a piece of yarn.

Reason for visit: *I need to call home.*

"Where do you want to call?" the receptionist asked in Italian when he finally got to the counter after what seemed like hours of waiting.

"Eritrea."

"The phone is over there." She handed him a ticket and pointed to a hallway a few feet from the furthest row of chairs. "When the person talking right now is done, you may make your call. You have ten minutes."

The woman carrying the baby was sitting on a chair facing the phone on a small table, staring out the window as she spoke softly. The baby was now limp in her lap, deep in sleep.

Life is already so tough for you, little one, Girmai thought, looking at the fuzz of curly hair peeking out from under the knit cap in the crook of the woman's arm. What he wouldn't give to hold his baby just like this. *Did my baby survive? Did Elen?* He could think of nothing else.

Girmai stayed at a respectful distance until she hung up and walked out, then rushed to the phone. He quickly dialed Berhane's number. Daniel moved around too much and he didn't want to risk calling an empty house. With each rotation of the rotary dial, he said a quick prayer and hoped Berhane was home.

"It's me," Girmai said when Berhane picked up. "I'm out."

Berhane said nothing, but breathed hard into the phone. Was Berhane being hesitant because the Derg had tapped his phone? They all took precautions to make sure that wasn't the case. It was unlike his friend to be so distant after all they had gone through together, after all this time apart.

"Berhane. It's me. I called to say that I'm—"

"Daniel is dead."

The words landed on his ear so softly that Girmai refused to believe he had heard them. He stretched the phone cable, circled the table, and leaned his head against the window. His breath fogged the view of the passersby on the street below.

"What happened?" His mind flashed back to the last time he saw Daniel.

I know we will do great things … Don't lose hope. We will be victorious … This is where we part ways …

"They caught him in the middle of an operation," Berhane said, his voice shaky. "It was an ambush."

Girmai put a finger to his other ear to block out the conversations behind him and clutched the receiver tighter.

"They really got him bad, Girmai. We couldn't save him."

Daniel had always been the one getting people out.

"They tortured him for almost a week, but he didn't talk. He succumbed to his injuries yesterday."

Girmai's eyes followed people walking on the street below, the normality of their lives making the news of his friend's painful death feel like fiction.

"I'm glad you're safe," Berhane continued. "Sorry to give you such bad news. We just heard. There was no bigger patriot; he did so much to advance our cause. We are grateful for him and his contributions."

"Yes," Girmai managed, the momentary elation at hearing Berhane's voice after months of running long gone.

What was I doing while my friend was dying? Hiding? Running away?

Behind him, two men hunched over a chess game in a recreation room beyond the hallway, children played with some overused toys in a corner, and women huddled together, whispering and laughing.

This isn't a fight, Girmai thought bitterly. *What am I doing here?*

Daniel's voice from their conversation in the valley came back to him: "To fight, we must survive."

He swallowed the tension rising from his chest. "What about my family?"

"They are all fine," Berhane said. "The Derg has let the factory continue to function for now. Araya is doing a good job of keeping the finances flowing. The kebele officials published a notice in the newspaper that all your properties will be up for auction next month. We've made arrangements. No one will purchase them."

"Thank you," Girmai said, nodding as if Berhane were in the room with him. He took a deep breath, preparing himself for the answer to his next question.

"Have you heard anything about Elen?"

The seconds dragged by before Berhane's response came through.

"They transferred her to Alem Bekagn a few days ago."

She is alive.

He went still and gripped the phone tighter at the mention of the name of the prison. The moment folded in on itself and it became hard to breathe. He didn't want to think about what he knew about that place.

"I just found out. The warden at Haz Haz got wind of the breakout plans we had for our people in Haz Haz. Someone must have talked. They transferred all the political prisoners with sentences longer than two years. Solomon is keeping the bar open and is taking care of Faven and Aman. I told him about Elen's transfer, and he called Alem to see if she could visit."

"How is she? Is the baby okay?" Girmai's head pounded. He needed to process the news about Daniel but had to get as much information as he could in his ten minutes of phone time.

"I have limited information, but as far as I know, she was heavily pregnant when she got on the plane to Addis. They have put her in the section of Alem Bekagn for pregnant women, new mothers, and members of the royal family they detained. The conditions are better there than in the other sections.

“Unfortunately,” Berhane continued, “there is no way to get her out. I am afraid she will have to stay until the end of her sentence. Our network in Addis is thin, especially after the withdrawal. She has two years left. The prison allows limited packages, so you can send her something small.”

Girmai closed his eyes and stretched his neck. The smudge Girmai’s forehead left on the windowpane blurred the passersby below. *She doesn’t even know I’m alive.*

Girmai’s brain suddenly kicked into gear. “I’ll call Alem and let her know I’m here. I need to figure out what to do next. I’m too far from everything here. I’ll try to get closer to get them all out.”

“Don’t set foot in Addis,” Berhane quickly warned him. “Though they haven’t extended the search there, the warrant for your arrest is still active in Asmara. Don’t take any chances.”

“I was thinking of going to Nairobi.” On his journey out of Eritrea, Girmai had heard about the growing Eritrean community in Kenya’s capital. It would be the support network he needed to put a plan together. Eritreans could get residency papers there and start a new life. He could also start a new business that wasn’t an ocean away from everyone he loved.

This isn’t any different from the other times I have started over. I can do it.

In just seconds, he was several steps into a plan, plotting how he would sell his assets in Italy and transfer everything to Kenya.

“Who do we know in Nairobi?” he asked Berhane as he glanced at his watch.

Five minutes left.

“We have people there I can put you in touch with,” Berhane responded without hesitation. “Derg spies are plentiful in Nairobi too, but they won’t be able to do anything to you once you have residency papers. You need to arrange that as soon as you arrive.”

“Thank you,” Girmai said, realizing he hadn’t asked Berhane how he was doing. “Hey, is your family okay?”

“We are hanging in there,” Berhane replied with a sigh. “The Derg has gone rabid with their Red Terror attacks. It is a wonder that we still have people left in this city. We have lost count of how many of our people they detained or killed. It is definitely in the thousands at this point. They've emptied the city. All the youth are gone, either to the field or into detention centers."

"Will you be leaving too?" Girmai asked him. "Maybe you should join me in Nairobi."

"I might get my family out if conditions are right," he said, "but I must stay for now. We are making progress here."

Girmai knew the EPLF had suffered massive losses. He shuddered to think about how many of those young people had died in the Derg offensive and the strategic withdrawal. To be pushed back so aggressively when they were so close to Asmara had been demoralizing for the entire movement.

"I met Kifle in Sudan," Girmai said, changing the subject.

"Oh, yeah?" Berhane's voice brightened. "How is that rascal doing?"

"He is as fine as one can be out there," Girmai said, suddenly missing his friend. "He seems to have learned his way around that area and has a new life now."

We all have to start again now.

"Let's keep in touch," he told Berhane as he looked at his watch again. "I need to call Alem now."

"Her phone line might be bugged," Berhane said. "You never know who is listening. Be careful what you say."

"I will," he said. "Thanks, friend. I'll call you next week at the same time. Hopefully, I'll have a plan by then. Stay safe."

He hung up the phone and picked up the receiver again.

Four minutes.

A man stood in line right by the row of chairs, waiting for his turn for the phone. Girmai quickly dialed Alem's number.

"Hello?"

"Alem?"

"Who is this?" The quiver in her voice spoke volumes.

"This is your friend. Do you not recognize my voice? I've just called to say hello."

"I don't know who you are," she said and hung up.

They must have already questioned her.

He put the handset down, picked it up, then dialed again.

"Hello?"

"Before you hang up," he said quickly, "watch out for that window!"

Silence.

Then her sobs broke through the static. "Oh my God! Oh my God! Oh my God!" she cried. "We thought we would never hear from you again!"

Girmai used his free hand to wipe the tears that welled up at the sound of her crying. The man in line for the phone locked eyes with him, then respectfully stepped back.

Girmai hunched over the receiver.

"I am so happy to hear from you!" Alem said when she caught her breath. "Where are you? Are you okay?"

"I am safe," he said, not completely answering her question. "How is our friend doing?"

"I visited her last Sunday," Alem replied. "She is so strong! I took her some food and a change of clothes for her and the baby. It looks like she's due any day now."

Light-headed, he lowered himself onto the chair beside the table and bent over his knees, his heartbeat pulsating through his whole body.

"Visiting hours are only once a week," he heard Alem say. "They didn't allow us to talk for long, but I am glad I laid eyes on her. She will be so happy with this news!" Her words tumbled over each other in her rush to get them out between her sobs.

She is alive. The baby is alive. He closed his eyes.

A boat, bobbing in the low tide, appeared before him. Anchored in low waters, waiting for the right time to sail toward the horizon.

"Alem?" His fingers ached from how tightly he held the receiver. He covered a tear stain on his pants with his elbow and wiped his eyes with his free hand. "Tell her I … I—"

He covered his quivering chin and tried to swallow the weight of the emotion expanding in his chest.

"I will give her your love," Alem finished for him. "She will be so happy!"

He cleared his throat. He had little time left on the phone.

"The baby," he said. "Tell her to name the baby Hiyab; I will tell her why when we meet again."

"Okay, I will."

"Alem?" he said. "Tell her we *will* meet again."

38

Alem Bekagn prison, Addis Ababa, 19 January 1979

Elen's eyes flew open as her abdomen tightened. She struggled into a sitting position, the sharp metal springs of her cot digging through the thin mattress into her skin.

"Oh my God," she gasped into the semi-darkness of the cell.

"Are you okay?" Tsion asked from the cot beside her. The coils under her mattress also squeaked in protest at her movements.

Elen tried to turn to look at her cellmate, but the pain radiating up from her sides immobilized her. More springs creaked as women stirred.

It had been ten days since Elen arrived at Alem Bekagn. Seeing all the mothers with their children in prison had crushed her.

All these kids are growing up here!

Elen had five cellmates. Tsion Andom, sister of General Aman Andom, had been arrested soon after her brother's death in a shootout at his home. Milite, a new mother, who lay furthest from Elen. Her six-month-old baby's constant suckling noises gave Elen a small measure of comfort, showing that it was possible to raise a baby in this place. Girmanesh, the other pregnant woman on the block, slept beside Milite.

"I'm almost as far along as you," Girmanesh had said to Elen when they met, her pregnancy almost unnoticeable under her loose dress.

Sister Hawelti and Sister Jember, nuns with medical experience, occupied the other two cots.

"The Derg's fear of the educated got us locked up here," Sister Jember had volunteered on Elen's first day. "They imprisoned us for crimes we haven't yet committed."

Although Elen and her cellmates slept on flimsy cots, she knew this wasn't the case for everyone at Alem Bekagn. The conditions in many other parts of the prison were very similar to the horror she had left behind in Haz Haz.

Being here is a luxury, Elen had told herself. *I have a bed, space, and a toilet far from where I sleep.*

As the contractions grew stronger, she repeated her gratitude over and over.

Though they couldn't see the men's sections, Elen had seen the cramped metal structures built to accommodate the overflow of prisoners. The women there slept on damp mattresses and battled lice that jumped from one person to the next. They used their time outside to dry their possessions in the sun every day.

Abeba was one of them.

"Let's count our blessings," Abeba had said when they embraced in the communal courtyard for the first time after their separation. "At least we can see each other during the day, and you are in a much better place now."

"Yes," Elen had agreed, hugging her tightly.

"Have you seen Halawit or the other women on the plane with us?"

"Some are with me, but I think many are on the other side," Abeba had told her.

Elen dreaded the nightly signal to return to their cells. The chilling nights left her on the wiry cot exposed to her nightmares, shapeshifting and rolling in her head one after another through each sleepless night.

And now this. I can't bring a baby into this.

Elen collapsed against the icy concrete wall when the contraction finally released its hold.

"Thank you, I'm okay," she said to Tsion and the others. She breathed through her mouth, making as little noise as possible. "Go back to sleep."

"Is it time? We need to call for help," Milite said.

"No, no. It's fine. I can wait until morning."

Milite's baby whimpered, and Elen focused on the gurgling sounds he made as he nursed to quiet her rising panic.

Focus on the positive.

She closed her eyes and thought of the courtyard, where the sun shone bright and the women found things to laugh about. A dozen children under five would run around, weaving between the women sitting together to wash their clothes in tubs with soap sent from home. Elen had brief moments when she forgot she was in a prison.

She quickly befriended Tsion, a woman who spoke her mind and instantly reminded Elen of her aunt Tsehay, who had once shown her a world of possibilities.

Tsion radiated beauty despite her shapeless dress and loosened braids. Elen had heard about this legendary woman. A renowned fashion icon, Tsion founded Tsion Tibeb, an Ethiopian fashion house that first made its name by blending traditional Ethiopian designs with modern '60s cuts.

"I've been here three years now, and who knows how much longer I have. They didn't even give me a trial," Tsion had said, blowing out a long breath. "I miss being creative, so I do needle-work whenever I can. It helps take my mind off this place. I'll make something as soon as I find some cloth," Tsion had promised, her eyes lingering on Elen's swollen belly.

Now, Tsion was whispering prayers in the dark, her voice calm and soothing. Faint moonlight filtered through a high window on one side, the courtyard lamp illuminating the other, its yellow light contrasting with the moon's blue.

Elen kept her body still as she looked around the room. The cots were close but not touching—a luxury after months of fighting for space in Haz Haz.

She caressed her belly with both hands. Her abdomen tightened again, as if a fist had taken hold of her lower back and begun squeezing its way to the center of her belly, the sharpness of the radiating pain forcing her upright.

"Oooff!" She exhaled sharply, but nothing would ease the pain.

"Elen!" Tsion sat up. "Is it time?"

Speaking was not an option now. Elen groaned as a spasm erupted at the base of her spine, pulling her abdomen taut. Her fists shook, gripping her dress as she swung her legs over the side of the cot, hoping a new position would help.

It didn't. She rocked back and forth until the pain subsided. Tsion was standing beside her, a hand on Elen's shoulder.

"It's gone now," Elen said.

"Do you think you can last until morning?" Sister Jember asked, also appearing at her side.

"I hope so," Elen replied, pulling her legs back on the cot and leaning against the wall.

She didn't want to call attention to herself. The night guards were on duty and, while they patrolled the hallways, it was unlikely that they'd open the cell door at this hour. Nothing good ever came from the doors opening at night.

Baby, please stay inside a little longer, just until morning.

She clutched her belly and forced herself to think of a good memory as the women shuffled back to their cots.

Alem had visited for the first time the previous Sunday. *Was that almost a week ago already*? Elen closed her eyes to replay the events of that morning, minute by minute.

Everyone in her cell had a visitor. They had followed the guard and eventually joined the other prisoners, who walked shoulder to shoulder to an open area enclosed by a fence. Elen's breath frosted in the early-morning chill as she walked to the fence standing before a deep ditch that separated the prisoners from their visitors.

Elen had no idea who even knew she was there. The crowd surged forward, rushing to the fence. Those who didn't make it to the front had to make do by shouting over those in front to talk to their family on the other side.

Elen locked eyes with Alem just as she braced herself against the fence with both arms to keep her belly from being crushed.

Her sister had been further down the line, struggling to push through the crowd.

"Please, I need to see my sister!" Alem shouted. Pushing and shoving, she inched closer to her side of the fence until she finally stood a few feet away from Elen, clinging to the wire.

"Alem!" Elen had screamed, pushing against the relentless pressure gluing her to the fence. "Please!" she yelled. "I am pregnant! Stop pushing!"

Her plea went unheard over everyone's shouting.

"Elen!" Alem shouted over the throng of people also pressing her into the fence.

"Ajokhi, haftey ma'arey, my dear, sweet sister. You are going to be okay," she said, rivulets of tears streaking her cheeks. "Stay strong. Don't cry!"

"Alem!" Her face slammed against the wire fence as a woman behind her pushed forward to get closer. All Elen could do was look at Alem through the wire and sob. She pushed her fingers through, desperate to touch her.

"Alem!" The name felt like it dropped into the ditch between them, hundreds of voices stifling hers. "Alem!" she yelled louder.

"When I come next Sunday, I will bring a change of clothes for you and the baby," Alem shouted over the din. "They said I could also send food. I will make you some nice injera, okay? Tell me what else you need."

The guards began to usher the visitors away from the fence before Elen could respond. She hadn't asked about Girmai, Faven, or Solomon. There hadn't been time for anything—except tears.

Elen shifted in her cot again and winced at the loud squeaks beneath her.

How many days away is Sunday? Elen tried to remember, breathing in heavily and massaging her belly.

"When it is your time, they will take you to the clinic," Milite said, cutting into Elen's thoughts. "It's not that far from here. We are with you, ajokhi. Look at me. Do you see? My baby is okay. It will all be well, God willing."

Milite's baby was quietly suckling in the darkness.

Will all be well? Elen wondered. *How can it be? How can anything be well when this child is to be born into fatherless suffering?*

Her eyes grew heavy as she leaned against the wall. She had barely settled when the next wave hit. Her back seized so suddenly she sat up straight, the movement faster than any she had made in months. The muscles around her spine cramped until she felt like she was ripping apart.

"I'm calling the guards," Sister Jember said. The springs in her cot squeaked as she got up.

"No," Elen said, agony drowning her words. "Please, I don't want trouble."

"You need help. We can't do this on our own. This baby is coming, and we don't even have any water in here!"

Elen's ears filled with her own groans. She was vaguely aware of movement around her.

"No, don't, please," she whispered through gritted teeth.

But Sister Jember was already banging on the door.

"No," Elen tried again, shaking her head as she clutched her belly. *What if they decide to torture me now?* Fear clawed at her. *What if they have been waiting all this time just to kill my baby?*

Sister Jember's banging brought the guard to the door. When he opened the peephole, a soft light streamed onto her face. It quickly darkened again as the guard peered inside.

"What is all this noise about?"

"Elen is in labor," Sister Jember said. "She needs to go to the clinic right away. The baby is coming."

"There's nothing I can do about that," the man replied flatly. "All the keys are with the prison warden, who is not here. She will have to wait until morning."

"She can't wait!" Sister Jember pleaded. "She needs medical attention. There's nowhere clean for the baby here, no water—"

"Shut up!" the guard banged on the door with something hard, making Sister Jember jump back.

Elen shrank at the sound, biting her lip so hard to stifle her groans that she tasted blood. Tsion squeezed her shoulder in silent comfort.

Sister Jember regained her composure, rising onto her toes to get her mouth close to the small peephole.

"Please, sir," she said, her voice more subservient. "She needs a doctor."

"I said she'll have to wait until the morning," he repeated, his voice high with impatience. "We do not open doors at night for anyone."

The guard was already walking away as Sister Jember started banging again. "Please help her!" she cried.

"Stop that noise, or you will regret it!" he banged back, much louder this time. "This door is not opening tonight."

His footsteps receded as contractions gripped Elen, one after the other until they flowed into one constant wave of pain.

Elen closed her eyes, letting her mind drift away from her body.

She was thirteen again, walking away from her family hut in Adi Nefas. Her chafed feet carrying her far from home, away from her mother.

Selas's hands were grabbing at the hem of Elen's dress.

"Elen? Don't leave. Stay with me."

She couldn't see her mother's face, only her calloused hands clutching desperately at her dress.

Elen kept walking.

I can't turn back now, Adey.

Her mother's fingers hardened and thinned into copper wires winding around her belly. The wires clenched tighter until she couldn't breathe.

"So," Ashagirie's face loomed before her. "Are you going to talk now?"

The electric shocks tore through her.

She kept walking.

Girmai came to her now, stopping her.

Girmai, they are killing our baby!

He stood just out of reach, the copper wires pulling her away from him.

"Girmai! I need you! Why are you just standing there?" she screamed. "Why did you leave me?"

Her body burned as Girmai kept staring, silently hovering over her.

"Girmai!"

His body began to fragment. His legs went one way, his arms another, until every piece of him scattered into darkness.

Are you dead? Elen screamed. *Did they kill you?*

She struggled against the wires, against the searing pain, but he was gone.

Where are you? Elen cried. *Don't you want to see your child? We made something beautiful together, remember? Girmai! Come back!*

"Let's move her to the floor," Sister Jember's voice broke through Elen's haze. "Put her down here. The baby is about to come."

"Elen," Tsion's voice reached her, garbled as if she were underwater. "We are moving you to the floor so it's safer for the baby. We are going to lift you now, okay?"

But I'm stuck, Elen wanted to say, holding her cramping abdomen. *Can't you see? There's no safe place for my baby.*

Arms hooked under her armpits and lifted her dead weight. Others dragged the mattress to the floor. Hands tucked balled-up clothes to cushion her head as they settled her down.

"Elen, hush! We are going to take care of you." Tsion stroked Elen's forehead.

Elen shook her head.

"No." The single syllable forced its way through her gritted teeth. "No!"

"Look at me, Elen!" Tsion knelt over her on the floor and spoke into Elen's ear, but only distorted sounds came through the pain. She cringed at metal scraping across the floor as someone pushed a bed aside to make more room.

"Elen, can you hear me? Look at me! You will make it through this. Be strong for your child!"

"Give her more cushioning for her head," Sister Jember called, her hands working swiftly between Elen's legs, pushing her dress further up.

A warm, wet liquid burst out of her, soaking through the mattress and spreading beneath her. The warmth turned icy in a matter of seconds.

"Milite, get my gabi," she heard Tsion say. "We need something to cover her. She is wet everywhere."

Voices echoed around her.

"I don't even have water to wash my hands."

"God help us!"

"Move over here."

"Give her space!"

Tsion pushed something into her hand.

Her rosary.

... Deliver us from evil, Lord, for yours is the kingdom, the power, and the glory, forever and—

"Push, Elen. I see the head. The baby is coming!"

With the burning came an urgent pressure at the bottom of her pelvis.

"Push, Elen!" she heard from somewhere in the room. "Your baby is almost out!"

Elen fought the dizziness threatening to knock her out and pushed.

She pushed against the voice of the soldier who found the newsletter.

Look what I found!

She pushed against the fear that Girmai was dead.

It's not mine. It's Girmai's. He must have left it here when he came to visit.

She pushed against her anger, against the dark future ahead of her.

We made something beautiful together.

She pushed until a tiny, fragile cry rang out in the cell.

"It's a girl!"

A girl, Girmai! Did you hear that? Will you ever get to hear that? Girmai? Where are you?

Elen reached out to hold her baby, but the darkness came first.

39

"It will be harder to bury her if she has a name." When Elen regained consciousness in the women's clinic the next day she told Tsion she didn't want to name the baby.

"Why do you think like that?" Tsion reprimanded her. Several patients turned at the sharpness of her tone. "May God not hear your doubt!"

Tsion held the sleeping child out to Elen, still weak from hours of labor. Elen didn't remember them bringing her here.

"How did they let you in here?" Elen asked, momentarily distracted by Tsion's presence.

"They are understaffed. They let us in to help. Sister Jember and Sister Hawelti come here too when there are too many women to take care of," Tsion said, still holding the baby. "Look at her! She is healthy and happy. Hold her, feel her. Your daughter is a fighter, just like you."

Elen stared at the little girl Tsion placed in her arms. Tsion's gabi was wrapped around her tiny frame and made her seem a lot bigger than she was. Someone had washed her, and her soft head smelled of the bar soap the women used to wash their clothes. A tuft of hair that came almost to her eyebrows escaped the cap on her head.

Then a cold dread swept over her.

She must be damaged. How could an unborn child survive that?

she thought, remembering the beating she took during the interrogation.

Elen slowly unwrapped the gabi until the baby lay naked underneath.

"We will figure out how to get her some clothes," Tsion said as she leaned forward. "I'm sure we can borrow something from one of the babies here."

Tsion kept talking, but Elen heard little of what she said.

Ten fingers. Ten toes. She felt around the tiny stomach, half expecting to find a deformity, a mark of the suffering they had both endured.

Maybe her brain is damaged from the beatings, Elen thought, feeling her tears well up again. *Who can go through electric shocks unscathed?*

She gently ran her fingers through the girl's head of soft, jet-black curls that stood up as Elen brushed over them.

She is so beautiful!

Elen barely noticed the saltiness of her tears until they dripped onto the sleeping baby's cheek. She wiped them off and rubbed her eyes.

I'm so sorry, my baby. You didn't ask for any of this.

"Elen!" Tsion said, putting a hand on her shoulder. "Shhh, Elen, you have to be strong for your daughter. She needs you."

The baby stirred at all the movement and the cold the open gabi let in, knotting her face into a scowl. Her tiny hands flew up as her eyes rolled open, and she gave a weak, stuttered cry.

Elen wiped her tears away, then quickly wrapped the baby up again.

"She needs to eat." The nurse, a fellow prisoner by the looks of her, was back. She inclined her head to Tsion. "She can leave here in the next couple of days. If she has any food sent to her, bring it here."

"A package just came in for her this morning," Tsion said to the nurse. "Can I bring that too?"

"No packages in here." The nurse quickly shook her head and glanced at the guard by the clinic's entrance. She watched Elen fumble with her dress to try to nurse the baby and then bent over to hold the infant's head up.

"Let her rest now. She can have the package when she goes back. There is plenty of time for that."

Elen kissed the baby's forehead gently, then lay back on the pillows propped up against the wall as she latched on. The cot was just as flimsy as the ones they had in the cell.

How long have I been here?

"Did I miss the visit day?" she asked Tsion as she got up to leave.

"Yes," Tsion said. "Alem brought some food and a small envelope for you; surprisingly, it is still sealed."

Girmai. It had to be. Elen clung to the thought though there was no reason to believe he made it out alive. *But … how else would an envelope make it through the guard check still sealed?*

"I will bring the food to you now," Tsion said, cutting into Elen's thoughts. "When you are ready to walk, one of us can help you get back."

"She will need to stay here for now," the nurse repeated. "She lost too much blood."

Elen blinked back her tears and held her baby tighter. All thoughts of the envelope dissolved as she relived moments from her night of labor. The damp floor, the women's voices.

"You will need all the rest you can get," the nurse insisted as she pulled the bed sheets higher over both mother and baby.

***

The next day Tsion and Abeba took turns visiting Elen. Elen was not sure how Abeba negotiated her way into the clinic section of the prison and was too exhausted to ask. Tsion unwrapped a large white cloth that covered a container full of injera soaked with shiro. "You have a nice present waiting for you when you get back. Sorry I couldn't bring that to you here. I told Alem you had a baby girl. She said she would bring some clothes the next time she comes."

Tsion looked at the white cloth and held it up to the light. "This is enough to make a dress for this young lady," she said, pleased with herself.

It took three days for Elen to feel stable enough to walk the expanse of space between the clinic and her cell.

"Look at this angel!" Abeba said. She wedged the bundled baby into the crook of her arm as Elen shifted into her cot.

"You have many mothers here, my love," Abeba continued as she made clucking noises at the baby, "but I'm your favorite. Don't tell the others, okay, ma'arey?"

Once she was settled, Elen opened her arms to Abeba to take her baby back as the other women crowded around the bed.

"What do we call her?" Milite asked. "Look at this angel!"

Elen reveled in their compliments, but wouldn't let anyone else hold her.

"I don't know yet," she said.

The women erupted into discussions of what the name should be and when Elen should name her. She watched them talk, happy for the company, until her eyes became heavy.

"Okay, everyone," Tsion said and stood up from the corner of the bed. "Let's give her time to rest. We will have lots of time with this little one."

Elen woke to dimming light, the baby still asleep in the crook of her arm. She put a finger under the baby's nose to confirm she was breathing, then angled her body up to a seated position.

Women were still chatting quietly outside the cell entrance. She was alone in the room. As she sat up more, a crackling sound under her stopped her short. She felt around with her free hand and pulled out a brown envelope.

To Elen was scrawled on the front.

The package! Her heart ached that she had missed an opportunity to see her sister.

Elen moved the baby onto her lap and secured her head between her knees. Her fingers shook as she opened the flap to expose a small, hard piece of paper.

She took it out.

Girmai!

He was looking right at her, his eyes black against the gray backdrop. The portrait captured him up to his shoulders. His jaw was sharper, his face much slimmer. An almost imperceptible smile creased the corners of his mouth lightly.

"You're alive!" she shrieked, then clamped her hand over her mouth and glanced over to the door. Relieved that the women hadn't heard, she studied the photo again.

Her eyes dissected every part of Girmai's face, his lips, those eyes she loved so much.

She didn't think she could cry anymore, but the tears burst out of her anew. The picture fluttered under her shaking thumb and forefinger.

Girmai! My love! You are alive!

There was something else in the envelope. She put Girmai's picture on the baby's chest and lifted out a gold chain.

They let this through? she marveled.

The kneeling woman engraved onto the round pendant had a defiant expression, contrary to being on her knees. Her back was straight as she held two scales on either side of her. Her arms were raised high, the scales level with her chest.

Justice.

Elen held the chain up and let the pendant rotate as she watched the woman appear and disappear.

She picked up the photograph and turned it around, reading what Girmai had written on the back.

You are my truth. Know that we will be together again.

Our daughter—name her Hiyab.

40

Addis Ababa, 7 July 1980

"Elen Ghebrekidan! Gabi ina metawekiya!"

The early-morning summons to bring her gabi and identification card meant one of two things: release or transfer.

Two women sat behind a table in a dingy office at the front of the prison as Elen gingerly lowered herself onto the only chair available by the door, its metal frame creaking beneath her. Hiyab lay fast asleep on her shoulder, her tiny breath warm against Elen's neck.

Metal cabinets on either side of the women brimmed with files. Boxes stacked on the floor overflowed with more folders, leaving the women little room to move.

One of them flicked through what looked like Elen's file and stretched out her hand without looking up. Elen handed her prison identification card with details of her entry and the duration of her sentence.

Elen shifted in her chair and moved Hiyab to her lap, adjusting the gabi over her to keep her warm.

"Your name came up for early release," one of the women said as she scanned Elen's file, cross-referenced the information with her card, and handed it back to her.

Elen stared at her, the words not entirely sinking in. Hiyab fidgeted on her lap and stretched, her eyes still heavy with sleep.

"I … I am leaving?" Elen finally managed, her voice barely above a whisper.

"Yes." The woman stamped her file. "You are allowed a phone call to arrange your pickup. She,"—the woman gestured to another woman by the door—"will show you where."

Elen left the inner office, her feet unsteady, and followed the officer.

She whispered the good news to Alem on the phone, giddy with the thought of this phase of her life ending.

Alem shrieked with delight on the other end of the line. "This is a blessed day! I will come get you tomorrow."

When Elen returned to the cell, Tsion rushed to her, already teary at Elen's joy as if she already knew. "What did they say?"

"I'm going home, Tsion!"

Ululations broke out in the cell, and others rushed to join in joy and sorrow. They embraced tightly and Hiyab, caught between them, squirmed in protest, her small voice drowned out by the noise.

"I'm so happy for you!" Tsion said. A film of tears coated her eyes. "Now you get to live your life! Raise this baby well. Don't let her forget where she came from."

Elen held up the tiny white dress Tsion had sewn for Hiyab, made from the cloth Alem had once used to wrap food. She caressed the blue embroidery Tsion had painstakingly sewn onto its hem and sleeves, feeling the love and care stitched into every thread.

"I am going to braid her hair," Abeba said to Elen later in the communal courtyard as she lifted Hiyab out of her arms and wiped tears from her face. "There is no way my baby is leaving here messy."

For the rest of the day, guilt lined the edges of her euphoria. These women had been her family here for a year and a half, and now she was leaving them behind.

"I will miss you," she said to Milite as she handed over the bathtub and all the other baby items Alem and Girmai had sent. It was time for these things to help others.

"May God bless your journey, my friend," Abeba said to her before they parted to their cells for the night.

***

Early the next morning, Elen and two other women walked through the prison to the ululations of those staying behind. Joy and sorrow rose together, their cries swelling to one aching sound.

Elen, wracked with emotions she could not contain, hugged as many women as she could on her way out, then made her way through the front prison gate, jumping at the loud sound of it closing behind her.

The deafening silence on the other side of the gate disoriented her. Alem stood waiting for her across the street and barely looked for passing cars before dashing across to her. The sisters embraced each other for the first time in years, Hiyab squirming between them.

When they finally pulled apart, Elen took in the garbage-strewn street and the road stretching into the distance. Behind her, the prison walls loomed dark and grimy, coils of barbed wire cutting harsh lines across the dull sky.

She turned her back on it and closed her eyes as Alem took Hiyab from her and showered her with kisses.

Dear Lord, may Your will be done on Earth as it is in Heaven.

She took a deep breath and lifted her face and arms to the warming sun.

Forgive us our trespasses, as we forgive those who trespass against us.

Elen felt the prayer reverberate through her. Finally, she opened her eyes, resolute. She would not look back.

"Here, wear this," Alem said, handing her two dresses once they got to the car.

Elen turned the matching dresses over in her hands and ran her fingers along the intricate patterns. The white of the zurias shone brightly in the gloomy day, the embroidered decorations vibrating with color.

"I had them made a while back and was saving them for this day!" Alem grinned. "You should go home in style. Come, change in the car."

Arriving at Alem's house after they stopped to take pictures in their new dresses was the homecoming Elen had dreamed of since her arrest. She carefully removed the dresses, washed herself and

Hiyab, and then put them back on. The fabric felt soft and clean against their skin, a small luxury that brought unexpected comfort.

Exhausted from the raw emotion of their sudden freedom, she let Hiyab wander around as Alem spread out the feast of injera and several sauces over her dining-room table. Alem handed the phone to Elen when Solomon called during his regular check-in call soon after Elen arrived.

"When are you coming home?" he had asked after their tearful hellos. "We all miss you so much!"

"I don't know if I can go back to Asmara yet," Elen said. The thought of returning filled her with an inexplicable heaviness, especially knowing that Girmai wasn't there. "Can you come here with the kids? I need to see them."

"I can't leave the bar," he replied. He cleared his throat and continued. "Things here are better now. You can come and see for yourself. Please come home."

Elen knew that things were anything but better.

"Maybe in a little while," she said softly.

With a substantial reward on Girmai's head, he wasn't going back anytime soon either. She fingered the gold pendant he had sent her and watched Hiyab.

"Can you please send the children to me?" she asked Solomon again. "Even if it is for a short time."

***

After several weeks, Solomon reluctantly arranged for Aman and Faven to travel to Addis with their grandfather, who had been visiting Solomon. By the time Elen's family got to Alem's house, the novelty of flying on a plane had yet to wear off Ghebrekidan. Wide-eyed, he sat at the dining-room table after hugging Elen and quietly watched her reunite with the children.

"Oh, my babies!" Elen cried, holding on to her children as if letting them go would make it all disappear.

"Mama!" they both shrieked. She felt every bit of the emotions coursing through them as they held on to her. It was as if they were breathing new life back into her soul.

Hopefully, time will heal us all.

41

Addis Ababa, August to September 1980

"Don't be sorry!" Elen's voice trembled through her tears as she sank to her knees at the sound of Girmai's voice over the phone.

"I am so sorry," he kept repeating.

"I knew what I was doing. We all did. Let's not waste our precious time looking back. Hiyab and I are out, and we are well."

"Hiyab …".

"Yes," Elen smiled, tears still brimming. "Our girl! She has your nose, and she might be even more stubborn than you."

I will see him again! Who knows when or how, but I will see him again. My child is not fatherless.

"Nairobi?" she said. "You're in Nairobi? What are you doing there?"

"I've been waiting for you," he replied. "I have a house and have restarted my business. We don't have much time to talk now; I can tell you more about that later, but Elen, we can build a good life here."

The rest came fast and she had to strain to keep up.

Girmai had arranged for Yonas, Rahwa, and Samuel to travel to Addis, where they would meet her and cross the border together. A trusted friend, Misgina, would guide them all the way to Nairobi.

He warned her not to return to Asmara despite her protests that her brother needed her.

"It's still too dangerous," Girmai said. "They are still looking for me. They know I'm in Nairobi but they can't reach me here. What they can do is use you to get to me. Even Addis isn't safe."

Elen stood frozen. The receiver pressed to her ear.

"You need to get a bus pass for yourself as soon as possible, Elen," he continued. " You have a cousin in the kebele office downtown, don't you? He might be able to help you. Do it as fast as you can. We will talk soon."

Then the phone line clicked dead.

***

Three days later, Elen visited her cousin's office in Arat Kilo.

"Elen, haftey, my sister," Tekleberhan greeted her warmly. His office was stark and dingy, with only his chair, table, and two plastic chairs for visitors. His two bodyguards stood outside his office after one of them closed the door.

"Your time at Alem Bekagn was unfortunate," he said. "I trust you are well now?"

"Thanks be to God, I am very well, Bere, hawey, my brother," she said, using his nickname to give him the illusion that she was calm as she explained her visit.

It's been a long time since I've had to pretend like this.

"I was hoping to take a break from the city and travel south to Hidlola. A friend offered his family house there so I could rest with my children after our separation all this time."

The lies slipped out smoothly, with the casual elegance that had worked multiple times in her bar. No one moved through county lines without passes, and he had the authority to give it to her.

"I understand, Elen," he said soberly. "Rest is indeed something we all need these days. I can give you only one pass, though," he said after a sharp intake of breath. "More than that is too risky for me. Movement is tight all over the country, especially to the south. The baby can go with you. She is under two years old, right? She doesn't need a pass if she is with you."

"But what about my two other kids?" she asked, suppressing the desperation in her voice. "I was hoping to spend time with them there."

"You'll have to come back to them in Addis," he said, shaking his head. "I can't explain giving bus passes to a whole family; too many people are crossing borders."

No amount of pleading would change his mind.

Elen left his office bereft, gripping her pass for one.

"How can I do this to them again?" she asked Alem as they watched the children play.

"I'm sure there's a way for us to get them to you," Alem replied reassuringly. "We can send them back to Solomon for now so they can continue the life they are used to until you arrive safe. You can't help them until you help yourself first. They can join you once you are in a stable place."

Elen watched Aman and Faven playing with Hiyab on the floor. They had bonded with her and had been inseparable since they met. She couldn't bear the thought of tearing the siblings apart, nor could she think about separating herself from her children after she had just gotten them back.

Yet she saw the truth in what needed to happen.

What good am I to them dead, or in prison again?

***

The room was still dark in the pre-dawn hour when Elen slipped a third dress over her body less than a week later. The change of clothes would come in handy; packing a bag would raise suspision. The thickness of the layers pinched her armpits when she lowered her arms.

The bedroom door was slightly ajar, and she could hear Alem in the kitchen preparing food for her trip.

Elen opened the door a little wider to let more light in, then stood over the bed to watch her three children sleep.

"Mama, will you stay with us forever now?" Faven had asked her two days before while they were sitting in the living room together.

"If it is God's will, my baby," Elen had said, guilt tearing at her.

I have no power to make promises about forever. Only God does, she'd thought sadly.

Now, standing over them again, tears welled in her eyes. She wiped them away quickly before grabbing the small cloth bag she had prepared the night before. Inside was the white dress Tsion had made for Hiyab, along with a few more changes of clothes for her. She also had the envelope with Girmai's picture that she carried everywhere. She touched the pendant on her neck for good luck, then said a little prayer before tucking it into an inner pocket of her dress.

She patted her dress pocket to make sure the pass was still there.

Elen tied the cloth bag with Hiyab's extra clothes. Once they reached the border, she would add her dresses to it. She couldn't give any impression that she was leaving the country.

"The guide will take you through to Hidlola on the bus," Girmai had told her. "You will have to walk over the border, then catch another ride to Nairobi. Misgina will be with you until you get here. Ajokhi, Elen, you are very close now."

She suppressed her sobs and picked up Hiyab from between Aman and Faven, gently tying her to her back. Hiyab was so used to being carried this way in Alem Bekagn that she barely stirred.

"Where are you going, Mama?" Faven asked, groggy with sleep. Aman opened his eyes at the sound of her voice.

Elen knelt beside the bed, giving them both tight hugs.

"I have to go away for a little while," she said finally, forcing steadiness into her voice. "Go back to sleep now."

I will figure out how to bring you to me, my babies. I have to.

She then slipped out of the room before they could ask more questions. In the kitchen, she grabbed Alem's elbow and glanced back to Aman and Faven's room.

"If they kill me, promise me you'll take care of them," she said.

"Elen, stop talking like that," Alem said and put the knife she was using to chop carrots down on the counter. "You have to believe that—"

"If something happens, promise me you will look for Hiyab. The birthmark on her right arm will help you find her."

"Don't say that!"

"Promise me!" Elen said as she clutched both Alem's arms. "Tell me you will go find her and care for her if you don't hear from me. I need to hear you say it."

"I promise," her sister sobbed.

A half-hour later, Elen stood opposite a row of buses parked on the other side of Revolution Square. Street children loitered on the corners begging, or selling small cones of roasted nuts. She adjusted the cloth holding Hiyab to her back, taking care not to trip on the cracks in the uneven sidewalk as she made her way to the bus. Hiyab was sound asleep as Elen followed the wave of pedestrians negotiating the cars to cross the road.

She had been free for two months.

"He is a dark man, taller than me," Girmai had described Misgina, the guide who would be taking her and Girmai's three other children to Kenya. "He will wait for you near the bus traveling to Shashemene.

"Misgina will have a light brown jacket on. Rahwa, Samuel, and Yonas will be with him. My friend Semere's three children might join if their papers come through. He and his wife Biri are here with me in Nairobi."

She and Hiyab and six children. Misgina would have to get the eight of them across the border. Guilt suffocated her at the thought of traveling with other people's children when she couldn't get passes for her own.

"Elen, I will make it right for all of you," Girmai had reassured her, his voice full of conviction. "We will bring Aman and Faven to us once you get through. I won't rest until I make that happen. Focus on the journey ahead of you for now. Be at the station before 6:30 so you can get to the bus on time."

Here she was, like so many years ago—at a bus station with a one-way ticket to freedom that came at the sacrifice of family.

Hiyab's weight dug into her shoulders as she navigated the crowded station, searching for the bus to Shashemene. She clutched the pass inside her pocket, her heart thudding.

"Elen?" A man startled her with a tap to her shoulder. The whites of his eyes contrasted with his dark, weather-beaten skin. Six children around the age of ten to fifteen stood behind him, sleep tugging at their eyes as they stood calmly together.

"Misgina?"

Her pulse quickened. Her future—and the safety of her children—depended on this stranger.

They nodded stiffly at each, bypassing the traditional cheek taps.

"Here, meet everyone." He stepped back, gesturing to the group of children.

"Nice to meet you," Elen said, giving the children a small bow. She forced a smile, pushing away the image of the two children she left behind.

Please, God, forgive me.

"It is time to go." Misgina looked up at the bus. They all shuffled after him as he made his way to the door, bus tickets for all of them in hand, while each held their own stamped bus pass.

"Tickets? Pass?" the conductor asked each person in the queue. Just like the first time she boarded a bus all those years ago, the conductor hesitated as he looked at the pass in her outstretched hand before waving her through.

42

The children didn't complain once during the five long days of travel, clinging to each other for comfort. Elen refused to let her grief over leaving Faven and Aman behind paralyze her.

I will get them out too, she repeated to herself over and over. *I must.*

"The fewer people who see us, the better," Misgina told her as he pointed to an isolated mud hut at the edge of a small clearing surrounded by acacia trees. "We'll spend the night here."

"Where is here?" Elen asked as she untied Hiyab from her back. She cleared her throat; her voice sounded hoarse and unfamiliar, and it took every ounce of energy she had left to speak.

Misgina had led the tired group on a winding route to bypass the sleepy border town and reach this hut.

"We are just outside Hidlola," Misgina said. "Kenya is just over those mountains. We'll be a lot safer once we're over them."

"That's the next part of our journey," he said in a controlled voice, as though he were trying not to alarm her. He pointed at an ominous-looking mountain range stretching endlessly in both directions. A thin brown path wound its way from the edge of the clearing and disappeared into the trees. Elen followed his finger, her gaze climbing the imposing mountains.

Elen hadn't seen anyone during the hour-long walk from the bus drop-off, and the isolation pressed down on her like a heavy blanket.

"All of you wait inside," Misgina instructed as the children filed obediently into the hut. Elen marveled at their resilience and how quietly they bore the weight of the long journey.

Yonas checked on his siblings during the entire bus ride. She felt herself soften at his quiet strength and protective nature. Eyob, the oldest of Semere's children, did the same for his sisters. The children mostly sat in silence, catching sleep when they could.

"I have to report to the village chief and let him know we're here," Misgina told her once the children were settled inside. "Everyone's on the lookout for refugees. The Derg border-patrol offers a reward to anyone who turns people like us in. We don't want them coming after us tonight, so I'll tell the chief I'm here with my wife and children to visit our family up the road. He'll probably wait until morning to verify the story in person. If anyone comes by, you stick to the same story, okay?"

He looked at Elen expectantly.

"I understand," she said, her voice steady, despite the exhaustion clouding her mind. She peeked into the hut and saw that the children, too tired to do much more than sit, had found places along the circular wall.

"What about food?" she said, glancing at Hiyab. They'd only had a few slices of bread before boarding the bus that morning, and it had been hours since their last meal.

"Once I check in with the chief, I'll bring something for everyone to eat. But we have to be ready to leave very early, so don't get too comfortable."

The words tugged at Elen.

When was the last time I was comfortable? She sighed as he disappeared down the dirt path.

I'm a refugee on the move, she thought bitterly. *That's what I am now. That's what we all are.*

She rubbed her eyes and lowered herself onto the dirt floor, positioning herself to see the mountains through the open doorway. She stared up at the cone-shaped grass ceiling, fighting back the tears, a constant preoccupation these days.

The children huddled close to each other. Hiyab toddled from Samuel to Rahwa, her little arms outstretched. *She must know they are sisters,* Elen thought. The unspoken truth pressed down on her. She had no idea how to tell the children—not this. Rahwa opened her arms and pulled Hiyab close. The two sat quietly together on the floor.

"You are such brave children," Elen said softly to all of them. "Try to get some rest. You've done well today."

Yonas's voice broke the silence. "Do you know how much longer we have left?"

Elen was surprised by how comforting it was to hear him speak. "I'm not sure," she replied, "but Baba Misgina knows this area well. He'll get us through. Your fathers are eager to see you all."

She smiled as the six children slowly surrendered to sleep, their heads leaning on each other's shoulders.

Though empty of furniture, the hut showed signs of recent use. Two small pots sat stacked on one side near the remains of a fire on a raised stone bed. A worn metal kettle and a couple of stirring spoons lay nearby.

As dusk fell, shadows swallowed the acacia trees outside and crept up the mountains. Elen welcomed the stillness, a brief reprieve from the constant movement of the past few days.

Her eyes had just begun to droop when Misgina returned with a bag of himbasha, which he set on the floor. Elen forced herself to shake off the weariness and got up. She broke the bread into pieces, gently waking each child and handing them equal portions. They ate quietly in the dim glow of Misgina's flashlight.

The pass her cousin had given her had gotten them through the intense checkpoints in Shashemene, Dilla, Hagere Mariam, Yabelo, and their final stop in Hidlola. She strained to see the darkening mountains ahead as she fingered the pass in her pocket. It had taken her as far as it could get her; it was useless now, offering no more protection.

***

"Wake up!" Misgina hissed, shaking her shoulder in the pitch darkness. "It's time to go."

Elen's heart lurched at the urgency in his voice. "What's happening?"

"We need to get over the border before daybreak," he said over his shoulder. "It's no longer safe here."

They all fumbled to their feet in the dark. Elen lifted Hiyab's limp body, grabbed her small cloth bag, and followed the others.

She stepped out into the crisp morning air. The sky was cloudless, and the full moon illuminated their surroundings enough for her to see clearly.

A slight movement near the acacia trees startled her.

She stifled a scream as she spotted a man standing in the shadows.

Misgina pushed her toward him. "This is our guide," he said, beckoning the children to follow. "He's from the Borana tribe and knows this area well. We need to leave now and follow him. The village chief will be here at nine to verify my story. We need to be as far away as possible by then."

Misgina checked his watch. "It's 4 a.m. We have a few hours before they come looking for us."

The Borana guide wore a checkered turban wrapped high around his head. His dark face and legs seemed to melt into the night; the thick gabi around his shoulders contrasted sharply with his thin knee-length shorts. He didn't say a word as he turned and started walking.

Misgina followed closely, urging the children to move quickly. They walked in a single file. The children led the way, followed by Elen and Misgina, who brought up the rear.

An hour passed before Elen broke the silence. "How long is the walk?" she whispered. They still had yet to reach the foot of the mountain range.

"Sololo is about thirty kilometers from here, just over those hills. We'll need to move quickly."

Elen looked up at the looming incline of the mountain range that stretched endlessly in both directions. There was no way around.

They continued in silence. The mountains seemed to glide further away with each step they took. Elen's shoulders ached from Hiyab's weight as she slept on her back. She ignored the burning in her legs and focused on placing one foot in front of the other.

They arrived at the foot of the towering mountain range just as the sun brightened the sky.

"Here, let me carry her," Misgina offered. "You'll need your strength for this."

Elen gladly untied the cloth that held Hiyab on her back and passed her to Misgina. She broke off a piece of himbasha she had saved from the night before and handed it to Hiyab, who had woken up during the transfer. The little girl immediately munched on it, dropping crumbs on Misgina's head as she sat on his shoulders.

Their guide darted ahead with the agility of a mountain goat while Elen scrambled up the steep and dusty path far behind him and the rest of the group. As the heat increased, the man folded the gabi over his shoulders. His muscles rippled with each effortless movement up the mountainside.

The children crab-walked behind him, their hands and feet scraping over the uneven rocks. After what seemed like hours of climbing, scraping knees, and struggling for breath, they finally reached the top—just in time to see the sun's warm orange glow spreading over the horizon.

Misgina set Hiyab down on a narrow plateau where they all collapsed to rest.

Elen brought out the last of the himbasha. She ripped pieces off and handed them to everyone.

Hiyab quickly grabbed her second piece, crumbs covering her lap as she ate. Elen knelt beside her. *She's lost weight,* she thought, noticing the dry patches on Hiyab's scalp where her braids had loosened.

The endless plains stretched before them, bathed in the morning light. Somewhere beyond that vast expanse, Girmai was waiting for them. Elen chewed slowly on her piece of himbasha, her mind racing.

We've come this far. We have to make it.

Suddenly, the Borana man crouched beside Misgina, murmuring something as he pointed back down the mountain toward Hidlola. Elen's stomach clenched at the urgency in his voice. She couldn't understand his words, but followed his finger and Misgina's gaze.

Far below, tiny figures were moving through the trees—people, maybe four or five of them, moving in their direction.

Misgina sprang to his feet. "We have to go now!" he said urgently. "They're coming. Give her to me. We need to reach the Kenyan side before they catch up."

43

The Borana guide moved quickly downhill, Misgina and the children racing to keep up. Elen's legs shook in uncontrollable spasms by the time they'd slowed to a walk once the incline leveled off.

They were several kilometers away, weaving through the acacia trees and the occasional thick, thorny bushes. The children ahead of her swayed with fatigue. Hiyab, still on Misgina's back, appeared and disappeared between the trees as the gap between Elen and the group widened.

"Wait!" she cried out, her voice ragged as she collapsed at the foot of a tree, her entire body seizing with spasms. Months spent in prison had left her muscles weak and unprepared for such an intense escape. She couldn't make her legs obey her any longer. She gritted her teeth and tried to massage the cramping pain in her thighs and calves, her hands trembling with the effort.

Misgina spoke hurriedly to the Borana guide. "Sit and rest for a little while," he instructed the children, motioning for them to gather under the shade of the tree. Elen slumped against its rough bark, her chest heaving with exertion.

Misgina crouched beside her. "We have to keep going," he insisted, his voice carrying a note of irritation. "We can't stay here. We're not safe yet. We have to push through."

Elen's breath hitched in her throat. "How can anyone be coming for us here in the middle of nowhere?" she asked, careful so the children wouldn't hear her desperation. "There's nothing here but trees and bushes!"

"You saw them coming," Misgina replied through clenched teeth. "We're responsible for these children."

Elen heard the words, but her exhaustion overrode the fear she knew she should feel. The mountains they had climbed were at a distance now and seemed smaller than the effort it took to get past them. She started to doubt her perception of everything around her.

Ahead of them, the scattered homes she had seen from the top were not visible from where they sat. The plains stretched far and wide in every other direction, with no soul in sight.

"Okay."

She willed her body to move and pushed herself off the ground. She gingerly stood up and stretched.

Something on the ground a few paces to her left caught her eye. A thick tree branch, an unnaturally dark patch of earth around it.

"What is that?" she asked, pointing toward the branch.

Misgina had already gotten the children up and was ushering them to the Borana guide. He followed Elen to the branch.

To her horror, Elen recognized the dark stain on the ground.

"Blood," Misgina said, waving the children forward.

The sight sent adrenalin racing through her. She backed away and kept moving with an energy she didn't think she could muster.

She kept her eyes on Hiyab's head bobbing above Misgina's shoulders and forced herself to follow and push through the pain.

This can't end here.

***

Stitched together with mud, dried reeds, and branches, a solitary hut appeared in the vast plains ahead. Scrawny cattle grazed on the browned grass nearby, their ribs starkly visible in the harsh mid-day sun.

The guide gestured toward the hut and Misgina nodded before turning back to Elen and the children. He gently handed Hiyab back to Elen.

"Wait here," he said.

Elen adjusted the cloth around Hiyab, securing her to her back once more.

Yonas looked up at her, his eyes wide with hope. "Are we going to rest here?"

"I think so," Elen said with a tired smile, giving him a gentle pat on the shoulder. "Come, there's some shade here. Let's sit."

By her rough calculations, they had been walking for eight hours. The relentless heat had slowed them down, and Elen's throat burned with thirst.

The children collapsed under the shade while Elen watched Misgina speak with a man who appeared to be the cattle herder.

Where did he come from? Elen wondered. *Maybe this is how people get caught—too tired to see what's right in front of them.*

Misgina returned with a triumphant smile. "We can rest here for a while," he announced, pointing to the grass hut.

Relief at those words gave Elen the energy to get the children up and help them into the cool interior of the hut.

"Is he leaving us?" Elen asked, seeing the Borana man wave and turn back toward the plains.

"Yes," Misgina said. He adjusted his shirt, his face unreadable. "He's taken us as far as he'll go. We are on our own from here."

Watching him disappear into the distance, she bowed her head and recited the Lord's prayer.

The sun blazed directly overhead as they settled into the hut, its interior significantly cooler than the sweltering heat outside.

"We're in Kenya, but not out of danger yet," Misgina warned.

Misgina's pass allowed him to travel between countries as a trader, but the rest of them had no legal documentation. It could mean a swift return to Ethiopia or a prison cell in Kenya if caught here.

"Stay out of sight. I'll see if I can find us something to eat."

Hunger pangs gripped Elen at the mention of food. She brushed her fingertips over her cracked lips and shook her head at the thought of her breakdown earlier in the day.

"The owner of these cattle will come in the next few hours," Misgina said before he stepped out. "I'll organize a ride with him for the next part of our journey. In the meantime, don't go beyond this area here." He gestured to the small clearing around the hut.

Misgina returned with a pot of fresh milk less than an hour later. He started a fire beside the hut.

"This should be good to drink once it's boiled," he said. "I'll be back with more food soon."

Elen stirred the milk absently, her mind drifting. When it started to boil over, she quickly removed the pot from the fire and set it down to cool. Inside the hut the children were asleep, their bodies curled up together. Hiyab lay across Samuel's lap, her tiny fingers clutching his shirt. Yonas and Rahwa slept beside each other, arms wrapped in an embrace.

Elen sighed, weariness seeping into her bones. She peeled the sticky fabric of her dress away from her skin and sat beneath a young acacia tree, giving the children more space inside the hut.

Elen hadn't realized she'd dozed off until a noise jolted her awake. Her eyes flew open just in time to see Sewit stumble out of the hut. Her foot caught on an elevated patch of mud, and she stumbled and stretched out her arms to catch herself from falling.

She knocked over the entire pot of cooled milk on her way down. The white milk turned brown as it spread over the dry dirt, which quickly absorbed it.

Elen couldn't help but wail. "It is all gone!" The tears she had kept in until now flowed uncontrollably.

"It's okay; it's not your fault," she comforted Sewit a few moments later despite her panic.

Misgina found her curled up into herself, moaning with her face in her hands as she rocked back and forth outside the hut.

"The milk is gone. It's all gone; I can't watch them die!" she wept.

Misgina's face softened as he took in the scene. "No use crying over it," he said with a small smile. "We're not going to die, Elen," he said firmly. "I know it feels hopeless right now, but we're going to get through—"

The distant sound of a truck engine caught his attention. His expression darkened immediately.

"Get inside," Misgina ordered, his voice low, urgent. Elen scrambled up, rushed over the wet milky spot, and crouched on the hut floor with the children.

She put her finger over her lips, grateful that Hiyab had fallen back asleep. "Stay quiet," Elen whispered, her voice trembling. She moved Hiyab gently onto Samuel's lap. "Can you keep her quiet for a few minutes?"

Samuel nodded solemnly and wrapped his arms around Hiyab.

Elen inched forward and peeked through a small gap where the dried reeds of the roof joined the mud wall.

Outside, dust swirled around a parked truck. A man in a shirt and canvas pants got out. His long black hair oddly contrasted with his dark skin gleaming in the heat. Sweat spread in patches around his armpits and neck.

The man didn't look Kenyan or Ethiopian. Was he Indian? Elen had never met anyone like him before.

The cattle herder appeared from behind a group of cows. He said a few words to the man and pointed at Misgina. The men shook hands.

The cattle herder began removing hay bales from the truck bed as the two other men talked.

She couldn't make out the words, but they sounded like those she'd heard on the BBC radio bulletins she would pass over while searching for the EPLF radio station. *Are they speaking in English?*

Misgina pointed at the little hut, and the man nodded and looked at his truck thoughtfully. He eventually shook Misgina's hand again and watched him return to the hut.

Elen scrambled back to sit on the floor with the kids before he got there.

"Let's go!" Misgina said.

By now they were all conditioned to obey his instructions promptly.

The man stood back and nodded, assessing them as they tumbled out. Elen could tell he was counting.

"This is Devinder," Misgina introduced the man to the group. "He will give us a ride to Marsabit. That's our last stop before we get to Nairobi. Kids, get in the back. Elen, you and Hiyab sit in front."

Misgina got onto the truck bed with the children. All the hay Devinder had brought for his cows now lay beside the truck.

The truck sped off in the late afternoon, leaving their temporary sanctuary in Sololo behind. It moved much faster and smoother than any of the buses had.

Devinder fell silent after the first few attempts at conversation. Elen couldn't understand anything he said to her. All she could do was nod and hold Hiyab tighter.

She sank into the soft seat and inclined her head to the open window to let the wind cool her down.

They drove in silence for several hours until the sun dipped in the sky. Despite her best efforts to stay awake, the rhythm of the truck lulled her to sleep.

***

Elen woke up with a start to the pitch blackness of night. Someone was shaking her shoulder roughly.

Ahead of them, a line of cars moved slowly through what looked like a checkpoint. Men in light-blue shirts and dark-blue pants were inspecting vehicles, peering inside windows and popping open trunks.

Devinder frantically waved at her to get out of the car. The truck shook with the movement of Misgina and the others jumping out the back.

Elen fumbled with the door handle and opened it. She stumbled out and slung Hiyab, still asleep, onto her back.

"This is the checkpoint into Marsabit," Misgina whispered, tension lining his face. "Come on, we need to get off the road."

They disappeared into the bushes and down onto a sunken, dry riverbed parallel to the road. Misgina motioned for them to duck low as the headlights from cars headed to and from the checkpoint lit up the night.

"We are lucky it is dark," Misgina said as if reading her mind. "We'll circle the checkpoint here and meet Devinder on the other side.

"How do you know he won't leave us here?" Elen's legs ached. The hours in the car had made them stiff.

"I have the other half of his payment," he replied. "He'll take us to a guesthouse for the night, then to Nairobi tomorrow."

They made a wide loop around the officers checking documentation, using the bushes to shield them from view. Car headlights filtered through the branches as their feet sunk into the sand of the dry riverbed with each step. Misgina then led them back up the river bank.

Devinder's truck, headlights off, was idling on the side of the road ahead of them. The only trace of light was from his cigarette, a glint that shone in the darkness like a lone firefly.

Half an hour later, they entered Marsabit, and Devinder stopped the truck in front of a motel. The young woman in the reception area half-listened to Misgina's story about him traveling with his wife and children as she wrote something in the hotel ledger. She smiled at him when he promised to pay her extra to keep them from "being disturbed during the night," and gave them the keys to a sparsely furnished room with two double beds. The musty smell suggested that it had been long since anyone had aired it out.

Elen got the children to wash up while Misgina went out in search of food. Soon after, he came back with a plate of injera and a jerry can full of drinking water.

Elen recognized the exhaustion pulling under his eyes. "Thank you for helping us, Misgina."

"Don't thank me yet," he said, putting a chunk of injera soaked in sauce into his mouth. "We are not out of danger yet. We need to be vigilant until we get to Nairobi."

Elen climbed into one of the beds with the girls, the tension of their uncertain future pressing in around her. The boys took the other bed. Misgina settled into an old armchair in the corner, his eyes heavy but alert.

She kept her eyes on Misgina for as long as she could, hoping to be as vigilant as he was, but eventually she drifted off into a black sleep. In it, she kept walking up steep inclines and down excruciatingly slippery slopes, one foot in front of the other, down endless paths. Death lay in wait around each bend. It grabbed her by the ankles and shook her until her teeth chattered. She resisted it as much as she could, the muscles in her arms and legs straining with the effort. Tired from the exertion of hanging on to life, tired of everything, she wanted to let go, to let herself go off into the peace of death. Maybe Hiyab could come with her, and they could both rest. Then Girmai appeared before her like a ghost. His hand grabbed her shoulder. "Come on, get up!" she heard him say.

"Get up now!" she heard him again, but it wasn't Girmai's voice. Misgina was standing over her, his voice desperate. It took a moment to orient herself back to the small room. It was still dark outside.

"Soldiers are at Reception asking to see the guest list. I am not sure how long the receptionist can stall them. Hopefully, what I promised her is more than the reward money they offer." He went around waking the children. "We need to leave out the back. Devinder is waiting. Let's go!"

Elen blinked the sleep out of her eyes and swung her legs off the bed. She helped Misgina get the other children up and hoisted Hiyab onto her back, still fast asleep. They quietly filed out the back door of the motel, away from the male voices in the reception area.

Devinder was waiting for them a block away in the driver's seat of a light-blue Peugeot 504 station wagon instead of his open-bed truck. The car was already in gear and moving before the last door closed.

He drove slowly without the lights on for the first few blocks of the empty street, then switched them on and accelerated.

Misgina turned to Elen and the kids in the back seat.

"Everyone okay?"

Half-hearted agreements were murmured in the car, though everyone was far from okay.

"This is the last leg of our journey," he said. "You all need to lie down so no one outside can see you until we leave Marsabit town. It will just be a few more minutes. I will let you know when we are clear."

Just before she lowered her head below the window line, Elen caught sight of the clock on the dashboard. Two-thirty in the morning.

May God be with us.

44

"So where does that leave me?" Helen asked, her voice cutting through the static of the phone line. Silence followed as Girmai grappled with how to say what he needed to.

The truth would sting. Girmai was about to sever their marriage by phone.

He took a deep breath and plunged ahead. "I will take care of you, Helen. I'll make sure you'll have everything you need. I just . . ." He struggled to say the words he knew would break her heart.

She stayed silent on the other side of the line. Girmai could imagine her sitting on his favorite chair with the phone cord extended to her ear from the receiver on the side table.

"I love her," he said finally.

He winced at the thought of her hearing his words alone. He was in Nairobi, she in Asmara, thousands of kilometers away.

No words of apology could undo the pain he was causing her.

He wanted to say so much more—*you are an amazing woman, the rock that held the family together when I left and even for the years before when I was physically there but not really present. I should have done better for you and the kids*—but his thoughts tangled in the thickness of his regret.

He wanted to tell her how much he appreciated her and all her sacrifices, especially the painful goodbye she'd said to their three oldest children, not knowing when or if she would ever see them again. He wanted to thank her for allowing him to take them, to give them a chance at a safer life.

But what came out instead was: "I will make sure you are taken care of." His voice sounded colder than he intended. "Araya has a good handle on the finances. You can trust him to run things. I confirmed the auction of my properties won't go through, so you'll continue to have an income. You'll have more than enough to sustain you. When Yonas, Rahwa, and Samuel arrive, I will take care of them and make sure they have every opportunity we never had."

Silence.

He rushed to fill the void. "I will do my best to care for our children and you."

He had no choice now but to wait for her response.

"Helen?"

The phone clicked. The dial tone rang in Girmai's ear.

He held the receiver in his hand for a moment longer before slowly lowering it to its cradle.

His gaze drifted out his office window to two of his transport trucks with trailers parked in the lot. One of the drivers had just pulled in and parked, and a third was making deliveries and would be in soon.

Girmai had invested heavily in these trucks, relying on their success to fund the operation that would bring Elen and the children to safety. His transport business in Kenya was doing exceptionally well, giving him the resources to secure their passage.

He tried to focus on the ledger in front of him, but the numbers blurred and the pen in his hand stayed still, unable to move. A sigh escaped him as he rubbed his eyes and forehead, then pushed his chair back and stood up.

He grimaced thinking of Helen—the woman who had done everything right and held their family together. He had hurt her in ways he couldn't mend. Maybe someday she would forgive him.

I had no choice, he thought. *I had to send for Elen. I couldn't live with myself if something else happened to her because of me. Her life and the life of our child were in danger, even after her release.*

His thoughts wandered to Daniel and the price he had paid—a terrible sacrifice for a freedom he would never see.

Ten days.

The last time he had talked to Misgina, the plan had sounded like it could work. They all had the passes they needed to get to the border, and Misgina assured him he had enough contacts between Sololo and Nairobi to get them through into the city.

"We will be out of touch after this," Misgina had told him the night before they got on the bus. "Hopefuly, we will see you soon."

Hopefully. A word that came without guarantees.

He tried not to think the worst, but knowing what had happened to Daniel made the waiting worse. Restless, he stretched to shake the tension from his body.

Girmai was itching to leave the office—just as he had been every evening for the past ten days—despite the profound sadness that awaited him in the large, empty house he and Semere rented, and the circular thoughts that consumed him each night. *What if they got caught? What if she'd been sent back to Addis?* The possibilities twisted through his mind, each one darker than the last, until he finally drifted into a fitful sleep in the early-morning hours. The mornings brought some relief, and he threw himself into his work with an intensity that didn't allow him space to think outside of business.

Just then, the transport truck he had been expecting pulled into the lot. The driver hopped out and headed toward him with a set of keys jingling with each step.

"I'm done for the day, boss," the driver said, handing him the keys. "All deliveries completed on time, just as you requested."

"Thank you, Thomas," Girmai replied, his English more fluent after more than a year of practice in Kenya. "We have a few more orders for delivery tomorrow. I'll see you in the morning."

A half-hour later, Girmai bolted his office door and got into his car. He waved at the guard at the main gate and edged the car slowly through Nairobi's industrial-area traffic.

As he drove into his housing complex, his blood started racing at the sign of a blue Peugeot station wagon parked outside. He slammed on the brakes and jerked his car to a stop behind it.

Leaving the car door wide open, he sprinted to the house and almost crashed into the front door. He fumbled with the knob before he finally swung it open.

Her back was to him. She was sitting at the dining-room table, the light streaming from the window capturing her exquisite silhouette.

His breath caught in his throat. He froze. He could hear sounds of children upstairs, but the sight of her immobilized him.

Was he dreaming?

She turned; the sight of her face almost made his knees buckle.

Her eyes were bigger than he remembered, and tears shimmered in them instantly. The whites of her eyes were bright, even without kohl to outline them. Her childhood scar, like an upside-down half-moon, sat prominently on her sunken cheek. Bones jutted out beneath the blue shawl draped over her shoulders.

He was already standing before her when she got to her feet. He wrapped his arms around her and held her tighter than he had ever held anyone. Her body felt frail, shaking with silent sobs. He loosened his embrace for a moment, fearing he might break her.

"I can't believe it," he whispered into her hair, breathing in her familiar scent. "You're here …"

She leaned back to look up at him. New lines framed her eyes and quivered with her smile.

"Girmai," she said, her voice cracking.

He pulled her close again.

"There hasn't been a day, not one second, that I haven't thought of you and wished for this moment, my love," he murmured.

Her body shook in his arms; he held her tighter.

"Every day, I said your name. I prayed for you," he whispered, his voice breaking. "I never stopped loving you."

He loosened his hold and cupped her face so he could look into her eyes. Her arms were still wrapped around his waist as he took in every detail of her face and gently wiped the tears with his thumbs.

"All that matters is here and now," she said.

"I want to spend the rest of my life making it up to you."

She smiled and rested her head against his chest. "We are together now with a chance at a new life. We are reborn."

She turned to face the living room behind him. Girmai loosened his hold on her; his eyes tracked hers. His arms fell to his sides when he noticed the small girl looking up at him from a couch.

The child's large eyes blinked at him, her tiny body stiff and tense as she gripped the armrest.

"She's never seen me hug anyone like that," Elen sniffed.

"Hiyab, ni'i, come," Elen said, waving to the little girl. Hiyab stood frozen, gripping the couch tighter.

Before either of them could move toward her, a chorus of joyful screams and hurried footsteps down the staircase grew louder. Yonas, Samuel, and Rahwa came bounding down the narrow stairs, their laughter filling the house.

"Baba! Baba!"

Elen stepped aside as Girmai opened his arms wide to catch them. The children collided into him in a flurry of hugs, each fighting for space as they laughed and cried in unison.

"My children!" Girmai said. "You are home now. You are safe."

He didn't bother to wipe his tears away, letting them fall as he kissed their foreheads repeatedly.

Just then, Misgina stepped out of the guest bathroom, grinning when he saw the scene before him.

Girmai pulled himself away from his children, rushed over to Misgina, wrapped his arms around him, and enthusiastically thumped his back.

"You brought my family back to me," Girmai said, his voice thick with gratitude.

Misgina's grin spread from ear to ear. "There are a lot of stories to tell, for sure," he said, glancing at Elen. "They were all very brave."

Girmai hugged him again, unable to stop smiling. "I can never thank you enough," he said.

Hiyab was still standing by the couch. She hadn't moved, her fingers still gripping its edges as she silently watched the scene unfold.

Girmai walked over to her, stopping just a few feet away. He crouched down, his heart swelling with love for this little girl who had never known him.

"Hello, Hiyab," he said gently. Her dark eyes took him in, wide and unblinking, her fingertips white with tension.

He stretched his arms out to her, smiling as he waited.

For a moment, she remained frozen, and he searched her face. A faint scar, no bigger than a fingernail, marked her cheek, and wisps of unruly hair framed her small face. Her oversized T-shirt hung loosely on her thin frame, the neckline stretched and browned from wear, revealing her delicate collarbones.

"This is your Baba," Elen said softly into Hiyab's ear. "Say hello. Give your Baba a big hug." She gave Hiyab a gentle nudge closer to Girmai.

She was more beautiful than he could have imagined despite the exhaustion that showed on her small, fragile body.

"This is your Hiyab," Elen said, smiling at Girmai. "Your daughter."

Girmai stretched his arms wider, his smile growing. *I will wait for you, baby girl, however long it takes. I'm here for you, now and always.*

Hiyab blinked up at him once more, then slowly let go of the couch. Her tiny hands reached out, hesitant at first, then with growing confidence as she stepped toward him.

When her arms wrapped around his neck, he scooped her up, closed his eyes and held her close to him, his heart swelling with a love that felt boundless.

He opened his eyes to see Elen behind Hiyab, face wet with tears, her smile—oh, that smile.

We made something beautiful.

Note

Dear reader, I am grateful that you picked up this book, that you spent precious hours of your life reading it, and that you have gotten to this point where I can thank you directly for choosing to be a part of our family history.

I initially wrote this story as an essay to my children so they could know the extent of their grandparents' sacrifices to make all our lives possible. As children grow, the essay also grew—into the book you are holding in your hands.

To understand why I wrote it—come back with me for a little while to Nairobi, 1988. It was an exciting day in third grade. I had been waiting for my turn for a long time. I was finally going to share my "All About Me" poster.

"Put in interesting information about yourself," our teacher, Sister Caramel, had said. "I want to know more about you—where and when you were born, how many family members you have, what makes you proud—anything about you!" Her enthusiasm washed over us all and I knew exactly what I was going to put on my poster.

This was the first time I had ever been asked to talk about me outside of school. Our strict Catholic school gave us no reprieve from the high expectations of obedience and discipline. The rigorous pace of academics was relentless, and I often got in trouble for not meeting the exact requirements of each assignment or rule.

I liked Sister Caramel; she was the only teacher who didn't shout at or punish us. The whole class was excited, eager to show off our posters. Watching a few students present before me gave me more inspiration and I threw all my creative energy into making this the best art piece I had ever created.

On my poster were my mother, father, and all eight siblings. I scattered them around the page to show how big and colorful my family was. I planned to tell them how I was the eighth of nine children and how full and noisy our house always felt. All my family members were smiling in my picture, but the one with the biggest smile was me. My colorful self-portrait had eyes only for my mother. I looked up at her adoringly as she stood beside me with long, curly hair brushing her stick-figure shoulders.

The poster was up. It was my turn. I cleared my throat and started my well-rehearsed presentation.

"I was born in Alem Bekagn prison," I said proudly.

Gasps and murmurs made me stand up straighter. It was time for them to hear about a true hero!

"Alem Bekagn is in Addis Ababa, Ethiopia," I continued. "My mother is my hero. She fought against the bad Derg government in Ethiopia so that Eritrea could be free. She fights for justice!"

I pumped my fist in the air for emphasis like I had seen my father do many times.

"My father had to run away when she got arrested because—"

"He is a THIEF!" Dennis's voice from the back of the room sliced through my presentation and stopped me cold. The entire class erupted in laughter; everyone was talking at once.

"You must be a thief too, because you have been in prison!" He was pointing at me; his stare began to shake my body. I turned to Sister Caramel standing behind me at the entrance of the classroom. She seemed shocked, but whether by my story or Dennis's words, I couldn't tell.

How could they not be proud?

All my life, I heard stories of near-death experiences, of courage and hope when there wasn't any reason to have any. My parents talked about their experiences during the Red Terror so often that I thought it was the norm.

For all of my childhood in Nairobi, our house used to be full of refugees who stayed until they found a more permanent place to be safe and start life over. My parents would pull out the mattresses and insist they stay until they got settled. My mother convinced me that I would have all the blessings I needed in life if I gave up my bed for our guests and I believed it. I fought my siblings to sleep on a mattress on the floor and would smile at the thought of my blessings piling up as I welcomed a tired stranger to use my bed to rest.

My parents taught me to love freely and welcome openly.

"We know what people have been through, and everyone deserves a good, peaceful life. Our duty is to help however we can. We wouldn't be here without the love and generosity of family, friends, and even strangers who lifted us up when we needed it."

That's the way my parents lived. Our house was always full; the kitchen was always busy with Mom producing vats of food for the masses; stories of survival were the background noise at any time of day or night. This was my normal.

Looking at Dennis and the rest of the class laughing at me that day, I felt othered for the first time in my life. It wasn't my world. It was theirs, and it had no place for someone like me.

I glanced at Sister Caramel's clouded face. My chest burned with the hope that she would say something, anything. She gathered herself slowly. I was visibly shaking by the time she raised her voice and silenced the class. I hoped her next words would be to admonish Dennis. I expected to hear her say that my story was a great one. But all she said was "You can carry on, Donica."

But I couldn't. I saw the uncertainty in her eyes. Did she wonder if Dennis was right? Did they think I made it all up? My vision wavered behind the tears I spent all my energy containing.

"I ..." The story stuck in my throat. I had rehearsed it so many times. I had visualized myself telling them about how my mother had saved so many people's lives. How, for so many years, she educated people on the struggle for independence and supported the Eritrean rebels in the field. How she got arrested and was tortured in prison while I was in her belly. How she survived. For me.

I had not once considered that the start of my life as one who had survived a year and a half in prison with my mother could be anything short of a miracle. I was so certain that they would be amazed at my mom's extraordinary bravery, resilience, and courage. So certain that they would be impressed that she taught me to always be on the side of justice and to choose to do the right thing even when that is the harder choice.

It had not occurred to me to plan for an alternative.

I walked over to my poster and tore it from the board where Sister Caramel had taped it up and ran out of the room, the sound of their laughter following me down the hall.

Confusion turned into embarrasement then into an anger that festered within me for the rest of the day as I realized that I was the only one of me in school. Everyone else was normal.

I took out all my confused emotions on my mother. Why couldn't she be normal like all the other mothers? Why can't my dad just be like the other dads and not a … fighter? Why did Mom have to go to prison—no one else's mom had!

That was the last time I spoke of my family's experiences for a very long time. Through my teens and young adulthood, I became adept at switching personas so I could fit into my school world. I blended in and became like everyone else. At home, I stopped asking my parents questions and ignored the hurt on their faces when they saw me harden and walk away whenever the subject of their past came up.

In 2001, I gave birth to my first child. Noah was the first personal miracle in my life. I remember looking at him in the crook of my arm after seventeen hours of hard labor—the most intense pain I ever felt. I was overwhelmed by so many emotions that it froze me, and all I could do was stare at him the whole night as I thought of my mother.

The Red Terror in Ethiopia and Eritrea was not just one coordinated massacre but waves of violence that lasted years. Killings were often carried out by local militia and young cadres, which makes an accurate documentation of lives lost hard to pinpoint.

Sources give different estimates, ranging from tens to hundreds of thousands. The truth is, we will probably never know. The Derg regime tightly controlled all media and communication, any form of journalism was suppressed, and most of the killings and torture went on without trial and with no official records to track the number of victims. Names were omitted from prison lists, prisoners were transferred without notice and may have died in various locations, bodies were disposed of in mass graves with no written record, and families were not allowed to collect remains. In fact, there were instances where they would be punished for asking, or had to pay a bullet tax: the cost of the bullets it took to kill their loved ones.

In 2018, I went with my mother to the Red Terror Martyrs Museum in Addis Ababa. We walked hand in hand among the pictures of whole families wiped out, we read descriptions of the extensive atrocities committed. It broke my heart to hear the familiarity with which my mother spoke as she described different torture techniques and the level of fear they had to live with for so long. I remember her looking at a wall covered in pictures of people from floor to ceiling as she said, "These are so few compared to all those we lost."

Back in the materinity ward, staring at my son just a few hours old, my mind kept going back to my mother. She kept me alive as a three-month-old fetus through multiple days of torture and beatings, and held on to life because of me. She gave birth to me in a prison cell. No water, no family, no hospital. She held on to me and loved me while she rode out her sentence for another year and a half. She nurtured me into the person I am today. Looking at my son in the dark of that night, I finally came to understand her love and the sacrifice that came with refusing to give up. This resilience was intertwined with the one value that my parents have impressed on me as far back as my memory stretches: gratitude.

I made a promise to myself to tell her story. I would tell my father's story too. My children, Gabriel, Noah, and Maria, would know where they came from and be proud of who they are. They would never carry the shame I once did. They would live knowing their inheritance—the legacy of love, courage, and justice.

My parents are brilliant storytellers and, despite all the trauma they have been through, they speak freely about their experiences and find healing in the act of sharing.

This story sits on the historical fiction shelf because I have recreated conversations, merged timelines, changed names, and added my own description to places like Alem Bekagn, which doesn't exist anymore. Most of what is in this pages has happened: the arranged marriage, the prison and torture experiences, the journey to refuge in Nairobi, and so many things in between. We have lived to tell the tale. The sadder truth is that thousands and thousands of people will never get to tell their story. May their spirits be honored and remembered within the pages of this book.

I also hope that we, the generations that have come after, can move beyond the shame my third-grade self once felt—and instead live our lives with pride, doing what we can to honor those who came before us so their loss is not in vain.

Donica Merhazion
Nairobi, Kenya, 2025

Donica, her daughter Maria on Tsion's lap, and her mom, Wubet, on the day of Maria's baptism in 2012. Maria is wearing the dress Mama Tsion made for Donica in Alem Bekagn.

Acknowledgments

Habtu, Mussie, Leul, Eden, Elsa, Yohannes, Semret, and Wina, it is my privilege to be your sister. Thank you for all that you are and for being a big part of who I am.

My friends, who doubled as beta readers and life coaches, this could not have come together without you. Lilly Bekele Piper, your friendship, enthusiasm, and unwavering faith continue to inspire and motivate me. Ruth Kuguru, thank you for putting aside your infinite obligations to read this story and for your thoughtful suggestions and constant encouragement. I am deeply grateful for our friendship. Marta Woodward, my sister, your writer's eye shaped so many parts of this manuscript. Thank you for taking the time to read it during such a busy chapter of your life. Yohannes and Eden, thank you for your love and your time. Sharing your feedback on the first drafts through a family lens was invaluable. Arman Dostmohamed, "thank you" doesn't seem enough to express my gratitude, not only for your input on this manuscript but also for the countless other ways you have been my thought partner and encourager over the years. Asli Kifle, I can't imagine my life without you in it. Since we were in the single digits, you've been my rock, the anchor that keeps me grounded. Thank you for your constant presence, even from the other side of the ocean.

Sagda Khalil, Sally Ratemo, Rahma Egue, and Jessica Joseph, my soul sisters! You are my tribe, the village that has embraced me in endless ways, wrapping me with love, laughter, and a constant listening ear. I am grateful for all the ways your friendship has added color to my life. Benjamin Piper and Amin Hussian, your unwavering, calm presence is all the reassurance and support one needs in life. In all life situations, I will panic only after you do. It hasn't happened yet! Thank you for keeping me grounded. Naigzy Gebremedhin, mountain climber and grandfather extraordinaire, your tenacity, perseverance, and your steady presence is the best thing any daughter-in-law could wish for. Thank you for being such an inspirational second father; I am grateful for you.

To my writing critique group, Carol Yee, Susan Puska, Jen Welsh, and Liz Kauffman, our long critique sessions and conversations were the highlight of my writing life. I learned so much from each of you, and I appreciate you so much. Your meticulous feedback makes me a better writer. Carol, my gratitude also goes to you for your meticulous writer's eye and infinite hours of feedback, which encouraged me to keep going.

Many thanks to Eric Koester, the Book Creators program, and New Degree Press for opening doors to a writing community that helped shape the early steps of this project. Mike Butler and Carol McKibben, your guidance through those mucky first drafts gave it the boost it needed to keep going. I am forever grateful for your encouragement and the ways you helped me see that this was a story worth telling. Fourie Botha, thank you for your keen eye; your polish and final touches have given this story its shine.

Anna Soler-Pont and Carla Briner, you advocated tirelessly for this story and believed in its worth. Thank you for being champions for me and for so many other underrepresented voices.

Jessica Powers, I can't thank you enough for seeing the potential in this story and for introducing it to the world. I am deeply grateful beyond what words can express.

Years before I joined Catalyst Press, I went out on a limb to try to publish on my own. I sent out a social media pitch for a few weeks with the hope of getting enough support to self-publish. So many invested generously without reading a word and contributed more than I needed to get the book printed. I am humbled by your faith in me. Thank you for your patience as I paused and pivoted, adding years to my promise to get this book into your hands. It is a dream come true to finally be able to share this with you.

Abraham Tesfu · Adda Tewolde · Adrienne Donohue · Akberet Girmay · Alan Bright · Alex Foto · Alex Hagos · Alicia Messing · Alistair Goold · Alpa Shah · Amanda Fine · Amreen Walbridge · Amy Longcor · Andrea Gagne · Andrea Wilson · Andromeda Restrepo · Angela Suther · Angelique Umubyeyi · Anita Shankar · Ann Abogi · Anna Long-Slade · Anne Chen · Anne Kneedler · Arman Dostmohamed · Aruna Varsani · Asli Haile · Aya Toure · Azeb Samuel-Britton · Beth Anne Pratt · Betsega Bekele · Betty Musyoka · Bill Parsons · Brendan Ross · Caitlin Coast · Caren Ouma · Carol Yee · Caroline Ashley · Caroline Blair and Michael Gebremedhin · Caroline Elias · Casey Blaschke · Catherine Baillieux · Cécile Lacorre Botzung · Cecilia Roberts · Christina Novinskey · Christine Katcher · Christy Dow · Clare Feinstein · Colleen Tighe · Cristina Zucca · Dan Suther · Dana Sandstrom · Danstan Bagenda · David J Joy · David Seruyange · Dayo M Fafiade · Dineo Motlepa · Donna Bracewell · Eden Beyene · Eden Tesfamariam · Edward Odunguli · Elisabet Kivimäki · Elizabeth Fafiade · Elizabeth James · Elizabeth Rees · Elsa Gebreyesus · Eric Koester · Farah Daoud · Fiona Thangata · Garity Line · Gash Hiruy Amanuel · Gash Tami Samuel · Gemja Adhanom · Haben Berhane · Haben Fecadu · Hanna Dagnachew · Haregu Gaime · Heather Vickery · Heidi Laws · Helen Tesfai · HP Boyle · Jacey Spratt · Jack Doutrich · Jackie Frank · Jaclyn Corrigan · Jaclyn Jones · Jaime Lee Jarvis · Jalan Sahba · Jeff Gettleman · Jen Welsh · Jennifer Barak · Jennifer Brinkerhoff · Jennifer Gray · Jerry Lavery · Joana Print · Joanna Johnson · Joanne Aubrey · John StClair · Jonelle Duke · Juna Patella-Ross · Justine Elliot · Karl and Barbara Baker · Kate Woods · Kathleen Chromitz · Kathleen Paffett · Katie Kimber · Katrina Kostianis · Katy Mitchell · Keela Lupton · Kelley Bunkers · Kelly Mott · Kendra Daly · Kirsten McGarigal · Kristi Belete · Kristin O'Planick · Laura and Francis Atemo · Laurie Fuller · Laurie

Walters · Leila Habtu · Lesley Potter · Leslie Blaha · Lilly Bekele Piper · Linda K McCarley · Lisa Kurbiel · Lisa Parrott · Liz Rees · Maria Ortiz-Malte · Maria Owen · Mariana Garza Vela · Marjanne Jansen · Marta Woodward · Martha Erickson · Martha Fa · Matias Belete · Maura Allen · Meg McNulty · Melanie Bustrum · Meley Kifleyeus · Merkeb Yohannes · Meseret Kassahun Desta · Metti Kanno · Michelle Barrett · Michelle Mennis · Millicent Karuri Obiero · Mira Boxer · Mona Bormet · Múkami Kinoti · Muluneh Sugebo · Mussie Tecleyessuse · Nadia Patel and family · Natalie Kneip · Naz Medhanie · Netsanet Solomon · Noah Flessel · Noah Naigzy · Oyuna Finch · Patricia Salleh Matta · Paul Montoy-Wilson · Paula Morgan · Pauline Afman · Rachel Jones · Rafaelle Patella-Ross · Rahel Tadesse · Rahwa Lillie Tekie · Rebecca Brady · Rebecca Prince-Ruiz · Rhian Gastineau · Robel Samuel Habtu · Robert Keating · Robert Onyango · Roice Fulton · Ruth Jones · Ruth and Kenny Kuguru · Sajda Khalil and Amin Hussain · Salem Ayele-Acolom · Samir Patel and family · Sarabeth Kawugule · Sarah Lout · Sally Ratemo · Sarah Patella · Saskia Hissink · Scott Lavack · Scott and Sarah Lout · Selam Emiru · Selamawit Mehary · Selome Samuel · Sem Tesfamariam · Sewit Ahderom · Shelly Maldonado · Sienna Loftus Burns · Sinikinesh Beyene Jimma · Sisonke Msimang · Sofia Tesfazion · Soraiya R. Shah · Sue Piper · Sue Vernalis · Suganya Kimbrough · Tamar Lawrence-Samuel and Thaly Germain · Tamara Cook · Tedros Abraham · Temesghen Debesai Asfaha · Terry Bahati · Thomas Araya · Tigist Yilma · Tolani Martin · Tracy Woodward · Tsigereda Wolde · Vaishali Tanna · Wendy Chamberlin · Whitney Fry · Will Clurman · Wina Merhazion · Yacob Fitiwi · Yerus Ghebremeskel · Yohannes Tesfamariam.

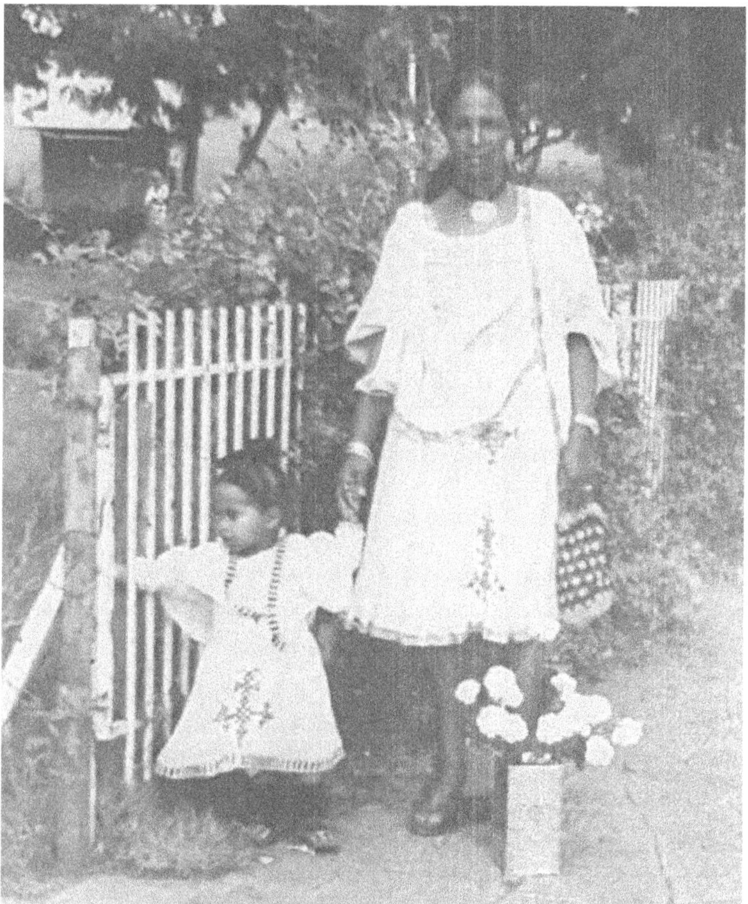

Donica and Wubet, the day they were released from Alem Bekagn.

www.ingramcontent.com/pod-product-compliance
Lightning Source LLC
Jackson TN
JSHW022051060226
97113JS00001B/1
9781960803337